THE

THRONE OF DAVID

From the Consecration of the Shepherd of Bethlehem
to the Rebellion of Prince Absalom

By REV. J. H. INGRAHAM, LL.D.

Author of "The Prince of the House of David," "The Pillar
of Fire," etc., etc.

Being an illustration of the splendor, power, and dominion of the reign of the
shepherd, poet, warrior, king, and prophet, ancestor and type of Jesus; in a
series of letters addressed by an Assyrian ambassador, resident at the court of
Saul and David, to his Lord and King on the throne of Nineveh; wherein the
glory of Assyria, as well as the magnificence of Judea, is presented to the
reader as by an eye-witness.

Fredonia Books
Amsterdam, The Netherlands

The Throne of David:
From the Consecration of the Shepherd of Bethlem
to Rebellion of Prince Absalom

by
J. H. Ingraham

ISBN: 1-4101-0085-5

Fredonia Books
Amsterdam, The Netherlands
http://www.fredoniabooks.com

THE AUTHOR OF

"THE PILLAR OF FIRE" AND OF "THE PRINCE OF THE
HOUSE OF DAVID" INSCRIBES TO THE

AMERICAN HEBREWS

THE PRESENT BOOK; ILLUSTRATING THE PERIOD OF HEBRAIC
HISTORY WHEN THE ROYAL LINE OF DAVID FIRST
RECEIVED FROM THE HAND OF GOD ITS
CONSECRATED CROWN.

UNITED IN AFTER AGES BY THE LAST PRINCE OF THE HOUSE
OF DAVID FOREVER WITH THE CROWN OF
THE SON OF GOD.

THE OUTLINE.

The author's plan, in illustration of the history of the Hebrew people, embraces three books. The first in order of time, though it was second in the order of publication, is "The Pillar of Fire; or, Israel in Bondage." The central figure of this book is Moses. It takes up the Hebraic history at the time of the sale of Joseph into Egypt, and closes it with the promulgation of the Two Tables of the Divine Law from Sinai. The present work, "The Throne of David," is an attempt to illustrate, after the same plan, the grandeur of Hebraic history, when the "People of God" had attained, under the reigns of David and Solomon, the height of their power and glory as a nation. The central figure of this work is David, Prophet, Priest, and King, and type of Him who, as the last Prince of His house, transferred the Throne of David from earth to heaven—from Jerusalem below to Jerusalem above! It presents David as a shepherd, and a poet; in his friendship with Jonathan; in his victory over the Philistine; in the splendor of his regal magnificence; in his fight from Prince Absalom; and in all the scenes of his later life. Absalom in his rebellion, and Solomon in his kingly glory, are leading features of the work. The aim of the writer is to invest with popular interest one of the most interesting periods of Hebrew history distinguished by the contemporaneous existence of four of the most wonderful men of any age; viz., David, Saul, Samuel the Prophet, and Solomon the greatest and wisest of men.

His aim in these books is to draw the attention of those who seldom open the Bible, to that sacred volume, by unfolding to them the beauty, riches, eloquence, and grandeur of the Holy Scriptures. He is told that the two preceding works have contributed, hitherto, largely to this result, and numerous letters in his possession from grateful writers bear testimony to the good which those books have done in directing attention to the Bible, the inexhaustible Fountain from which they were drawn.

The Bible is a legitimate field for human research. Like the globe, its mines of gold and silver are by man lawfully penetrated and worked for their treasures! Every sermon gathers its wealth of thought from its sacred placers; every commentator finds in the golden sands of its rivers of Life his riches of illustration. The pious Art painter portrays with his pencil its holy incidents; and the religious sculptor chisels in marble his devout and elevated conceptions of the forms and features of its prophets, priests, kings, and martyrs; even the ideal human form of the Divine Son of Mary, without rebuke and without impiety, Art, devoutly and reverently, commands the marble to reveal, so far as the lofty conceptions of concentrated genius can reach, the unknown and heavenly lineaments! Destroy all pictures and statues which illustrate sacred characters and scenes, and Art would be destroyed with them; for upon the incidents of the Old and New Testaments nearly all pure Art has hitherto been nourished; and to illustrations of their holy scenes it is indebted for nearly all of its glory and splendor.

A writer, therefore, whose high office it is to make known the Scriptures, who, with becoming reverence and with right motives approaches them to illustrate with his Pen scenes and characters therefrom, labors in a lawful field of duty. The Pen is but another instrument wherewith consecrated Art may delineate the characters of Holy Writ; and, equally with the Chisel and the Pencil, be permitted to present them to the imagination of the devout reader. These present books come, therefore, within the legitimate province of sacred illustration. They are delineations of historical portions of the Bible, presented in the form of " Letters " in order to secure more familiar and vivid expression.

The Third Book of the Series (but which was the first in order of publication), " The Prince of the House of David," illustrates the decadence of Hebraic power, as " The Pillar of Fire " unfolds its beginning; while its final culmination is presented in " The Throne of David." The central figure of " The Prince of the House of David " is Jesus the " Son of David," our most blessed Lord and Saviour. The time of that work embraces a period of about four years, from the appearing of John the Baptist to the ascension of our Lord.

Thus the three books cover the whole field of Hebraic history, from the Bondage in Egypt to the reign of Solomon, and thence to the crucifixion of Jesus. There is no necessary connection between the books. They may be read in chronological order (which is best), or separately, or the last named, first.

We now commit this work to the readers of "The Prince of the House of David" and of "The Pillar of Fire," with the prayer that it may inspire them with a desire "to search the Scriptures" for the treasures of wisdom they contain; and above all for the knowledge of "the way of Life" revealed in their sacred pages, which ever lead the devout reader to the Cross as the only solution of the mystery of this present life, and the true key to that of the world to come.

CHRIST CHURCH RECTORY,
Holly Springs, Miss., January 26, 1860.

AUTHOR'S INTRODUCTORY EPISTLE TO THE READER.

The twin-valleys of the Euphrates and Tigris received the first families of the human race after the flood. Nimrod, the great-grandson of Noah, whom sacred history and tradition term "a mighty hunter," or "warrior," and whom profane history calls the first "king of men," is regarded as the founder of Babylon, the oldest kingdom of the world.

Ninus, a prince of Babylon, invading the beautiful valley of the Tigris, founded, not long after the dispersion at Babel, the city of Nineveh upon the banks of that river. These two cities became the centers of two monarchies which long rivaled each other in splendor and power. Nineveh ultimately gained the ascendency, and, extending her scepter over the plains of the Euphrates, placed one of her own princes upon its throne as tributary to her crown.

In the progress of centuries Babylon recovered her independence, and advanced to a position of wealth and grandeur that subsequently rendered her the second city of the earth, Nineveh still retaining her imperial supremacy as mistress of the East! Her kings were warriors and conquerors who made the science of arms the noblest study of man, and regarded war his highest happiness. In times of peace they devoted their leisure to adorning their capital with superb palaces, gardens, terraces, lakes, and monuments of unrivaled magnificence.

The obscurity which veils the history of those early ages of Oriental dominion and splendor has concealed from us, in a great degree, the true condition of that venerable empire for nearly a thousand years of its most ancient progress. Profane history, borrowing her light from the dim torch of tradition, casts but here and there an uncertain illumination into the deep twilight of those dawning ages of the world. Now it reveals a Ninus the Great, extending his dominions to Ethiopia and the Mediterranean; and now a queen Semiramis, represented as enterprising and magnanimous, martial and powerful, who completed the conquest of all the East! Then a brilliant and luxurious monarch Ninyas appears, who adorns his empire and prefers pleasure to the hardy enterprises of military glory.

A long line of princes more or less indolent and effeminate follow in a succession of luxurious reigns, covering several centuries, when, under the reign of Teutames IV., one of these kings, we hear of the re-conquest of Babylon and Media, and also of an embassy from a Pharaoh of Egypt to his court. This was the king Mœris, successor to the Pharaoh who was destroyed with his armies in the Red Sea.

Here, then, the obscurity of mere tradition, which hitherto had presented us but dim representations of the past of Nineveh, is removed by the full light of positive history bearing upon it. Egypt and Assyria, of which Nineveh was the capital, are hereby placed contemporaneously on the same historic page; and henceforth belong, equally, to the legitimate domain of profane history.*

But allusion to Nineveh does not appear in the sacred traditionary records of the Jews until about two hundred years after the conquest of the Promised Land; nor in the sacred Scriptures until several centuries later; that is, under that name.

Yet the splendor, power, and wide dominion of the Assyrian Empire was not unknown to the Jews. The neighboring kingdom of Tyre had received ambassadors from Nineveh long before the time of Saul; and the Jews were always on terms of friendship with Phœnicia; but until the time of Saul the Israelites and Assyrians were not brought into relations of polity and ordinary national intercourse.

The time and the occasion on which the Assyrians may be supposed first to have held official communication with the people of God are, so far as is known, revealed in the following pages.

Samuel was then the Prophet, Priest, and Lord of the Twelve Tribes; for his rule as a Judge of Israel had not only become absolute, but in the exercise of power he was supreme Dictator. Vice-gerent of God, controller of the Priesthood, and Judge by the voice of the people, he governed without opposition by

---

*The cuneic inscriptions revealed by recent investigations at Nineveh, as far as translated, promise a complete history of Assyria up to a period much earlier than the era of the call of Abram from Chaldea.

the dictates of his single will. Under his long and able administration of affairs he consolidated the government of the Jewish tribes, and having shown himself also a soldier in their wars with the Philistines, they were inspired with the idea of making him their king! Noble in presence, grave with wisdom, venerable with years, he commanded even the admiration of the enemies of his nation; and his fame as a "Seer" extended to the kingdoms of the heathen around him, while his name was spoken even with reverence at the haughty and luxurious court of Belus the king of Assyria.

At this time the city of Nineveh, where Belus reigned monarch of all the East, including Babylon, was at the height of its magnificence and power. Its population was more than a half a million. It was a four days' march to compass its lofty, tower-embattled walls. Every house was inclosed by gardens, and the top of the walls was for miles ornamented with trees and beds of flowers. Its palaces and temples, shrines, altars, and statues were without number; its terraces, lakes, walks, and colonnades forming an endless labyrinth amid the most charming artificial scenery.

Enthroned in his palace in the center of his mighty metropolis the youthful Belus, not yet twenty-five years old, and recently come to the inheritance of the scepter of Assyria from his mother Arphaxa, administered the government of his vast kingdom with wisdom and prudence beyond his years. Instead of giving himself up to indolence and luxury after the example of many of his ancestors, he sought to enlarge his dominions eastward to the Ind, and southward to the "Sea of the Sun," westward, and northward, and also to form alliances of friendship and commerce with powerful nations such as Phœnicia and Egypt.

His mother, who was an Egyptian princess, the daughter of a royal ambassador to the court of Nineveh from that of Thebes and Memphis, on the day before her death, calling him to the side of her couch, said to him:

"My son, I am about to depart this life to enter into the world of the gods! To you I intrust the scepter of my realms. I know you will wield it with mercy and judgment; for I have, from your childhood, trained you to this great end! One promise before I die I ask of you!"

"It is granted, royal and beloved mother, ere the words are formed on your lips," answered the prince, kneeling by her pillow and bending over her with glittering eyelids, and in deep emotion.

"I wish you to strengthen your empire by an alliance, stronger than that of a treaty, with my native country. The haughty Pharaoh now on the throne is a prince of a new dynasty, unknown to my father's royal House. Send an embassy to him congratulating him on his accession to the double crown of Thebes and Memphis, and ask in marriage his daughter as your queen. I have heard she is fair and gentle. He will consent! And thus the two most powerful nations that divide the globe will dwell in peace; for without such an alliance war would be the natural attitude of two great empires, each ambitious to rule supreme on the earth!"

"I would rather conquer Egypt and subdue her proud Pharaoh to my scepter than wed his daughter, were she fairer, dear mother, than the evening star," answered Belus, with a smile.

"Nay; let there be peace! Secure your crown by this alliance. Promise me you will ask the hand of the Egyptian princess, and so be at one with the powerful Pharaohs."

The prince bowed his head upon the jeweled fingers of his still lovely mother, and answered.

"I obey, dear mother!"

"May Assarac, the powerful and wise god of your race, bless you," she answered, laying her hands upon his youthful brow.

One year after the death of the queen, and the new king had placed the affairs of his kingdom on a firm basis, he recalled the promise he had made to his mother; and sending for one of the young nobles of his court he spoke to him:

"O Arbacas, companion of my childhood, friend of my manhood, faithful and true in all things, I have sent for thee to confide to thy trust a sacred mission, by command of the queen, my mother, now blessed with the divine gods. Thou knowest my mother was a princess of Masr, a niece of Pharaoh, daughter of his brother Thothmis, who came to my grandfather's court on an embassy of friendship, asking him to unite with him in a war to crush the twelve warlike Republics of the Chaldean Israelites, and divide their country by the great Sea between us that our borders might unite! My royal grandfather Nabopolassar refused, preferring in his sagacity that these Jews should continue to hold their country as a safe separator between Egypt and Assyria, not caring to have the powerful monarch of the Nile too near a neighbor. But in order to soften his denial and prevent hostilities arising out of his politic refusal, he proposed a union between his son (my royal father Arphaxad) and the prince-ambassador's fair daughter who was with him. The marriage secured and sealed a peace! My mother, who took the name of her husband, and who has ruled so well and powerfully since my father's death, when near her own, commanded me to send to Egypt for a wife, also from thence. I obey her. I have confidence, dear Arbaces, in your judgment, wisdom, discretion, and ability. I have selected you, young as you are, for this delicate mission. I wish you to be ready to depart within thirty days. It is a long journey and requires unusual preparation. You will take with you a befitting retinue—not large enough to alarm the lesser nations whose territories you traverse, yet numerous enough for protection against insult and to give dignity as you enter Egypt to your embassy. You will take with you full royal equipage, with a large train of household officers and servants as becomes the representative of a powerful Assyrian king, and your own rank as a Prince of the Blood; for are we not cousins but twice removed, my dear Arbaces? The tent of cloth of gold which was my mother's you will also take with you to be the abode, as you return, of my future bride. If she be but half as fair as my mother, I shall be happy, my friend; but if she prove as plain and dark as an Ethiop maid, I will be content; for will she not be my mother's elect?"

A slight smile played in the young and handsome king's eyes as he spoke these words, and soon afterward the tall and comely young prince Arbaces left the presence.

Thirty days elapsed, and the military escort of the ambassador, consisting of eight hundred horsemen in burnished armor with helmets of gold, and two hundred chariots, was drawn up before the lofty gate of the magnificent "House of Nimrod," the hereditary palace of the Ninevite kings. In the ornamented square in front, guarded by two gigantic lions, stood the statue of the "King of men," a colossal monolith, towering seventy feet into the air, holding aloft above his head a spear, the golden point of which first caught the blazing rays of the morning sun.

The horsemen and chariots were drawn up in a crescent open toward the palace. In a private audience room within it stood the young king in the act of taking leave of Arbaces.

"Farewell, my cousin! The God of Ninus and the Controller of the stars attend you. Do not delay. I shall expect your return within four months. Convey the jewels I have intrusted to you, to the maiden with your own hands, presenting her therewith my heart's lowest homage.

"I have directed you to take the route through the land of the Jewish people, in order that you may have audience with their mighty Seer and Friend of the gods, Isamel, and secure with him a friendly alliance, so that he may not be won to the interest of Egypt (if this nuptial embassy fail), but be bound to Assyria forever! A people, even though it have no king, that can bring into the field one hundred thousand fighting men, as the caravan chiefs from thence report, is not to be despised as an enemy or as a friend. See this Prophet of the gods, therefore, whose fame is so wide, and make the alliance sure to us. Learn, while there, something of their policy and mode of government, and unravel to me how they can have authority or laws without a monarch."

"I will not fail, my noble prince," answered Arbaces, "to record everything of interest I meet with, and from time to time will send you by caravans my letters, or bring the tablets with the records of my journey to you in person on my return."

"Present the Chaldaic-Jewish Prophet Isamel this jewel, and ask him to consult the gods to know if my reign will be long and prosperous; and you will also ascertain their real feelings toward Egypt."

"Without a doubt, they still partake of the ancient hostility. A people once in bondage to a kingdom will never love it well," answered Arbaces.

"True; no real amity can exist. It was from one of their sacred books in the temple of Assarac I had interpreted to me by a priest, then my tutor, the account of their wonderful deliverance by a mighty warrior who divided the sea with the sword of his god, and turning the fiery blade toward Egypt destroyed, at a blow, the whole host of the pursuing king. I have felt a desire to learn more of their wonderful history; and if, when in their land, thou shouldst find other books that continue it, purchase and bring them to me. Remeses, Prince of Damascus, whose letters to the King of Phœnicia were given by a Syrian ambassador, four hundred years ago, to one of my ancestors, wrote that he left them in the wilderness seeking some country which their gods commanded them to conquer and settle in."

" I have also seen those ancient letters of the Syrian Prince Remeses to King Sesostris his father, written more than four hundred and fifty years ago. I remember his description of that mighty nation of the Hebrews and the power of their gods," answered Arbaces.

" If thou canst hear of farther writings of that people's progress and conquest of the land wherein for four hundred years they have now dwelt without a king, see that a copy of the books be obtained; and what thou seest, my Arbaces, in thy travels write me, in order (as Remeses wrote his father and king), the events as they transpire, and I will on thy return have them inscribed on vellum and bound in a casket of gold, and placed with the other royal books in the archives of the Palace of Ninus."

" It will be too great an honor, most august king," answered Arbaces modestly; " but I will do what lies within my poor ability to preserve for your perusal a clear history of the events which are before me in the strange countries which I am about to visit."

After some more words of friendship, which became rather the parting of brothers than of a king with a subject, the monarch embraced his ambassador and took leave of him at the door of the audience chamber.

The Prince Arbaces, preceded by a stately chamberlain, clad in a purple tunic embroidered with stars and flowers, and wearing upon his head a tiara of velvet with the crest of a brilliant serpent's head, and covered with a net of woven threads of gold, passed through a stately hall open above to the clear azure sky, and decorated with the most elegant figures painted in vivid colors upon cedar-wood panels. Above the noble entrance to this magnificent hall was placed the emblematical winged circle of the god Assarac, dazzling with the radiance of precious stones.

Leaving this hall, he traversed a corridor, the columns of which were richly gilded, and the cornices carved and covered with plated gold, while the architrave consisted of the rarest woods worked with surpassing skill. Compartments or shields, on the plinth of the columns, were surrounded by elegant moldings with borders of polished acacia-wood inlaid with ivory and silver; while the spaces between the pilasters were divided into oval and square depressed panels, painted with flowers and the beautiful forms of ideal animals.

Another apartment which he traversed was lined with sculptured figures, standing in noble attitudes. Kings, warriors, and priests were represented in processions amid the sacred groves. He walked upon alabaster slabs which recorded in letters of gold the achievements of the monarch who had built that portion of the palace.

He now crossed a court of fountains, and came to a majestic doorway guarded by gigantic winged lions with human faces of the most benign and kingly aspects. At this entrance stood a number of the palace guard, who saluted the prince ambassador with military homage as he passed through the portal. At the extremity of another court he walked through a gateway guarded by colossal winged bulls of white alabaster, while above the gate were sculptured the most elaborate and elegant designs of a mingled sacred and warlike character.

He now reached the vestibule of this vast palace of the Assyrian Kings, to the magnificence and grandeur of which a hundred monarchs had contributed, until it covered a half a league square with its kingly edifices. This lofty room was painted and decorated with gold and azure, ivory and cedar, in every part. Along the sides were represented winged priests crowning kings, processions of chariots and horsemen, and the august ceremonies of religion—all sculptured in pure alabaster and colored with the most brilliant tints of the artist's pencil. Over the gateway was represented as a colossal figure in colors the first Sardanapalus in an attitude of adoration before the starry heavens, holding a golden cup in his hand filled with offerings.

This gorgeous gate led to the outer portal of the palace; and Arbaces, passing through the lines of guards in brazen armor, came where his horse was held by two Indian slaves, and mounting him, he rode to join his legion. Placing himself with his chief officers, all glittering in gold and steel, at its head, it wheeled into column and dashed onward through the superb avenue which led from the front of the "palace of the kings" to the western gate of the city.

This avenue was broad enough for the two hundred chariots to drive along it abreast. It was lined with palaces, before the pillars of the gates of which reposed majestic winged bulls; or alabaster lions of colossal size, having faces of men; or stood statues and winged animals of the most ideal yet elegant forms. Statues, in stone, of serpents in vast coils crouched at the doors of temples; gardens, lakes, terraces, and fountains adorned the fronts of these palaces, which extended in uninterrupted splendor and beauty four miles along the avenue, before they terminated in a vast quadrangular castle which defended the gigantic gateway of the city.

Passing through this portal the Prince Arbaces was followed by his brilliant escort until, crossing the Tigris,—which is made to environ the whole city as a means of warlike defense, by a bridge supported by one hundred piers, each a colossus,—they came in sight of the royal caravan in waiting a mile from the gate, by the fountain of Ninus.

This caravan consisted of two hundred camels, bearing tents, and provisions, and other equipage for the long journey into Egypt; of three hundred led horses, four hundred mules, and wagons fourscore. It was an equipment such as was provided for a warlike expedition to a remote province, only the whole was more costly and superb in its character, as became a nuptial embassy from the king of so great a realm as that of Assyria to a haughty Pharaoh of Egypt.

At a given signal the caravan moved onward; and as each division had its captain or chief, with a royal supervisor over all, who took the whole responsibility of the conduct of this vast retinue, the young ambassador had only to ride at the head of his legion and leisurely pursue his march westward.

After the third day they had left the beautiful valley of the Tigris with its pleasant and familiar scenes; and, taking a southwest course, the seventh evening Arbaces riding forward came in sight of the Euphrates winding through its charming valley far distant, and shining in the setting sun like a tortuous serpent with scales of burnished gold, lying along the undulating horizon. Upon its banks glittered a bronze roofed temple, and along its shores shone the palaces of the priests; for this was a sacred city of the ancient empire of Babylon. One hundred miles below stood Babylon in glory and magnificence only second to Nineveh, and governed by a prince appointed by the Assyrian monarch; for the two dominions were now united under one scepter.

"I would gladly," said Arbaces to his chief-captain who sat upon his horse near him, "have taken our course more southwardly and passed Babylon in sight, if not through it; but I will do that on my return from Egypt; for I would fain behold the southern capital of our vast united empire!"

"It were better, my lord prince," said the gray-bearded chief-captain with deference, "not to trust the fair princess or even yourself with so small a retinue with Belesis of Babylon. It has been rumored of late that he is ambitious to make himself king; and that he already conspires to win the army in Babylon over to his interests. Your presence there might bring the matter to a head by the temptation which it would present to him to seize upon you as a hostage, or you and the princess on your return! As your highness is the king's cousin, he might feel that he could dictate terms to Belus with your person in his power. No, my prince, let us not trust the wily governor of Babylon. We are now in his Euphratian realms and near enough to his metropolis."

"Say you so?" answered Arbaces; "then ought the king presently to know that he cannot confide power to that ambitious Babylonian prince!"

"His majesty suspects the purposes of his viceroy; when they are confirmed, the sun is not far off, which, rising on Belesis with his vice-regal crown on his head catching and reflecting its beams, will set upon him shorter by crown and head," answered the old noble, with stern decision.

Encamping upon the broad, flower-enameled plains of the stately Euphrates, the next morning they crossed it near the temple of Bactris by a bridge adorned with statues of sacred figures; while at the extremity, in a grove before the temple, was placed as a guard a symbolic statue compounded of a man, a lion, an ox, and an eagle. Past it was the "sacred way" by which none but the priests could enter the holy place.

The caravan wound slowly around the consecrated grove, and Arbaces stopped by the side of an altar where stood seven priests, the chief with wings, as a part of his costume, of the most brilliant plumage of Oriental birds, extending from his shoulders to his feet, giving him an aspect of singular majesty and glory. His white beard flowed to his girdle.

He was reverently saluted by the young Assyrian ambassador, who asked for his blessing and prayers. The High Priest, who was about to offer up the usual morning sacrifice, received him with benignity, and having learned the object of his expedition, said:

"If thou passest through the land where dwelleth the mighty

Hebrew Prophet Isamel, convey to him the homage of Dodanah, the chief priest of Bacchus; for we have heard of his wonderful power and favor with the gods of his land and that he calleth lightning from the skies with a wave of his wand! We honor the prophets of all gods! for, though the deities are as numerous as the stars, their power is derived from one and the same Supreme Spirit of the Universe. But this is a mystery of our religion, O prince, and revealed only to the pious, which I believe thou art, being cousin to the great king, and taught in all that concerns the great and good to know. But the ignorant see the Supreme only in marble and in symbols. But *we* perceive Him through the mind and thought, and need no material form in order to worship Him!"

The High Priest having thus affably conversed with Arbaces, as to a person of wisdom and prudence, directed the morning worship to proceed, as the sun at that moment lifted the edge of his shield above the horizon.

The six priests immediately struck each a cymbal held in his hand, lifting their voices in a sonorous chant, while the venerable High Priest, taking sacred fire from a censer, kindled a fagot of fragrant wood laid upon the altar.

In a moment it blazed high in the air, when an eighth priest advancing placed a serpent of bronze upon the altar and a beautiful youth swung incense before it, offering it worship.

The priests chanted as they beat their cymbals:

> "Hail wisdom and light !
> These are the powers of the Universe !
> These create all things !"

> "There is nothing greater than light ;
> There is nothing superior to wisdom,"

answered the High Priest, holding the serpent up to the morning sun now in full splendor above the horizon.

"The essence of all things is light," chanted the youth who swung the censer, upon whose breast hung a winged circle of gold.

> "Light is hidden under all that shines !
> Evil and light can never dwell together !
> The spirit of darkness flies before light !
> Sun, moon, stars, lightning, fire—these
> Rule the Universe—these are the essence of God !"

Thus chanted responsive the priest and his assistants in slow and solemn measure, while Arbaces and his officers in reverent attitudes of worship stood by.

When the whole ceremony of the morning rites was over, the High Priest invited Arbaces to enter his palace and refresh himself for a few hours after the fatigues of his journey. But the young soldier urging haste in his mission declined; and receiving the blessing of this chief of the Magi rejoined the still advancing caravan.

Their course now was due south for two days and then for four days directly west. On the fourteenth day after leaving Nineveh they came in sight of a range of high, dark mountains, from the summit of which, the chief of the caravan informed Arbaces, was visible the valley of the river of Ammun or Jordan.

The prince was overjoyed at the sight of this vast gigantic mountain wall; for its level summit, unbroken for leagues by any indenture, gave it the aspect of a wall upreared, as tradition declared, by the antediluvian giants, to keep out the great flood from their abodes. He knew that the Jordan flowed through the land of the Hebrews, and that he should be half-way in his journey to Egypt on crossing it.

Galloping forward with a hundred of his bodyguard as a protection against any attack from the parties of wild horsemen which, armed with long lances, for two days had been hovering on the wings of the caravan, he in three hours reached the mountain, and in another had wound his way upward to the top.

Wide and beautiful exceedingly was the prospect which burst upon his eyes. From the western foot of the mountains stretched a fair green valley, dotted with villages, small fenced cities and castles, and waving with fields of golden corn, rich with vineyards, and verdant with secluded vales studded with flocks and herds.

"This is a land of plenty as well as of loveliness. It truly flows with milk and honey. This must be that country of the Hebrews—the rich and glorious land promised to them four hundred years ago by their leader Musis, as is written in the rolls of Remeses of Damascus. And can there be such a peace and prosperity among a people without a king to rule over them?" exclaimed Arbaces with animation.

"It is rumored, my lord prince," said Ninus, his armor-bearer, a tall youth of humble birth, and fair countenance, with the courageous looks of a lion, "that they have a god for their king who dwells in a tent of gold and silken curtains, in the form of a star of pure fire, on which no man but their chief magician can look and live."

"Where heardest thou this tale, Ninus?" asked the prince.

"My mother's brother, my lord, was a merchant of pearls and precious dyes; and once a year made a journey with others to the city of Damascus, the fairest town for beauty of site and riches on earth. Once he extended his journey into Egypt, passing through the Hebrew country. He said it was a brave people, but chiefly tillers of the soil and shepherds; that they had no king over them as other nations, but professed that their god was their only king; and they showed my uncle from a distance the gorgeous tent, which they called a tabernacle, wherein their great king-god dwelt. They had, however, a sort of governors called Judges, men and even women, whom for great exploits in war or some extraordinary favor done the nation they elected for life to rule over them; but that they could do nothing save by the authority of the king-god."

"This is a very strange government," answered the prince; "and I am glad you remember so clearly what your merchant uncle used to relate to you thereof. But we will soon see for ourselves. What a fair land! Behold the river between us and that hill-country; how, like a silver thread running through a green mantle, it meanders along the emerald valley; now flashing in the sun as it hurries on its swift course; now hidden by cliffs; now glimmering amid the trees!"

As they rode along the mountain ridge they saw walled cities, which hitherto had been concealed, reveal themselves beyond the river, with numerous castles perched upon high rocks, while all the valleys teemed with population. Soon a bright sea, farther to the south, became visible and seemed to receive the river, though its mouth was not in sight.

It was night before the whole caravan and armed retinue had crossed the dark mountain by an easy pass which, at a distance, was not apparent, but that led them into the valley not far from the river.

Here the Assyrian company pitched their camp, while the shepherds and villagers, alarmed by the descent into their peaceful vales of so large a party of strangers, like a small army, fled to their cities and strongholds. The alarm was sounded from hill to hill by the peal of trumpets which, caught up by the mountain echoes, were repeated again and again amid the narrow dells.

Prince Arbaces thought it best to remain quiet in his tent until morning, and then ride to the gate of the nearest citadel and explain his object in coming into their country.

All that star-lit night, while the ambassador's camp was still, save the dull tread of the mailed soldiers that paced about it to keep military watch upon its weary travelers in their deep sleep, came from across the valley the metallic ring of blows on iron and brass; the sounds of a surprised people preparing their armor and weapons of war in order to meet the events of the coming day.

Having now, in this epistle, laid broadly and plainly the foundation of our book, we shall here close it, leaving the pen of the youthful Assyrian ambassador to record the events and scenes which subsequently transpired in the progress of the important mission intrusted to him by his king.

January 26, 1860.

THE THRONE OF DAVID.

LETTER I.*

ARBACES, THE AMBASSADOR, TO BELUS, KING OF ASSYRIA.

CITY OF JERICHO, NEAR THE JORDAN.

SIRE:

In obedience to your Majesty's commands, I have availed myself of my first leisure to record in the leaves of my tablets the scenery and incidents which have struck me as worthy of observation during my journey from the banks of the Tigris to those of this remote river. Descriptions of the interesting countries through which I have passed, with allusions to the manners and customs of the people, I will not here repeat, as I have made a careful history of them for your Majesty's perusal when I shall return from my embassy.

After a journey of fifteen days I reached the valley of Jordan, and, crossing the river the following morning, pitched my tent outside of the gates of this city. Here we have been reposing for several days, in order to recruit the weary and restore the energies of all after our fatiguing march, much of which lay over arid plains.

Our first sudden appearance in this lovely valley created both surprise and fear; and the inhabitants took up arms to attack us and drive us back to the dark mountains from which we had emerged. Not less than seven thousand men were collected for this purpose in one night and were discovered marshaled upon the plain before us in hostile array at dawn.

Not wishing to appear like an enemy where I wished to be at peace, I gave orders that not one of my legion should leave the tents; and advancing with only my armor-bearer, Ninus, and my venerable chief captain, Nacherib, I walked toward one who seemed to be their leader.

As I drew near I could see that but few of the host carried

* About 1050 B. C.

proper weapons of war, or wore steel armor, there being visible but here and there a helm and nodding plume in the whole forefront of the array. The greater number were armed with shepherd's crooks, hunting-knives, bills, wolf-spears, and instruments of labor; yet they bore themselves with a bold face, and were ranged in companies and battalions with the regularity and precision of a well-drilled army. A few ensigns fluttered above their heads, the pennons flashing in the morning sun.

I was struck with the noble bearing of the leader, who seemed a mere youth, though he towered above the ordinary height of men. He wore a helmet and cuirass, and held a sword in his hand.

Seeing me advance in a peaceful manner some paces before my two officers, he also came forward, and saluting me with a courteous wave of his sword, said, in a Chaldaic dialect not unlike our own speech, so that I plainly understood his words:

"Who art thou, my lord! and whence comest thou with an armed legion and so great a retinue? Is thy mission one of peace or of war?"

"Peace, my lord captain," I answered. "I serve the King of Assyria, and am going on an embassy into the land of Egypt; but have a message to deliver by the way to the great Seer and Judge of thy country, Isamel, the friend of the gods! Thou didst last night behold an armed legion enter this valley with me. It is but my bodyguard given me by my master, the King of Nineveh, to protect me against the wandering bands of the wilderness; but, as thou perceivest, not numerous enough to make war. If thou hast authority in this land, I crave permission to cross the Jordan, and go on my way to the palace of your governor, Isamel."

When I had done speaking, the youthful warrior came near to me, and again saluting me, said:

"We welcome thee, O Assyrian, to our land! The aged prophet, Samuel, whom thou callest Isamel, is at his abode in Ramah, at least two days' march for thy caravan, westward. He is a man of God, virtuous as judge, undaunted in duty, gentle in heart, yet with a lion's courage against evil. But thou errest, my lord, in supposing he is now the Judge of Israel. We have now a king like the nations around us!"

"This news had not reached our ears in Assyria," I answered. "Is the Prophet Isamel no more?"

"The Seer of God's people," here answered a grave and elderly personage, with the scars of battles on his brow, who with others of the Hebrews drew near, "still lives, my lord of Ashur. He is yet, as ever, loved and honored for his great age, profound wisdom, and celestial virtues. But becoming too aged to rule the land, disturbed by a long war with our hereditary foes, the martial nation of the Philistines, although often delivering us from them by a divine courage, he yielded the authority to his two sons! But these men inherited not their father's ability and wisdom, nor the friendship of God, and all the land rose up under their weak rule and demanded of the Prophet to elect and anoint over us a king in their place. The Prophet would have dissuaded us from having a king, saying: 'He will take away your possessions and make your sons the servants of his palace, drivers of his chariot, his horsemen and guards of his body, and your daughters slaves to do the labors of his household! All of you will be at the service of your king, and without power to follow your own way, but only be made the obedient servitors of his power. Then you will repent and wish again for the liberty to elect your own Judges, as you have done for four hundred years, even since the days of Joshua and the elders of his day.' But, my lord of Ashur, the multitude did not hearken to the words of the Seer, and were so clamorous for a king that he anointed a young man by the name of Saul of Benjamin, son of Kish, a mighty man of valor whom God pointed out to him."

"And is Saul now your king?" I asked of the grave Hebrew who had spoken.

"He is, O most noble lord, and has been for some time. He is a notable warrior, and has fought for us, and won great victories against the Philistines at the head of our armies. As a soldier he has no superior; but he is of a gloomy, sad, melancholy, wayward temper of late, and the whole land sighs for the mild and firm dominion of the wise and good Prophet."

"Thou speakest boldly of thy king," I said, surprised at this freedom of speech, where each word might be reported to his monarch, and his imprudence cost him his head.

"So do all men, my lord, who are men," he answered. "God has given a king to us in his anger, as was said, and we now feel it. Even the great Prophet has of late departed from him in displeasure, to see him no more, on account of his impieties and cruelties! Nay, God seems to have deserted him."

"Happy the day," said the young chief, "when his brave and wise son, the Prince Jonathan, shall be king in his father' place."

I was amazed, your majesty, at the audacity and boldness o speech of these Hebrews! They are a fearless race, saturnine in complexion, with brilliant black eyes, raven hair, and face: full of intelligence and genius. I like them much. I learnec from them why they were not armed any better. It seems tha their conquerors, the Philistines, have once overrun the coun try and disarmed the whole land, city by city, leaving then only implements of toil! Under their king they hoped in some measure to retrieve these disgraces, but he had achieved nc permanent good to his kingdom by his victories, the Philistines still holding part of the land, and constantly offering battle.

After some further conversation, the chiefs, satisfied of the peaceful character of my retinue, retired from the field, anc reported to the council or senate in the principal city of the valley, four miles distant.

In a few hours a messenger came to me with an invitation to go to the city, and permission for my caravan to encamp near the gates, by a certain sacred fountain.

With pleasure I accepted this courtesy of the Hebrew people and resuming our march we crossed the Jordan at a ford kindly indicated by the young chief, who having first come over, guided us to the western shore, the water having been nc deeper than our saddle girths. Thus we all safely passed the swift stream, and in an hour afterward had reached the pleas-ant field, shaded by a grove, where we were to encamp. How shall I describe to your Majesty the beauty of the scenery, on all sides presenting a singular mingling of the wildest rocks, with the most lovely vales! Fields of corn shining as if a snow of golden flakes had descended upon them, charming vales, pleasant pastures, gardens, vineyards, villas, castles, and forti-fied cliffs; with the ever present flowing river, and the dark mountains beyond, with the bright deep blue sky above, all com-bined, afford to the eye the most delightful entertainment.

The populousness, too, of this land is wonderful to behold. The people fill the fields, the roads, the avenues, travel to and fro among the hills, crowd the gates of the towns, throng the paths to the spring and to the river; and are in gardens, vine-yards, shops, bazaars, and market-places innumerable. In As-syria, all our population is centered in the city, save a few shepherds and rude tillers of the soil. Here the country has the life of a city; and the inhabitants are not peasants nor rude serfs, but intelligent and active, self-possessed men, free from all the awkwardness and ignorance that is supposed to characterize the rustic. The very plowmen have the bearing of metropolitans and civilians near a court, and walk and speak with a striking air of independence. All can read their sacred books (which are the most wonderful in the world), and have the ability to copy them. Descended from the same Chaldaic ancestry, twelve tribes born of twelve brothers, they are equal in rank, bear a striking natural likeness to each other, and have one language. In speech as well as in blood they are allied to Assyria, through Abram their chief. Though I have been here but nine days, I have already learned much of their manners, customs, religion, and polity. The elders, venerable and dignified men, chosen in every city for their wisdom and years of experience, have been courteous to me beyond expression.

On the first day of my arrival I had hardly got my tent pitched ere a deputation waited upon me from Jericho, the chief city in this valley. I was about to dine. They were pleased with, and greatly admired the elegance of my silken tent, the beauty of the plate upon my table, and the exquisite shape of the furniture. I seemed to them as a great king, from the magnificence of my appointments, and they treated me with but little less distinction than they would have shown your majesty in person. I invited them to dine with me, but they excused themselves, saying they had prepared a banquet, of which they came to invite me to partake, inasmuch as they desired to show their regard for the high and mighty Prince, my master, by their attention to his ambassador, who had honored their country by passing through it. Attended only by Ninus and the brave Nacherib, I accompanied them to the gates of the city. Upon my way I perceived that the army which had been collected so suddenly from both sides of the river to oppose my march had as suddenly dissolved, all the persons who had assembled at the war cry hastening again to the occupations from which the alarm trumpet had called them. There seems to be among them no standing army, save a bodyguard of two thousand men for the king's person, and a thousand for his son, the popular young Prince Jonathan; but all the males are trained soldiers, except a tribe of priests, and are ready for war and the battlefield at the summons of the moment.

Upon passing into the great gate of the city several noble-looking men, most of them with flowing white or gray beards, rose up from seats placed in the corridor each side of the entrance, and saluted me with graceful dignity. A large throng of people stood around observing me with curiosity. One of these elders then addressed to me a few words of kind welcome to the city, and expressed the desire of his fellow-citizens to render my brief sojourn pleasant among them.

I replied in a suitable manner, and was then invited to a seat by his side upon a sort of dais; for I perceived that this principal gate was made use of as an ordinary hall of council for the senators of the town, being the most public place within the walls. Here they were accustomed to receive the visits of their friends, the homage of the citizens, and honor from all, young and old. No one passed them without an obeisance of respect; and I observed, while I sat there, that sometimes they would gently detain a passing young man, and give him some words of advice or of mild reproof.

After a conference of some length, during which it gave me satisfaction to reply to many inquiries which they made about Assyria and your majesty—and it pleased me to hear their remarks and expressions of surprise at many of the things which I communicated to them—after an hour passed thus agreeably in their benign society, came the steward of the chief elder and informed him that the banquet was prepared. I accompanied him, followed by the other elders and some of the chief citizens, with the two military chiefs, the younger of whom I learned was called Joab, a young soldier of great promise as well as prowess. But I pass over the incidents of this feast, as it presented no particulars sufficiently interesting to detain your majesty. It was chiefly characterized by simplicity and temperance.

By the close of the second day I had become acquainted with many of this remarkable people, and held many conversations with their Rabbis or men of learning, who readily gave me access to their sacred books, and cheerfully recounted to me such events in the history of their nation as my curiosity led me to make inquiries about.

From these books, and from their remarkably clear traditions, as well as from a personal record which I have had the

privilege of perusing and copying, I am able to furnish your
majesty with an interesting account of the history of this nation from the time when Remeses the Prince of Damascus
terminated his letters to King Sesostris to the coronation of
their first king, the warrior Saul, now upon the throne.

As your majesty possesses a copy of the roll of parchment
on which the ancient epistles of Prince Remeses (written now
four hundred and ninety years since) are inscribed, on reference to them to refresh your recollection, you will learn that
he parted from the leader Musis, or Moses, as his countrymen
term him, in the desert of Arabia about two months after the
departure from Egypt. It was the intention of the Prince of
Damascus to have accompanied the Hebrews in their march to
the conquest of the land their God had promised them; but
having offended their Deity by worshiping the golden calf,
Apis, a god of Egypt, in the justice of His divine anger He
decreed that they should be withheld from the possession of
their promised country until forty years had passed.

Prince Remeses alludes to this in the following passage in
his parchments, which, as nearly as I recollect, reads as
follows:

"Moses informs me, my dear father, that in punishment of
this sin of the Hebrews, their God will cause them to wander
blindly many years in the wilderness ere He bring them to
the land promised to their fathers, and will subject them to be
harassed by enemies on all sides; some of whom have already
attacked them in their march, but were discomfited by the
courage of a Hebrew youth, called Joshua, who promises to
become a mighty warrior and leader of Israel, and whom Moses
loves as an own son.

"In view, therefore," continues the letter of Remeses, "of
this long abode in the desert of the Hebrews, I shall to-morrow
join a caravan which will then pass northward on its way into
Syria from Egypt. It will be with profound regret that I shall
bid adieu to Moses, to Aaron, to Miriam, their venerable sister,
and all the friends I have found among this wonderful people.
Will not the world, which has beheld the wonders worked for
their release from Egypt, watch from afar the further progress
of this army of God?"

Thus writes Remeses at the close of his series of Letters to
his father, King Sesostris; and from that time we, in Assyria,
have learned nothing more of the history of this people, save

that at this moment they are inhabiting this beautiful land, twelve powerful nations united under one king, a realm of warriors, priests, and wise men, simple and pastoral in their habits, patriarchal in their customs, and eminently favored of the gods.

As everything relating to such a people whose past history is constantly intermingled with that of the divine gods is of deep interest, and as your majesty enjoined me to make myself acquainted with whatever concerned their polity and customs, their religion and government, I shall briefly avail myself of the narratives of their sacred books, of their private records and written traditions, and of the conversation of their learned men, to which I have given all my time during the past eight days (being delayed by the illness of some of my people), to present to your majesty a clear outline of their history, taking it up where it was dropped by the Prince of Damascus.

The interval of four hundred and ninety years up to the present day could not be otherwise than abundant in events of the deepest interest. While I shall consult brevity, I shall at the same time endeavor to give a distinct outline of their extraordinary career.

When the warrior prophet, Moses, had descended from the mountain of Heaven with the tables of alabaster on which his God had inscribed with his finger the laws He desired the Hebrews to observe, say the sacred books, and beheld the people worshiping the golden god of the Egyptians, he, in his great grief and anger, cast the tablets upon the earth and shivered them into fragments. Destroying the idol, he slew three thousand of its worshipers! and for their sin, the intentions of their mighty God were so changed toward them that He plagued them in their passage through the wilderness in such a manner that they lost their way continually for the space of forty years, even until all who were over twenty years of age when they left Egypt had died, and were buried in the sands or amid the rocks of the desert, save two great and good men, Joshua and Caleb. These, alone, were saved for their faithfulness, virtues, and courage.

Moses having atoned to his God for the idolatry of the people, by the blood of the offenders, went again up into the mountain at His command, and received a second time tables of the law from Heaven. These laws are still piously preserved and obeyed by this people; are inscribed in letters of gold upon the walls of their civic temples, or synagogues, and proclaimed once in seven days aloud in the entrances of the cities. They are ten in number, and embrace all human duty to the gods and to man.

They command the worship of one God; forbid the adoration of material idols; the profanation of the sacred names; command the observance of every seventh day as holy; obedience to parents; forbid murder, impurity, theft, false testimony, and avarice! Such pandects, methinks, are worthy to be received by all people.

Their God also directed them to erect a movable temple in the form of a vast royal tent, in which to preserve the sacred vessels and to perform worship to Him. Their holy books give a minute description of this tabernacle. It was gorgeous beyond expression. In Nineveh I know of nothing, luxurious as all is there, which can surpass it in magnificence. It was divided into courts and compartments from the outer to the most inner and sacred, and contained altars for sacrifice and incense, and an interior secret throne for their God, whose symbol was like a burning Eye, dreadful to behold, and blinding for mortal to gaze upon.

This tabernacle still exists in this land, and when I have seen it I will more particularly write of it to your majesty.

For forty years the nation wandered through the terrible deserts which lie beneath the blazing center of the sun. Their sacred books record forty-two encampments, or one fixed rest a year, continuing sometimes only weeks, sometimes many months. In their march they constantly traversed and retraversed their former track, now going north, now bending their painful course west, and again eastwardly, only, after many weary days, to change again the direction of their labyrinthine track toward the south! Thus, like a blind man groping in a field to find an outlet, this great nation of three millions of people, of which six hundred thousand were fighting men, groped up and down and across the mighty deserts of Afric, seeking vainly, mourning sadly, for the land promised to their fathers and to them, and which they had come forth from Egypt with great power and glory of deeds to find and conquer. How terrible the judgments of their God! How fearful his displeasure!

Whithersoever they went they bore the tabernacle with its holy altars and sacred Ark, where dwelt the divine light of the glorified presence of their God. Morning and evening sacrifices of animals burned upon the high altar, and the priests and people ceased not to propitiate the righteous anger of their offended Deity.

As this mighty nation was descended from twelve chiefs, brothers and sons of one man, grandson of the Assyrian Abram, so the descendants preserved, even when they numbered tens of thousands of souls in each line, their lineage distinct. They were not so much one nation as twelve nations governed by one law, under one leader, worshiping one God! Of these twelve clans, or tribes, one was set apart as sacred to the priestly office. The men thereof were not to bear arms, but reserve themselves for the holy duties of their temple or tabernacle.

On the march these twelve tribes formed as many armies, each under its own standard and chiefs. Seventy Elders assisted the leader Moses in council and judgment of cases. During their whole sojourn in the wilderness they were miraculously fed by a sort of supernatural or celestial food of the gods, which was secretly conveyed to the earth by night, and found by the people in the morning! Also flocks of birds followed them as by an irresistible spell upon them! and along their path in their marches, however arid, hot, and sandy the desert was under their feet, there flowed with refreshing coolness a stream of pure water clear as crystal, and which never deserted them for the forty years of their remarkable wandering; thus in punishing this people, their powerful God remembered mercy, and preserved their lives, when He might have permitted them to perish. This wonderful stream of living water had originally been created by their leader Moses, by opening with a stroke of his rod a rock in the desert about three months after they had come out of Egypt, when they complained for want of water and charged him with bringing them into the wilderness to die of thirst. From that fountain, which so marvelously gushed forth out of the dry rock, the stream flowed ceaselessly, and wound about across the desert after them, " as if," says the personal record I have before alluded to, " it possessed intelligence and benevolence; as if it were not so much a rivulet of water as a bright and liquid serpent with a divine and living spirit inhabiting it, and directing its course by love and pity in order to refresh and save the weary and the wandering."

In addition to this wonderful phenomenon, the sacred books of this people state that the garments which they wore when they departed out of Egypt remained all the while unimpaired by time and exposure; while their sandals continued for forty years unbroken and as fit for service as the day they first bound them upon their feet! If this be all true, which I cannot at all doubt, what a God of wonders and power must be this Deity of the Hebrews! How extraordinary his acts! Commanding them in punishment for transgression to wander forty years in a desert, yet providing, with a Father's care and love, for their meat and drink and apparel, where otherwise they could never have obtained them, and without which they would speedily have perished! How different his character from that which priestly traditions give to our gods Assarac, Ninus, and Ophic, who are represented as utterly destroying and mercilessly exterminating their foes! All things done by the God of the Hebrews show, not only his resistless power, but reveal surpassing Goodness, wondrous Patience, and perfect Love.

That a nation so powerful in numbers and warlike with armed men should create alarm in the countries along the borders of which their march extended, your majesty will readily conjecture. Some of these nations met them with all their military forces, and gave them battle in order to prevent their advance through their country. Rumor of their numbers and the mighty miracles of their Deity had gone before them; and all the kings, whose dominions lay near their line of progress, hearing that they were seeking the conquest of some country in order to supplant the inhabitants and dwell therein themselves, trembled for their own dominions; and uniting together attacked them with overwhelming armies. In some of these engagements the Hebrews were victorious; and routed and pursued their enemies with terrible slaughter; in others they suffered most disastrous defeats, and were driven back from their line of march and the sight of green vales and fair cities, again into the depths of the wilderness; and thus between their hopeless wanderings and their relentless foes they seemed ready to despair, and sighed for a return to the bondage they had borne in Egypt as a happy relief to their present miseries! Was ever a nation, for whom the gods had done such mighty works, so afflicted by the gods? Their pitiable condition recalls the tradition of Sephaxad, that lesser god of ancient Assyria, who would scale the superior heaven by climbing the edge of the rising sun! in punishment of whose ambition the supreme god Assarac caused the sun to turn on its axis with him, so that Sephaxad continued climbing to this day this ever turning shield of light, but never in the least progressing.

At length the gods of the Hebrews, or, for me to speak more accurately, rather God (for they recognize and adore but one Deity), appeased by this forty years' patient endurance of his anger against their sin, which, as I have written, was withdrawing their worship from Himself and fixing it upon a molten image of an Egyptian god, mercifully put a period to their aimless marches, and elevating before their hosts the fiery standard of his glorious power, bade them follow and it should bring them to the land of their hopes and prayers!

This standard was a wonderful column of light, which by night shone with the brilliancy of a thousand moons, and lighted up the whole camp for miles around the sacred tabernacle over which it suspended itself in the air. It had preceded their march during all their movements in the forty years of their desert wanderings. It had indicated when and where they should encamp, by advancing and becoming stationary over the appointed place; and when to move onward again by going forward. By day, it had the appearance of a bright cloud let down from the heavens, and borne gently onward by the wind a few hundred feet above the earth. Yet its motion was not produced by the wind, says the private journal of "Caleb the Good," who has left on record a most interesting narrative of what befell his people in their journeying, and which record, now before me, is preserved in the archives of the Levites in this city. In the sand storms of the desert the column of cloud remained as immovable as if it were an aërial pillar of alabastron; and when the atmosphere was breathless, it moved forward with a motion within itself, "as if the Spirit of the Lord dwelt in it," adds the record from which I transcribe.

Hence this people did not so much *lose* their way in the desert as were led out of it by their God! How must the hearts of this mighty nation of wanderers have bounded when at length, near the close of a long and painful day's march, Moses stretching forth his rod toward the land they were to take possession of, suddenly cried in a loud voice, "Behold yonder lofty ridge of mountains northward, ye men of Israel! Lo! from their highest peak is visible, to the eyes of him who standeth thereon, the land of Abraham, of Isaac, and of Jacob.

the land flowing with milk and honey, which the Lord hath
promised to you for an inheritance, and of which He is now
about to place you in possession! Let Israel go forward! Behold the Pillar of Cloud advances!"

How these stirring words (taken from the brief record of
them made by the warrior and holy man, Caleb), must have
thrilled through every bosom! How changed now, alas! was the
material of this mighty host! It still numbered more than
three millions of souls; but they were not the men who crossed
the Red Sea and commenced, forty years before, their solemn
march. There were still six hundred thousand fighting men,
but they were not the men who had fought the first battles of
Israel near Mount Sinai! The mighty legions, now moving
in twelve armies to the conquest of the land of promise, are
composed of men under forty years of age; not one has ever
seen Egypt! They were born, not slaves of Pharaoh, but free-
men of God in the free desert. Their erring fathers have laid
their bones in its sands for their sins; and these come in to
take the promised inheritance with clean hands and hearts.

The elders and rulers of the people are none of them above
sixty years of age; and these are of those who were yet beardless when their fathers came out of Egypt. Not a beard that
left the shores of the Red Sea (save those two men Joshua and
Caleb), stood by the waters of the Jordan. Even Moses, their
august and venerable leader, when he at length came near the
mountain called Pisgah (the lofty summit of which, on the
other side of Jordan, I have seen to-day from the top of this
city's highest tower), made known to the people he had so long
led, that his God would not permit him to tread upon the soil
of the pleasant land he had for forty years yearned to enter.
This prohibition, he told them, was on account of his own sins
of infirmity in not bearing patiently with the murmurings of
the people; and, in his despair, almost questioning, himself, the
wisdom and goodness of his God.

What a lesson must this stern justice in their Deity's divine
character have taught this people! How careful must they
have been to keep his laws and avoid all transgression against
him! He who could entomb in the wilderness a whole nation,
and mark with his displeasure its faithful and venerable chief
for a few acts of impatience, how surely, they felt, will He visit
them with the dispensation of his retributions!

When the great and wise Moses had taught the people at

great length a code of moral laws, full of wisdom and truth, for their government as a nation, carefully laid down the policy they ought to pursue after establishing themselves in the promised land, and had given them a plan for the division of the country by tribes, and strengthened them with the wisest counsel, he eloquently pointed out to them the rewards which virtue, and the punishments which vice would bring to them. He then assembled his elders and captains, and solemnly informed them that his God had made known to him that he should be graciously permitted to behold from the top of the mountain over against Jericho the glory of the land to be possessed by the people of Israel; but that he should only see it! for after seeing it, God had said "in that very mount thou shalt die and be gathered to thy fathers."

How painfully touching must such an announcement have been from the lips of Moses to his people! To most of them he had been as a father from their infancy. He doubtless knew every face, and was loved and honored by all. And now how sorrowful must it be to them and to him, to be separated from them at the moment of the achievement of the great end for which he led them forth from Egypt, and in sight of the long-wished-for country, which, alas! by the fiat of his God he was forbidden to enter at the head of his conquering hosts!

But we hear no murmur from this mighty man! At the age of one hundred and twenty years he submits like a gentle child to the will of his mighty God. Taking leave of his friends at the foot of the mountain, and leaving a nation in tears, he ascends, attended by a few favored elders, whom he instructs in wisdom as he goes up the side of the mountain. Though his locks flow white upon his shoulders, and mingle with his snowy beard upon his breast, his eye is not dimmed nor his natural force abated. Near the summit he embraces tenderly his friends, blesses his noble general (Joshua), to whom he formally surrenders his place, authority, and power; while the aged Caleb kneels at his feet and bathes them in tears.

The voice of God from the summit calls him from their embraces! He hears the familiar sound, and spreading his hands over them, and over the kneeling nation in the plain below, he blesses them in silence, and then with moistened eyes turns away, and soon stands upon the mountain top.

Says the record of Caleb, "His majestic form seemed to expand and tower in stately beauty as we beheld him gaze off across the valley of Jordan, and let his piercing glance wander over the broad fertile country which lay, like Eden, between the two glittering seas! When he had surveyed it on all sides from his elevation, a bright cloud descended above him, which transfigured, but did not conceal him; and we heard a voice from above the cloud, as the voice of God, which said:

"'This is the land which I sware unto Abraham, unto Isaac, and unto Jacob, saying, I will give it unto thy seed! Behold, this land of Canaan I give unto the children of Israel for a possession forever! Lo, I have caused thee to see it with thine eyes; but thou shalt not go over thither!'

"When the voice had ceased speaking," continues the testimony of Caleb, "the face of Moses became like the sun! All his form and flowing robes were resplendent with light ineffable; and the cloud slowly enfolding him, he was borne as if supported by invisible beings from the place where he stood on the top of the mountain, and disappeared forever from our eyes.

"In awe we waited until we took courage to approach the holy place he had left, when we found all solitude. Nothing was visible around us but the rocky peak descending sheer into the dark mountain ravines! Silence like the eternal stillness of the upper sky reigned supreme!

"God had taken him from us, and buried him in mystery and holy secrecy from the eyes of all men! His sepulchre no man knoweth; but there are many that believe he was translated like Enoch to heaven, in the bright cloud which enshrouded his majestic and venerable form, and which many Seers who looked assert took the form of a mighty angel, even of Michael the Prince of Heaven!"

Thus reads the parchment of Caleb the good.

Farewell, my beloved cousin and king! I will soon take up my pen to address you another letter.

Your faithful
ARBACES.

LETTER II.

ARBACES TO THE KING.

AMBASSADOR'S CAMP, BEFORE JERICHO.

MY DEAR COUSIN AND KING:

We still linger in this romantic valley, not from choice, but from compulsion, as our invalids are but now sufficiently restored to health to move forward. This is the twelfth day since we encamped here; and yesterday I would have resumed our journey, but a messenger whom I had sent, by the advice of the elders of the senate, to the king to ask permission to pass through his territories, has but a few hours since returned with the royal consent. As his majesty was neither at Gibeah nor Gilgal, his usual abodes, but at the city of Hebron, farther south, where he is building a palace, my messenger was longer on his mission.

The king, with that grace and courtesy which singularly characterizes this refined people, not only accorded me the liberty to traverse his dominions, but has sent hither his son, the eldest Prince of his House, with an honorary escort of two hundred of his bodyguard, to accompany me to Hebron. I was walking in front of my tent, enjoying the soft air of this delicious clime, and watching the groups of dark-eyed, laughing maidens gathered, with their pitchers upon their heads, about the fountain which gushes forth near by in a grove of the tall palms that stand so grandly all about this city, when I heard the clear ring of a trumpet sounding from a narrow dale between the vine-clad hills that rise west of Jericho.

I looked and beheld emerge from the pass three or four mounted men in armor, one of whom was richly attired and seemed to be their chief, followed by a body of foot soldiers, whose shining steel casques reflected the sunbeams. They were marching into the valley, cheerfully sounding their trumpets before them. My chief captain, Nacherib, at once fastened on his helmet, and seizing his sword, marshaled my bodyguard into battle array, suspecting a surprise. The warders from the gate of the city at this moment responded to the bugles of the advancing party, which again replied with a stirring flourish of a score of martial instruments, among which were heard drums, cymbals, and cornets.

"That is not a warlike challenge, my noble captain," I said, hearing this stirring music, "but rather a salute of honor."

"True, my lord prince," answered the prudent old warrior, "but one must always believe armed bodies of strangers hostile until we prove them to be friends."

At this moment I perceived my messenger (who was Ninus, my armor-bearer), whom I had sent to the Hebrew monarch, detach himself from the van of the advancing troop and gallop across the valley toward me. In a few moments he alighted at my feet, and saluting me, said:

"Fear no treachery, my lord prince. This company, which you see advancing, is a guard of honor commanded by the youthful Prince Jonathan, and sent by King Saul to conduct your highness to his presence. The monarch, whom I had to seek in three cities and found in Hebron, received your message gladly, and expressed his desire to see in person the ambassador of the great king of the east; and as a proof of his sincerity he entertained me with the most distinguished courtesy, and has sent his son, the prince royal, to attend you to his capital!"

Upon hearing these welcome words I immediately mounted my horse, and at the head of one hundred of the most splendidly-attired of my bodyguard, rode slowly to meet the Hebrew prince. When I had come within three bow-shots of his party I halted, and leaping to the ground advanced on foot toward him. The Israelitish prince followed my example, and we met midway, saluting each other with military courtesy. I was at once most agreeably impressed with his appearance. He was a mere youth, with the down scarcely shading his lip, and in height not above the ordinary stature of young men. But there was a noble frankness in his clear, open eyes which revealed within a soul ingenuous and pure! His brown hair fell in shining waves upon his shoulders, and was parted above his fair forehead, which seemed to be the very throne of truth. Without being regularly handsome, his face was singularly attractive, and especially when lighted up by the fine, warm smile of sincere good-will with which he greeted me, as, coming quickly nearer, he extended his open hand to clasp mine! It seemed from that moment we were friends and to be friends

forever! Your majesty must not charge me with enthusiasm.
There are very few men to whom my heart goes out, or to
whose hand-clasp my own fully responds. When he spoke, his
voice, rich and musical in its pleasant cadences, completed his
conquest over me!

"My noble lord of Nineveh," he said, "the king my father
welcomes you, by me, to the land of the Hebrew people! He
is not ignorant of the glory and power of Assyria. He desires
you will accept my escort and visit him at Hebron. His court
is usually at Gibeah, but he now sojourns at the former place,
which he intends to make the capital of his kingdom!"

"I accept with pleasure, noble prince," I replied, "the invitation of your royal father. I can, however, pass but a brief
time at his court, as my mission is to that of Egypt!"

"So I have learned from your messenger," answered the
prince.

I then invited him to my tent, toward which we walked side
by side; while I intrusted the reception of his bodyguard to
the military courtesy of my chief captain. The dark-clad Hebrew troop, escorted to the camp of my one hundred brilliant
guards, took up a position near them, and soon the Assyrians
and Israelites were seen intermingling, curiously examining
one another's arms and armor, and conversing together like old
comrades and men of the same blood. And are not these Hebrews of the race of Chaldean Assyrians? Their language is
still so similar to ours that we converse together with facility.
The magnificence of my retinue, the superb helmets, corslets,
and coats of mail of my chosen company of one hundred Ninevite young nobles whom your majesty gave to guard my person
and tent, the beauty of their swords, golden helmets, and fal-
chions, the richness of the saddles and trappings of the horses,
and the elegance of the animals themselves, for the Hebrews
have but few horsemen, were all subjects of admiration and
remark.

In the meanwhile I sat in my tent with the amiable Hebrew
prince placed opposite to me. I entertained him with the richly
preserved fruits of India and the soft, golden wines of Media.

"You live in great splendor in the Orient, my lord prince,"
he said, glancing around upon the silken hangings of my traveling pavilion and at the costly appointments of everything
within.

"Our king is the most opulent of all princes on the earth,"

I truly answered him. "Nineveh is a city of palaces and of luxury. The empire of Assyria is unbounded in extent eastward and to the south. It embraces numerous lesser kingdoms, provinces, and governments; and the once mighty Babylon is subject to its scepter."

As he manifested deep interest in our affairs, and asked many questions about your majesty, I gave him a history of the power and splendor of your dominions; spoke of the vastness of your army, of the exhaustless wealth of your treasure-houses, of the magnificence of your court; but more than all, I described to him, O king, your majesty in person, the wisdom and prudence of your reign, and how you were loved and honored by your subjects.

When I had done speaking, the noble Hebrew modestly remarked:

"The glory of a kingdom, my lord, lies not in the gold and silver in its coffers, in the grandeur of its palaces, nor in the splendor of its court, but in the virtue, wisdom, and justice of its monarch!" From this admirable sentiment, which he finely expressed, his features being animated with all its spirit, your majesty will perceive something of the excellency of his disposition and the dignity of his thoughts.

When I had answered all his inquiries about Assyria, which he warmly expressed a desire one day to visit, I put many questions to him, in my turn, about his own country and people. When, from my observations, he perceived that I had some knowledge of the history of his nation up to the period of the eve of their conquest and the death of Moses, he appeared to be much pleased, and said that it would afford him great pleasure to communicate to me any further information I desired to obtain, while we should be journeying leisurely toward his father's court.

We were now interrupted in our pleasant intercourse by a delegation from the city, composed of its chief men, who, having come as far as the outer guard of the camp, sent in to ask permission to pay their homage to their prince.

With the heightened color of modest diffidence the young Hebrew arose, and was excusing himself to me, saying, he would go forth to them, when I expressed a desire that he would receive the deputation where he was; but he said that he would prefer to meet them without and accompany them to the city. I then arose and went with him to where they awaited his coming, and was gratified to behold the affectionate reverence with which he was received by the white-bearded elders, and the unaffected simplicity and kindness of his tone and manner in addressing them. Happy will this people be, O king, when this ingenuous prince shall come to rule over them! Wisdom and mercy, justice and truth, will be the ornaments of his throne.

To-morrow we resume our journey, as all my retinue are refreshed and vigorous for the march, with their long and pleasant repose in this lovely vale of the Jordan. In the leisure which this delay has given me, I have been studying the sacred books in the Hall of Scrolls at Jericho, and especially the records of " Caleb the wise," which I have four scribes engaged in copying for me, as I may not take it away, and greatly desire to have the narrative in my possession.

I now write in my tent by the light of the swinging lamp of chased gold, my mother's gift, which used to be suspended in my chamber in my palace at Nineveh. The sight of it recalls vividly the familiar room; and I hardly realize that I am many hundred miles distant from the apartment it used once so cheerfully to light up. But I fear this is a feeling of homesickness, my royal cousin, which, I am told by travelers in far lands, seizes upon the heart of the exile instead of the body! I will not yield to it. I will write still. The prince is to-day a guest in the city! My soldiers are amusing themselves, some with songs and musical instruments, others dancing in the moonlight, others listening to the romantic legends of a traveling story-teller from Arabia, who has wandered into the camp. From a distance, borne on the soft breeze to my ear, I hear the trumpets of the warders upon the walls of the city as they sound the signal for changing the guard, and proclaim the hour of the night.

I will here resume my narrative, your majesty, of the wonderful events which followed the death of the great Hebrew leader, Moses, upon the mountain of Pisgah, in sight of that land, to the very portals of which, after forty years' painful wanderings. he had at last led his people!

To his chief captain, a man renowned for his valor and wisdom, he resigned his authority. This warrior's name, according to Caleb, was Oshea, which signifies a Saviour. In the sacred writings he is called Joshua. Upon him Moses had solemnly laid his hands, and communicated to him a portion of his spirit and divine glory that the people might unquestionably obey him. Already his prowess in their battles with their many foes had commanded their respect, while his piety equaled his bravery.

After the departure of Moses to the dwelling-places of the gods, this chief took command of the countless hosts of the Hebrews, and advanced at their head to make conquest of the land that God had given them; not, however, bestowed as a free gift, but to be won by their arms, Jehovah himself fighting for them.

Having marched until they came in sight of the Jordan, approaching it from the deserts of the south, Joshua, their general, encamped, and despatched spies across the river to see and report to him the appearance of this country, and the character of the inhabitants. Their glowing accounts of its abundance and beauty filled the Hebrews with joy, and they became impatient to be led across the river to enter upon its possession. But it was then the time of the harvest in the land, in the middle of April, when this river overflows its banks, and is very deep and broad, spreading sometimes three thousand cubits wide over the valley, at which time its current is so strong and swift that nothing can cross it. Small boats that attempt it are carried down the stream with resistless velocity, reaching with difficulty the shore, far below. Caravans arriving at this period are compelled sometimes to encamp many days on the shore, until it subsides and sinks within its proper bounds and becomes fordable. Such was its condition two weeks ago when I crossed its shallow ford with my retinue, guided by the young Hebrew soldier Joab.

The ancient Canaanites who dwelt this side of the river were not ignorant of the presence, a few miles off on the other shore, of the vast multitudes of the Israelites, for the Hebrew spies had been discovered in Jericho, and pursued to the river. The King of Jericho, supposing the Hebrew hosts would pass on toward Chaldea, the land of their great ancestor Abram, which rumor had noised was their real destination, and not suspecting they would enter his territories any more than those of the kings along whose borders they had hitherto marched, contented himself merely with watching their vast camp from the top of his palace. He felt the more secure, inasmuch as the swollen river, then nearly a mile in width, with a current swift as the flight of arrows, presented a secure barrier between his dominions and the Hebrews, to the passage of any body of men.

After the visit of the spies, he commanded all boats to be brought to the western side and secured, and dismissed any apprehensions of danger which he might have entertained.

But what are the devices of kings or of men against celestial powers? The fate of his kingdom was sealed! Forty years had those mighty hosts there encamped in twelve armies, with their thousand banners glancing in the sun, been seeking his kingdom and those adjacent to him of his fellow monarchs, and like hungry eagles who have discovered their long-scented prey, they were not now to be turned aside, they nor their God! from their determinate purpose! This land for forty years had been the theme of their talk by day seated in their tents; and in the weary tramp through burning sands! In their troubled sleep beneath the stars of the desert they had dreamed of it, and fancied that they cooled their arid lips with its rich clusters of grapes, and bathed their brows in its fountains of cool waters! They were not *now* to turn aside! Not all the waters of the Great Middle Sea would have stayed their advance! Their God, who had divided the watery plain of the Red Sea before their fathers, could open a highway across the Jordan for his people!

Secure at least in the protection of this now great river, the king, and his courtiers, and his army, enjoyed themselves in banqueting and in their pleasures. In his cups that day the monarch of Jericho defied the hosts of Israel, and waving his goblet of wine toward their camp from his palace window, mocked them and their God!

Then it was that Joshua was commanded by the voice of his God to rise up and marshal his armies, and put in array all the people in the usual battle ranks in which they marched when led by Moses, saying unto him:

"As I was with my servant Moses, so will I be with thee; and this day I will magnify thee in the sight of this people, that they may know that I have made thee leader of them in his stead. Before thee lies the land promised to Abraham, Isaac, and Jacob. Enter in this day and possess it."

But Joshua answered, saith the record of Caleb, "I have seen the river which lieth between. It is risen high above its banks and no man may pass over, for the current is both broad and deep." He was answered after this manner:

"Thou shalt see the waters of Jordan cut off as at the sea of Egypt. Command the priests, the Levites, that they take up the Ark of the covenant and bear it toward the river. Let the hosts of Israel follow by their armies, but be careful to leave two thousand cubits space between them and the Ark of God."

When the God of the Hebrews had further spoken to the Hebrew general, and given him some directions, Joshua left the celestial presence, and instructed the elders, Levites, and people according to the command he had received. Then the captain and chief officers of the host passed in and out among all the companies repeating the orders of their general, that the people should follow the Ark at a reverential distance, and prepare to go over Jordan.

The sight alone of the swift and perilous river filled with consternation the timid, and the women and the children, who, not having seen the dividing of the waters of the Red Sea before their fathers, did not realize that the Jordan could be divided so that it might be crossed dry-shod.

The twelve priests of Israel took up the sacred Ark of their God, and moved slowly forward until they came to the brink of the stream when, at the voice of Joshua, they stood still. The van of the marching hosts of Israel also halted two thousand cubits distant, while, as far as the eye could see, the prolonged column of the Hebrews stretched eastward to the mountains till their remotest companions could not be distinguished as men, but seemed to be rather the shadows of clouds slowly passing along the earth at their base. The king and his court and his people from the towers and walls of Jericho, of Ai, and other cities, beheld this amazing spectacle with mingled awe and mocking.

In the midst of his derision at the idea of their attempting the passage, an old courtier whispered in his ear, " Beware, O king! Their God, forty years ago, opened a passage for this mighty multitude whom you deride and scorn, through a great sea, so that they went over on dry ground. Observe their compact movements! They have some scheme in view, by the confident manner they approach the banks and take their stand!"

" Is not that the shrine of their god, those twelve white-robed men bear?" asked the king, beginning to feel ill at ease, and drinking a deep draught from his wine cup.

The question was not answered: for a great shout from all the towers and walls which were lined with people caused the startled king to look again toward the river.

But I will transcribe the scene which followed, from the parchment of Caleb the Good:

"When," says this record, "the twelve Levites had reached the brim of the river, they stood still until the ceaselessly advancing columns of the Hebrew legions, one after another, deployed out into the plain facing the Jordan. For five hours they thus came, rolling on, wave after wave, battalion after battalion, host following host, each with its standard and ensign of its tribe and family displayed, until their front stretched along the river and parallel with it six thousand cubits, or more than a mile and a half in line; while its depth in the rear toward the southeast was two leagues, including the necessary spaces between the tribes and companies for the baggage, cattle, camp furniture, and, besides, for the women and children. The whole plain was covered with their dark masses to the bases of the black mountain of Nebo.

"At length the Hebrew general elevated the sacred rod of Moses which he held in his hand, and commanded the priests to enter the water, carrying the Ark. There was a brief instant of hesitation on the part of the bearers, and many of them glanced at the face of Joshua to see if their leader were in earnest; for it seemed to them certain destruction to attempt to take ten steps into the foaming and roaring waters before them. He replied to their hesitating regards by a quiet but firm wave of the hand, signifying his wish for them to advance.

"The priests, which had borne the Ark to the water's edge, then obediently raised it from the ground upon their shoulders; and the two foremost, side by side, entered the river. As the soles of their sandals were dipped into the water the waves retreated from before them in a remarkable manner. The twelve priests, amazed, steadily moved forward, and began to chant a sublime hymn, commencing:

"'The waters saw thee, O God, and fled!
The Jordan is driven back at thy coming.'

"Continuing still to advance, the twelve bearers of the Ark entered the revealed bed of the river, a short distance, their feet scarcely wetted by the retreating stream. Here by the command of Joshua they halted!

"Now a sublime and awful spectacle exhibited itself before our eyes! All the broad river above the Ark was suddenly arrested in its course, and began to pile itself up into a wall of roaring waters, each moment heaping its waves higher and higher, as if struggling with stupendous energy to turn back on itself rather than pass the Ark of God! That portion of the river below the Ark being deprived of its natural supply by the sudden stopping of that which was above it, shoaled rapidly in its bed, each moment becoming shallower with the fleetness of its downward flight; so that where the priests' feet stood, and thence, quite across to the western bank, the stones, gravel, and sand, soon became visible!

"In this manner the waters above the Ark being stayed by the power of God so that they could not pass the terrible place where It rested, and the waters below it flying away as if with terror from its Presence, there widened every instant a broad road in the bed of the river opposite the front of the Israelit-ish line. It was a wonderful sight to behold one-half of Jordan fleeing away, until, far as the eye could see, its waters con-tinued no longer visible, leaving, for two miles, its bed dry from shore to shore, while the northern half stood fixed, foam-ing and rising in heaps, a wild precipice of boiling waters, seek-ing to rush downward, but held back, as it were, with bit and bridle, by an invisible Hand!"

How amazing is all this, your majesty! How awful the power of this God of the Hebrews! Here is recorded a miracle as wonderful as that which is written of the dividing of the Red Sea! But I continue my narrative from the parchments before me.

"When the children of Israel," says the writer of the record, "beheld this manifestation of the presence and greatness of Jehovah, the waters standing upon a heap on one side and fly-ing wholly away on the other, they set up a great shout of joy and of wonder, which must have made the walls of Jericho shake.

"The king from his terrace had also witnessed the sight of his river rent in twain, one part leaving his dominions, and the other rushing back on its course overwhelming trees, vil-lages, cliffs, with its reverse torrents. He trembled with fear, and stood gazing in mute horror upon the sublime and appall-ling scene before him.

"The priests who bore the Ark were now commanded by Joshua to lift it upon their shoulders and march on until they came to the middle of the bed of Jordan and there stop. Then came after them, walking into the river bed, dry shod, the

Levites, four hundred in number, bearing the rich curtains and pillars of brass, hangings of purple and broidered work, and other parts of the tabernacle and its furniture, with all the sacred vessels appertaining to the sacrifices therein. In the midst of the river the priests stayed the Ark. Then those who bore the tabernacle kept on past them and reached the other shore! The van of the main body was now commanded by Joshua, who stood on the land, to move forward; and magnificent was the sight! In column, with not less than a mile and a half of front, the bannered hosts marched toward the river. There was no sound of trumpet; no voice heard, only the deep tread of the tens and hundreds of thousands of men! Entering the bed of Jordan the van occupied up and down its length a space as far as a man could be distinguished by the eye from the end of one wing to the end of the other wing. Their onward march now ceased not! Hour after hour the mighty current of the human river flowed athwart the dry bed of the suspended Jordan, until at length the vast multitude overflowed the valley on the other side, and filled the whole plain with their terrible hosts.

"When the last company had reached the banks, the Ark, which until now had stood immovable in the middle of the river-bed, was lifted up again by its consecrated bearers and borne landward. No sooner had the last priest's sandals touched the grassy bank, than Joshua, who came over last of all, turning to the Jordan, extended toward it the rod of God in his hand, when lo! the accumulated wall of waters gave way! and, as a fierce courser, long held in by the curb, plunges madly forward when released from restraint, so the mightly Jordan, unbound, leaped into the abyss; and with the roar of rolling thunders, and in the shape of a gigantic cataract, it poured its imprisoned waters once more along its deserted channel! All Israel stood, and beheld, amazed, the sublime sight!

"From his palace the king, who had watched with consternation the crossing of the countless hosts of the Lord, also beheld the return of the river to its bounds, and saw the unloosed, dark flood rush wildly toward its sea. That which had been a barrier, as he believed, between him and his foe he now saw was to become the bounds of a prison-house for himself and his people; shutting within the land his dreaded foes. Already he had assembled his army about him within the gates, confident in the strength of his lofty walls! He now beheld

the vast multitude pitch their camp in the green plain (first
setting up twelve stones, brought by them from the bed of
Jordan, as a memorial), by tribes and by companies, with the
tabernacle erected in the midst and the dread Ark of their
God near it! As the day closed the smoke of burning sacrifices rose from the altar of the Hebrews, and the voices of
the priests were heard chanting a conquering hymn to their
God. Night at length veiled the scene; and silence, unbroken
save by the calls of alert sentinels on the walls of Jericho,
and the rushing of the wild waters of the river, reigned over
city and encampment, over town and tent."

Here closes the second book of the record of Caleb, the Wise.

Thus, your majesty, did this wonderful people enter the
land promised them as a possession! Was not such a triumphant and glorious entrance a full reward for their long
years of wandering? Was it not a just recompense for all
their sufferings? How must this people have adored their
mighty God for His marvelous works in their sight! What a
profound impression of his majesty, power, and omnipotence
must this miracle of the Jordan have produced upon their
minds! Who among them all would henceforth dare to disobey
His commands or murmur against His divine will! What a
manifestation to this barbaric King of Jericho, of the greatness
and strength of the God of the Hebrews! How impotent must
he have felt his own power before such an exhibition of that
of the Lord of the Israelites! Like another Pharaoh, he must
have trembled, even while he defied!

The next day there was made a great national feast to their
God, of unleavened cakes. The morning after this, to the great
consternation and surprise of the Hebrews, when they went
early abroad from their tents, as aforetime, for forty years
past, to gather the manna which fell from the heavens for
their sustenance, lo! none was to be seen upon the earth! It
had never failed them before! When Joshua perceived this,
and that they looked to him for relief, he made known to them
that now they had come into their own proper inheritance, the
land of Abraham, a land of corn, wine, oil, and fruit, a land
flowing with milk and honey, they were to gather of the
abundance thereof and eat, as they were to have manna no
more! All around them the wide plains were teeming with
golden corn ripe for the sickle; and as God, to whom belongs
the whole earth and man upon it, saith the chronicle of Caleb,

had given the land and its productions to them as their rightful heritage, the people gladly hastened to gather the corn and fruits, and provide food for their families.

The King of Jericho, shut up in his strong city, had observed all that was done in the camp; and as he beheld no battering rams or engines of war among them for the assault of cities and castles, he said to his chief officers:

"They will soon waste the plains, these Egyptian slaves, and march on like locusts! They will not assail me here, for they know they cannot enter my gates of iron and brass, or make a breach! We have our granaries well stored for a siege; we will wait in quiet until hunger drives them to other kings' dominions."

In the meanwhile Joshua was troubled in mind to know how he should get possession of the city, for it was the key to the land. He walked first with his officers, and then afterward alone all around the great and strong place which stood, in the pride of its citadels and towers, the glory and strength of the plains. But his chief captains united in saying that it was impregnable, and that it could not be taken except by a long siege, by which to reduce them to capitulation through hunger and thirst.

In the evening of the third day, records the book of Caleb, as the Hebrew general was slowly walking before Jericho, and gazing musingly upon its loftly battlements lined with archers, spearmen, bowmen, and mailed soldiers, and saw the formidable slings between heavy beams with which they could discharge huge rocks into the plain, and was doubting if it could ever be taken, when from between two palm trees there suddenly stepped before him a tall young man with a drawn scimitar in his hand! Immediately the Hebrew warrior-chief drew his sword, advanced upon him, and cried:

"Art thou for us, or against us?"

"I am a captain in the hosts of the God of Israel," answered the young man, whose face was like a god's for beauty and courage, while his eyes beamed with celestial splendor. "I am against thine adversaries, and am come to fight on thy part!"

When the Hebrew chief heard these words he fell prostrate to the earth and worshiped him. Then the youthful and glorious captain of the Lord's hosts said to him:

"Loose thy sandals, for the place whereon thou standest is holy!"

When Joshua had obeyed he looked up, and lo! a celestial light shone from the person of the warrior of God, and his robes were radiant as the glory of the morning.

Then said the captain of the hosts of heaven, "Thou seest that this city, even Jericho, is straitly shut up because of thee and thine armies! None come out or go in. But lo! I have given it into thy hand, and the king thereof, and all its mighty men of valor! But thou must first command that the priests who bear the Ark, preceded by seven more holy men of God, each with a trumpet in his hand, shall compass the city seven days, once each day, blowing with their trumpets continually. With them thou shalt send a body of tried men-of-war to guard them from assault; and the Seventy Elders of the people shall also go with them. On the seventh day thou shalt assemble the whole army of Israel in all their companies, and march seven times around the city; and the seven priests shall sound the trumpets as they go before the Ark, ceasing not until they return whence they set out. At the end of the seventh circuit of the city all the priests shall sound long and loud with their horns, and the trumpets of the Hebrew hosts shall mingle their voices in the peal, and all Israel shall shout with the voice of God! Then shall the Lord deliver the city into your hand!"

The celestial vision, for such it was, after some further instructions, disappeared from the eyes of the Hebrew leader, who joyfully returned to the camp, his confidence in the help of his God confirmed anew.

Obedient to the command of the Divine man with the sword in his hand, Joshua sent forth on the following morning, the priests with the Ark, seven more with trumpets, the senate, and the guard of a thousand men-at-arms. For six days they made a solemn circuit of the city, while the king and his mighty men, his courtiers, and his concubines at first wondering at the sight, after the third and fourth day laughed, and derided, and mocked this strange procession, from their terraces and battlements. They shot arrows and slung missiles of war, in hopes to reach them, but Joshua had forbidden the priests coming within bow-shot of their walls. On the morning of the seventh day said the merry king to his courtiers:

"Come, let us see if this unmeaning procession maketh its appearance to-day also! By the gods of Jericho! it is full time! Nay, they will not march! They are weary looking at the outer walls of my fair city to no purpose! What can have been their purpose in taking the air for six days past around about our battlements? But their odd tramping has come to an end, I hope!"

"Nay, my lord king," said one of his captains, coming in with haste. "The whole army of the Hebrews, their whole people to a man, are in vast motion like a sea, and are coming on in terrible grandeur, their Ark in advance, and above it shining a strange and terrible light, like the angry fire of a human Eye!"

The king and his courtiers hastened to the battlements! The report of his captain-at-arms was indeed true. Like a mighty river, heaving and dark with the swell of a coming storm, the armed hosts of the Hebrew people were to be seen flowing along the plain, and slowly drawing near, each moment encompassing the city closer and closer, as a huge serpent gradually coils about its victim. They marched with banners on high and trumpets sounding, and the fall of their feet was as the sound of many waters, and their tread upon the earth shook the plain, and caused the red wine in the jeweled cup of the king, which he had left standing on his table of porphyry, to tremble with tiny waves! This mighty multitude gradually filled the vale, and rolled its swelling human waves high up along the sides of the overhanging hills. The king, pale and silent, looked on! Ridicule and derision ceased to have place upon his white lips. A cold terror settled on all hearts! Until now he had no conception of their countless numbers! What could mean this mysterious march of seven days! and this last one in battle array, and so grand and terrible with its display of power in numbers! Onward they come! they pass the citadel! and the great circuit is at length completed, and they have not attacked. The king breathes earsier! But hark! They come again! The Ark enveloped in its burning cloud, the priests, the elders, the men-of-war, Joshua, and the twelve armies following, all resume their awful advance, while their trumpets peal continually, making now one unbroken roar during their whole compass of the walls. When a second time they have terminated the circle of the fated city without any show of attacking it, the king faintly smiles with assurance, and his courtiers attempt a jest, but with pale and uncertain mirth. They recall the recent passage of the Jordan! and they fear that such mysterious demonstrations as these mean something! The inscrutable character of these encompassing marches awes and troubles them! The courtiers, as becomes these royal sycophants, strive to amuse the monarch with their faint wit upon these strange evolutions.

But the king looked grave, as a third time he heard the advancing trumpets, and beheld the Ark re-appear beyond the grove of palm trees, the point where it always first came in sight.

When, however, for six times the mighty host had compassed the city without halt or purpose, the fears of the king disappeared; and he lightly joined in the jests of his flatterers.

"Without doubt, your majesty, these wandering Hebrews are lunatics, and this is a sort of mad march round and round they are doing in honor of the moon!" said one.

"Nay, but rather all blind; and in trying to find their way out of the valley perform these endless circles about Jericho," said another.

"Then," said the king, with a smile and an oath, "I will give the richest quarter part of my kingdom to the man with two eyes who will show them the way safely out of my dominions."

"Peradventure," said a third courtier, "the man with two eyes would shortly be without a head to keep them in, were he to venture thither."

"One would imagine," said a soldier in gilt armor, who was a captain of men-at-arms in the palace, "that they expected to see walls fall down to let them in, or at least the gates fly open at their trumpet calls."

And so the king and his people jested, but only to conceal their secret fears.

The seventh time that day the host of the Lord encompassed Jericho, and then facing it, stood still, every man with his sword in his right hand.

"See! Have they not come to a halt?" cried the king, who, perceiving that nothing was done to the city, had quite recovered his gayety, and was making great mirth with his friends at this strange pastime of going round and round his capital seemingly without end or aim. But when he perceived that they had stopped and turned every man his face toward the city, and in silence seemed to await some event, his heart was troubled, and the hearts of all his people with him. Ascending quickly the highest tower of the citadel accompanied by a few of his officers, he turned and looked around him. The sight made his knees shake. He saw that the dark host of the Hebrew armies completely inclosed his city without a break in the fatal chain. It was a terrible spectacle to him, to behold that formidable wall of armed men surrounding his wall of towers and battlements of stone.

At a distance he discerned a party of horsemen galloping along the line. At their head, mounted upon a noble charger white as snow, was a gray-haired warrior, with a burnished helmet and a mailed form, and waving in his hand a white rod. His sword was in its sheath. He rode rapidly along the line of the close ranks of the Hebrews, and at intervals reined up to address a few words of command; and then, followed by his escort of mounted men-at-arms, he would gallop on again. The king knew him to be the leader Joshua. He felt that now something menacing the safety of his city was about to be attempted. What, he could not divine! But he was ill at ease.

"What can they do?" he said to his chief captain, looking for courage and confidence into his pallid face. "Are we not shut in with gates of brass and bars of iron? Are not our walls too high to be scaled? Besides they have no ladders nor other engines of war! Yet this spectacle is terrible! I feel like a man who wakes and beholds across a chasm a lion crouching and bending his piercing gaze upon him. The chasm is wide, yet the lion *may* achieve the great bound and clasp him in the embrace of death! I know they cannot mount the walls; yet I do not feel secure! This silent expectation is fearful! What a dark and menacing aspect they present!"

At this instant the air was rent with the peal of a thousand trumpets. The warlike sounds grew louder and louder, longer and longer, until one fierce roar of brazen horns appalled all ears within the city. The very towers shook, and the citadel on which the king stood with his officers vibrated beneath their feet. With a cry of terror the monarch called upon his officers to fly for safety below, for the tower was falling. Suddenly the trumpets ceased their clamor! Silence like that of midnight succeeded for a moment, and then, while the pale King of Jericho still stood on the tower, hesitating and petrified with fear as he knew not what judgment was about to come upon him and his city, the voice of the Hebrew general was heard through all the plain which was in front of the king's gate, crying:

"Shout aloud. O Israel! The sword of the captain of the Lord's hosts shall fight for you this day! Shout with the voice of one man, for the Lord hath given you the city!"

The tens of thousands and hundreds of thousands of men in the army of Israel at once lifted up their voice! It seemed as if the heavens would fall and the earth rend, so loud, so dreadful, so like the thunder of the voice of God, was this fearful war-shout of three millions of people in one wild, fierce, menacing battle-cry! The king in nervous terror shrieked a frantic response, and his courtiers answered it like men gone mad with affright! For not only did the awful voice of the multitude appall their hearts, but they beheld suddenly appear in the air above the Ark a man with a sword in his right hand whose stature overtopped the highest towers of the city! They saw him, at the great shouting of the people, shake his gleaming falchion in the air, stretch it forth toward the city, and strike! Like a flash of lightning it seemed to encircle the walls and cleave them close to their foundations, so that towers, gates, battlements, citadel, and the walls fell over all about the city in the same instant level with the ground; leaving the interior of Jericho, with its palaces, temples, streets, and dwellings, exposed to the eyes and approach of all Israel surrounding it. Only one little part of the wall with an obscure inn thereon stood firm! The sky was darkened with the clouds of ascending dust which, reaching a certain height, hung like a pall over the now wall-less capital!

"Advance and take the city and destroy all within, in the name of the Lord of hosts," cried Joshua, advancing before them!

Then with a great shout of victory the Israelites moved, each man straight forward from the place where he stood, and entered the city sword in hand. It was soon taken. All the inhabitants were put to death! Joshua sought for the king, and found him in his palace lying dead, with his sword, upon which, in his despair, he had thrown himself, sheathed in his heart!

Here, your majesty, end, for the present, my transcripts from the records.

The city having been plundered of its gold, silver, iron, and brass, was set on fire and burned to the ground. Thus the first conquest of the Hebrews was achieved in a manner altogether in keeping with their miraculous history. Where hu-

man means are ineffectual their God lends them the aid of his
mighty power; but first he bids them work for the end, as if
they expected to accomplish it solely by the means made use
of, alone!

Why they should have been commanded to compass the city
so many times, thirteen in all, or what virtue there is in the
number seven, my dear Belus, I do not profess to know. The
result, however, was, as I have stated, that the lofty walls in
which the King of Jericho trusted fell instantaneously at the
shouting, and exposed the city to the mercy or vengeance of
its foes. One only house stood with the wall beneath it. This
was the abode of a poor woman, an innkeeper, who saved the
spies of Joshua when pursued, and hid them in her house until
they could go out in safety and secrecy. Her house was singularly preserved amid the general overthrowing of the walls;
and Joshua generously saved her and all her kindred from the
universal slaughter which followed the miraculous taking of the
city.

I will now close this very long epistle, your majesty, describing scenes enacted here nearly five hundred years ago. To-
morrow, escorted by Prince Jonathan, I take up my line of
march for the court of Saul.

Farewell,

Your faithful
ARBACES.

LETTER III.

CITY OF RAMAH, IN THE LAND OF JUDEA.

MY DEAR COUSIN AND KING:

Your majesty in this letter will learn what events befell me in my journey from Jericho to this place, and what transpired in my interview with the Seer of the Hebrews, at whose palace I have been for the past two days a guest.

The young Israelitish Prince, Jonathan, who had been sent by his royal father to escort me from the province of the Jordan, was ready with his bodyguard of two hundred Hebrew men-at-arms, early in the morning after my last letter was written. The sun had not yet risen when his trumpets rung musically through the valley, the wild notes coming back in melodious echoes from the surrounding cliffs. I was soon in the saddle, and rode forth to meet him, my own legion being already in order of march, marshaled before my tent, under the command of the brave Nacherib; who, with his silvery locks flowing beneath his steel, gold-inlaid helmet, his burnished cuirass, and mounted on his noble war-horse shining with polished scales of mail, looked the personification of Belassar the god of war!

The caravan was already alert and in motion westward under its chief. I lingered to receive a courteous farewell from the elders of the city, who expressed, in parting with me, their respect for Assyria and for your majesty, and a desire that friendship might be cemented between the two kingdoms forever. I warmly reciprocated this sentiment; for I assure your majesty that if we can maintain terms of amity with this warlike people, they will afford the best safeguard and frontier westward for your kingdom in reference to Egypt and its ambitious Pharaohs.

The signal was now given to march, and the prince and I, side by side, rode forward, when there approached us from the gate of the city the tall young warrior, Joab, who had assembled the seven thousand men to confront me, when at the head of my retinue I descended into the valley the other side of the river! The young man was on foot, but armed as when I first beheld him. He was of large frame for his youth, and wore his armor awkwardly, as if more of a herdsman, which he really was, than a warrior. But in his large expressive eyes burned that resolution and courage of soul which, in the moment of danger, had given him the undisputed leadership of the hastily-gathered army which had met me beyond the Jordan.

Upon coming near he said to the prince, "My lord Jonathan, permit me to go up to Hebron in your company. I wish to become by profession a soldier, and to serve the king with my sword!"

"That thou shalt, if it please thy humor, good Joab," answered the prince, with the smile and tone of one who had knowledge of him. "My father needs brave, hearty, and strong arms about him! You shall go with me, and I will take you into my own bodyguard, until the king shall call for your service. These barbaric Philistines will soon give us all enough to do! They menace us again in the west!"

"I will gladly serve in your bodyguard, my lord prince," answered the strong-armed and stout young soldier; "for I know that, young as thou art, thou art a master in war, and that thy legion is a training school at-arms!"

"You do me too much honor, my brave Joab," answered the ingenuous prince modestly. "Thou shouldst be near my warlike father to learn the art of doing battle against one's foes!"

"Thinkest thou, my prince, that all men in Israel do not know thy prowess and skill at the weapons of war? No man has forgotten thy victory over the Philistine hosts singlehanded, save that thy armor-bearer was with thee!"

"Not worth thy or their remembering," answered the prince, smiling, and riding forward, adding, "Thou hast no horse, Joab?"

"No, my lord! I have always been afoot!" he answered.

"Then thou shalt henceforth ride, young man," I said to him, and ordered one of the led horses to be brought up, which I forced him to accept; and mounting him he rode near us.

The Hebrews, as I have said, have not many horses. Their armies are chiefly foot-soldiers, and their chief captains fight on foot. It is only a few of the most distinguished commanders and officers of the royal guards who ride on horses. The king has a battalion of chariots of war; but in this hill-country armies of infantry are more easily marched from point to point and maneuvered with more facility in battle. With us, being a nation of horsemen, a captain on foot would be a degrading position for him; but here even their greatest leaders have led their hosts dismounted. Horses are, however, coming more into use, and the king is to organize a legion of six thousand mounted men!

As we crossed the beautiful and fertile plain toward the hills, I turned to take a last view of the vale of Jericho and its surrounding scenery. The beams of the rising sun were just lighting up its loftiest towers. The river flowed peacefully past far distant amid gardens and vineyards, and above the dark mountains of Nebo with the loftier shoulder of Pisgah, where Moses died, floated a group of purple clouds, their summits gilded by the sun's rays into a blaze of glory. How peaceful and fair to look upon was all the scene! The valley waved with corn, like an emerald sea, while in all parts of it amid groups of palms, and fig, and pomegranate trees, were visible the walls of the pretty white villas and cottages of the dwellers in this vale of repose. Even the hill-sides and rocks and cliffs were verdant with grape-vines and hanging with gardens! Every foot of ground was cultivated, and plenty and peace, security and happiness seemed to make their abode here. Amid all, like a noble diadem crowning the whole landscape, rose the battlements and towers of the city, a fair and imposing finish to the captivating picture.

"How charming all this view!" I said to the prince, who had regarded my admiration of it with natural pride and pleasure.

"Yes, my lord," he answered, "it is a fair land the God of our fathers gave us for a possession. You will find innumerable lovely scenes as you journey through it."

His words recalled to my thoughts the passage of the Jordan and the fall of the walls of Jericho nearly five hundred years before; and I said:

"Who that gazes on this fearful scene could imagine the river, so placidly flowing in its bed, piled on heaps there by yonder village of Adame, and roaring backward on its northward course like a cataract!"

"Or," said he, taking up my thought, "who can conceive

the spectacle this valley about Jericho presented, when the armies of the Lord, led by Joshua and marshaled by the shining captain of the hosts of heaven, marched along it in their mighty circuits of its walls!"

"What a sight all that must have been!" I exclaimed. "How the sound of the priests' trumpets and the shouting must have awakened the echoes of these now silent hills! How little the present seems to reveal the past!"

"It would seem that the echoes still should linger of those three million voices," he said. "But all is changed! The Jericho of to-day is another city altogether! The first was utterly destroyed by our fathers with fire."

"So I have read," I answered, "in your sacred books, and also in the chronicles of Caleb the Good."

"You have then an interest in knowing something of our history, my lord prince?" he remarked.

"I am deeply interested. I have with me copies of your sacred books and other parchments which I shall carefully peruse. One feature in your history I cannot understand. How is it," I asked, "that your nation, since the death of the venerable chief, Joshua, under whom it nearly completed the entire conquest of this land, has had no other great captain or leader? I am told that your royal father is its first king, and yet it is more than four hundred years since the death of the conqueror!"

We had by this time entered a defile, the sides of which hid the city and Jordan with its valley from our sight. The royal Hebrew bodyguard now marched in the van with two hundred of my own guard, the caravan moved along in the center, and my main legion came last directly in our rear. We had, therefore, only quietly to keep the road, and had leisure to converse, Joab and our armor-bearers being the only listeners.

The prince was about to reply to my inquiry when a richly dressed Hebrew, mounted on a large fine mule, with a retinue of seven or eight foreign-looking servants, drew near by a road leading from a handsome stone villa, and craved permission to join our company, as he was traveling to Hebron. It was granted to him, and the prince, who knew him, presented him to me as one of the chief architects of the kingdom going to assist the king in planning his palace.

"Of what nation are those slaves?" I asked, struck with

the dark saturnine countenance, glittering black eyes and small stature of the architect's servants; for Hebrews they could not be.

"These swarthy men," answered Prince Jonathan, "are descended from the ancient inhabitants of the land!"

"I supposed they were all exterminated," I answered, again regarding the eight servitors, being much struck with the looks of cunning and duplicity which seemed to be a marked characteristic of the faces of all of them; looking like persons not to be fully trusted and to be kept in subjection alone by fear.

"They are a singular exception," answered the prince. "Their history is a remarkable one. They are Gibeonites! Their fathers dwelt in a small kingdom not far west from where Joshua crossed the Jordan. Hearing of the fall of Jericho and the successive conquests of the Hebrews, this wily people, with others whom they prevailed upon to unite with them, hit upon a stratagem to save their lives, if not their territories. They selected ambassadors, whom they clothed in tattered garments and worn out sandals, and gave old sacks for their provisions, and disguised them altogether as travelers who have been many weeks on a weary march from a distant land!

"Presenting themselves before Joshua, they told him how they came from a far country, having heard of the power and glory of his people, and desired on the part of their king to make a treaty of friendship with him. They, moreover, said that their clothes and sandals were new when they started from home and otherwise so deceived him that, believing they were a people dwelling far beyond the land which he was commanded by his God to take possession of, he entered into covenant with them of peace and friendship. Having succeeded in their deceitful mission, these ambassadors (who dwelt not two full days' march from the Jordan) returned home. When at length Joshua, extending his conquest and destroying all the people of the land with the sword as he went, came to their country and recognized the men, and knew that they were Canaanites of the land whom it was his duty to destroy, he was justly very angry at the deception they had practiced upon him; but having entered into a solemn league of friendship with them, he felt he could not now exterminate them. They humbly plead, that, in order to save their lives they had been compelled to adopt the wily course which they had done,

THE THRONE OF DAVID.

Thereupon Joshua, calling the chief men of the Gibeonites together, said to them all:

"'I have sworn and will truly keep my oath, to be at peace with you so far as not to take your lives! But from this day your whole people shall become hewers of wood and drawers of water to the Hebrews!'

"Thus were they condemned to perpetual servitude," added the prince, "and here you behold after four hundred years their descendants, servants among us!"

I regarded these slaves with no little interest, your majesty, after hearing their history; and I cannot but express my wonder at seeing how they have inherited looks of duplicity, a trait which is evidently still their birthright, judging from their treacherous-looking countenances.

Seeking now, as we rode on, further information from the intelligent young prince about the past of his people, he said:

"You desire to know how we were governed after our great chieftain, Joshua, died! First by a Supreme Senate of seventy elders with whom he left his authority; but after about fifty years of this rule the armies, dissatisfied with the pacific government of the elders, elected their own chief and gave him absolute authority to rule and judge them. These Judges were often military dictators, and their power at length became as absolute as that of crowned princes. There was even a heroic female Deborah in the line of our Judges. From Othniel the first Judge twelve Judges have reigned, with intervals of disaster and of submission often to our foes, down to the present generation. The last Judge was the prophet Samuel now living at Ramah, an aged Seer and servant of God!"

"Will you explain to me, my prince," I said, "how a Judge of Israel with absolute power and a king can both exist in the land at the same time?"

"Samuel the Seer continued to govern our nation with almost imperial authority," he kindly answered; "as a prophet, he held over the people undisputed sway and commanding influence. His talents, virtues, wisdom, piety, and firmness, as well as his great experience in governing, gave them unlimited confidence in him. But at length, through the weight of years, he transferred his powers to his two sons, dividing his authority between them. These men were deficient in the great qualities of their father; and unable to bear longer their inefficient rule, which was felt more keenly inasmuch as we were at war with the Philistines and required an energetic head, they waited on the prophet in a great body, and demanded a *king* to be placed over them! The prophet at first refused to hear them (for he was still the actual statesman and counselor of the nation, guiding his weak sons in their office by his experience and wisdom), but at length yielded to their importunities, and by the command of God anointed my father, then a young man, king. He was, at the time this high honor befell him, dwelling among the mountains of his nativity, and wholly unsuspecting the distinction to be conferred upon him. The people, when they saw him, confirmed by acclamation his choice; for he was of lofty stature, with a singularly commanding person, and of undoubted courage, having shown proofs of his daring and warlike spirit in minor conflicts with parties of the enemy in the passes of his native hills. Not long after this the King of Ammon beyond Jordan invaded our land, and the new king, promptly putting himself at the head of the Hebrew soldiers, routed the enemy with great slaughter. My father was then crowned with great rejoicings, and prepared to consolidate his throne. But the Philistines, a warlike and fierce people of the west, whose country lies on the borders of the Great Sea, and who have not ceased since the days of Joshua to dispute our possession of this land of our fathers, declared war against the newly-crowned monarch. The Hebrews, proud of having a king like other nations to lead them forth to battle, rallied in great numbers and full of hope around the royal standard. These wars continued for many years, with occasional intervals of truce; and in these my father strove to strengthen his kingdom, adorn its cities, improve his army, and elevate the people. His reign was for many years happy and glorious, and his prosperous wars added distinction to his name. Moderation and clemency marked his treatment to his enemies, and resentment and revenge were then strangers to his bosom."

Here the prince sighed and looked sad and thoughtful. Perceiving that something painful was upon his mind, I rode on in silence; for I recollected what had been told me at Jericho of the gloom which had settled upon the mind of King Saul; and that from being a wise and magnanimous prince he had become cruel, unjust, and revengeful, and sought even the lives of his best friends.

The royal youth would no doubt have resumed the subject in a few moments, so abruptly broken off, but at this instant a

man came bounding with the speed of a wolf down a narrow
defile between two hills, past which our road wound. He came
in sight of us so suddenly that he could not check the impetus
with which he was running soon enough to escape our observation, as he quickly tried to do. No sooner, as he turned to fly,
did the eyes of Joab fasten upon him than he rode toward him,
and seizing him by the hair, took him captive.

"Who art thou, with blood upon thy hand?" demanded the
prince, before whom his captor led him.

"I am a herdsman, and have just slain a wolf which attacked my flock," answered the man, pale as death.

"Why then fly as if thou hadst murdered a man?" demanded
Joab, still holding him by the collar of his tunic.

The man looked at a loss to reply, and held down his head.

"My prince," said the rich Hebrew architect, "he is evidently a murderer flying to one of the cities of refuge for
shelter from vengeance! See, there come pursuers down the
dell in full cry after him!"

At this the man made a sudden dive beneath the horse on
which Joab was mounted, and so successfully as to leave his
rent tunic in his hand, and darting across the road he disappeared in a dark forest of oaks ere his flight could be arrested.
When his pursuers came up, they stated that he had, three
hours before, in a village twelve miles to the south, slain a
shepherd, his fellow and brother of the speaker, and now was
seeking refuge probably at Sichem, a chosen city farther north.

When these angry men had gone forward again on their
path of vengeance, and we had resumed our progress thus
momentarily interrupted, I inquired of the prince the meaning
of a city of refuge for murderers!

"I will gladly answer your inquiry," he replied courteously.
"In the division of this land by Joshua to our fathers he appointed, by the command of the merciful God, several places as
'cities of refuge,' so that if any man slew another by accident
he might fly thither from vengeance. This privilege was not
to shield the murderer, but to protect the innocent; for a man
who unwittingly slew his fellow, not intending it, might be
killed therefor by the by-standers who knew not the true facts,
and so unjustly perish. 'Therefore,' said Joshua, 'whosoever
killeth any person unwittingly, or unawares, may fly thither
for refuge from the avenger of blood!' For instance, my lord
prince, this man, who is now bounding across the country on

his way to a city of refuge, may have slain his victim unwittingly; but the dead man's friends pursue with vengeance, as you have seen, to slay him, not giving him opportunity, if they should overtake him, to show his innocence of evil intention. Now, if he reaches the gate of the city of Sichem, and can but lay his hand upon the gate-post, he is safe; nay, the city extends its protection, for a bow-shot beyond its gates all around, to the flying man-slayer! Standing in the gate he asks shelter and protection from the avenger of blood. The elders of the city are called by the chief captain, and in their ears the fugitive makes known the circumstances of the crime for which he flies, declaring the deed to have been accidental. The elders then appoint a certain officer of the city to receive him, who conducts him to a safe abode in the heart of the city, where he is to dwell until the death of the High Priest of the land! If the pursuers come to the gate and demand him, they ask in vain. If they can prove, however, before the Senate and Judges that the slaying was malicious, then the murderer is given up to the executioner of the land and stoned to death."

"Why is the unwitting slayer released on the death of the great High Priest?" I asked.

"So reads the law," he answered, "that in such an event the slayer shall peaceably return to his own city and home; and whosoever then slays him shall be put to death! There is a tradition that the death of the High Priest is the type of the death of a divine High Priest, Prince and Son of God, who is to come out from heaven in the future ages, and die for all who have done evil, in order to release them from their guilt! and that this pardoning of murderers in the cities of refuge at the death of the High Priest is to keep before the minds of the nation the divine Priest to be sacrificed and die for the whole people! 'for,' says the tradition, 'we are all guilty before the holy Lord God.' All this is obscure, my lord of Assur; but if you converse with the Seer, Samuel, at Ramah, he may be able to make it clearer to you; for it is his privilege and office to know the mysteries of God and reveal the future! We can pass through Ramah to his abode by deviating somewhat from our direct route to Hebron, and if you wish to see the venerable prophet and friend of God, while your caravan proceeds direct to Hebron, I will go on with you with my bodyguard. Near Ramah is Bethel, where my royal mother now resides, whom I would gladly pay my respectful duty to, as I have not see her for many weeks, having been in the interval with my father at Gibeah, at Mizpeh, and at Hebron, at all of which places he has either winter or summer abodes which he is adorning and enlarging; for our land has hitherto been without kingly residences. Hebron, however, will ultimately become the king's capital, as my father regards it with more favor than any other of the cities of his habitation."

In such conversation, your majesty, we beguiled our way, which gradually wound in among lofty precipices and led over bold hills, most of which were crowned with walled villages or castles; while the prospect from their summits was full of interest to one coming from a land so little diversified as Assyria, about Nineveh. Hills, rocks, dells, valleys, in romantic confusion, all teeming with life and rich with culture, met the view. The names of several places were made known to me by the Hebrew architect, whom I found a person of intelligence.

At one of the castles which we came to, the captain thereof appeared at the gate and offered us hospitality; but we declined the courtesy, preferring to dine in our own tent on the road. He, however, detained the prince two hours on some affairs, while I rode slowly forward, attended by Joab, the young soldier of the Jordan. This young man I found had an imperious will, and was as rude in speech as brave in heart. He seemed to regard me, however, with partiality, and to be ready to communicate any information in his gift. As we rode on he said:

"I see that thou thinkest highly of the king's son Prince Jonathan! Thou mayest, lord of Assur. Young and fair as he appears, he has a lion's heart. His eyes, which seem as soft as a woman's, can blaze with the light of battle! To see him in his blue-broidered tunic and golden armor, with the plume in his silken bonnet, one would fancy he were only a fair-day prince, who loved rather to hear the voices of singing women than the trumpet-cry of war!"

"What has he achieved in arms, my friend?" I asked, seeing that he wished to talk about his prince.

"I will give thee, my lord, one instance of our royal prince's brave deeds. When the last foray of the Philistines was made into our land, the king went out to meet them, and laid siege to a garrison where they were fortified. They could not, however, be dislodged for want of proper war engines and arms.

Weary of the delay, the young prince called his armor-bearer, the bearded man whom you see riding there by that man-at-arms, behind us, and said, 'Come, let us go and see these Philistines! Peradventure we may find a weak point where they may be attacked!' So going secretly out of the camp at the close of the day, they descended through a defile, and came before the garrison! Finding that there was no way by which the army of the king, his father, could get up to it, but only here and there a place where one man could put his foot, he called out aloud to the Philistines and said:

"'Come forth and let us fight our battles in open field! In the name of the Lord we will destroy your hosts!'

"Then the Philistine captain, coming to the top of the rock, called to Prince Jonathan to come up and take the garrison, as he seemed so bold!

"'Such a challenge to the son of the king shall not be refused while I have a sword, and a hand to wield it,' cried the prince, in a sort of divine fury; and calling to his armor-bearer to follow him, he commenced climbing the rocky sides of the garrison. In a few moments the daring young soldier, closely followed by his armor-bearer, drew himself over the verge, and leaped, sword in hand, into the very midst of his foes! He came so suddenly upon them, and his aspect was so terrible, and he threw himself upon them with such vengeance, the while uttering his battle-cry, that those who resisted were cut down, and others, flying, alarmed the garrison, and created a panic throughout the whole Philistine hosts; for it was believed from the noise of fighting and the ringing blows of steel on iron armor, that the whole of the king's army had scaled the cliff and were attacking them! The prince alone slew twenty men in the space of a few yards before him, while his armor-bearer, keeping close to him, warded off the blows of those who had courage to oppose him. It being dark, the enemy could not distinguish friend from foe, and, in the confusion, parties attacked each other. Thus the dismay each instant grew, until the whole army in and beyond the garrison commenced to fly along the passes of the mountains, pursued by the prince and his armor-bearer, slaying as they went, and uttering their fierce battle shouts. The noise of the conflict reached the ears of the king, his father, in his tent; and it was told him the Philistines were attacked, by whom they knew not! He soon ascertained that Jonathan and his armor-bearer were missing from the camp. He then rose up, he and his army, and followed in pursuit, and the fight and chase lasted till the close of the next day, when weary with slaughter and with pursuing, the king and his army halted and encamped for the night, laden with spoils! This daring exploit of the prince, as well as his piety and virtue, has endeared him, my lord, to all the people, as you may well believe."

While Joab was speaking, Prince Jonathan came riding up and rejoined me. I regarded him now with deeper interest. What courage and noble qualities lay hidden under that calm, pleasant countenance, which was almost effeminate in its fairness, added to the soft, shining tresses which fell in waves upon his shoulders!

We now rode on, but at our ease, to keep within the slow traveling pace of the caravan. At night we encamped in a vale by a well, and the next day continued our advance amid agreeable scenes, while on all sides the density of the population and the great number of villages surprised me. For miles the valleys are like a continuous village; while on the rocks and among cliffs, almost inaccessible, are perched habitations, gardens, and vineyards; kids, goats, and sheep seem to cover every projection of the hills in great numbers, and herds of fat cattle roam the green and secluded glens.

I have not spoken of the beauty of the females of this favored land. They are seen everywhere moving about without restraint, sharing, with affectionate interest, in all that concerns the welfare of the community; kind, affable, cheerful, and intelligent, they are worthy to be the daughters and wives of a manly and truly domestic race like the Hebrews. Concubinage or duality of wives is unknown among this virtuous people. The females, therefore, retain a certain dignity of aspect and a feeling of self-respect which is not observable in the bearing of the ladies of Assyria. Here woman is the companion of man: as his wife, often his judicious counselor in difficult and doubtful cases, and the sympathizer of his sorrows; his tender nurse in sickness, his truest, best, most unselfish, and most faithful friend always.

In personal appearance they are not tall, but their forms are the impersonation of grace, both of outline and motion. They have raven black hair, very abundant, and long, and beautifully glossy, in which they take great pride as woman's most lovely adornment and her "crown of glory," as one of our poets has it, braiding it in shining bands, and adorning it with precious gems and dust of gold. Large and brilliantly brown eyes they have, warmed by feeling and ardent with animation, their dangerous fire tempered by long, sable eyelashes which, when they drop the eyelids, rest in a curved fringe upon the cheek. Their power of expression surpasses all that I ever beheld in woman's eyes; and a sure captive will the unwary youth become who suffers himself long to gaze into their fascinating depths.

The personal beauty of the Hebrew women is universal in their years of maidenhood and early wifehood. What, with their massy and richly-bound tresses, their eyes of fire, their lips more brilliant than the hue of the pomegranate, the soft, olive tone of their complexions, the gazelle-like grace of their movements, the exquisite shape of their heads, and delicate smallness of their hands and high-arched feet, the singularly attractive melody of their voices when they speak in the low, musical tones peculiar to them; all these present a charming combination of attractions that will convince your majesty that I at least have a full appreciation of the extraordinary loveliness of the gentler Hebrews. Add to this their cheerful dispositions, their kind and obliging manners, and the intelligence with which they are gifted, and one cannot withhold from them that praise and commendation which is so deservedly their merit.

In the national history of the Hebrews there stand out prominently several of the sex who have reflected honor upon the whole people by deeds of heroism performed for their country, or else by the loveliest exhibitions of faithfulness and truth, or by sacred devotion to the will of parents, or of obedience to the gods. Of these are Deborah, the prophetess, and warrior, and Judge, all in her own person; Ruth, a foreigner by birth indeed, but adopted into the Hebrew nation, and of whom their poets love to sing the gentle praises; and a young and beautiful daughter of a great warrior, Jeptha, who sacrificed her, herself consenting, to the gods (or rather to his ' God,' as I shall say when writing of these people), in fulfillment of a vow on the occasion of a great victory; and Iael or Jael, allied by blood to the priestly line of Israel, who slew with her own hand Sisera, the powerful and cruel general of her nation's foe, and thereby delivered her country from servitude.

These noble women are all subjects for the poet's harp, and

are household names in the land. It is a peculiar feature of
the Hebrew character that the men honor the female sex even
above their own; concede to it the highest places and the first
acts of courtesy in mixed assemblies. This consideration in
itself elevates woman, and renders her worthy of the homage
and regard paid to her.

How different all this from woman in the East, your majesty,
where the sex is regarded as but so many beautiful toys created for our luxury and pride, and far beneath in intellect a
husband and a father! Only here and there, as in the noble
exceptions of Semiramis, Sardanapala, and Arsephaxa, all
powerful and virtuous queens of Assyria, does woman in the
East assert her true rank by nature, which, doubtless, is to be
the companion and friend and prudent counselor of man, both
as kings and subjects.

I see your majesty smile at my eulogy of the sex and at my
admiration of the Hebrew females. If Egypt's fair daughter,
to whom I am sent to ask her hand for your majesty, be half
as fair as Adora, the beautiful daughter of the chief senator
of Jericho, your majesty will have a bright jewel to wear in
your coronet. If I had not hastened from the splendor of her
eyes I should have been consumed by them to ashes.

But to resume the narrative of my journey hither. At the
close of the second day's travel we came to where two roads
met. One of these took a direction southwardly, but the other
led westward toward Ramah, the abode of the Seer, and so on,
to the shores of the Great Sea, which the prince informed me
was visible from a mountain not far from the place where the
prophet dwelt.

As it was my desire to see this holy and venerable person,
and present to him your message and signet-ring, I gave the
caravan orders to continue on the way southward, under the
charge of my captain, Nacherib, and, encamping before Hebron,
await my coming. Retaining only my personal guard of one
hundred nobles, the prince having also kept one hundred of
his men-at-arms, sending the residue under Joab with my caravan as an escort through the country, we were about to go forward toward Ramah, when Nacherib, who had just put the
caravan in motion on its road, came riding up as if with a
message.

"Your highness," he said, "I had best halt the whole body!
I see a large force winding its way in this direction through

the valley below us, and if we proceed we cannot avoid meeting with them!"

The prince and I immediately turned our horses' heads and rode one side to a slight elevation from which the southern road was visible for a league. Half that distance off I saw advancing a long train of camels and laden mules preceded by a party of horsemen carrying slender lances.

"It is a caravan, doubtless that from the country of Sheba, which is expected yearly about this time on its way to Syrian Damascus," said the prince, after a moment's scrutiny. "But let us spur forward and ascertain!"

Followed by a portion of my hundred horsemen, as a protection in case of surprise, I rode rapidly forward with the prince, and we soon came so near that the armed troop in its van stopped and drew up in line of battle. I then halted my guard and Prince Jonathan rode forward alone. No sooner was he perceived by the strangers, than their chief, a dark warrior of gigantic stature clad in chain-mail, detached himself from the main body of his command and came galloping into the open space on a coal-black charger of magnificent size, superbly caparisoned. He rode as if man and horse were but one animal, moved by one will and one power. It was a superb display of barbaric horsemanship, and as he rode he held his long lance in rest, but not leveled in an attitude of hostility, but pointing skyward above his head. He was followed at a little distance by one who bore his shield and sword.

I at once rode to the side of the prince, who said to me:

"I am right. It is the annual southern caravan from the kingdom of Sheba, which lies by the south sea, and destined for Syria. I know well their faces and style of armor, and have before seen this chief about two years ago!"

"Peace and amity," cried the prince, as he came up within a few paces of the warrior.

"Even so! We are for peace and amity, this being a caravan of merchants, my lord," answered the chief.

"You are welcome to pass through our land, sir captain; for we also profit by your merchandise. Didst thou stop before Hebron?"

"But one day, my lord, for rumor came suddenly that the Philistines had moved with a great army from their fastnesses, and were to march upon Hebron. So we hurried on to be out of reach of foes which make no distinction, and plunder where there are treasures. Thou seest I have but four hundred armed men with me, enough for security against the bands of the men of Esau in the deserts, but not to withstand battles with hosts harnessed for war!"

"Thou hast done well to hasten thy march," said the prince. "Pass on thy way in peace! This is indeed news," he continued, turning to me. "So this armament so long threatened by our foes is come to a head, and Hebron is menaced by our implacable scourge! For your sake I am grieved, as I fear the enemy will possess themselves of the passes south, and delay your march toward Egypt."

"In that case," I answered, "I will not remain idly waiting a passage to be opened by your arms, or their pleasure, but join in the war with you with my thousand trained Assyrians, and so bring it to an end the sooner, that I may peaceably proceed on my mission!"

"These tidings," continued the prince thoughtfully, "should take me at once to Hebron. But the king in person is enough there! I will assemble our armies in this quarter, and send them to my father. I still will go on to Ramah! There are several garrisons on the way, and also there, the soldiers of which I must dispatch to the south. Besides I would, in this new peril, ask of the man of God what will befall in this war! My poor father used to consult him! But now there is no intercourse between them! My father offended him by sacrificing, without waiting for the prophet whose sacred right it was alone, and I fear displeased God, also; for he seems, alas! to have been, since then, under a dark cloud of divine judgment! As painful as it is for a son to say this, I cannot withhold the truth from you. My father was on the eve of an engagement, and wished to offer the usual sacrifices to propitiate the God of battles, and win a blessing upon his arms! He waited until the time of the evening oblation, and not seeing the prophet appear, seized the sacrificial knife in his impatience, and with his own hand slew the victim! He lost the battle! Thus Heaven frowned upon him for the act, and the prophet in displeasure denounced his unlawful proceeding as high impiety, and declared to him in the most solemn language, that henceforth he should not prosper in his reign, and that the day was at hand when his crown and scepter should be taken from him and given to another, chosen of God! Since then the prophet, who once loved and honored my father, and

who privately consecrated him at his election, himself, as King
of Israel, and again consecrated him at his coronation before
all the people, has turned his face from him, nor spoken with
him either words of anger or of kindness. This displeasure
has had its natural effect upon my father, and filled his soul
with that gloom and depression which, most noble prince
Arbaces, you will not fail to observe when you come into his
presence!"

During this revelation of the king's infirmities we were
slowly riding back again to the place where the two roads met,
the caravan of the strangers from the south being once more
in motion, and coming after us. I could not but feel and
express my sympathy with the amiable and sorrowful prince,
who evidently loved and honored, with the profoundest respect
and affection, his unhappy father. After a few moments he
added:

"It is my wish to see the prophet, to entreat his interposition
with the God of our fathers to pardon my father's act of
usurpation of the priestly office, and give him prosperity in this
war, and in all his reign. Not that I desire this prosperity on
my own account, noble sir, for it does not grieve me to be
deprived of the succession to my father's crown; but alone for
his peace and honor do I desire it."

"How, my prince, are you to be deprived of your kingdom
at the king, your father's, departure from this life?" I asked,
with surprise at his words. He answered:

"The prophet has pronounced, and his word is the fiat of
God, by whose inspiration and knowledge he speaks, that the
kingdom shall be given to another at his death! Not to *me!*
Another is to rule Israel, not of my blood or of my name!" he
continued, with earnest feeling. "But he who is to wear my
coronet is worthy! Heaven has consecrated him beforehand!
His anointed and youthful brow but waits for the crown of
my father!"

He rode quickly onward, as if to give some orders to Joab,
without saying more, leaving my mind in a state of suspense,
and with increased interest in this noble and good prince,
whose life, evidently, is also shaded by the cloud which overhangs the path of his royal and doomed father.

The stranger caravan, interesting to the eye from the varied
costumes of the foreign people who composed it, now came
creeping on up the winding ascent in a long picturesque line;

while my Assyrian retinue of nine hundred men were drawn
up at a distance on a hill, their burnished armor gleaming in
the radiance of the sun, awaiting the passage of the merchants
and their guard of four hundred men, led by their gigantic
and warlike chief.

The whole company having passed on, the spices which the
camels bore filling the whole atmosphere with fragrance around
us, my caravan, which had drawn aside to give room to the
strangers, once more advanced with its head toward the south.
The prince gave Joab and Nacherib warning to be on their
guard against any bodies of the Philistines who might be secretly penetrating the country; which precautions I carefully
enjoined upon my chief captain, also, to observe. We remained watching the two caravans, which got out of sight,
going in their opposite directions, about the same time; and
then, spurring forward, we made all haste to reach Ramah by
noon. Onward we dashed up the rocky defiles, my bodyguard
of a hundred Ninevite horsemen and that of the prince, divided
into fifties, preceding and following. There were, besides these,
but four of us in the party, the prince, myself, and our re-
spective armor-bearers; the Hebrew architect having gone on
with the caravan.

Our road was at one time amid romantic defiles, the sides
of which were hung with vines, and to which the cottages of
the vine-dressers almost seemed to cling for support; at another
over rocky ridges fortified with castles and guarded by garrisons; now we traversed lovely vales, and now threaded our
way through a long village of white stone houses with flat roofs
on which we saw the inhabitants either walking for air, reading parchments, or copying them, the women pulling flax,
weaving, carding, or engaged in needlework; while many were
at their meals upon the roof, which was protected by fancifully
colored awnings with fringed curtains, looking precisely like a
tent pitched upon the housetop. These awnings were tasteful
in shape, and rich and gay in material and in colors according
to the wealth of the householder; and so were the occupations
of the family beneath them, either humble or leisurely elegant,
according to their condition. It was a lively and happy scene.
Want seemed to be a word unknown. How soon, I thought,
could all this fair picture be changed by the invasion of a wild
band of those armed Philistines, who seem to have been for
generations the terror of the land, and its implacable foes! I

felt a curiosity to know something of these dreaded adversaries. The prince kindly answered my inquiries; and from him I learned that they are a warlike remnant of that conquering family of ancient Phœnicia, called Palestines, a race of Shepherd warriors, who invaded Egypt (before the time the fathers of the Hebrews went thither), and with their well-trained armies conquered Lower Egypt and set up a foreign dynasty at Memphis. After reigning for six generations, being driven out of Egypt by a Theban conqueror, they retired into Palestine with only a remnant of their former numbers; but since then they are much increased in power and warlike arts; for their glory and happiness is in war! When the Hebrew people conquered the adjoining kingdoms, fearing for their own, they became their most vindictive enemies. The Hebrews have not so much sought to conquer their country as to defend their own from their invasions. To this day they continue to be a scourge to this people of God; and what is singular their incursions always follow the commission by the people of Israel of some national sin! It is moreover openly said by their Seer that God permits these foes to exist as a living instrument for the chastisement of the nation!

How wonderful the God of this people! How constant his watch over them now for five hundred years! With what numberless displays of his divine majesty does he aid them in danger! With what ceaseless severity does he visit them when prosperity leads them to forget their dependence upon him! Is He not the most powerful of all gods, as well as the most terrible in his manifestations of Himself? Who of the gods of Assyria—Assur, Ninus, Assarac, Belessar—which of them have ever pretended to any such power and glory? If the God of the Hebrews, your majesty, did not limit his care and providence to this people alone, but manifested himself to all nations as *their* divine Protector, I should regard Him as the Lord of the whole earth and the Arbiter of the fate of all kings and dominions, even as of this! But as he limits his care to the Hebrews he is evidently their national Deity as Assarac is ours! yet how much more powerful is the Hebrew God! Nay, his power, it would seem to me, could fill the world, and that if He chose He could lord it over all lords, and rule in heaven and on earth God of gods and King of kings! The more I learn of His ways and dealings the more I revere and honor his mighty name! But fear not, your majesty, that I shall be drawn into infidelity and become a Hebrew! The gods of Assyria are the true gods for an Assyrian, until a mightier Deity like this of Israel removes them from their celestial thrones and reigns over us in their place.

We at length came in sight of the brown battlements of Ramah elevated upon a steep, which, on all points, was capped with turrets, giving it a warlike and commanding aspect. Winding our way through pleasant and populous suburbs, the vine-dressers and laborers in the fields pausing to regard with wonder the splendid appearance of my bodyguard in their foreign armor and plumed crests, we came before the eastern gate of the city. Here we were challenged; but the Prince Jonathan being instantly recognized by the chief keeper of the gate we were permitted to enter, my guards following, riding two and two. The streets were narrow and closely built, and the roofs and lattices were thronged with people to gaze upon us; for at first the alarm had been bruited about that we were a party of Philistines who were approaching the city; but on learning that we were friendly Assyrians from the far east, their curiosity to see us was unbounded.

After going through half the place, which is not very large, we came to a house not very ancient in appearance, and with a look of superior dignity to the others. This, I was informed, was the palace of Naioth, the abode of the late Judge of Israel, Isamel the Seer. Here we alighted, and the prince sent in his armor-bearer to ask audience of the man of God for himself and an ambassador from the court of Nineveh.

But, your majesty, I will defer my account of the interview to a subsequent letter. Meanwhile, with my prayers to the gods of our country long to preserve you in health to sit upon the throne of your long line of heroic and pious ancestors, I subscribe myself,

Your cousin and faithful subject,

ARBACES.

LETTER IV.

ARBACES TO HIS KING.

CAMP NEAR HEBRON, CITY OF THE KING.
MY BELOVED MONARCH AND COUSIN:

I will now proceed to relate to your majesty the interesting circumstances connected with my visit to the venerable Seer of Israel. While the armor-bearer of the Hebrew prince was in the palace, the people in great numbers gathered about us and hailed with glad voices of loud acclamation their king's son, whom many recognizing had pointed out to all others.

What with his distinguished presence among them, and the curiosity excited by my Assyrian guard of young nobles in their cuirasses of gold, silver saddle bows, and rich scarlet cloth-housings, and, above all, their beautiful Persian horses, the scene around me was exciting and novel.

"Long live our prince!" cried one.

"May he soon be our king!" said another boldly.

"Nay, this is treason, my friends!" exclaimed Jonathan, looking round sternly and rebuking them with flashing eyes, "you speak like traitors to your king who use such language. You mean well, but I cannot hear it!" he added, more gently, as he perceived that they were abashed and humbled.

At this moment the gate of the court opened and the prince's armor-bearer, Heleph, reappeared, accompanied by the steward of the palace, an aged man attired in a loose gray robe, and with snow-white hair and a flowing beard. He approached Jonathan with courtesy, and said, at the same time saluting me in a marked manner:

"The prophet, my master, desires me to conduct you, my lords, to his presence."

We followed him into the courtyard, which was inclosed by corridors and with a fountain in its center, while tall palms grew from the midst of the court, the broad tops of which effectually shaded its pavement from the sun. The columns were crumbling with age and covered with moss or half concealed by neglected vines. The house had for three hundred years been the abode of the Judges; and when Samuel gave up his authority from the weight of years and infirmities, after he had passed threescore and ten, he still retained it as his abode, but resigned two others belonging to the Judges, at Gilgal and Mizpeh, to the king. Here had dwelt for a time Samson, the mighty destroyer of the Philistines; here Deborah, and here nearly all the stern old warriors and famous Judges of the land.

Crossing the paved inner court and ascending a flight of stone stairs, the steward preceded us along a gallery to a spacious chamber that was placed immediately over the gateway through which we had entered. The door was ajar. The steward knocked softly, and a voice within bade us enter. We obeyed, and stood in the presence of the man of God!

I beheld before me, seated by the window which threw its light upon a table beneath it covered with parchments, a man of august and venerable aspect. Large and majestic in person, stooping a little with great age, he presented the ideal of the father of gods as I have often conceived his appearance in imagination. He was elevated a little above the floor upon a sort of carved throne, or chair of state, of ancient workmanship, once the tribunal of the old Judges, robed in a rich garment of woolen, dyed a dark crimson, over which was the ephod or sacred mantle of the Hebrews. About his waist was a girdle of linen, and he wore a full white tunic, fringed, and similar to what I have seen upon the chief of the Levites! Upon his head was a small blue cap, worn to supply the loss of his snow-white hair, a few thin locks of which curled down about his neck like shining threads of silver. His majestic face was one on which Heaven had impressed the seal of the highest expression of humanity. Upon his lofty forehead authority sat enthroned as upon her native seat. His awful eyebrows, stiff and black as night, not a single hair turned gray thereon, hung like a crag above his imperious eyes, lending to them a depth and power inconceivably grand and impressive! Their fire was not dimmed, nor their piercing regards dulled by his great age; but rather his soul seemed to be concentrated in their light with star-like brightness. His high, arched nose indicated a strong and resolute character, firm and bold; while the proud and commanding air of his closed mouth bore testimony to a life of rule and absolute power over men, leaving its record there as if chiseled in marble.

Withal, I fancied I could discover a certain elevated, chastened, and divine expression on his features, caught from frequent communion as the oracle of his people, face to face with his God! Time, while it had softened, had not wholly removed from his noble features a certain sternness and awful severity which sufficiently betrayed the former absolute dictator, powerful Judge, haughty prophet, and imperious priest. He looked, perhaps, like all he had been, only tempered by the veil of repose, with which Old Age ever invests her children.

At his feet, seated upon cushions before low tables, were two scribes in blue cassocks and white linen robes which came down to the sandal. They were engaged, as we entered, with pens of reed in taking down from his lips words dictated by him to them. Now the two youths were suspending their labor and were gazing upon us; for our entrance had interrupted the prophet in his work. I saw freshly written "Shopeteim," or "Judges," at the head of one of the parchments before them. All around the room, which I subsequently learned had once been the hall of Judgment, were many seats arranged, and tablets on stands placed before them; but they were all unoccupied. There was no sort of ornament on the walls, no decoration of any kind; on the contrary, an air of desolation and decay reigned over all. The very palace itself seemed to sympathize in the decadence, in the person of their present aged and reverend occupant, of the long and brilliant succession of warrior-Judges!

The Seer, upon beholding the son of Saul enter, smiled with that benignity which so becomes old age, and extending his hand to him, said:

"Welcome, Jonathan, my son! I am too infirm to rise——"

"Not to me, holy father, not to a youth like me," interrupted the prince, kneeling reverently and kissing the hand of the Seer with the profoundest respect and affection. "I rejoice you are so well, and that our God has so long spared your excellency to us!"

"But my days," he answered gently, "will soon come to a close, my child! But God will take care of his people Israel, and accomplish the work for which he has raised them up and made them a great nation."

"I would, my lord, that the king and thyself were friends. My father truly grieves at the past! It is breaking his great heart! He mourns until his mind is fearfully dark, and his words and acts strange. Entreat the Lord our God for him, O father!"

"Nay," answered the Seer, his brows bending sternly, and a light of displeasure kindling in the deeper darkness beneath them. "He must bear the judgment of God as all men must who transgress his laws. I am grieved to hear of thy father's sad condition. I have no power to help him, my son! The will of God will be done on earth, and no man can hinder the work of his hand or oppose the decrees of his word gone forth. None shall let or hinder Him! Thou, my child, art innocent, and I know good and pious at heart. But it is the unchangeable law of sin that the innocent offspring shall suffer for the guilt of their fathers."

"I bow in submission to the law of my God," answered Jonathan humbly, his voice tremulous and low, still kneeling before the Seer.

"Thou hast forgotten, my son, the stranger who came in with thee!" said Isamel, regarding me with fixed observation.

"Pardon me, my venerable father, I thought only of my unhappy parent," he said, rising. "This is the most noble Arbaces, a Prince of the court of Assyria, and cousin to its great King Belus, who is on his way as an ambassador to the court of Pharaoh; but, passing through Judea, seeks your presence to make known to you the respect his monarch entertains for your excellency, and to ask of you certain questions."

I advanced, as Jonathan thus formally presented me, and bent my knee before the august and awful Seer, whose looks and manner deeply impressed me, saying:

"May your mighty God, who reveals himself in glorious majesty, bless and honor your highness above all wise men on earth, and preserve you in peace and health many years to come! I consider myself happy, venerable Seer, to have the honor of seeing, face to face, the mighty prophet of the Hebrews, whose fame has long since reached the court of Nineveh. Permit me to present the congratulations of my king, and his kind wishes for the prosperity and glory of your nation."

"I thank thee and thy great king, young prince, and in return wish him health and peace, and the wisdom of the knowledge of the true God, who is Jehovah, King of kings, and Lord of the whole earth, and Maker of all men, whose aged servant I am permitted to be." Then regarding me attentively, he inquired, "How long hast thou been in this land?"

"It is not quite one month, your highness, since I left the banks of the Tigris," I replied, rising from my knee. "I have been nearly half that time in your beautiful and abundant land, every step in which I have been interested."

"I trust you will find your visit in Judea agreeable," he courteously answered.

The venerable Seer then invited me to sojourn with him a few days, saying, pleasantly, he could not give me princely entertainment, but that if I would fare as he did and the school of the prophets under his roof, I should be a welcome guest.

After some further interesting conversation with the august Hebrew, whose presence more and more impressed me with awe and respect, the steward conducted me to a chamber along the corridor. As I proceeded thither I perceived in a second or interior court, which also contained a garden, several youths and young men in dark tunics and caps, variously engaged. Some were walking up and down the terrace reading from leaves of parchment, others conversing, others engaged in exercise; and three or four in copying with a stylus, beneath a tamarind tree.

"Who are these, and what is their pursuit?" I asked of the steward, having left the prince conversing still about the king his father, and the menacing invasion of the Philistines.

"This is the 'School of the Prophets,' my lord," answered the old man proudly. "Has not the fame thereof reached thy land?"

To avoid making a reply which might wound the kind old servitor's national pride, I inquired the number of the young men.

"Seventy, your highness. That is the sacred number, neither more nor less. When one leaves, another enters. This school was founded forty years ago by Samuel (in that the sons of Eli proved so evil), that the prophets of the people might be piously instructed in their holy duties."

After I had found my chamber, and seen and talked with Ninus my armor-bearer, who informed me that my bodyguard were well cared for, I walked along the corridor to observe the young candidates for the high office of prophets of God. They all seemed to be happy, and by their appearance to come from among the best families of the land; though here and there was one with less refinement than his companions, and evidently from a more rustic district. There was one youth of singular grace and beauty of person, who was reading by the fountain, and wholly absorbed in what he studied, whose appearance greatly pleased me.

While I was observing him a trumpet sounded a few brisk notes, and all the young men left their pursuits, and crossing the court entered a door beneath the portico and disappeared. The handsome young student, not hearing the signal at first, was the last to go in. Prince Jonathan at this moment stood by my side. He had just left the presence of the Seer. His face wore a profound aspect of sadness that was very touching. But seeing my look of sympathy, he gently smiled and said:

"Do not let my sorrows render you sad, my lord. I had hoped that I could appeal successfully for a blessing on my father, and prosperity to his arms in the war! But it is the will of Jehovah that he shall not prosper! What am *I* to oppose God? I do not blame at all the holy prophet. He has but uttered what God commanded. He sincerely mourns for my father, and pities him, even while he is firm in his purpose to see him no more! But we will not speak on this subject. How grand the prospect from this terrace! I perceive you were admiring it. From yonder height of Mount Ephraim you can see, in certain conditions of the atmosphere, the Great Middle Sea, beyond the illimitable horizon of which all is a mystery and marvel to mankind!"

"This prospect is varied and beautiful," I answered; "but my attention was fixed upon the court below, which a moment since was filled with young men, who have just entered beneath the portico by that palm tree."

"You have seen the disciples of the prophet," he said; "this is the School of Seers for the nation! It is a high privilege to be admitted into it. Here they are taught by seven of the wisest Rabbis of the nation, each gifted with the spirit of prophecy, knowledge of the law, and of all religious duties and holy rites; and they also know the mystery of communing with God, the highest privilege of man! This school is supported by the gifts of the people. The youths have now gone in to their noonday meal. The place is free to all. Will you accompany me?"

I gladly accepted his companionship; and, descending the terrace into the garden, he first pointed out to me the rooms occupied by the young men. They were perfectly plain, with a lion or leopard's skin laid upon the tiled floor for a bed, a bench, and pitcher for water, and an iron lamp: this was all their furniture. Entering the hall I saw the whole company standing around a long, narrow table, upon which were set earthen vessels of bread, cups of water, and lentils, with dried fruit in abundance. This was their frugal fare, but they partook of it with evident satisfaction. At the head of the table was another one much shorter, by which also stood the seven noble-looking Teachers of the School of Prophets. I looked for the young man whose fine appearance had so struck me when in the court, but could not discover him. After they had ended their humble meal a signal was given and one of the Rabbis commenced to chant. The young men responded all in one voice till the roof rung again. The second Rabbi recited a part, and the seventy youths answered antiphonally as before; and thus seven verses were nobly hymned to their God in fine manly voices and with the most wonderful melody.

They now, at another signal, formed in line and marched at a slow movement along the hall, mounted a broad flight of stairs, and entered a large upper apartment around which they arranged themselves in attitudes of reverence. At the upper end, upon a platform covered with blue cloth, the seven prophet-teachers took their seats. Then a door opened and the venerable Seer came in from his chamber. All rose, crossing their hands upon their breasts, and bowed with affectionate respect. He took his seat just above the seven sub-prophets, and opening a roll of parchment which he held, he proceeded to read from it, to his attentive audience, a treatise upon the moral obligations of all men to love one another as children of the same common Father. He closed with enforcing the virtues of purity, truth, temperance, and industry, and reminding them of the omnipresence of their God, who judged men by their hearts.

When he had concluded this beautiful essay seven young men came forward and took their stand by a sort of choir-desk, where stood a harp and several smaller musical instruments, such as the sackbut, psaltery, trumpet, cornet, and ten-stringed lute.

The young man who had so attracted my attention I now saw leave one of the seats where he had been out of view, and go to the harp, over which he ran his fingers as a prelude to one of the most sublime and touching pieces I ever listened to. The prince no sooner fastened his eyes upon him than, with an exclamation of surprise and pleasure, he made a half spring forward as if to address him! but this impulse he instantly checked, saying:

"It is the young shepherd of Bethlehem!"

He stood up and eagerly regarded him with the most friendly interest, like one who suddenly discovers a very dear friend. I could not ask him any questions, I was so rapt with the performance of this beautiful youth upon the harp, and with the rich and harmonious tones of his voice; for he played but a few passages before he began to sing a hymn addressed to his God!

"Praise ye the Lord.
Praise God in his sanctuary;
Praise him in the firmament of his power;
Praise him for his mighty acts;
Praise him according to his excellent greatness;
Praise him with the sound of the trumpet;
Praise him with the psaltery and harp;
Praise him with the timbrel and dances;
Praise him with stringed instruments and organs;
Praise him upon the loud symbals;
Praise him upon the high sounding cymbals;
Let everything that hath breath praise the Lord.
Praise ye the Lord."

How breathless all listened to the magnificent anthem! How noble and graceful his attitude! how grandly he strikes the harp strings! How calm and holy his countenance! How full of adoration his aspect! What a light of devotion burns, like altar fires, in his upturned eyes!

When he had ended, the other players played upon their instruments their parts; and then the seventy pupils chanted sublimely theirs; and the Seer, raising his hands solemnly to heaven, spoke a sublime recitative to his God; when all, harp, cymbals, trumpet, and voices, united in one mighty swell of praise.

I was overpowered by my sensations! My heart was dissolved within me already by the sweet melody of the youthful harper. Tears came into my eyes! Harmony of sounds had never before impressed me so and moved my soul!

The Seer now spread out his hands and blessed them; and shortly afterward the students retired, not in procession, but leisurely, conversing with each other and their teachers. Sev-

eral approached the Prince Jonathan, and with great demonstrations of affectionate respect saluted him.

"Who," I asked him, "is the youth who played so wonderfully upon the harp?"

"I am now going to embrace him!" he answered. "Will
you come with me, my lord Arbaces? See, he advances!"

"David!"

"My friend and prince!"

These mutual exclamations were followed by a warm meeting between the harpist and the son of King Saul; the last
speaking with ardent and delighted feeling, the former with
modest diffidence, yet with evident strong attachment to his
prince.

"How long hast thou been in the School of the Prophets?"
asked the king's son, releasing him from his embrace. "I believed thou wert still at Bethlehem!"

"I have been here but a few weeks, noble prince," answered
the humble youth, with looks full of friendship, if not of love,
for this amiable and warm-hearted young man of high rank.
"The holy prophet, Samuel, sent for me to come hither to
study, and I have obeyed him. I estimate deeply this privilege
of knowing books, and being versed in the wisdom of this far-
famed seat of sacred learning."

"I rejoice at it, my dear David! Here you should be! You
know, as well as do I, your high destiny, God-elected! It becomes you to be here to prepare yourself therefor!"

This was said in a tone that was unconsciously sad. The
youth pressed his hand, and without a word (for both their
hearts seemed full from the presence of a common thought),
they walked away together hand clasped in hand! I followed
them with deep interest with my eyes, and a desire to learn
more of the noble and beautiful boy, for scarcely was he twenty
years of age, who seemed to be so loved by the kind prince.

The Hall of Praise and of Prayer was now deserted by all,
save the Seer, toward whom I advanced, as he seemed to
await me.

"Come with me into my chamber, my lord of Nineveh," he
said, with an air of venerable courtesy. "Since the prince and
the youthful shepherd, David, are gone away together, you will
be left alone for a time. I will now give thee audience, and
hear thee in behalf of the request made by your prince."

I passed an hour with the man of God. The awe I at first

experienced in his presence was not lessened, while a profound feeling of filial affection became mingled with it. He won my heart while he continued to command its deepest and most reverential homage. I will, when I return to Nineveh, your majesty, reveal to you his answer to your inquiries. We spoke of the Hebrew king. This led to an allusion by me, not without hesitation lest I should be venturing on forbidden ground, to his malady. He said gravely:

"You will find Saul, O prince, an unhappy monarch! The spirit of God has departed from him for his impiety and disobedience. He is a man to be pitied. His scepter will soon be taken from him, and be given to him whom God has anointed."

Here the Seer paused, and turning to the table took up a parchment-roll closely written. As he saw me look with curiosity at several other scrolls, and glance at those upon the desks where the two scribes had been writing, he said:

"I perceive you possess a mind which takes pleasure in investigation. These parchments contain in progress the history of the three hundred and ninety years of the rule of the Judges from Joshua to myself, the *last* of the Judges of Israel! In the roll upon the shelf above the table is the book of Joshua, written by himself up to within a few days of his death, and completed by me. The five large scrolls with purple covers in the niche by the window comprise the Five Books written by our great law-giver, Moses. They are our sacred Records, and the seal of God to them bears testimony to their truth as the voice and word of Jehovah! That small scroll in a silver case is a history written by the young man who performed upon the harp with such skill. It is called the "Story of Ruth," who was the mother of his grandfather! It was written by him in his nineteenth year at Bethlehem, at my request, in order to preserve the genealogy of his family. It is a poem of great beauty, for the youth is, by nature as well as by divine inspiration, a true poet!"

"I am already interested in the young harpist, my lord," I answered, "and, with your permission, I will read his book."

The Seer kindly gave me the permission. There entered at this moment one of the seven prophets or teachers of the school, whom I had noticed while in the "Hall of Praise," from the remarkable intelligence of his face, and a certain air of independence and courage by no means unbefitting one who was to be a censor of evil men, as all prophets must be. He acknowledged my presence with a slight but respectful bow, and was going to the shelves for a book when the Seer said to him:

"Nathan, my son, place in the hands of the Prince of Assyria the Book of Ruth: and if you have time transcribe a copy for him. He desires to know all he can of our polity, religion, and literature, during his short sojourn in our land! As you are familiar with these subjects, I desire you to attend him, and afford the prince whatever information he may require."

I thanked the venerable prophet for this favor; and the young teacher, after giving me the book, said with a pleasant smile, "It will gratify me to be of service to your highness."

The Seer then retired to an inner closet or oratory, where he was accustomed to pray, and closing the door left us in the Judgment hall. I passed two hours examining the manuscripts therein, some of which were richly illuminated with brilliantly colored headings to the chapters. The polite teacher then led me along the terrace to a room which contained copies of nearly all the books ever written in the known world: Egyptian, Assyrian, Phœnician, Indic, Arabian, Babylonian, and parchments from the land of Tarshish, in the farthest east, and from the Isles of Grecia in the farthest west, which, in his life of nearly ninety years, the learned Seer had gathered by means of merchants and travelers, often offering to chiefs of caravans large sums in gold for books from strange countries!

"And is there in your seminary of the prophets anyone so learned as to be able to read these parchments in their own languages?" I asked, holding in my hand a massive volume bound between rolled-out plates of silver, and written in beautiful but strange characters.

"No one but the prophet our president," he answered. "He has the knowledge of all the tongues within them! That book you hold in your hand is an Arabic book, treating upon the stars, from the land of Idumea, the chief city of which is wonderfully cut out of the side of a mountain. You perceive, graven upon the silver cover, a picture of that city!"

From this "Chamber of Wisdom," as it is called, we walked along the corridor, as he intended to show me the view of the Great Sea westward, which I had expressed a curiosity to behold. We passed a column in crossing the garden which seemed to be a monument to the dead. Seeing me observe it and admire its carved plinth and the symmetry of its form, he said:

"That is the only remaining pillar of a great temple to the dragon god Bel, which once stood where this old palace of the Judges is placed. It was destroyed by our fathers, all but this column, which Joshua commanded to be left as a memorial of the gigantic architecture of the powerful nation of idol worshipers he had conquered. It is now still more famous as the tomb of the mighty Samson, once a Judge and prophet in Israel, as well as a warrior!"

"I have already, to-day, read," I answered, "in the parchments of the Seer, a narrative of this Hebrew hero, who perished, I believe, about seventy or eighty years ago by pulling down a vast theater upon the heads of his enemies, destroying them all with himself!"

"Yes! He was the strongest, though not the largest of all men, and nobly died avenging himself upon the foes who had put his eyes out in sport. His body was subsequently recovered from the ruins, and buried by the side of this column, which has now become his monument. When he was a Judge of the people he dwelt here two years of the time; and one morning, after a slight shock of an earthquake during the preceding night, he saw that this column leaned over so that it threatened each moment to fall and crush beneath it that wing of the palace. In the presence of the Seventy Elders, his council, and the governor of the city, and many others, he came down, and placing his hand against it, with one effort of his mighty strength he restored it to its level, upright as you behold it now! When, therefore, he perished between the columns of the house of the Philistines, it was deemed fitting that he should rest here; and now it is called no longer 'Dagon's Pillar,' but the 'Pillar of Samson.'"

We now passed a series of rooms which the young prophet informed me were the apartments of the women of the families of the former Judges. "There," he said, pointing to a spacious room now tenantless and ruinous, "the courageous prophetess Deborah had her lodgings. In that door she stood when she made known to the Hebrew Judge and general, Barak, God's command for him to attack the barbaric Canaanites, who held a portion of our nation in bondage. When he refused to go for fear of their great army, she indignantly cried:

"'Wilt thou have *me* to go with you?'

"'Is not God with thee?' he answered. 'Come with my army and I will meet Sisera and all his hosts; but if thou remainest behind I will not stir horse or foot from Mount Tabor where my army lies.' The prophetess put her ephod upon her shoulders, and taking only her sacred wand, marched forth with him. Sisera, a brave and experienced, though youthful general, was defeated and, losing his chariot in the battle, fled on foot, and was taken and slain by a woman called Jael, to whose tent he came for shelter."

"I have also read that narration," I answered, "in the writing of your Seer."

"You will then recollect that she cut off his head with her own hand. It was sent hither to the prophetess Deborah, and laid by the messenger upon this stone by the door; but she humanely commanded it to be sent back and buried with his body, which, at her request, Barak had conveyed to his mother who, from her lattice, was waiting his return as a conqueror, when she beheld approaching his headless body brought back upon a bier of boughs."

"When did this heroine live?" I asked of the intelligent and interesting young prophet.

"About two hundred and fifty years ago. Here is an apartment," he continued, "which is invested with pleasing yet most painfully touching associations. About one hundred years since there was a noble and brave general, whose name was Jeptha. He had a fair daughter, called Phigenia. Her beauty and gentle character made her universally beloved. Her warlike father idolized her, while she returned his fond affection with all the tender ardor of a daughter's love. It was a pleasing sight to see them both together, and witness his prideful regard as he gazed upon her lovely face, and met the soft eyes of filial trust and confidence with which she looked up to him. When he came from the wars she would be the first to descry, from the tower of his castle, his tall form and waving crest; and the first, when he entered the gate of the city where he dwelt, to welcome him with joy and gratitude at his safe return; while he would bend over from the saddle and lift her slender form to his mailed bosom, and kiss her cheeks with tear-sparkling eyes and words of parental love. When he reached the palace, she would, with her delicate fingers, untie the fastenings of his brazen helmet, arrange his gray locks, and attend to his comfort in the thousand ways known only to pure and unselfish filial love.

"At length the King of Ammon, who reigned on the east of

Jordan, invaded the land. Jephtha was called upon by the people to become their leader in the war, and they invested him
with authority as a prince and a Judge over them: the highest
office in the nation. His daughter was at this time sojourning
in Mizpeh at his house with her friends. But when he became
Judge of Israel he forthwith sent her to Ramah with his
sister to make ready this palace, as he intended after the war
to dwell here. For eighteen years the Philistines had op-
pressed our nation and conquered us in every battle, so that
we were in a measure subject to them, and for that period had
no Judge in Israel. The election of so distinguished a soldier
as Jeptha caused great joy; and all the people sent offerings
to Ramah, and also to Gibeah to repair the houses of the
Judges, which had been suffered to fall into desolation.

"The people of Ramah rejoiced that their Judge was about
to make his habitation among them, and gave their money
freely to restore it; and his fair daughter had soon the palace
ready for the reception of her father when he should return
from the field.

"In the meanwhile Jeptha, on the east of Jordan, had been
making preparations to give battle to his adversaries. On the
eve of attacking them he stood before his captains, and raising his right hand to God made a solemn vow, which he sealed
by the oath of God, that if the Lord would give him victory
over the army of Ammon and deliver their adversaries into
his hand, on his return to Mizpeh whatever came forth out of
the gate of the city to meet him he would offer it as a burnt-
offering unto the Lord his God! Little did the warlike father
suspect who would meet him. Phigenia, his daughter, having
got this palace all in readiness, and anxious to hear news from
her father, and obtaining none after three days' suspense, said
she would go as far as Mizpeh, as she could sooner there get
tidings from the land of Ammon whether there had been a
battle and her father were safe. So she returned with her
maidens and friends to Mizpeh. Hardly had she entered within
the walls of that city ere a messenger came into the town,
running and saying that a great battle had been fought, and
Jeptha victorious! The next day from the battlements the
conqueror, with a small war-worn retinue attending him, was
discerned galloping across the valley toward the gates. The
whole city went out to hail their deliverer; and as they drew
near him, falling back a little, they let Phigenia advance first

to meet him, at the head of a company of the maidens of Miz-peh with timbrels and dances.

"When he looked up and saw her he uttered a great cry of agony, and leaping off his horse to the ground rent his man-tle, and covering his face, refused to embrace her, saying:

"'Alas, my daughter! alas! How camest thou hither to meet me and to break my heart?' And she said (while all stood amazed at his grief):

"' What grieveth thee, O my father? Art thou not covered with glory? Has not God blessed thy sword with victory? I have come forth to meet thee, like a loving and fond daughter, to hail thee conqueror of Ammon, when thou hidest thy face and turnest from me in sorrow! Art thou wounded, O my father, and in pain?'

"'Wherefore should I not hide my face and weep?' he an-swered, gazing upon her with a haggard visage. 'Listen, my child! I vowed a vow to God before the battle that, if he would deliver Ammon into my hand, I would sacrifice as a burnt offering to Him the first object that met me on my return home! Lo! Thou art come, alas, alas, to make thyself the victim! Would God I had fallen on the field by the sword of Ammon, or lost the battle with infamy, ere my eyes beheld thee here! But I have sworn to God thy death, and thou must die!'

"Then all the people with the maidens lifted up their voices and wept sore at these dread words; but the lovely Phigenia, with a firm voice though with a marble face, said:

"'My father, if thou hast sworn, thou canst not forswear thine oath! Do with me according to thy vow! Hath not the Lord given thee victory over thine enemies, thus accepting thine oath? And wilt thou withhold the sacrifice, or shall I the victim? No, my noble father! I am ready to die—to have purchased thereby this victory of my country and the glory of thine arms!'

"'Ah, dearly purchased by thy sweet death, my child!' he answered, falling upon her neck and holding her lovely and slender form long in silence against his mailed heart. At length he stood up and said, with husky words:

"'Thou shalt not die! Heaven will spare my child!'

"'Then what price wilt thou pay back to God, O my father, for the victory? I am no longer thine, but consecrated by thy vow to heaven! Better I should meet my death on the altar of fire than thou shouldst be false to thine oath on the field of victory.'

"'Yes—there is no hope—none—no—alas! Thou must be slain!' he said sorrowfully. Then suddenly added firmly:

"'Prepare thyself for the sacrifice, my daughter!'

"'Not now—oh, not here, my father!' she thrillingly cried, as he drew his sword and made a sign to her to kneel! 'Thine oath named not the hour! I will not shrink—oh, no, I will not shrink from the death! But spare me two months, O my father, to prepare myself for the altar of sacrifice!'

"Gladly the poor father caught at this respite and bade her go, and with her maidens make ready to be offered up, at the end of that time, a burnt-offering to God!"

Here the youthful prophet Nathan paused. I had listened with the deepest and most painful interest to his narrative.

"Was this beautiful virgin sacrificed by her father?" I asked.

"Alas, yes!" he answered sadly. "She at once came hither to stay until the expiration of the two months, during which time she lodged here in this place with her friends; save that every day she would go into the groves of the hills, which you behold near the city, where a holy prophetess dwelt, and lament in touching songs her fate, to be doomed to die so young! for life was naturally dear to her. She also prayed much there, and sought to consecrate herself with the aid of the prophetess by prayer and fasting for the sacrifice. At length the day came for the fulfillment of the dreadful vow made by her father! He had passed the intervening time in his house at Mizpeh clothed in sackcloth, and spoke to no man for nearly three-score days. Then came he hither, and in the little vale which you behold from this angle of the wall he erected an altar with his own hands. In this room before you the hapless virgin was attired for the sacrifice in robes of pure white, wearing on her head a crown of white roses. She went firmly forth at the hour of evening sacrifice, descending with her train of weeping maidens through the gate of the court below, and so across the hill which you now see covered with olive trees, and thence entered into the vale. By the altar stood the dark and stern father, his drawn sword in his hand! He appeared like a marble statue rather than a living man. Thousands looked on in religious awe from the walls and hillsides.

"The sweet victim, embracing her young friends, released

herself from their clinging arms and approaching her father, would have knelt before him for his blessing; but he forbade her with a gesture, and said, 'Let me kneel and ask thy forgiveness, O dear lamb, for my rash vow, and for the deed my hand must do in its fulfillment this day!'

"He knelt down before her, all the while keeping his eyes turned away that he might not look on her face, and she placed gently and lovingly her folded hands upon his head, and said:

"'I have nothing to forgive, my father! I die for my country's victory, and for thy honor before God and the people of Israel! Now, farewell!'

"For a moment she rested in his arms, then kissed his forehead, and gently disengaging herself, with a firm step ascended the altar. He rose and followed her—tottered to her side like a man overcome of wine—and as she kneeled in an attitude of prayer upon the wood laid for the burnt-offering he sheathed his glittering sword in her snow-white bosom; then kindling the fagots with his torch, he fell to the earth insensible, and lay there as one dead."

"It is a sad, sad tale," I said, perceiving that the prophet was silent. "Did the father live?"

"He never smiled again! He lived a few melancholy years, weary of existence, and unfit for war or rule, and died the sixth year after his fatal victory, at Gilead, where he was buried, for he never entered this house of Naioth in Ramah after her death. His head reposes upon an urn containing the ashes of his lovely victim!"

I thanked my intelligent guide for this touching narrative, and surveyed with renewed and tender interest the room consecrated by the last presence on earth of the hapless, yet amiable, courageous, and pious Phigenia.

We then continued our way out of the city to the hill-tower, from the lofty top of which I beheld for the first time the mighty Sea of the West. My emotions deprived me of speech! I could only gaze with wonder and awe! How shall I describe the spectacle, to give your majesty an idea of its sublimity and illimitable grandeur! It appeared to my eye as if I could see off the earth into boundless space; for the sea and sky were both of the same azure tint, and the meeting line of water and air was not perceptible. There was in fact no visible horizon! The far distant strand of Palestina, full twelve leagues west of us, but more by the roads, seemed the jagged edge of the world! I never experienced before such ideas of vastness and remoteness. The atmosphere was pure as crystal. As the sun declined, the narrow belt of sea became silvered with its light, and looked like a brilliant river without a farther shore flowing around the verge of the world! Your majesty must pardon a little enthusiasm in one who beholds such a sight for the first time!

My guide, whose grace of manners, gentleness of speech, and intelligent conversation attracted me more and more toward him, and who seemed to have a profound acquaintance with his country's history, and to know how to instruct without ostentation, now directed my attention to the surrounding scenes. In one direction he pointed to where Joppa lay, a famous seaport, but not in sight; gave me the names of the mountains which we stood upon, those all about us, and indicated with his hand the direction of Hebron, south. The valley of the Jordan, the dark mountains of Nebo beyond, and, also, the Sea of Sodoma lay to the east.

On our return from the summit we crossed the little valley of the sacrifice of Phigenia, called the "Vale of the Oath." It was a gloomy spot, overhung with rocks on one side, and deserted even by flocks and herds; and since that day, one hundred years ago, no man has tilled or sown thereon! I stopped near a pile of stones, half buried and covered with wild vines and moss. It was the remains of the altar of Jeptha! left as a lasting monument of his rash vow! On our walk we had just passed a beautiful garden when we came to a large mausoleum all in ruins, and apparently of great age. Perceiving that I regarded it with interest, the prophet said:

"This is called the tomb of Joshua! But there is another sepulchre in the rocky sides of the mount of Bethel, which is also claimed by the Benjaminites as his burial-place. There is no doubt that this was erected as a sepulchre for one of the ancient Canaanitish kings, and his coffin removed by the conquerors; doubtless the body of Joshua was placed here! At least tradition, which is history to us, gives its testimony to this effect."

While I was meditating upon the spot, and recalling the glorious career of the Hebrew conqueror, and the ingratitude of his nation in permitting his sepulchre to perish, or to be in doubt as to the place of his burial, the Hebrew prince and the young harpist of the School of the Prophets appeared walking in the path, side by side. The prince at once joined me, excusing himself for neglecting me. I replied, I had been in good hands, and had derived much information from my companion.

"In that case," said the prince, smiling, "I will not take any blame to myself. My lord Arbaces, this is my friend David of Bethlehem, of the School of the Prophets!"

The youth, who had just asked of Nathan some question, met my salutation with modest frankness, blushing like a maiden; evidence of a right and noble disposition, and of an ingenuous nature uncorrupted by the world. I could not but regard with admiration his extraordinary beauty, of which I have before spoken! He seemed a superior being, especially when I recalled his wonderful performance on the harp, and his voice so rich with melody and pathos. Here a fourth person joined us, a young man in the dress of the School. His name was Asaph, and he brought a message to the prince from the Seer. We all went toward the palace together, when I parted with the intelligent prophet, expressing warmly my obligations to his courtesy, for he had given me full four hours of his time. The handsome Bethlehemite also left us at the foot of the terrace, the prince taking his hand, on separating, with the affectionate manner of a twin-brother.

It was my privilege to occupy the same apartment with the royal prince. When I seated myself to recover from the fatigue of my walk, I related to him what I had seen and heard. We discussed the conduct of Jael in slaying Sisera: the prince giving it as his opinion that "she was justifiable as he was an enemy of God; as in permitting him to go in safety she would have been condemned as an enemy to her people: she had no alternative but to do as she did." On the contrary, I contended, your majesty, that the rights of hospitality are *always* sacred; and the enemy who seeks protection under its shield cannot be harmed by the host without crime.

Of the fatal vow of Jeptha we also spoke. I said that "a rash vow is a great wrong; but if it involve a greater wrong, the *least* of the evils should be chosen. He had better have been perjured than for his oath's sake commit a crime which has no parallel.

"Your God, my noble prince," I added, "would rather have forgiven the vow than received the unnatural sacrifice."

"As Jeptha alone was guilty," said the prince, "he alone should have been the sufferer. He ought to have sacrificed himself rather than the innocent Phigenia! Suicide is a crime, and so is murder! He could have chosen between the two! But she has left to the world a noble and touching memory, and a sublime example of filial obedience and piety. Her sacrifice has made her immortal."

After two days passed as guest of the venerable Seer, at whose feet I also sat with his School of youthful prophets to listen to the words of wisdom that fell from his lips, I at length bade him farewell and received, kneeling, his blessing. He desired me to convey to your majesty his remembrances, and to ask you to read a copy of the sacred books of his people which he has presented to me for your acceptance. He says your reign will be happy and prosperous if you continued just and virtuous, but that sins and oppression in kings (evils happily unknown in your majesty's rule) are more severely punished by the God of the heaven and earth than the transgressions of other men! That "kings are vicegerents of the supreme King on high, and should rule with equity and judgment." He showed me how all the wars in which his nation have been involved were actual scourges of their God sent upon them for national transgressions.

Having taken a kind leave, at the foot of the stairs, of my intelligent friend Nathan, who promises to become a leading man among his countrymen, young David came forward to me and grasping my hand said, in a manly way and with graceful dignity:

"I am sorry, my lord prince, you have come to find our country troubled by the hordes of the Philistines, whose presence will perhaps prevent you from going, at present, farther south than Solima or Hebron. News is come within an hour that they even menace this place."

The prince had already heard the tidings, and ridden to the gate to learn their origin. There I found him, not long returned from a visit of filial duty to his mother at Bethel, surrounded by the captains and officers of the garrison. I learned that an army of four thousand men was within ten leagues of Ramah, having already occupied several towns on their route. The prince promptly sent a force of eight hundred men to defend a pass in the mountains of Ephraim, made some valuable suggestions to the general who commanded in those parts, and at length rode forward with me on the way to Hebron, his own and my bodyguard escorting us.

On our way we passed the rocky heights of Solima with a bold castle crowning the southern eminence, still held by a pagan garrison of Jebusites; the place having withstood since the days of Joshua the assaults of the Hebrews. There it towered in strength and pride, an inaccessible fortress of the ancient masters of the land in the very heart of the kingdom. Your majesty may suppose that I gazed upward toward its frowning battlements with deep interest, from the narrow valley which it overhangs and through which we traveled. Upon my expressing my surprise to the prince that so small a castle should have held out for more than four hundred years, he said that it was formerly the citadel of the chief city of the land, Solima, once the capital of the kingdom of a wise and virtuous Syrian prince, Melchisedek, and that " Joshua conquered the city itself, but left the citadel to be subsequently and at leisure reduced; but other places demanding his attention, it remained unattacked up to the time of his death; and since then, though often assailed, it has never been conquered. The garrison is, however, peaceful, and seldom molests our people."

The same day we passed across a portion of the plain of Mamre before Hebron, where the three great Kings, Abraham, Isaac, and Jacob, lay buried in the cave of Machpelah; which interesting spot I have visited since I arrived here. In it also reposes the embalmed body of the eminent and virtuous Prince Joseph, once governor of Egypt, who, at his dying, commanded the Hebrews to bring it with them from the land of the Pharaohs and here bury it; thus singularly prophesying not only their departure from Egypt, but their conquest of this land.

In the plain of Mamre I found encamped my caravan, and retinue of Assyrian soldiers. The next morning I entered the city, and was conducted by the Hebrew prince into the presence of King Saul.

Your faithful
ARBACES.

LETTER V.

ARBACES, THE AMBASSADOR, TO BELUS, KING OF ASSYRIA.

AMBASSADOR'S CAMP, PLAIN OF MAMRE, BEFORE HEBRON.
MY DEAR COUSIN AND KING:

The city before which I am encamped, your majesty, is one of the oldest in this part of the earth, even older than ancient Tanis, once the capital of the northern Egyptian realm. It is said to have been founded by a giant named Habro, or Hebra, of the race of the old kings of Palestina. When Joshua conquered the land it was the stronghold of a Canaanitish king, who himself was of gigantic stature, of the family of Anakim.

It is built upon a bold and rocky hill, and looks with its lofty battlements, immense walls, and strongly founded towers, to be impregnable. Hence the king has recently selected it to become the capital of his kingdom, when he shall have completed his palace, and strengthened and enlarged its fortifications. It is partially encircled by the vale of Machpelah, a portion of the valley of Mamre, of which with its gardens, and white flat-roofed villages, and groves of palm trees, and enclosures of fig, pomegranate, and apricot trees, it commands a noble view. Around this vale stand precipitous hills, which are separated by deep passes, that approach close to the walls in one direction; but a small number of soldiers can prevent an enemy from penetrating through them to the city. Without doubt it will be made by the monarch the strongest city in this extraordinary kingdom of walled and battlemented towns and garrisons.

I regret to have to inform your majesty that the apprehensions of the prince are realized. The Philistines have actually thrown out their advanced troops so far as to cover the road towards Egypt, and intercept all travel in that direction. They have a two-fold motive, perhaps, both to plunder caravans and cut off supplies from King Saul in Hebron. I shall, therefore, be under the necessity of remaining here until a battle is fought, and the way opened; which I trust will be in a very few days.

The king is diligently assembling his army, and the prince is active in lending his efficient aid. In case of an attack upon these troublesome foes, I shall not withhold my services and those of my battalion of Assyrians. A spy reports that the force south of Hebron numbers ten thousand men, which evidently intend some important movement. The king is strengthening the city at every point, and troops are pouring in from all parts of the kingdom, brave looking men, but poorly armed; for this nation has not yet recovered from the loss of all its arms in the early days of Samuel, when the Philistines, mastering the country, took away from it every sword, spear, battle-ax, and weapon of war. The little intercourse of the Hebrews with other countries, and the total absence of commerce among them, has been an obstacle to their replacement. Almost the first inquiry made of me by King Saul, after I was presented to him, was, " if arms in abundance were in Assyria, and if your majesty would permit your merchants to sell one hundred thousand weapons of all arms to the Hebrews? "

Courage and zeal will not effect much in war without serviceable weapons. The profound policy of the Philistines in disarming their conquered foes is now clearly apparent. An hour since a thousand Hebrews marched past toward the town. Not half of them were armed in a soldierly manner; and these not uniformly; while the rest either carried sharpened bits of iron or steel secured to the ends of staves, or shouldered reaping hooks; and, indeed, many of the swords I saw had been rudely shaped out of sickles and scythes. An army, thus imperfectly armed, however brave the material, cannot have confidence in itself on the field. The Philistines, on the contrary, are well harnessed for battle; are mailed in iron, and defended by helm and cuirass. Besides, they have battalions of chariots of iron with broad, curved knives secured to the ends of the axles, while their horsemen are numbered by thousands, all clad in panoply of steel, and wielding formidable lances. Moreover, they have, as I am told by the Hebrews, a bodyguard of one hundred giants, sons of Anak, who attend their king, who is also a gigantic warrior, six cubits or more in height, or nearly ten feet! He is with the main army west of this, so report the spies, encamped in a large plain which is darkened by his countless hosts. The division south of us I have seen; for, doubting the accuracy of the observations of the men of Beersheba, who brought the report that they held the southern high-road, and resolved, if the way should appear to be at all open, to strike my camp and advance, without an hour's delay, rapidly toward Egypt before it should be wholly closed against me, I took fifty men with me immediately, and started off in that direction. After four hours' riding I reached an elevation over which the road wound, and beneath me saw a sight which confirmed the report, and depressed my hopes of being able, for some time at least, to continue my journey in the direction of the Nile. In a narrow plain, across the green bosom of which wound the yellow, dusty highway toward Egypt, stretched the long, white line of the camp of the thousands of the Philistines. Their number had been exaggerated, as I perceived there could not be, in all, more than five thousand men. As my eyes fell upon them they were going through military evolutions. Chariots in long lines were wheeling across the plain; bodies of cavalry charged hither and thither; men-at-arms in columns were marched and countermarched; bowmen were discharging flights of arrows, and spearmen throwing their long weapons at imaginary adversaries. Banners fluttered, plumes tossed, swords flashed, helmets gleamed, lance-points glittered in the sun, and the noise of the chariot wheels, the loud thump of hoofs, the tramp of many running feet, the wild shouts of the chiefs, and wilder answering cries of the soldiers filled the air; while over the strange and warlike scene rolled clouds of dust reflecting a hue of gold from the beams of the setting sun!

I turned away satisfied that, if this were the highway down to Egypt, I must be content for a short time to remain encamped in the beautiful vale of Mamre.

I have since learned that by retracing my way to the Jordan and recrossing that river, I can gain the wilderness of Moab and Edom, and by a longer route of great hardship, through a country of dangerous and fierce people, whose hand is against all men, ultimately reach Egypt. I would, far rather than risk this route with its increased distance, cut my way, O king, with my thousand brave guard through the camp of the Philistines. I shall remain here a few days and see what will be the issue. We have already been detained nearly one week, and are all impatient at this delay, which I trust will soon terminate.

I will not recount to your majesty the particulars of my interview with the Hebrew monarch. The day following my arrival at my camp, the prince, who had left me the evening previous to hasten to the presence of his royal father, came out to my tent and said that King Saul desired then to see me. Passing on foot through the massive portals of the city, which was crowded with troops, I accompanied the prince along a street narrow and steep, which seemed to be lined alone with stone barracks for the accommodation of the garrison. Beyond these we entered a fine square surrounded by various castellated edifices, with towers intermingled, and all ancient and imposing in appearance. This square was filled with illy-armed Hebrew soldiers, who were being drilled by their captains, while on every side from the inner courts was heard the sound of forging-hammers beating iron into weapons of war. Crossing this animated place we traversed a short street which led into a noble courtyard, on two sides of which were fair gardens; the third was open to the plain of Mamre with its verdant valleys and cliff-like mountains, while the fourth was occupied by a half-erected palace on which numerous workmen were employed. Near it stood the Hebrew architect, whom five days before I had parted with at the cross-ways where we fell in with the caravan from the far-south land of Sheba. The palace builder recognizing me, saluted me with dignity, and desired us to admire his noble building, which, being in good taste and admirably proportioned, I praised as it deserved, when he remarked " that after it should be completed it would surpass all other palaces in the world." I could not but smile, your majesty, at this little exhibition of vanity when I recalled the one hundred and seventy superb palaces within the walls of Nineveh, the least of which is more noble and beautiful than any edifice I have seen in this land, and especially when I thought upon the magnificence of the " Palace of the Kings," half a league square, and your royal mother's alabaster palace, its roof of beaten gold, and its columns of silver, marble, and cedar-wood, inlaid with ivory and pearl!

Thence we proceeded toward a singular tower very large and square at the base and rounded at the top, with an iron gate leading into it.

" That is the ' house of shelter' for men-slayers when they fly red-handed to this place from the avenger of blood," said the prince; " for Hebron is one of the cities of refuge. This is their abode at night, made secure to protect them from secret assassination should their adversary steal into the city to slay them. In the day they go about their occupations like others. Thou seest at the grated window one of the fugitives, whose pale face shows he is too ill to-day to be abroad."

At length the prince stopped before the portal of a low wall which, from the appearance of the foliage rising above it, inclosed a garden. A sentry in a coat of mail and iron head-piece, and armed with a battle-ax, paced to and fro in front of it, while two other Hebrew soldiers similarly accoutered stood within the entrance also on guard. Upon beholding the prince, the sentinel saluted; and we passed into a spacious area paved with stone, and containing a fountain, shaded by a single palm tree. Opposite to the entrance I saw a large stone edifice, which seemed like most of the public edifices in this land, to have been once a temple or palace of the ancient Canaanites. Between a double row of trees, chiefly the oleander and myrtle, with here and there a flowering acacia, we approached this mansion.

In the massive and carved old doorway stood two men-at-arms, tall, strong, mountaineer-looking fellows, armed with short swords. They wore helmets with a low crest, bright red tunics, corslets of steel, or cuirasses of polished iron, or of thick leather, gilt and embossed; with greaves of brass: altogether a singular armor! These soldiers were of the tribe of Gad, and a part of the king's bodyguard; bold, fighting-looking men, and would evidently do their work thoroughly on the field of battle. They did homage to the presence of my princely companion, who conducted me to a broad staircase, so shallow that I was not surprised subsequently to hear that the king, in one of the fits of madness that sometimes come upon him, had once spurred up them on horseback.

At the top of the stairs we came upon a wide corridor, at the end of which was a door, where also stood a sentinel. Many persons were walking up and down this entry, or ante-chamber, waiting for audience. Some were chief captains in full armor; others, elders of the city in flowing beards and long robes; others, citizens of distinction, richly attired; others, persons who came to sue for mercy or for justice, or to present petitions. To all of these the prince, in returning their respectful salutes, spoke a word, now of promise, now of hope, now of sympathy, now of confidence. Among them whom should I discover but the governor of Jericho, who had just arrived in obedience to a summons from the king! He recognized, and met me with great cordiality, and when I asked after his fair daughter Adora, the greatest heiress and most beautiful virgin in Israel, of whom I have before written to your majesty, he answered that he had brought her with him, and that she was at the house of his brother, the captain of the city. Upon hearing this news I must confess to your majesty that I was not a little gratified; for the presence of so charming a person would serve greatly to relieve the tedium of my compulsory stay at Hebron; for at Jericho I saw her often at the house of the chief governor and elder, her father, and learned to esteem them both as valued friends.

"Does the king know thou art in waiting?" asked Jonathan of him.

"I have sent in word by the chief chamberlain, your highness, about an hour ago," he replied.

"I will recall you to his mind. Is thy business pressing, my lord?" he continued, addressing the noble-looking governor.

"It may be to his majesty. He desires to hire sixty talents of gold for this war! I am here to say that I and my friends can oblige him with it all!"

"I rejoice to hear it, my good governor! I know my father needs money to pay his army. With your kind aid all will go favorably! I will let him know you wait."

Here I overheard a low voice say to someone, "He will see no one to-day, I fear. The dark spirit is upon him."

"Will my lord of Assur do me the honor to dine to-morrow with me and my daughter at my brother's?" asked the governor of me, as we were passing on.

"I will gladly accept your excellency's invitation," I replied; "for all my time hangs on my hands. I only fear you will see me too often!"

"Do not fear that, my lord Arbaces," answered the stately and handsome Hebrew ruler, smiling.

We passed by the sentinel, and entering, I found myself in a large and beautiful apartment adorned with sculpture. Gilded panels, enriched by painted flowers, were set between ranges of columns of polished marble, inlaid with ivory and colored woods, and burnished to the hardness of porphyry. At the lower end were hangings of various colors richly variegated with needlework; and the ceiling was decorated to represent the azure vault of heaven studded with stars of gold. The opposite extremity of this noble room was filled by a throne elevated three steps above the floor, and overhung by a splendid canopy of cloth of gold. Behind the throne, which was a magnificent chair of ivory, inlaid with devices in silver, and covered by Tyrian velvet of a dark purple hue, enriched by needlework, was a great window through which came blowing the cool breezes from the mountains of Adoniram, which were visible not far off with their rugged shoulders and dark, brown sides, dotted with flocks and herds.

The throne was vacant. On each side of it stood a tall, bearded man in steel armor, leaning upon a long two-edged sword that shone like silver. In front, kneeling upon an embroidered cushion, was an Ethiopian page, richly attired, who seemed patiently to await orders to go and come. By a column, on which was fastened a leaf of brass as a writing-table, stood a long-haired secretary without a beard, his reed in his hand, and his silver ink-horn hanging at his girdle that bound, by a gold buckle, the long blue gown which he wore beneath a short, green tunic. He was not writing, but engaged in conversation with a gorgeously clothed and pompous-looking chamberlain, who, with his green wand in his hand, was awaiting the commands of the monarch.

Walking at great strides up and down the long hall, his eyes fixed upon the floor, his arms folded across his herculean chest, and his large, noble features overcast with troubled thought, I beheld the king himself. It could be none other! It was not necessary for the young prince to look at me and say in a low tone touched in sorrow:

" There is my father! "

His majesty took no notice of us, but walked by to the foot of the throne, and then returned to the lower end of the room, thrice, before he seemed to be aware of our presence in his audience chamber. I had therefore an opportunity of observing him. He was the most magnificent looking man I ever beheld! Tall, with almost the proportions of a splendid giant; yet, from the perfect symmetry of his limbs, carrying himself with a firm, graceful, and noble air! His head was grand! and covered with short masses of curling locks, which were black as night! His ample forehead reminded me of the godlike brow of the statue of Sardanapalus in front of your majesty's palace. He seemed to be about fifty-six or fifty-eight years of age, a few silver threads woven into his heavy beard, which covered only his upper lip and cheeks, betraying that he had passed the goal of fifty. He was royally attired in a suit which was half-armor, half-citizen's costume; his majestic breast being protected by a corslet curiously woven of silver chains, while a silver helmet with a white plume flowing around the golden crest covered his head. Over his broad, kingly shoulders was thrown a short crimson mantle clasped by a pair of steel lion's claws. A short dagger was stuck, unsheathed, in a broad belt of leopard's skin, which confined his coat to his waist. There was an air, partly of barbaric splendor and partly of courtly ease, in his appearance and bearing. Without question, he was a man of decided intellectual character and strong passions, with undoubted power over men, and whom it would be madness willfully to enrage or disobey.

As he paced up and down, his great noble eyes wore a sorrowful and heavy look: they seemed to hold no light in them; but, like mist-hidden stars, to be under the veil of the cloud resting on his soul's horizon! His proud, fixed lips, the bent brow, the awful expression of settled gloom betrayed the strength of the terrible emotions which tore and lashed his haughty spirit, chafed by the anger of his God and the displeasure of the powerful prophet! It was painful to gaze upon this wreck of the once proud, ambitious, and generous-hearted king, of the lion heart and eagle eye, who had been chosen, above all his fellows, to be anointed the first king of his ancient race! I thought I could see the storm rolling across the darkening sky of his soul, as fiery thought after fiery thought flashed like forked lightnings from his surcharged brain at the reflection that he was the mark of his God's wrath, the abandoned of his Spirit, the victim of his vengeance! He seemed at one moment to cower under this pressure, and dropped his head lower and lower; but the next, as I watched his face, I thought I could see a look of defiant despair developing itself amid the gloom. I was not mistaken! He stopped near us, raised his majestic head with an air of fierce anger, and shaking his open palms toward heaven with eyes kindling he cried, with fearful emphasis and in appalling, passionate tones:

"I defy the God of Israel! Sacrifice? So I did! Who should let me? Was I not priest as well as king? 'Twas not to Baal, nor to Ashtaroth, nor to the gods of the accursed Philistines, I slew the victim, but to the—— What! art thou come, my son?" he suddenly spoke in a natural and even tone, as at this moment his eyes rested upon us! The transition, from his sublime and terrible appeal to Heaven to this pleasant tone of voice, was like magic most wonderful. "I did not notice thee! I—I——" Here he passed his hand slowly across his forehead as if collecting his thoughts; and the cloud slowly passed away, and with a benign and noble, yet touching voice, as if the waves of emotion still trembled a little even after the dark simoom of passion had passed by, he continued:

"I hope you have not waited! This youthful stranger is, I doubt not, the Prince Arbaces of Assyria! I welcome you to my poor court, noble ambassador. My son has spoken of you so favorably that I already regard you as a friend. I rejoice that you came into Judea! It is my desire to hold relations of the strongest friendship with your monarch! At present we are a young kingdom, and it will require time to give us position and name among the kingdoms of the earth! I trust your royal master, Belus, is well and at peace in all his realm."

"He is well, your majesty," I answered, "and would have sent a personal message to you by me; but so infrequent is the intercourse between my country and the west, and Belus has been so short a time on the throne, that he had not heard that your people had changed its government to that of a monarchy; although I have learned that you have been many years king!"

"Many years!" he repeated, slightly frowning, and then smiled; "yes. But if not long enough to have made my name known on the Tigris, I have reigned, I fear, to little purpose; for I have not even expelled the Philistines from my borders! But, young prince of Assyria," he added, stamping his foot with sudden fury, "how can a king reign and conquer and bless his kingdom, with Heaven armed against him, Hell leagued to destroy him, and earth's most powerful Seer hurling prophecies of evil upon his poor head?"

"My dear father," said Jonathan, touching his arm and speaking as tenderly as he would to a child, "the holy prophet holdeth no anger! He is but the mouth of God! He pities you, and——"

"*Pities!* Samuel of Ramah *pity* Saul the king? The haughty prophet may beware! By the head of my father, if he pities me, I will slay him did he cling for safety to the very wings of the cherubim!"

This was spoken with insane violence. His eyes shot forth fire. His face flushed with his burning blood! His whole

mighty form was dilate with strong wrath! He foamed at the
mouth; he shook his clenched hands toward Ramah as if he saw
visibly the prophet: he laughed aloud! He stood before us
a madman!

Suddenly a rapid and troubled gesture, made by the prince
to a distant part of the hall, was answered by a strain
of music upon a stringed instrument, evidently from unprac-
ticed or trembling hands. The irate monarch, whose whole
pride of character had been suddenly and sharply wounded at
the idea that he whom he regarded as his enemy pitied him,
paused at the sound, turned slowly toward it, and fixing his
terrible eyes, blazing with supernatural splendor, upon a gallery
where two players dressed in white stood performing, he seèmed
for a moment to be listening; but a false note being struck, he
uttered a shout of vengeance and scorn, and drawing the dagger
at his belt, he sprung forward with death to the unhappy
players in his eyes.

"Mockest thou me! Darest thou?" he called to the unhappy musicians. In a moment I stood before him. It was an
act wholly impulsive!

"Oh, king, most wise and good! Thou art too just to harm
the innocent, or stain the purity of thy scepter by a deed of
blood on those poor harpists, thy slaves!" I said, with a firmness and force which I am since surprised at, as well as at the
result. For an instant, as I stood in his path, the glittering
steel which he held waved in his hand, irresolute above my
heart! I held his blazing eyes steadily with mine. Jonathan
would have come to rescue me from what he believed certain
death (for my sword was undrawn), when with a sudden change
of purpose he sheathed again the bloodless steel, his face relaxed its stern and violent expression, his eyes parted with their
fierce fire, and with a look of amity and regard he laid his
hand upon my arm, and said:

"Thou art right, prince! Saul the man is not so mad that
Saul the king forgets justice and mercy! I see thou dost not
think I am mad, like this Samuel and the rest of the Hebrews!
Thou seest in me only an unhappy king. Thy voice, I perceive, has neither pity nor reproach! I am now calm! The
dark spirit that at times possesses my soul has flown! He cannot bear words of kindness! Prince, pardon my discourtesy
to thee!"

How my heart bled for him! Deeply did I sympathize with

this poor monarch, who seems to be cast down with a consciousness of his madness, and keenly mortified by its exhibitions; alternately depressed by the idea of the displeasure of his God, and grieved at his sins by which he has incurred it; now melancholy with despair of reconciliation, now maddened by the certainty that his kingdom is to be taken from him, and his scepter given into the grasp of a stranger! I am sure that your majesty will feel deeply for the unhappy Hebrew king, and that you will wish that his great punishment might terminate after a due time, and the heavenly powers, propitiated, secure to him and his posterity his kingdom.

He was now thoroughly composed. What had first excited him was explained to us. An hour before we came in he had received an impudent and haughty challenge from the Philistine king, written with the blood of one of his spies (who had been taken and slain) upon a piece of sacred parchment of the holy law. It had been shot into the window fastened to an arrow, and fell at the side of the throne as the king sat thereon giving audience.

One should know, in order to comprehend the full insult of the challenge, with what superstitious reverence the Hebrews regard their sacred parchments. If a man see a fragment on the ground he dare not pass it lest one of the names of their God be upon it, and it be trodden under foot! It is a great crime in any way to desecrate it; but *one* of his mysterious names no man ever wrote or dares to write! The Scribes express it by a blank space! But others may lawfully be written. The Philistine knew this. Moreover, blood is deemed sacred by the Hebrews! To make use of it, as was done by the Philistine, was therefore a two-fold insult; not to speak of the slaughter of the poor spy whose life supplied the stream in which the reed was dipped. The boldness of the bowman, who could approach so near the walls, unseen, as to send through the window a shaft with the challenge secured to its feathered end, increased the wrath of King Saul. In vain the bearer of the bold challenge was sought for! The king, in the meanwhile, commanded his scribe to read it.

"To Saul of Kish, King of slaves, Goliath of Gath sendeth greeting: By this writing he challengeth him to single combat for his crown! In the valley of Mount Gebo, before Socho, he awaiteth Saul the Hebrew, King of slaves! Why should thy army all perish? Come forth out of the city and let us two men-at-war decide our quarrel. He that conquers shall have both kingdoms and wear both crowns. Send me speedily thine answer, thou dog of a Hebrew, son of Kish the herd."

There is little to marvel at that King Saul, with his morbid and irate temper, should have been thrown into a great rage by this missile! The arrow, with the challenge, I saw lying upon the floor as we entered, but had then no idea of their signification.

Having conducted me to a seat by his throne the dignified king now quietly conversed with me about Assyria, the number of the chariots, horsemen, and footmen in your majesty's armies, inquired as to your age and personal appearance, was amazed when I described to him the vastness of your dominions, and the magnificence of Nineveh with its million of souls. He inquired about your forges of armor, your mines of iron, of gold, silver, and copper; your pearl fisheries on the South Sea, and your fleets trading to remote Tarshish * in the east, and to Ezion-geber on the Red Sea of Ethiopia. He said he would gladly purchase arms in Assyria for his people, and desired me to ask your majesty to dispose of as many as would fully arm his hosts, which I promised to do; and he has resolved to send a caravan to Assyria with me on my return from Egypt, in order to bring them hither. We conversed an hour. The prince seeing the placable mood his father was in, secretly removed the arrow and its message from the hall, and disappeared; and as he passed through the ante-room he benevolently, though reluctantly, granted in the king's name the prayers of all who waited, and sent them away joyful; and forbidding anyone to intrude into the king's presence that day, he went to aid the generals to organize the army.

Poor young prince! How heavily his father's calamity weighs upon him! His position, too, is singularly anomalous! I have just said he granted the petitions of those poor people who sought the king's clemency or favor, but granted them reluctantly. He felt that in doing it he was usurping a right which was not justly his, for though he was the king's son, he knew he was not to succeed him in the kingdom; and therefore had no authority to act in the kingdom, as one who was by and by to reign might, perhaps, lawfully do! I have already

* Now the island of Ceylon.

stated to your majesty that the scepter was to be taken from
Saul by the God who conferred it upon him in his earlier
years, and given to another; that the prince not only knows
this, but is well aware who the person is who is to supplant
himself in the royal succession.

This evening, while I was seated in my tent, reflecting upon
the extraordinary scene which occurred to-day during my visit
to the king, the curtain of my tent was raised and the prince
entered. I received him with more than my usual friendly
warmth, and he took a seat by me. After a moment's silence
he said:

"My dear Arbaces, you have now seen my father, and can
understand his calamity. I am sure you sympathize with me,
and feel deeply for him with your generous nature. Once how
heroic, noble, majestic a king was he, until that unhappy day
when he usurped the sacred office of Sacrificer to God! It has
cost him his peace, his mind, his reason, the loss of the Spirit
of God, and ultimately will cost him the loss of his throne!
But I will not intrude our griefs upon you. I have come' to
say that my father has decided to march against the Philistines
without delay. There are twenty thousand Hebrew soldiers in,
and within an hour's march of, Hebron. We move the first
division at sunrise to-morrow. I have come to ask you if you
would like to accompany me, as I go with it! Do not think
I am soliciting your aid, I only desire your company; and have
thought you might wish to see a battle; for unless the enemy
prove too great in numbers we shall offer him battle within
three days. He is encamped about thirty miles to the north-
west, in a broad plain inclosed by mountains. His hosts are
reported by our spies to be very great. We shall advance with
the army we have with us, and leave orders for any fresh
bodies of troops to follow."

"I will not only go with you as a friend, my dear prince,"
I said; "but I will take with me six hundred of my bodyguard,
leaving the residue to guard my encampment. I now offer you
and the king the assistance of my brave Assyrians! Be sure
they will do good service."

The prince warmly thanked me, and then said, "I will make
known your kind offer to the king; but I fear his pride will
lead him to decline it; for if the victory is won, he would desire
the whole glory should be with his own army; and if he is defeated, he would be mortified to involve in the disgrace the

soldiers of an ambassador who is merely passing through his kingdom on a mission of peace to a foreign potentate."

"I see, my dear prince, you speak your own sentiments as well as those you think will be your royal father's," I answered with a smile. "At all events, I will accompany you with my guards; and if there prove to be no need of their service, they shall remain neutral."

At this moment the prince glanced his eyes upon the little roll of parchment called the "Story of Ruth," which I had been reading by the light of my tent-lamp when he entered.

"I see you interest yourself, noble Arbaces, greatly in our writings," he said.

"They are deeply interesting to me as well as wholly new," I replied. "Your whole history is wonderful! Beginning with the calling of Abraham out of Assyrian Chaldea by a voice from the heavens, and coming down to his obedience, and his march from the Euphrates to the Jordan guided by a dove (which at night shone like a star, as one of your ancient books records); to his wars here, and to his kingly dominion in this very land, Hebron, his chief seat of authority, while this plain was his burial place; to the romantic incident of Isaac his son sending to Chaldea for his wife, and her being brought to him veiled; to the wonderful career of Jacob; the selling of Joseph; the famine which drove them into Egypt; the sudden eleva-tion of the youthful Joseph to power; his revelation of him-self to his brethren; first their amazement, and then their terror lest he should avenge himself on them, and their joy at his forgiveness; their presentation before Pharaoh; the death of Joseph, and his dying injunction that his descendants should take his bones to this very plain where his ancestors had been buried; and the extraordinary fact that one hundred and eighty years afterward the descendants of himself and brethren did actually leave Egypt and come to this land and bury the bones of Joseph with his fathers in this cave of Machpelah, which I can by day behold in full view from here, my tent door; the power of your God exhibited in the dividing of the Red Sea, and of the Jordan, and in many other mighty deeds! all these events and incidents are parts of a wonderful history, such as mere human invention could never approach in interest or in marvels. From the beginning to the end it possesses a sin-gular harmony of proportions and dependencies, one event lead-ing to another, and the whole wrought out from foreseen and foreshaped circumstances by a Wisdom and Power which must have perceived the end from the beginning. Before its narration all the legends of our Persian poets are insignificant and weak. What will be the ultimate end, who can foresee? But without doubt there is a Future before you commensurate with the Past, and which has been in part foreshadowed by the Past."

When I had ceased, the prince regarded me a moment steadfastly and said:

"You understand our nation. Without doubt, we are working out some mighty problem in which God is interested, and of which we are but the blind instruments. Our prophets plainly teach us that whatever we do, we but prefigure something yet to come—that all our national events and our religious rites are but types of some great thing to be developed in the ages yet future; that our tabernacle, our sacred Ark, our altar of incense, our lamb sacrificed morning and evening, our seven candlesticks, our shew-bread, our holy of holies, our High Priest, the breastplate and ephod, the urim and thummim with its dazzling light, the scapegoat, the jubilee, the offering of atonement and expiation; all are not what they seem, but foreshadow a mighty Reality yet to come forth out of the splendor of a glorious future! They teach that all we are as a nation, in all we are and do, we hold but the place of the scaffolding by which a fair temple is upreared, which, when the holy edifice is completed in all its symmetry and fair proportions, is removed and cast aside as of no further value, now that the end for which it was made use of is achieved! We are a mystery to ourselves."

"I should gladly hear all that your priests can reveal of your religious rites and usages," I answered.

"I will give you the opportunity at an early day," answered the prince. "We were speaking of the Book of Ruth. It was written by the youthful David, my friend whom we saw at Ramah. It is a noble and sweet poem, though not rhythmical; but taste and feeling, and to know the art to touch the finer chords of the soul with the pen, make the poet! What a lovely character is his! How courageous yet how diffident! how ingenuous his disposition! how true are his instincts to the purest emotions of our nature! I love him, Arbaces, passing the love of maidens, and he not only returns my full affection, but I believe that my friendship is necessary to his existence. In each other's presence we are perfectly at peace!"

"I am interested to learn more of him," I answered; "for he made upon me a deep impression not only from the extraordinary beauty of his face and the manly grace of his bearing, but especially from his marvelous skill on the harp, and his harmonious voice, which is full of sweetness and power!"

"You shall hear all that I think will interest you, my dear prince," said the royal Hebrew youth as he replaced the flexible parchments of the Book of Ruth in their chased silver casket. "My friend is the son of the Hebrew Elder, Jesse, and was born at Bethlehem, the rocky castellated hill we passed an hour after leaving the fortress of the ancient and unconquered Jebusites, on the right hand. His father is a man of mark and of substance, and also a shepherd following the honorable pursuit of our patriarchial forefathers. This worthy citizen is, moreover, the grandson of Ruth, the wife of Boaz, the owner of the wheat field where she gleaned after his reapers. Thus Jesse is not of our pure Hebrew lineage, for the beautiful Ruth was from the land of Moab!"

"Who was Moab?" I asked; "and where is his country?"

"On the east of the sea of Sodoma," kindly answered the prince. "Moab was one of the sons of Lot the nephew of Abraham, born to his eldest daughter after the destruction of the cities of the plain. This unnatural child became the head of a powerful nation. He was born about the same time with Isaac our great ancestor!"

"If, then," I replied, in my desire to obtain full information of this people, "the Moabites are descended from a nephew of Abraham, Ruth being of his race traces her ascent equally with you Hebrews to the grandfather of Abraham, in whom both you and the Moabites meet! She can, therefore, hardly be called a foreigner! This rich shepherd Jesse, therefore, her grandson, has the same blood that Abraham had in his veins!"

"True," courteously answered the prince; "but by the command of God all collateral kindred to Abraham were cut off, and only the immediate descendants of the kingly patriarch recognized as the people of God's peculiar care. He has never called himself the God of Lot or of Moab, but only of 'Abraham, Isaac, and Jacob'; this is his name to us in the Past, Present, and forevermore! Moreover, the descendants of Lot's daughter through her son Moab have run in a diverging line from ours for nearly nine hundred years!"

"Pardon me, my dear prince, for this interruption," I said. "Be so kind as to proceed."

"When my father had displeased the Almighty by his usurpation of the priestly office, and sparing where he should destroy, as well as by two or three acts of impatient and reluctant obedience to His divine authority, He commanded His Prophet Samuel to go and anoint another king over Israel, saying, 'I have rejected Saul from being king!'"

"Who was Saul, thy royal father, O prince, in his youth?" I inquired. "Was he distinguished by any remarkable lineage? —descended from Moses or Joshua or any of the warrior Judges, that he was chosen in the beginning as the first king of the Hebrews?"

"No," he answered; "my father was of the smallest tribe— the younger brother Benjamin's tribe—of the people. His father was a man wise in council, brave in battle, and eminent for his great strength and valiant deeds. He was a tiller of the land; and herdsmen, with a few men and maid servants, and his sons also, served him in the care of his herds. With our God, my Prince Arbaces, human distinctions are wholly disregarded. As once he chose Abraham, the son of a carver of idols, out of Chaldea to be the father of our nation, and Moses, of humble parentage, to lead them out of Egypt, and Joshua, the son of a poor man, to conquer the promised land for us, none of them being of kingly lineage, so chose he out Saul, the son of Kish the herdsman, from the valley of Mount Ephraim, to reign over his people, when they demanded a king. In stature, dignity, courage, and generous qualities my father was worthy of this high distinction, from what I learn of those old men who knew him in that day!"

"I should suppose so," I answered, "from the majesty of his form now, and his striking appearance, although it is plain I behold only the splendid wreck of the former grace and dignity which he possessed."

"No more than the wreck, no more, my prince!" answered Jonathan, with a pensive look shadowing his fine face. "Samuel anointed him king in the presence of many of the lords and high captains and chief estates of the land, and eventually crowned him with full regal authority. The early years of my father's reign were prosperous and happy. He strengthened himself in his kingdom, he expelled our enemies from all our borders, which in the time of the rule of Samuel's sons they had invaded, and he carried his victorious arms beyond our country into Syria, and in all his battles was conqueror. But one of the nations (called the sons of Amalek) which treacherously did our fathers great mischief when they were wandering in the wilderness, Samuel the Seer had commanded him to destroy utterly, by the express direction of God. My father conquered the Amalekites, but saved the King Agag and a portion of the spoil, against this command. This, also, caused God's anger to be kindled against my father, and was another reason of his rejection as king! Yet with the people he was honored and admired as a successful warrior, as a wise ruler! But who can stand against the anger of the Almighty!"

"Thy God is terrible in power, and glorious in majesty," I answered, with awe; "who can offend him and escape punishment? Aaron his great High Priest, for his rebellion at the waters of Meribah, and for not preventing the people in the wilderness from worshiping the golden calf, was forbidden to see the promised land! There is something singularly impressive and touching in the departure of this aged and magnificent prelate to ascend the mountain of Hor to die for his sin! There is something awful and inexorable in the fiat of his God, which commands him to go up in the sight of the whole congregation, as if he would show them that the best and gentlest of men must expiate their errors and sins against him! The spectacle seemed to convey to them the lesson, 'If thus I cut off my consecrated High Priest Aaron (and forty years after his sin and yours is committed), how shall I spare you, when you sin and break my laws?'"

I can imagine, your majesty, the noble chief priest of this people in his pontifical robes, his flowing beard and silvery locks, his form bent with one hundred and twenty years, slowly ascending the elevated plain of Mosera, and crossing it painfully, commence the steep ascent of the peak of Hor. I see the vast multitude of people follow him with their sorrowful gaze! As the way wearies him, he leans upon the arm of his tall, strong son Eleazer; while his patriarchal brother, the equally venerable Moses (soon afterward to ascend Mount Pisgah, farther north, and die alone, with the angels of God to bury him), walks by his side, discoursing with him of the sublime and mighty truths of that other life, in which the Hebrews believe. When the three reach the mountain top, with the blue skies bending over them, and the broad plains of Mosera and the valleys beyond, dark with the hosts of Israel, watching them from afar, I see the aged Pontiff begin slowly, and with trembling hands, to divest himself of the magnificent robes and gorgeous insignia of his priestly office! First he removes from his patriarchal head his mitre, with its veil of lace of blue and fine linen, arranged in numerous ample circular folds confined by a broad plate of pure gold, on which is inscribed:

"HOLINESS TO THE LORD."

He places it meekly upon the brow of his son and successor, who kneels at his feet. Then he takes off his breastplate dazzling with the light of its twelve precious stones. He removes the splendid ephod of fine linen entwined and embroidered with gold, blue, scarlet, and purple threads, and adorned with plates of wrought gold; but his aged fingers cannot undo the clasps of the beautiful girdle of the ephod, and his venerable brother aids him, but with difficulty, as his eyes are blinded with tears! This holy ephod he places in the hands of Moses to retain, until he is wholly disrobed of his priestly apparel. Then from his shoulders one by one he removes the brilliant onyx stones inclosed in ouches of gold, which had held the chain of gold that fastened the breastplate, and attaches them upon the knobs of the ephod, held in his brother's hands. Now the long white linen robe, which distinguishes the High Priest's rank, and is an emblem of his purity, still fragrant with incense and the rich perfume of the holy anointing oil, he divests himself of, and solemnly invests the stately form of his son therewith. Over it he puts the ephod, and also places the glittering onyx stones on his two shoulders. Upon it he fastens the breastplate with its twelve stones, in four rows: the first containing a sardius, a topaz, and a carbuncle, very precious stones; the second row contained an emerald, a sapphire, and a diamond; the third row a ligure, an agate, and an amethyst; and the fourth row a beryl, an onyx, and a jasper; all set in ouches of gold with wrought gold borders. Each stone was a signet, bearing engraved thereon one of the names of the children of Israel.

Thus did the august and aged Pontiff divest himself of his insignia and marks of power as vicegerent of God on earth, and transfer them, on the mountain-top, in the sight of all the people and in the sight of Heaven above, to Eleazar his son to be the High Priest in his stead! This sublime abdication of the Hebrew pontificate by the command of his Lord being accomplished, behold the majestic man of God kneel toward the people and bless them! then folding his hands upon his breast, with one look of faith, resignation, and meekness upward, bow his august forehead to the ground, and give up the ghost.

"In the whole history of the departure of great men from earth," I said, addressing Prince Jonathan, "no account equals the sublime spectacle of the death of the High Priest, Aaron! That of Moses not long afterward was indeed impressive, but it wanted the details of transfer of authority which rendered the abdication and death of his brother so dignified and touching."

"My dear Arbaces," said the prince, "I am pleased to find you so skilled in our history! Hitherto I have regarded the death of Moses, followed by the mystery of his sepulcher, the more interesting of the two incidents. You are right in giving preference in sublimity and tenderness to that of the High Priest! But what led us to this subject? Were we not discoursing of David?"

"I had alluded to the awful severity of your God in punishing sin, with immediate reference to your royal father's sad rejection," I answered.

"True, Arbaces," he replied; "our God is a consuming fire to those who disobey him; but of long-suffering, pity, and great kindness to those who walk in the way of his divine laws. His power is infinite to punish or to bless. But I will now resume my narrative of my young friend David, the son of Jesse."

But, your majesty, I will defer this interesting history to another letter. I feel assured that nothing concerning this wonderful people, whose God ever walks among them, invisibly seeing all they do, powerful to protect, and terrible to avenge, will be uninteresting to you.

Farewell, and may the gods of Assyria be evermore your majesty's friends, and the foes of your adversaries.

ARBACES.

LETTER VI.

ARBACES TO THE KING.

CAMP BEFORE HEBRON.

YOUR MAJESTY:

A sandstorm from the south deserts swept over the King's
city and the plain of Mamre this morning with fearful power.
It darkened all the air so that the sun gave no more light than
the stars at midnight. Our encampment was thrown into the
wildest confusion. Half our tents were blown down and swept
away, and for a time destruction and consternation prevailed.
The winds roared with ungovernable fury. Trees were uptorn
and whisked across the valley like autumnal leaves; and even
the towers of Hebron shook, and one of them fell with a great
crash into the moat beneath! The atmosphere was surcharged
with yellow sand, so that it could not be directly breathed without danger of suffocation to all life. It lasted an hour, and did
the work of days of devastation in that brief time. The armies
of Saul, which had been marshaled by the chief captains and
high lords and generals to march forth to the war, were thrown
into disorder, and fled for shelter, or cast themselves in terror
upon the earth.

This destructive visitation has of course delayed the advance
of the army of the king for a day or two, as it will take some
time to reorganize and marshal all the dispersed forces. My
own tent withstood the storm, at least so far as not to be
blown over; but it was damaged and disordered. It is now
near sunset, and we have almost wholly restored everything to
its former condition. Quiet and order prevail immediately
about me. I will, therefore, resume my pen, and give you a
transcript of the residue of my conversation with the prince,
within the door of my tent last night.

"I will inform you," said Jonathan, "how and where I first
met with David. I had been hunting the gazelle with Prince
Ishbosheth, my younger brother, who had promised his sister
Michal to capture a fawn and bring it alive to her, when we

came to a small valley west of Bethlehem, up which a wild brown coney had bounded, and after which the Egyptian hunting dog of my brother took at full speed. At the same moment I caught sight of a graceful gazelle perched upon a point of rocks not far up the glen, and fitting my arrow to the bow-string, hastened with my brother in the direction taken by the dog. The ravine brought us into a narrow defile closed in by nearly precipitous rocks. Up the sides, leaping from projection to projection, the terrified rabbit ascended, while the gazelle, still visible on the topmost spur, seemed to be too intently and curiously watching some object beyond us to see us. Ishbosheth, light and swift of foot, was soon halfway up the crags, leaving his dog baying below. I quickly followed him, and upon reaching the summit was about to draw my arrow to its head upon the gazelle when Ishbosheth, who was a little in advance of me, cried, ' Come, quickly! Look in the vale below.'

"At first I could only see a flock of sheep flying in terror from some object, invisible to me. But drawing nearer the verge I beheld, nearly ninety feet below me, and not three bow-shots off, a sight that paralyzed me. In the bosom of the deeply shaded dell a mere youth was combating for his life with a large and powerful bear. At his feet lay a bleeding lamb, over which he stood as if to protect it. In one paw the bear hugged closely its bleating dam, while with the other it struck like a man at the brave young shepherd, for such his dress betrayed him to be, who, heedless of death, with his shepherd's knife inflicted rapidly wound after wound in the breast of the monster, until the paw relaxed its hold upon the now dead sheep and the enormous brute fell over upon the earth a corpse. Scarcely had this gallant victory been achieved, and as he stopped to pick up the wounded lamb at his feet, a loud roar shook the cliffs and resounded along the dell like deep thunder. It was followed by the appearance of a young lion, who bounded forward and suddenly crouched within twenty feet of the young shepherd. Seeing his peril, I sent the shaft I had intended for the gazelle, full-aimed at the lion's body. It fell short and pierced the sward forty feet this side of him. Ishbosheth followed it by another equally unsuccessful, at the same time uttering a loud cry to warn the youth of his danger, and to frighten the lion. To reach him in order to succor him (which was our first impulse) was impossible, as the face of the cliff from which we looked down into the dell was an unbroken perpendicular wall for several hundred yards on each side of us. The youth, hearing our shouts, looked up. His face was pale, but full of the light of a fearless heart. He smiled confidently as he awaited the bound of the lion, grasping in his right hand his blood-dyed knife, and closer sheltering in his bosom the wounded little lamb. For a moment the lion and the youth looked into each other's eyes with the steadiness of the sun shining in its strength. Neither blenched! The young man slowly retired, step by step, with his eyes full upon the great beast's eyes, which glittered with a steely-blue light, when in two bounds the lion was at his side —and only at *his side!* for as he leaped toward him, intending to light with both paws upon his breast, the cool and nerved youth lightly, at the very moment of mortal peril, stepped aside. The lion sprung past him, and as he did so the long herdsman's knife flashed on high for an instant, and was buried to the hilt in his heart. The animal plunged forward and fell headlong across the dead body of the bear. The victorious combatant then ran, and drawing his knife forth from the heart of the lion, he raised his arm heavenward, with the point of the weapon downward, and with the look of a priest who has just slain the sacrifice, he offered up thanks to God for his victory and his safety.

"Such courage, presence of mind, humanity, and piety in one so young, for he was scarcely eighteen," continued the prince, "at once awakened in my bosom the deepest interest in a youthful hero, who single-handed had thus slain a lion and a bear, and rescued so humanely his little lamb from its foes. My brother and I expressed our admiration and joy at the issue with shouts of triumph! and, hastening along the ridge of the precipice, after a quarter of an hour we found a steep pathway leading to the valley below. We soon found ourselves upon the level, and at length reached the spot where lay the dead lion and the bear! But it was a solitude! We looked around in vain to discover the youthful hero of the well-fought field. We approached the two slain animals, and saw that they were both of the largest size! The bear had not less than eight deep wounds in his body, while blood upon one of the claws showed that the victor had not got off without harm. I resolved to ascertain whither the young shepherd had gone, and a remark of my brother that possibly he was lying down somewhere bleeding from his wounds, made me more determined to hunt him up, and know what had become of him.

"We left the little dell, and going round a high rock at its entrance came to a gentle eminence on the top of which a large flock of sheep stood trembling. We drew near, when I heard the sound of a shepherd's lyre, and a clear triumphant voice singing a song like a pæan of victory. Advancing further we came to a group of rocks around which the sheep were collected, where stood the victor holding a rude triangular harp, having strings of unequal length, upon which he was playing, while he chanted these words, evidently composed as he sang them:

> " 'I will say of the Lord he is my refuge and my fortress!
> My God, in him will I trust.
> He shall cover me with his feathers,
> And under his wings will I rest.
> A thousand shall fall at the side,
> And ten thousand at the right hand,
> Of him, who makes the Lord his refuge,
> And the Most High his habitation.
> He shall tread upon the lion and the bear,
> The young lion and the dragon shall he trample under feet;
> For he that dwelleth in the fear of the Lord,
> Shall abide under the shadow of the Most High God.
> Blessed be the Lord for evermore.
> Amen and Amen!'

"The flock, under the influence of his melodious voice, seemed to dismiss their terror and peaceably to listen.

"When this hymn of confidence and victory was ended, he looked and beheld me standing near, regarding his seraphic countenance, pale yet beautiful, with deep interest. He laid the lyre upon the rock and advanced toward us, his left hand wrapped in the fold of his shepherd's mantle, against which he had held the rustic harp.

" 'You are strangers,' he at first said. 'Have you lost your way?' He then added: 'I think I see here the king's sons!'

" 'You are right; we are the sons of Saul,' I answered, supposing he had, as proved to be the truth, seen us in the city of Mizpeh where we then dwelt, and which most Hebrews visit once or twice in a year. 'I have not lost my way, young shepherd; but we witnessed your brave combat with the bear and the lion! We could not reach you in time to save you, the unequal combat was so soon ended to your glory. I have hastened hither to take you, brave Hebrew youth, by the hand,

and tell you how I admire your courage and that you and Jonathan, son of Saul, must from this hour be friends! I see by your face that I shall love you by and by for your virtues, as now I honor you for your bravery. No man-at-arms, no warrior among our chief captains, no lord of ten thousand men could have won a more brilliant victory. What is thy name? It will yet be spoken in the land, if thou livest, by the side of those of the greatest and best.'

" 'You praise me, O prince, beyond my deserts,' he answered, blushing. 'I have only done my duty: as a faithful shepherd is bound to protect his lambs from their foes! It was God who gave me the victory, and not my own arm, and to Him be the praise! I am called David, the son of Jesse, and I am a shepherd!'

" 'And also a skillful player on the harp, and an heroic poet,' I said, smiling, 'if that hymn was yours.'

" 'I was but giving God grateful praise for my victory and my life,' he answered. 'Besides I find my music soothes my poor flock when terrified. It is the voice of peace and security in their ears!'

" 'You appear to suffer,' I said, 'and are wounded! I saw that the claws of the bear were stained with blood.'

" 'Yes! The flesh of my arm is torn a little,' he said lightly; 'but it will soon be well. We mountain shepherds do not heed slight scratches from wild beasts if we come in contact with them in defense of our flocks.'

" The more I heard him discourse, O Prince Arbaces, the more my heart went out to him. I forgot gazelles and all else in his company. At eventide I accompanied him as he drove his flock across the valley to their fold, near the abode of his father Jesse. It was late when my brother and I left him, and returned to the town of Bethlehem, whence we had come out on our hunting expedition.

" Our fair sister, who, as well as my brother and myself, was then on a visit to the warlike Abner, my father's uncle, and general of his armies, was not at all pleased that we had forgotten her gazelle for a lion-fighting young shepherd, and said she cared not how handsome or brave he was, for she liked him not to cause her so great a disappointment. The next day I made to her a promise to hunt a gazelle the following morning, when, as I was speaking to her, the youthful shepherd presented himself at the gate of the courtyard, carrying a beautiful fawn upon his shoulder. I at once sprang joyfully to meet him.

"He said modestly, 'I heard your brother, O prince, say yesterday, how disappointed his sister, the princess Michal, would feel that he did not capture a gazelle to bring to her. Here is one I have this morning taken, and have brought it hither, hoping to be permitted to present it to the king's daughter!'

"Upon this my sister looked perplexed, and her generous blushes told how sorry she felt for having spoken such severe words about the youthful shepherd, whose beautiful countenance, and dark, expressive, yet bashful eyes made her cast down her own. Instead of suffering me to reward him, she seemed resolved to make amends; for rising, she went to him, thanked him in the handsomest manner for his kindness, graciously accepted the gift he had brought, and presented him with a ring of gold from her own hand. His youthful diffidence would have led him to refuse the jewel; but I insisted he should retain it. As my sister wished to take the gazelle home with her to Mizpeh the following week, the young shepherd gave her some directions as to its care and nourishment, for which she expressed herself very grateful.

"I then took him over the stately house of my uncle, and showed him the gardens and whatever was interesting; and when he left to return to his flock I accompanied him some distance beyond the city gates, and took leave of him by embracing him. We there pledged to each other firm and abiding friendship; for our hearts had grown together, his to mine and mine to his, every hour of our pleasant intercourse. He was so refined and so courteous; so ingenuous and modest; so intelligent and amiable; and withal so brave and humane, that not to have loved him would have been not to love any of those qualities which seemed, in him, to have their natural home."

Here, your majesty, the Hebrew prince, who in himself seems to combine all the noble virtues he had just enumerated, paused in his narrative; for at the very instant the loud clangor of a brazen bugle rang from the battlements of the city was answered from the citadel, and then responded to from the camp, while the cliffs and hills gave back in reverberating echoes the warlike notes.

"It is the signal for changing the guard on the walls, and

to announce that 'all is well,' in city and camp," he said, after a moment's attention to the sounds.

At the first blast I feared that it was an alarm of danger, and that the enemy were near. But as our outposts penetrate nearly to the camp of the Philistines, we should have had early intelligence of a hostile movement.

"I will now resume my narrative," said the Prince Jonathan, turning toward me. "For several months the youthful David and I met only to increase our mutual regard. At length my father's spirits became so profoundly depressed by the consciousness of the anger of God, the departure of his Divine Spirit from him, and the threatened loss of his crown, that a gloomy, apprehensive melancholy seized fixedly upon his soul. Resort to the most skillful of the court physicians for remedies for his diseased mind was naturally unsuccessful. They could not minister to a disease that was seated beyond the reach of human art. He passed his days in stern silence, and with a fixed look of despair impressed upon his noble features. He refused to recognize his wife or children; and at times became so violent in the paroxysms which came upon him that no man dared approach him.

"In hopes of aid I sought the Seer Samuel, who was then at Gibeah, not far distant. The prophet answered me that God had spoken, and his word must be accomplished, that he had taken the Spirit of the Lord from Saul my father, and given him over to an evil spirit because he had not obeyed the Spirit of God. 'God is not a man that he should repent or lie; what he hath ordained must surely come to pass.'

"Such was the reply I received from the sympathizing prophet. I then returned to my father in great sorrow of heart. As I drew near the house an aged, dark-browed man whom I had never before seen, clad in a foreign attire, met me and said:

"'Art thou the king's son?'

"I answered him, 'Yes.' He then said, 'Thou and the Elders and the chief physicians seek to find a cure for the malady that is upon my lord the king. I am a stranger who has visited far-distant lands. Many years ago I was at the court of Sheba, the kingdom whence come the rich pearls of the merchants. The king thereof, whose chief city is called Meroë, had a son, the sole heir to his throne, who was afflicted with gloom and melancholy not unlike what hangs upon the soul of thy royal father. He would refuse all food, and stand for hours, yea, whole days and nights, in the far corner of his chamber, and gnaw his finger nails and rivet his glazed and burning eyes upon the floor without ever moving the eyelids. He became emaciated to the bone, and his visage was terrible with the impress of despair.'

" ' By what was this caused ? ' I asked of the old man.

" ' It was caused by his love for a maiden who was torn in pieces by lions as she was traveling in her palanquin to her father's palace near the seaside ! ' he answered me. ' At length one of the physicians, an Egyptian magician, finding all incantations failed, thus spoke to the King of Sheba his father, and said:

" ' " If my lord, the mighty king of the south, will see his son restored to health and the evil spirit depart from him, let him order the sweetest minstrelsy to be performed within his hearing. Let the king command the most skillful musicians in his kingdom to play melodious airs and the most pleasing within their art, and the prince will be restored to himself. For, my lord the king, the fiercest hearts have been tamed by music; and there was a princess of Persia, who, being lost in a forest, was met by a wild beast which began to crouch in order to spring upon her, when she commenced chanting her death-song, according to the faith of her fathers; for she was a Sabaen ! Her voice was so sweet and thrilling, that the monster remained transfixed, listening to the wonderful music! his fiery eyes lost their burning glare and became as soft and gentle as a fawn's; and his whole attitude showed that he was fascinated by the melody of her song. This perceiving, she drew near to the lion, still softly singing, laid her hand upon his shaggy mane, and led him by her side until she came to the gate of her father's palace; when the sentinels seeing the strange sight shot at him with their crossbows and slew him; but he died licking with his tongue her delicate white hand ! "

" ' When the King of Sheba heard this,' continued the aged stranger, ' and was further informed that the loss of reason in man often allied him in ferocity to the wild beast of the desert, he commanded the most cunning players to play before the prince. The result was he was wholly cured, and to this day sits upon the throne of Sheba a wise and powerful prince. Now, my lord,' continued the venerable stranger to Jonathan, ' let someone who plays cunningly on the harp and sings with wonderful melody, be sent for to play before the king your father. Without doubt he will be restored thereby to health; for music hath a charm to soothe the ferocity of a mind where despair hath taken the reins.'

"Such," said Jonathan to me, "was the counsel of the venerable stranger in the foreign attire, who, having finished speaking, courteously left me, and I saw him no more. I at once sought the chief physician and grand-chamberlain, and high-steward, with all the lords and men of estate at court, and made known to them what I had heard. They were all in favor of trying the tranquillizing effects of music, and, at my request, two of them went into the presence of my father (for he could not bear to see *me*, and was always most violent when I came near), to propose it to him."

"Perhaps," I ventured to say to Jonathan, "the consciousness that he had wronged you by causing the turning away of the inheritance from you embittered his mind."

"Without doubt it was this, my dear Arbaces," he sadly replied; "but I do not feel that my father has wronged me! I have no desire to reign, if it be God's will to deprive me of the succession to the crown. David, as a shepherd, is happy; and a life of lowly duties is the safest if not the happiest. The crown of a king is lined with a bonnet of nettles, and his scepter of gold is often like lead in his grasp! When the physicians and wise men came into the presence of the king, he was seated upon the ground with a fixed gaze upon vacancy and his visage all marred by suffering. As they entered, he sprang to his feet, and cried furiously:

"'Who dare intrude! I am king still, and by the Ark of God! I will let no man scorn me! They say I am mad! No, no!' and his tone here fell to a touching pathos. 'I am only heartbroken—heartbroken—that—*that is all!* I have sinned, I have repented, I lie in the dust, I cry for mercy, but the great brassy skies are turned into one vast throne of justice! The prophet hath said my repentance is not sincere, and therefore God will not accept it! That it is only remorse! Is *this* remorse? Look ye! See my haggard eyes and hollow cheeks! Behold my thin hands and my wasted form! Can *remorse* do *this!* No, no! I have repented in the dust, I grovel in the earth, I lay my face where the worm crawls, I prostrate myself under the very ground in my humble contrition! But all is vain! The haughty prophet says it is not repentance, only

remorse, and God hears not remorse! I only ask for my kingdom for my son, though I perish! What come ye for?' he
abruptly demanded, as if noticing them now for the first
time.

"'My lord,' said the chief physician, for unseen I heard
all," continued Jonathan, "'without doubt an evil spirit is permitted by the Lord to be upon thee, and troubleth thee, in this
manner! Let my lord the king now command thy servants to
seek out a man who is a cunning player on a harp, and, peradventure, when the evil spirit is upon thee he shall play upon
the harp, and the cheerful and animating sounds thereof will
soothe thy troubled spirit!'"

"My father no sooner heard them than he cried with eagerness: 'Haste! provide a man that can play well and bring him
before me! Thy medicines, O physician, touch not the sore!
We will see what virtue lieth in this prescription of music!'

"Then, previously instructed by me, the grand-chamberlain
said: 'There is a young man, son of Jesse of Bethlehem, who
is a cunning player on the harp, a youth of valor and warlike
deeds, modest in demeanor, prudent in conduct, and wonderfully comely in person, and the Lord is with him!'

"'Who knoweth where this Jesse, the lad's father, dwelleth?' cried the king.

"'We can presently find him, O king,' answered the chief
physician.

"The light of hope at once brightened my father's countenance. He bade the messengers depart with haste, and under
his own signature sent a message to Jesse the Bethlehemite,
reading thus:

"'Saul, the King,
    "'To Jesse, the Ephrathite, Tribe of Judah: Greeting.

"'I hear thou hast a son, called David, a shepherd, who is
skilled on the harp. If rumor hath told the truth of him, send
him hither to me, I have need of him. It shall fare well with
him, and he shall be sent back to thee in safety.'

"The message was at once placed in my hands by the chief
physician," continued the prince, "and I gladly hastened to
the valley where David kept his flock. As I drew near I beheld
the stately-looking Jesse and his seven tall sons at work in
the field preparing a threshing-floor for the coming harvest,

As I came to them I asked if David were not in the valley with the sheep? Jesse smiled and said:

"'Noble prince, I fear thy frequent notice of the lad will make him vain! I marvel that such a friendship should spring up between the son of a king and the son of a shepherd.'

"'Were not Abraham, Isaac, and Jacob, our fathers, shepherds?' I answered pleasantly. 'But I have a message for thee from King Saul!' I then placed the missive in his hand. He read it with a respectful air, and then replied:

"'The king does us too much honor!'

"'What is it?' asked the black-bearded Eliab, the eldest son, in a haughty way peculiar to him.

"'The king has sent for David,' answered Jesse, with a look of paternal pride.

"'The boy will next fancy his cross-headed crook a scepter, and weave him a crown out of the hedge thorn,' responded Eliab bitterly; 'and he will ere long strut about us as Joseph of old, and bid us make obeisance to him, and say, "Hail, David, King of Israel!"'

"'Silence, my son! If thy brother is honored by the king and Prince Jonathan, is it not also thine own honor? There is surely something yet to show itself in the youth! Hast thou forgotten the visit of the Seer two years ago, and his anointing him?'

"'And what has come of it?' cried Abinadab, the next to the eldest, with a sneer in his narrow and envious eyes. 'Hasn't he still kept to his sheep?'

"'We expected to see somewhat come of so much cackling as was made when the Seer mocked us seven brethren to empty his horn of oil on this pretty boy's head,' growled the third brother in a hoarse voice; 'but the prophet hath not been here since; and the boy's pride is left, like his sheep's wool, to dangle upon the hedges.'

"'Hist, men!' said Jesse. 'The lad had no pride. He sought not the honor, whatsoever may come of it. Go and find my son David,' he continued, addressing me, 'and take him with thee to the king.'

"I departed from them, and at length beheld David afar off with his flock, leading them to a well to water them. When he saw me he stood still, and awaited my coming."

"When Samuel anointed the son of Jesse," I now inquired of the prince, your majesty, "did he inform him for what purpose it was done? Did Jesse and his brothers certainly know?"

"I will anticipate my narrative, and tell thee, O Arbaces, about that," answered the prince. "When the Lord had caused the King Agag, the haughty and vain Amalekite, whom my father had spared, to be slain, and the booty he had possessed destroyed, he called Samuel to Him, and said, 'I have rejected Saul from being king. Fill thine horn of anointing with holy oil, and go to Bethlehem, and to Jesse the Ephrathite there, for I have chosen me a king among his sons.' But the prophet hesitated, saying, 'If Saul heareth this, he will slay me.' But the Lord said, 'Go to Bethlehem, and there sacrifice unto me a heifer. Call Jesse and his sons to partake of the sacrifice, and thou shalt anoint the young man I shall name unto thee.' So the prophet came into Bethlehem, and his presence there filled the city with alarm; for the Seer Samuel was regarded as the dispenser of the judgments of God; and the people of Bethlehem trembled for fear he was to visit them with some retribution. 'Comest thou peaceably?' they inquired of him. He answered, 'Peaceably. Let the elders of the city sanctify themselves, and come and sacrifice with me before the Lord. Let Jesse and his sons be also called!' When the prophet looked upon Eliab, who was of lofty stature, and bold countenance, 'Surely,' said Samuel, 'this is the Lord's anointed, who is to reign instead of Saul.' But the Lord said, 'Look not on the countenance nor the form; for I have refused him! I, the Lord, look upon the heart!' Then Samuel said to Jesse privately, 'I have a great honor from the Lord, for one of thy sons. What is the name of the second young man?' Then Jesse answered, 'His name is Abinadab'; and he bade him rise and walk before the prophet. But the Seer, instructed inwardly by the voice of God, said to Jesse, 'Neither hath the Lord chosen him!' Then, one after another, Jesse made the seven of his sons present to pass before Samuel, when the prophet said to their father, 'The Lord hath not chosen either of these! Are here all thy children?'

"And Jesse answered with an air of disappointment, 'There remaineth David the youngest, a mere lad, who is with the sheep!'

"'Then,' said the prophet, reassured, 'send and fetch him; for we will not sit down to the feast until he come.'

"Then Jesse sent his servant with haste into the field after his youngest son, who found him with the flock, and peacefully amusing him by playing upon his rustic harp, which, with his clear, sweet voice, they heard borne to their ears on the breeze even before they discovered him.

" 'Haste; thy father sendeth for thee!' said the messenger. 'I will remain with the sheep till thou returnest. Make all diligence, for the mighty prophet of God of Ramah is there, and he has killed the sacrifice, and they only wait for thee to sit down! All thy brothers are there!'

" Then the youth hastened to obey his father, wondering why he should be sent for. When he entered their presence the eyes of Samuel rested upon his ruddy and beautiful countenance, softly shaded by exposure to the sun and winds of the desert, and the Lord said, 'Arise and anoint him, for *this is he!*'

" Then the man of God arose, and commanding the embarrassed and blushing boy to kneel before him, he poured upon his head the holy oil of consecration from the same horn of anointing with which he had anointed Saul, my father, King, many years before. No sooner had this sacred rite been performed than the Spirit of inspiration from God departed from Saul as he sat in his own house, and at the same instant descended upon David. Under its influence the consecrated youth seized his harp and struck it to a sublime symphony which seemed to be caught from the harps of angels. All were amazed at the rapturous adoration of his countenance, the holy light in his eyes, the celestial brightness of his form! This lasted only for a moment; and he then retired modestly as if seeking to withdraw himself from notice. Samuel went forth after him and said to him privately:

" 'David, son of Jesse, thou art now the chosen and anointed of the Lord to rule his people Israel. Keep in thy heart the secret until the day thou shalt be called to do God's work. Be true and faithful to thyself and to thy God, and all will be well with thee; but depart from the precepts of the Lord, and his Holy Spirit, given thee this day, will be taken away from thee. God chose thee for the beauty of thy piety, not of thy form, for he sees the heart; for thy righteousness, truth, fortitude, and obedience to thy parents, and for the purity of thy soul. Keep thyself pure, and thy reign, when thou shalt be called to the throne, will be famed throughout the earth for its splendor, power, and glory. Thy arms shall be victorious against all thy country's enemies, thy life shall be long and thy fame great, and thou shalt leave a name to posterity higher than that of any of the kings and potentates of the world. But if thou in thy prosperity forgettest God, He will bring upon thee evils instead of blessings, and thy gray hairs shall go down with sorrow and humiliation to the grave.'

"When the prophet had thus solemnly addressed him, he left him and returned to Ramah, and David, in a state between joy and fear, hardly realizing what had passed, returned to his flock in the desert and gave himself up to meditation and prayer, humbly and devoutly looking to God for guidance and strength to do all that should be required of him."

"Then," remarked I to Prince Jonathan, "the real purpose of the anointing was not known to Jesse or his sons?"

"No," answered the prince. "They believed it was to select him as a prophet; and as the Seer has since taken him to Ramah and placed him in the School of the Prophets, this opinion is recently fully confirmed in their minds. Jesse, the father, has regarded his son from that time with reverent curiosity and expectation; but the brothers whom Samuel one by one passed by, to send for David from the sheep-fold, have envied him and entreated him unfilially; so that it is alone my friendship which sustains his noble heart in its solitude."

"And you, my generous prince, you," I said, admiring the unselfish character he had exhibited, "knowing all this, have taken him to your bosom as your dearest friend. How wonderful is this! How opposed to what are the impulses of our nature! Was it before this anointing and supplanting you in the throne that you first saw him in his encounter with the lion and the bear?"

"Yes; it was after that encounter, Arbaces, he was visited and consecrated by Samuel. Our friendship had long before this anointing been sealed by mutual attachment!" he answered.

"And when you heard that your friend had become your rival in the succession, did it not shake your friendship?" I asked.

"No; but rather confirmed it, my Arbaces," was the frank and beautiful reply. "I felt then that God loved him whom I loved, and that he ought to be still dearer to me than before. I had already heard from the prophet, and also from words which fell from my father's lips, that another was to be chosen to wield the scepter, and that my claim as hereditary prince royal would be set aside by God. As I have before told you, this news pained me at first, but all ended in humble submission to the will of Jehovah in my heart. When at length I learned that the prophet of God had been to Bethlehem and consecrated my beloved David, my bosom friend, to be Prince of Israel in my stead, I can truly say I rejoiced at the tidings, O Arbaces, for I had long ceased to expect to receive the throne. I rejoiced, therefore, and blessed God that his choice had fallen on one so worthy."

"You have a noble and godlike nature, my dear prince," I cried, with enthusiasm, grasping his hand, and warmly pressing it to my heart. "In such a trial a man will either act above or below his instincts; show the God within him or the evil spirit of the earth! You have acted above humanity! How did you meet after this news? How did the young shepherd, conscious of what his new position was, deport himself in your presence?"

"I first heard of the consecration," answered Jonathan, "from one who was at the sacrificial feast in Bethlehem. He was a Levite of rank, and my friend. *He* well knew that the consecration was not priestly, but royal, and that the youth on whose head the sacred ointment was poured was ordained to become a king, not a priest! Upon hearing this intelligence, I requested him to keep it a secret in his own breast that it might not reach my father's ears (for though he knew that God would choose another, he knew not whom it would be), and then I hastened to find this shepherd prince to congratulate him on this honor from God. I found him amid his flock. Upon beholding me approach he turned aside his face' and pressed his hands together upon his breast in an attitude of sorrow and distress. I understood what was in his heart by this troubled gesture, and hastened to relieve him from his painful situation by flying to his side, putting my arm about his neck, and embracing him with the tenderest affection!"

"How good, how noble, how great you were, O Jonathan, most virtuous of princes!" I exclaimed, unable to repress my admiration of the sublimity of his exalted character.

In all the histories given by our poets of our august and divine heroes not one, your majesty, comes near in conception to the character of this Hebrew prince. I had already seen,

but a few days past at Ramah, full proof of his love and affection for his "rival," if this word I can make use of, where
rivalry there is none!

The prince, taking no notice of my admiring language, continued his narration:

"My dear David, instead of returning my caresses, burst
into a profusion of tears, and walked from me profoundly agitated, saying, 'If thou knewest all, my lord, thou wouldst despise thy David instead of embracing him thus!'

"'All!' I replied; 'what hast thou done?'

"'Ruined thee, my dearest friend! Robbed thee of thy
birthright! I have been to thee, O Jonathan, more cruel than
was Jacob to Esau! But,' he cried, suddenly turning toward
me and clasping his hands imploringly, 'forgive me! I will
tell thee all! I knew it not! I would have refused the consecration if I had known to what I was dedicated! But I will
conceal nothing from thee, even though it cost me thy friendship, as it ought and will do! Nay, it ought to make thee
spurn me! Listen!'

"'Cease to afflict thyself, dear David,' I replied, moved by
his emotion even to tears. 'I know all! Thou hast been highly
honored of God! The prophet of the Highest has anointed thee
with oil above thy brethren, and thou art set apart to reign over
Israel at my father's death! I have heard all, you see! Let it
not distress thee! Whom God hath chosen was before, and
shall be still, the chosen of my heart!'

"'Who told thee?' he asked, regarding me with doubt and
looks of wonder.

"'Eli, the Levite, who was present,' I replied, with an en-
couraging smile in my eyes. 'The celestial fragrance of the
holy oil is even yet about thy princely head, my David!'

"'And thou despisest me not?' he exclaimed.

"'No, but love thee doubly since now thou art so beloved
of God!'

"'Dost thou forgive me?' he asked, still hesitatingly.

"'I have nothing to forgive, my David! Thou hast no
blame!'

"'Yet I would have refused——'

"'Say not so!' I cried, alarmed, 'or thou wilt displease the
Almighty who has chosen thee to reign over his people! If
not thyself, some other one would have been anointed to this
end; for the decree is written in the records of Heaven. that

the kingdom shall depart from my father and his house! It is the will of the unchangeable God! Let us both meet His will by holy submission! Let us bear our sorrows patiently! for I know thy grief is sincere and deeper than mine, in that thou shouldst thus seem to show thyself an enemy to thy friend!'

"'Then thou forgivest me?' he asked, with a look of happiness.

"'With all my heart!' I answered, opening my arms. 'I will reign in thy heart, and thou on my throne, and we shall both be king!'

"He bounded into them, and I folded him to my bosom, kissed his beautiful brow, and sealed at that moment our friendship beyond any event of time to mar or break!"

"Worthy of each other, noble brothers in love and friendship!" I exclaimed, deeply touched, your majesty, by this exhibition of attachment so divested of all self, so superior to human nature! The prince, after a brief silence, now said:

"I think I have brought up sufficiently prominent and clear the past, in reference to these subjects, my dear Arbaces, and you will now be able to follow me in my resumed narrative of later events with less embarrassment, and with far greater intelligence of the facts I shall communicate. I was about describing to thee, before this deviation, to make the past plain to thee, O Arbaces, not yet wholly familiar with our national history, my visit to David when, two years after this consecration, I bore to him my poor father's message to come to him with his harp. If not too late in the night, I will finish my narrative. As I said, I found him leading his flock to the well, at which, Abraham, Canaan the son of Ham, and even Noah, the father of our race, had drunk. He awaited my coming. We embraced, and I made known to him my unhappy father's commands.

"'I will obey them if my father bids me go,' he replied; 'for thou knowest it becomes me to do all I can to render the king happy. But, my brother and friend,' he said modestly, 'I am but a mountaineer, and an indifferent player! The sheep love to hear my voice, and listen to my music, but I am not skilled to play my harp before kings!'

"'Hast thou not resting upon thee the Spirit of the Lord?' I replied. 'Is not music the gift of God to man? Come with me and bring thy harp!'

"I prevailed over his diffidence, and brought him to his father Jesse, who not only commanded him to obey the king, but sent by his hand bountiful presents to Saul, of bread, wine, and venison. When I returned to my father with David, I entered his chamber, and found him seated at his table in his right mind, and about to refresh himself with food. I did not hesitate, therefore, to appear before him. Upon seeing me he spoke very gently, and called me 'his son,' and desired me to sit at the board with him, saying, 'Would I had a bit of good venison and new wine to set before thee, my son!'

"At this moment, so singularly favorable, I called to David, and presented him to the king, saying, 'This is the son of Jesse, for whom my father sent! He has obeyed the king's commands; and brings with him a gift from his father, the Ephrathite.'

"Hereupon David, who was not free from embarrassment, bowed himself before the king with graceful dignity, and presented the presents, saying, 'My father prays for the king's health, and humbly asks him to accept these little gifts by the hand of his son!'

"The king regarded the face of the young shepherd steadily for an instant, seemed to be struck with its beauty and noble expression, and said with a look of benignity and pleasure:

"'Welcome, young man! I accept thy gifts, and command thee to thank thy father for me! What is thy name?'

"'David, my lord,' he answered.

"'I am marvelously pleased with thy appearance. How wouldst thou like to become my armor-bearer? Hast thou borne arms?'

"'Once against a party of the Philistines with my father, and brothers, and neighbors, three years ago!' he quietly replied. 'But my vocation is that of a shepherd, O King!'

"'Thou art famously skilled with the harp, I hear?' said the king.

"'I but amuse my hours in the desert with a poor instrument, your majesty,' he answered.

"My father then commanded a harp to be brought, and David standing by it, played upon it before him with such masterly power, and accompanied it with his voice so tenderly, that when he had ended the king expressed his pleasure in the warmest words; and taking a bracelet from his arm he placed it upon that of the harpist, saying in a most kindly tone:

" 'Thou shalt stay with me! Thou shalt be my armorbearer, and chief singer, and stand in my presence, and ever go in and out before my face.'

"Thus was the destined heir to my father's throne brought to his presence, and taken into his service. The following day the dark spirit of evil settled upon the king's soul. David seized his harp and commenced playing a battle-piece, which drew quickly the warlike monarch's attention. He then changed it to a plaintive air, and followed this by one full of animation and sprightliness. The king heard and was refreshed in his heart, and the dark spirit of evil left him, and he presently wholly returned to himself and his former cheerfulness. From that time David was necessary to his health and happiness; and his playing on the harp never failed to dissipate the clouds of melancholy which enveloped his soul. At length the king, my father, seemed wholly restored to his right mind, and David besought him for permission to return to his father's house, and to the care of his flocks; for, as he said to me, he felt ill at ease in the presence of the man whom God had mysteriously ordained that he should succeed in the kingdom!

"For a long time he dwelt at Bethlehem, returning to his former simple habits of life, and forgetting the cares and splendor of the court. He had, however, strengthened my love for him, and also carried away the heart of my beautiful sister Michal, to whom he had some time before presented the gazelle. I was not aware," continued Jonathan, "that he had been summoned by the Seer to the Prophet's School at Ramah until I unexpectedly met him there a few days since, in your presence. But the prophet wisely seeks to prepare him for the high position for which God has destined him."

Here the Prince Jonathan ceased his long and, to me, interesting narrative. The midnight moon had already gone down beyond the hills west of Hebron, and Arcturus shone in the north like a great diamond of trembling light; the sweet influences of the Pleiades were shed upon the earth from the upper skies; and near them marched the mystic Aldebaran in his triangular field of stars; while the sacred serpent wound its colossal length across the arch of heaven. It was a still and thoughtful hour. We were seated in the door of my tent, and for some minutes gazed musingly upon the stellated splendor of the illimitable dome above us. I could not but thank Prince

Jonathan in the sincerest manner for the pleasure he had conferred upon me by his conversation; and I assured him I should henceforth take the deepest interest in the life and fortunes of the youthful David.

"I regret," he said, "that the cure of the king's malady, though for a long time relieved by David's art, was not permanent. It has within a few days come upon him again, since this new war has been declared by the Philistines against him. You had, however, an exhibition, when you were presented to him, of the painful form his melancholy takes when the evil spirit is upon him. You saw me make a sign to the choristers, hoping their music would soothe him; but they being unskillful, the king, whose storm-tossed soul had been charmed into perfect peace by the superb performances of David, evinced his contempt for them as you beheld. If he continues in this gloom of soul, I shall send a messenger for my friend to hasten hither from Ramah and once more try the power of his skill."

The prince now rose to return into the city; and, as I could not prevail upon him to remain until morning, he was about to take his departure accompanied by his armor-bearer, when three tall men in plain iron armor passed in sight full in the glare that shone out of my tent, and were about to be challenged by my sentry, when the prince stopped, and said:

"What, sons of Jesse! Do I find you here all armed for the wars?"

"Yes, my lord," they answered. "We are Eliab, Abinadab, and Shammah, and are come up from our father's house in Bethlehem thus far on our way to Hebron, to offer our services to the king against the Philistines."

"Come, then, with me," said the prince, "I go into the city. My father, the king, will gladly accept the services of three such stout men-at-arms as ye are."

"Yes, we are not armed with harps and dulcimers and such woman's trumpery, but carry stout swords and battle-axes, and know how to cleave helm and cuirass when need serves."

This was said by one of them with a tone and allusion, your majesty, which I plainly interpreted as a sneer aimed against their honored younger brother; for these were the three elder brothers of David, still, it seemed, burning with jealousy and envy against him. Yet how little did they suspect that the anointing they had witnessed was to give him authority as

King in Saul's seat! How little Saul himself had suspected that the hand which struck the harp so boldly and sweetly in his halls was the one which was destined one day to wield his scepter!

The three men, following the prince across the plain, were with him soon lost to view in the veil of night.

Your faithful
ARBACES.

LETTER VII.

ARBACES, THE AMBASSADOR, TO BELUS, KING OF ASSYRIA.

CAMP OF SAUL, VALE OF ELAH.

MY ROYAL COUSIN AND KING:

It is with no little satisfaction that I commence this letter, knowing that you will so soon receive it, as well as those which I have hitherto written, and that I shall not be compelled to retain it, as I feared I should be, until my return from Egypt. The day after to-morrow a courier, who came to the Hebrew court from the king of Damascus to propose to King Saul a sale of arms from his far-famed armories, returns into Syria, and will be the bearer of my packages of letters to its capital. Thence, after three weeks, a caravan for the Euphrates will take its departure, and this Syrian courier promises to place my parcel in the hands of the commander thereof. From Babylon it will reach you by the regular post by which you receive letters from your viceroy, Belesis.

It will gratify your majesty to know that I am in excellent health, and that my caravan is encamped, during our detention, in the salubrious vale of Mamre, where there is both water and much grass for the horses.

You will perceive that this letter does not bear date at the place from which I wrote my last. In order to explain to your majesty where I now am and wherefore I am here, it will be necessary for me to take up my pen at the point where I laid it down at the close of my last epistle.

Your majesty therein learned that King Saul was actively engaged marshaling all his armies to go forth and offer battle to the haughty Philistine chief, who had sent to him an insulting message to come forth and fight with him in single combat, and in this way settle the war between them.

Three days after the destructive sand-storm which I spoke of in my last letter, the Hebrew army poured forth from the city into the plain of Mamre, and took up their position in marching columns. Although illy armed, and by no means presenting a brilliant and warlike appearance, they were a formidable host, darkening half the valley with their numbers.

To the eyes of one accustomed to behold your majesty's magnificent armies ready for battle: the splendor of its arms; the gorgeous variety of shining costumes; the blazing of ten thousand helmets; the waving of a sea of snow-white crests; the glitter of wide fields of spears; the richly-caparisoned Euphratean horse, ranged in squadrons a thousand deep; the terrible lines of elephants with their lofty towers bristling with armed men; the hosts of barbarian archers, javelin-men, Tigrian spear-men and bow-men; the iron phalanxes of Babylonian battle-ax men-at-arms; the superb battalions of chariots of ivory and gold; the vast armament of engines of war for sieges, with the ten thousand gay banners of every color flaming above the war-burdened plain—to eyes familiar with scenes like these, the unpretending display of the Hebrew army afforded but slight interest.

There were but few horse, while the foot-soldiers were of all arms and accoutered with but little regard to uniformity of costume. Not an elephant was in the whole field. The king's bodyguard of two thousand men and that of the prince were an exception to the general somber aspect of the armed hosts. These guards were magnificently helmed, cuirassed, and mounted, each man, tall and comely, and wearing a helmet of burnished brass, a silver corslet, and over his breast a gorgeous sash of fine crimson cloth, fringed with gold, which as he galloped at full speed flew out behind him, giving to the whole corps a strikingly picturesque appearance.

At length, when all were marshaled in the plain, the king, accompanied by the prince and his lords and chief captains and generals of his staff, rode out of the city gates and entered the field. His majesty drew near my tent, where I sat in my saddle at the head of five hundred of my Assyrian bodyguard, which I intended to offer to the king! He reined up his magnificent charger near me, saluted me with dignity and kingly grace, and said:

"My lord of Assyria, I regret to leave a guest I desire to honor for his own and his royal master's sake; but thou knowest the borders of my kingdom are invaded by a large army that must be met and conquered. I hope soon to drive them back to their seashore, and also thereby open the road for you to Egypt!"

"It is my purpose, with your royal permission, to attend you, O king," I said; "I offer you my services, and those of my bodyguard!"

The eyes of King Saul slowly traversed the warlike front of my splendid Assyrians, with the light of soldierly admiration each instant kindling in them brighter and brighter.

He was a noble object as he sat there in his war-saddle fully armed! He wore a coat of scale-mail, which fitted his noble form so flexibly and elastic, as to display not only the shape of the royal wearer, but even the contour of his superb limbs, and the development of the muscles. Greaves of polished plates of steel, bent round to the shape of the knee, covered his legs, which were encased in mid-leg boots of brass, the toes bent in a graceful curve upward, and fastened to the ankle by a massive chain of gold, which also held his brazen spurs. At his thigh hung the royal scabbard of lion's hide, covered with plates of silver, and studded with bronze bosses, while around it coiled a brazen serpent, in many a carved fold. The heavy sword, four feet in length, was shut within the sheath, but its massy ivory handle was adorned with two lion's heads, where the hilt was united with the blade. Chains of bronze held the sword and scabbard to a broad belt, or cincture of leopard's skin, embossed and set with studs of gold and precious stones.

Over his majestic shoulders hung open on the breast a short mantle of purple silk, worked with threads of blue, red, and gold, in rich devices of scarlet pomegranates, and other fruits, entwined with vines. The border was of fur. About his neck was clasped a collar, ornamented with brilliant pearls. His royal helmet of polished brass imparted, by its height and graceful form, dignity to the wearer, being encircled by a band of gold, on which were inscribed sacred words. A cloud of eagles' plumage danced from the superb crest. The visor was raised, and revealed his majestic countenance, which, though pale and sad, was that of a warrior-king! At his saddle-bow hung a ponderous battle-ax, and by a leather thong swung a heavy mace, with a carved wolf's head. His mounted armor-bearer carried his large embossed shield, javelin, and spear, with his royal quiver of arrows at his back. The noble animal on which the stately king sat wore housings of mail and plumes, while colored tassels with silver bells adorned his crested head, and shook with constant ringing as impatiently he champed his golden bit, and curved his arching neck as if conscious of the dignity of his majestic rider.

"Thou hast a brilliant bodyguard, Prince Arbaces," said the monarch with looks of pleasure, as he completed his inspection. "I may not need thy aid and that of these thy valiant men! But I invite thee to attend me to the field. My son holds thee as a friend, and will thank me therefor!"

The prince smiled, and warmly thanked his royal father. We then rode on across the plain; and the king, soon reaching the head of his army, gave orders to the columns to march forward. Our line of progress brought us near an angle of the city, where a large number of the citizens with the priests, and the wives and daughters of the officers, stood to wave farewell to the departing warriors. By my side rode the handsome and lordly-looking Governor of Jericho, Isrilid, mounted upon a superbly caparisoned horse, the richly embroidered headpiece and tassels of which, he proudly told me, were the skillful work of his fair daughter. As we passed the place where these spectators of our march stood, I beheld the beautiful Adora advance toward the king attended by two maidens. She carried a wreath, while they bore baskets of flowers, which they strewed before the path of the monarch. Gracefully laying her hand upon the gilded bridle of his charger, she arrested him for an instant, and placed the wreath upon the arched helmet of the horse's head.

"Nay, fair maid," said the king, "crowns are bestowed after victory, methought."

"Upon the brows of warriors! but before victory upon the head of the noble steed who is to carry the kingly soldier into battle," she answered smiling.

The king bent his head in acquiescence, but without answering her, yet evidently not displeased, and rode on; while her father reining up, spoke and said, "Since thou hast come hither, daughter, to see our march, and do the king this honor, I will kiss thee good-by again!"

"Wilt thou return within the three days, sir?" she asked earnestly, regarding her father with affectionate solicitude.

"Yes, my daughter, as soon as I have well seen how the Philistine army is posted!" he answered.

"Go into no danger!" she said affectionately. "I shall charge the Prince Arbaces," she added, with a bright smile, "that he keep you under his wing, my dear father!"

"In that case I shall have to be in the fight, child," he said pleasantly; "for be sure the Prince of Assur will not keep his sword sheathed while there is a battle going on, if I judge him aright."

"This is not the prince's quarrel, dear father," answered the captivating maiden, glancing upon me with her brilliant eyes. "He is on a peaceful mission to bring back a fair bride to his king, and he dare not run any risks of war which might prevent the object he has in view. I have a great curiosity, Prince Arbaces," she added, in a playful tone, "to see the beautiful Egyptian princess on your return."

"One need not go so far as Egypt to see beautiful virgins," I answered unintentionally in so marked a manner that she colored with enhanced loveliness, and looked so conscious and embarrassed that I feared, your majesty, I had unwittingly paid her too pointed a compliment; and flattery, as your majesty is aware, I am by no means given to; on the contrary, the sight of a beautiful female has always made me timid rather than bold, and I do not think I ever had the courage to compliment one before.

By this time the van of the army drew so near that Adora had only time to receive her father's farewell and return to the side of the way where the crowd of tearful females and citizens stood, when the leading column of the army came up!

"A sweet, dear daughter, my lord!" said the proud father, as his eyes followed the superb figure of his child as it receded from him among the groups of people. "She is my heart's treasure! So pure, so intelligent, so gentle, and yet so high-spirited! She well inherits the noble qualities of her princely ancestors!"

"What, my dear governor," I said, "are there princes in Judea besides the house of Saul?"

"No! I allude to her mother's royal line," he answered. "Adora is not a Jewess by maternal descent. Her mother was a princess of Tadmor in Syria of the Plains! Her grandfather was king of that superb City of Palms! The blood of an heroic race of kings runs in her veins! She is but two removes from the crown of Tadmor. Thou knowest of that realm, O prince! The chief city is ten miles in circumference, though of late years it has lost much of its grandeur."

"I know that the land of Tadmor," I answered, as we rode on side by side through a defile which the head of the army was just entering, "is a province of Assyria, and that its king is tributary to Belus, king of Nineveh; that it is one day's caravan journey from the Euphrates, and remarkable for the splendor of its temples, the magnificence of its palaces, and the beauty of its gardens, though situated upon an oasis in the Orient-Syrian desert! Hast thou been there, O Isrilid?" I inquired; deeply interested in this unexpected intelligence, that the splendid Adora Isrilid is a daughter of the race of the Euphratean kings who built Tadmor, the third city in the world. Your majesty will conceive that I experienced a freshly awakened interest in her.

"When I was a young man," answered Isrilid, "I was led by the spirit of adventure, being rich, to visit distant lands. I found myself in Damascus, and hearing of the glories of the East, I joined myself to a caravan going thence across Arabia-Deserta to Tadmor. There, after many adventures, I was made secretary to the king, having, thanks to my father's care, no mean scholarship, and by and by finding me faithful I was raised from step to step until I became his viceroy; for his majesty had become attached to me and given me his confidence. At length I married the youngest of his two daughters, a maiden of beauty as resplendent as that of Adora who is her daughter! The king at length died, and his son, jealous of my influence, imprisoned me. By the aid of my devoted wife I escaped. Disguised, we joined a caravan going to Tyre, and after many years' absence and great vicissitudes I returned again to my native land. Adora was then a lovely child seven years old. I found that my father and two uncles had died, leaving me the sole heir to three noble estates, for they were as princes in wealth. I was appointed by King Saul, the senate of Seventy confirming, governor or lord of Jericho and its province twelve years ago. Such is the brief story of thy friend Isrilid! and thus it is, O prince, that Adora is a princess in her own right!"

When the governor had ended his narrative I expressed my pleasure at hearing it, and at his present prosperity. I rode on some time musingly, when the Prince Jonathan came to my side and joined our company. He was in cheerful spirits, not only at the prospect of soon meeting the enemy, but at the quiet state his royal father's mind was in. I had not beheld the princely young Hebrew in his armor before. Instead of the gorgeous housing, burnished plate-mail, and brilliant decorations that covered the royal charger which carried his father with such stately pace, his horse, slender and graceful as an antelope, was unprotected save by a plain breastplate of brass and a brazen headpiece. Neither crest nor mail was placed upon him, but his limbs were free to move as with light and dainty step he bore along the youthful prince who rode with a grace and ease of horsemanship that would have captivated the eye of an Euphratean horseman. He, himself, was clad in a dark-green suit of armor, plain, without boss or precious stone, but becoming and elegant, which set to his graceful form like woven silk, although it was knitted of links of iron. A dark-green scarf crossed his chest, and by his side hung his straight, narrow sword without a scabbard, fastened to his black girdle by a silver chain. He wore a close, pointed helmet, bronzed and visored, but without crest or plume. At his saddle-bow hung a quiver of steel-headed arrows and a polished cross-bow of cedar wood. He had neither stirrups nor bridle, but guided his beautiful courser by the tones of his voice. In his hand he held a long lance, the point of which glittered like fire in the sun's rays. His fine, frank, generous features were alight with pleasure at the sight of the proud hosts around him moving to battle! I said to him:

"My dear prince, your armor is, pardon me, plainer than becomes your rank. Permit me to present to your highness for this war a suit of Assyrian armor which I have in my pavilion. I can send for it by my armor-bearer, Ninus! Indeed, I laid it all out for the purpose of some time offering it to you."

The prince smiled quietly, and said, "I thank you kindly, Arbaces, but I cannot wear royal armor. It becomes me to appear harnessed for war plainly, as you see me. Such splendid armaments as you speak of are fitter for the true prince of Israel, my friend David, than for an humble citizen like me. Should my father fall in battle to-morrow, I should be no longer a prince! Nay, no roof in the land of Israel, however lowly, could call me its lord. I should be a mere wanderer; for all my father has are his crown and sword."

I painfully felt the force of his words. We rode on in silence until we emerged into a noble plain, when Saul and his body-guard marched ahead, and the mighty army followed, column rolling along after column, across the broad green valley. The head of the leading battalions was penetrating the gorge of distant hills ere the rear squadrons had disengaged themselves from the defiles on the east of the valley.

That night Saul encamped partly in a vale, partly on the hill sides, and within but a day's march of the plain on which we knew the Philistine army to be reposing in battle order. During the night our camp presented a grand spectacle with its numerous tent-lights and blazing fires like stars for multitude. The hum of the people was borne over the vast plain like the roar of the Tigris, when swollen, heard afar off. Before morning there were several alarms, and two or three conflicts on the wings of the camp with roving bodies of the enemy seeking plunder or maneuvering to throw the new troops into disorder. At early dawn the bugles sounded the advance, and once more we moved forward; and now in imposing battle array, our flanks protected by clouds of archers and by the few horse which appertained to the army, against the wild, barbaric riders of the desert, some thousands of which were enlisted and fighting against Saul in alliance with the Philistines. All day, as we moved along the road toward Joppa, we saw small bodies of these fierce warriors hovering upon the ridges and embracing every opportunity of cutting off any lingering parties of our army.

Toward evening we left on the right flank the rocky heights of Bethlehem, and crossing a wild and bold series of mountain ridges pitched our camp in the deep valleys among them. We had now approached near the main army of the enemy, according to the reports of our spies. The most vigilant watch was kept up all night throughout the camp. The army slept, sword in hand, ready for the battle-cry should the Philistines attack our position. But the night-watches all passed quietly.

I occupied a pavilion near the king's, Jonathan and Isrilid sharing my hospitality. As the morning star was fading into the amber-tinted sky of dawn the early rising king stood at my door and said:

"Come with me, Prince Arbaces, and let us behold the Philistine encampment."

We ascended an eminence west of our camp, and as the sun rose in cloudless splendor we saw before us a vast plain from which the thin white haze was slowly dissipating itself into the clear atmosphere. A range of low blue mountains lined the distant horizon. Along their sides was visible a white, league-long line of tents of war. The base of the hills betrayed a dark shadow varied by lights and color, and in front of it gleamed a stream of silvery, broken, waving light, like a narrow river glittering with ten thousand shining and dazzling waves in motion.

"Behold!" said the king, "the camp of the Philistines! That dark shadow varied and broken on the hill, this side of the tents, is that portion of the hosts of Goliath who have been in arms all night, and now, relieved and unarmed, are reposing upon the ground. That long shining stream of moving waves of light proceeds from their front of battle, composed of their tens of thousands of armed men! the bright tremulous motion is the reflection of the sun upon the myriads of spears, helms, crests, swords, javelins, from shield, corslet, and headpiece!"

"It is a sublime spectacle," I said. "Their numbers seem to be immense!"

"It is not by numbers Israel is to be conquered or to conquer," answered the king, with a shade of the former gloom of his spirit passing across his face. "The host conquers, be it large or small, on the side of which the Lord God of Hosts and of Israel fights! No power of arms or strength in numbers of men can avail us, if He hides his face from us, or them, if He turns it upon them in wrath!"

The center of the vast plain was unoccupied, save that here and there a war-horse, which had escaped from its owner, was either quietly feeding upon the rich grass or dashing up and down in wild freedom. A single lion was seen cantering along farther north, driven from his lair in the cliff by the approach of our troops; for by this time the army of the Hebrews was in full march across the hills on which we were standing, and descending into the valley at their base.

From the elevation upon which we were, not only the dark, brown walls of Bethlehem, three miles to the westward, were visible, but eight miles distant northward the castellated square tower of the Jebusite fortress, overlooking Solima its city, was discernible. To the west the remote walled towns of Azekah and Socho could be dimly seen, between which stretched the line of the Philistines, their center resting on a strong fortress upon the side of the mountain in their rear.

King Saul now led his army down into the valley of Elah, and leaving one-third of the men to pitch the camp on the hillside, he marshaled the residue of his fighting men in order of battle on the plain, and rode along their whole line reviewing them and giving earnest orders to his lords, generals, and high captains as to the disposition of their several commands.

This done, he directed ten thousand of his men to commence fortifying his position, by digging a deep trench in front of it, and throwing up a parapet with the earth on the side toward his camp. This was done in order to prevent a surprise in the night, and in case of an attack to stop the chariots and horsemen of the enemy. As this fortification, which, with so many men employed, was thrown up before night, joined the mountain on one side and on the other side, it completely inclosed the army of King Saul.

As the Philistine hosts were so much greater in numbers than the king's, he resolved to await in this position the arrival of his whole army; for there were seventy thousand men of Israel yet to march to his standard from beyond the Jordan. Therefore, not feeling himself strong enough to meet the enemy with his present force, he resolved to defer offering the Philistine battle until he could equal him in numbers; for the unhappy king had no confidence that the help of his offended God would supply the lack of numbers, as in the former days of his regal glory ere he disobeyed his laws!

Thus encamped and intrenched, King Saul impatiently awaited his expected reinforcements. The second day Isrilid, Governor of Jericho, hastened back to his province to forward the talents of gold which he had loaned to the king. The tedium of the delay was sometimes varied by the chase of the leopard or the lion, which were from time to time started from their lairs, when they fled terrified across the plain, pursued by the younger and lighter Hebrew soldiers, with bow and javelin.

On the fourth day as the prince and I were slowly riding along the foot of the mountain beyond the parapet, now watching for the appearance of wild beasts, now surveying the inactive line of the Philistine foe, a leopard, frightened by the shouts of a foraging party of Saul's men, bounded from a defile immediately before us. The prince has a great passion for the excitement and perils of the chase; and he at once pursued. I was in a moment by his side. The beautiful and savage beast ran in a direct line across the plain. We were soon far from our own camp, and approaching that of the Philistines, which in our eagerness of pursuit we took no heed of, when we heard far in our rear a faintly sounding trumpet calling the retreat.

It was from the king's camp, where our rashness in advancing so far into the plain had been perceived. We turned, and for the first time realized our great distance from the encampment. We were also close upon the leopard, which already carried an arrow in its side from the prince's bow.

"A few moments more, and if we do not slay the leopard," said the prince, "we will obey the call and ride back to camp!"

As he spoke he launched his javelin with such precision that it struck the animal behind the shoulder and hurled him over upon the earth. At the instant of its fall I heard a tramp of horses' hoofs, and looking up beheld a body of Philistine cavalry and dromedaries sweeping in a curve across the plain toward us, the riders with lance in rest and flying over the ground with the fleetness of the wind. The prince, who had already alighted and was disengaging his javelin from the body of the expiring animal, at my warning looked up and beheld his danger. He leaped into his saddle and cried:

"Let us fly, Arbaces! It is my folly that has brought you into this imminent peril!"

"Do not concern yourself, my prince, about me," I said. "I have enjoyed the chase as keenly as you have done. They are too numerous for us to attempt to offer them battle! We must trust to the speed of our horses!"

"To the camp then for our lives, Arbaces!" he cried. "There are full three-score of them, and Idumean riders too, whose steeds are as fleet as eagles!"

There was not a moment to dally in hesitation. We shouted to our brave chargers and gave them the rein for the camp! Fortunately we were both admirably mounted. It became now a reversed chase! the hunters of the brute were now in turn hunted by men! No sooner had we wheeled to make our escape than the pursuers shouted their wild and terrific battle-cry, and clashing their swords and spears against their shields came thundering on, each moment the advanced horsemen gaining upon us little by little. We now saw that there was commotion in our camp. Armed men leaped upon their horses and the drawbridge over the moat fell, and a score of mounted Hebrews dashed across followed by the king, who soon took the lead of all! This was a gallant show of aid for us, but our foes had but one-quarter of the distance to traverse that our friends had to reach us. Every moment I expected we should fall into the hands of our pursuers, four of whom, Amalekites mounted on dromedaries, were now within bow-shot of us, and their long, slender arrows already flew past us!

Suddenly I wheeled upon the foe, receiving upon my shield a lance which fell at my feet shivered by the blow, and hewed down with my sword the barbarian who was about to transfix me, and also checked the advance of his fellow, who, however, launched his glittering javelin at the prince, as he turned to combat with a splendid, gayly-appareled warrior who pressed him closely. My brave friend, engaged sword in hand with his antagonist, was heedless of the flight of the javelin, which pierced the flesh of his right arm. I was by his side in a moment to cover him from the battle-ax of his antagonist, who fell cloven through the helmet. The next moment we would have been overpowered and slain by the rapid approach of others of the foe but for the presence of Saul himself! Colossal in size and mounted upon his gigantic white charger, his eyes blazing with war-fire and his visage terrible with rage, while his voice roared like that of the lion in his fury, he charged alone upon our foes, swept them aside like stubble with his great sword wielded in his left hand and his bronze-headed mace held in his right!

The rest of the Philistines, beholding with consternation this warlike champion thus coming upon them like the powerful and wrathful god of war, checked their advance and suddenly wheeling about galloped away to a safe distance, leaving seven of their number, horse and rider, in the dust of the plain. The followers of the king now coming up continued on and charged them with confidence in a speedy victory, while the king bending from his saddle drew the javelin from his son's arm, mildly reproving him for his rash boldness.

"Forgive me, my dear father," he said. "I know now I was wrong, since I have imperiled your life as well as that of Prince Arbaces; but in the heat of the chase I did not know we were so near the Philistine camp!"

"It is well it is no worse, my brave child," he replied. "Prince Arbaces, I saw the aid you gave my son. It was opportune and skillfully effected. We will now ride back to camp; for the Philistine army is not to be conquered by a stripling like thyself, my brave boy!" This was spoken to Jonathan, who appeared not to heed the anguish of his wound.

"I did not in my own person, my dear father and king, expect

to fight their army," answered Jonathan, returning the smile
—so rare on his gloomy sire's face. " But you need not look
so anxious, sir! My wound is but trifling. See! our men are
chased! "

This was true. The overbold Hebrew horsemen had not
counted the cost of their charge, and were received by the rallied Philistines so warmly that after a brief conflict they turned
and fled, pursued by their shouting adversaries to the place
where we were. Saul, drawing himself up to his full stature
and swinging his formidable sword, charged and stopped the
pursuit! The foiled riders contented themselves with sending
a flight of lances at the person of the king, which, caught on
his shield, helmet, and breastplate, and headpiece of his war-
horse, were shivered like crystals.

We at length regained our intrenchments, and the prince's
severe wound was medicated and bound up by my own skillful
Indraic physician.

The noble king had well calculated the result that would
follow his intrenching himself where he was. His object in
doing it was to draw the Philistine general out of his strong
position which he had taken up along the hillside, expecting
Saul to attack him there. But when the strategic barbarian
monarch perceived that the Hebrew chief had taken up a permanent position partly on the hill and partly on the plain, and
appeared to expect his attack, he reluctantly abandoned his
original plan of tactics, and moved with his whole army further northward and nearer to us, so that only a narrow valley
instead of a wide plain as before separated us. A rocky eminence also protected the rear of the Philistines' main body.
This change of position was made the morning after the prince
received his wound. The sight of the foe marching nearer, and
pitching their camp opposite to us, gave King Saul the highest
satisfaction. He felt that the next move would be to assail
him in his intrenchments, when he intended to pour from the
hills and defiles the chief weight of his army upon him. To
have crossed the plain, to attack a foe provided with horses and
chariots armed with scythes, would be to expose himself to be
surrounded and cut to pieces. So King Saul quietly and prudently waited in his encampment, until the Philistines should
weary of the delay and march out to give him battle.

Midway the valley flowed a sparkling brook at which the
pitcher-bearers of both armies went to draw water, who, being

all unarmed, peacefully talked with each other from bank to bank, leaving the active work of war to those who wore helm and sword. This pebbly brook, which a deer could bound across, was therefore neutral ground.

The morning after the armies of the Philistines had settled themselves in their new position, covering the opposite hill and half the valley, which is called Pas-dam-mim, with their glittering numbers, Saul shut himself up in his tent, and it was whispered that "the dark cloud was upon his soul!" This news was brought to my pavilion by Heleph, the armor-bearer of the Prince Jonathan, who lay upon a couch suffering from the pain of his severe wound.

"Do not let it be noised in the camp," he cried, with earnestness, "or the whole army will be paralyzed. Who of the people knows it?"

"The Prince Ishbosheth told me," answered Heleph.

"Go, dear Arbaces," implored Jonathan, "and see if it be so! My father will admit *you* into his presence. If possible, have it kept secret. It may pass off in a day! How disastrous!"

I immediately sought the king's tent. His high-steward met me at the door.

"Is the king ill?" I asked.

The old servitor shook his head sorrowfully.

"The evil spirit is with the king," was his sad and troubled answer. "It came upon him in the night! He sprung out of sleep and seizing his sword seemed to meet an invisible enemy! Then he cast the weapon away, crying, 'Shall I fight against a foul spirit with a sword of iron?' He then sunk upon the side of his couch, and has not moved since, his face all the while buried in his hands, at times groaning, not as in pain, but as a man mourns for the dead!"

I went softly in. The king took no notice of me. I ventured to lay my hand upon his, gently. He moved not! I spoke words of kindness and sympathy! He remained silent. I appealed to his warlike name, to his kingly pride, and to his army waiting their leader! He moved not, but great sighs betrayed the profoundness of his emotion. At length he removed his hands and looked up into my face! Gods of clemency and pity, your majesty! I never beheld such a countenance! It will haunt me to my dying hour! It was a dead man's face, but stamped with a living, unutterable woe! The hollow, black eyes seemed profound wells of tears, deep, deep

beyond the plumb of human sympathy to fathom. They seemed
to look out at me from the infinite shades of everlasting tor-
ment! The awful forehead was furrowed with great lines of
grief, as if the plowshare of despair had passed over it! His
haggard cheeks were valleys of grief, and the expression of his
mouth was that of one from the prayers of which Mercy has
turned her ears forevermore! It was the countenance of a
fallen god mourning his lost throne, conscious it can be regained no more—no more! in whom hope is dead while impotent
remorse remains!

I could not speak! My heart was full of tears! I slowly
and silently replaced his two hands over his face, as if it were
a deed of mercy to leave him to his woe which no man should
dare meddle with!

It was in vain to keep the secret from the army! Days and
nights he sat under the cloud of the dark spirit which had so
mysteriously usurped the throne of his soul. From the royal
pavilion the shadow passed over the whole camp, and each
countenance reflected the gloom of the king's. The army was
dispirited! Evil was predicted! Men deserted by night in
companies, feeling that their God would be against them in
battle! Jonathan, with fever burning in his veins and unspeakable sorrow in his heart, rode through the army and addressed the men, urging them to remain loyal and not increase
their evil condition by yielding to superstitious fears. He encouraged them to believe that the king would soon recover, and
that God would fight for them.

His personal popularity prevailed in a degree. It was a
touching spectacle to see the pale young prince, who was so
weak that he had to be lifted to his saddle, show such a
courageous and noble spirit in those dark hours. But he returned to my tent and fainted away.

Early the third morning, after the evil spirit, for such it
seemed, had again possessed the king, I was standing upon a
cliff watching the Philistines, who, during the night, had
changed their front and advanced to within half a mile of our
intrenchments with two-thirds of their army, leaving the re-
mainder encamped on a hill which they had fortified and held
in case of a retreat. This near approach looked like an intention on the part of their general ere long to attack us.

While I was observing their long, mailed front, their archers,
chariots, cavalry, men-at-arms, spear-men, and mounted Idu-

mean troops, and a battalion of hired Amalekites eight hundred dromedaries strong, each under its own chief and standard, and showy with varied armor and costumes, I was attracted by a body of about seventy men of gigantic size, clad in coats of steel, and wearing brazen helmets and greaves of brass, marching out from the line. Their leader was in height a colossus! Tall and enormous as they were, he towered a head and shoulder above them. He could have stood by your majesty's royal elephant and laid his arm across her back, as an ordinary man stands by a horse of large size and rests his hand upon his neck. Ninus, my armor-bearer, on beholding him, uttered a shout of terror and amazement. Prince Ishbosheth, a fair youth and younger brother of Jonathan, came near, and seeing them, said to me:

"Those are the far-famed sons of Anak! They are of the race of giants whom Joshua drove out from the land of Anakim!"

The sight was soon beheld from other parts of the camp and created great excitement. "The sons of Anak! The terrible Anakim!" cried the most timid; and all was confusion.

I watched them with deep interest! They moved across the valley in solid phalanx. The very earth seemed to shake with their combined tread. The clang and ring of their coats of mail, and chains, and huge swords as they stepped were terrific. Their shields were like great round tables of bronze. Their weapons of war were in proportion to their stature and enormous strength. I had heard rumors before, your majesty, of this family of Anakim, which have a city of their own in Palestina, where all of them, male and female, are giants; but now I beheld their chief men—human monsters six cubits, or nine feet, high—who formed the bodyguard of their mighty king.

When they had advanced, three cubits * at a stride, near the intervening brook, they came to a halt; and their chief, leaving them, advanced alone to within a bow-shot of the brook (from the banks of which the water-carriers of both armies fled away in terror toward their camps), and standing, he lifted up his voice and cried unto the armies of Israel. In height with helm and crest he was nearly eleven feet. He wore a brazen helmet upon his head, and was clad in a coat of mail woven of scales of brass, each scale the size of a man's palm, and

* A secular Hebrew cubit was eighteen inches in length.

riveted one to the other. Upon his legs were greaves of brass, and a target of brass between his shoulders. A cuirass of steel covered his ponderous chest, and at his thigh hung a great two-handed sword, a weight for a man to lift. The staff of his spear was like a weaver's beam, and the spear's head would have weighed six hundred shekels of iron. He was full seventy years of age, and his black, massive beard and thick locks were mingled with gray. Before him marched a strong man, with difficulty bearing his enormous shield bossed with spikes of iron and bound with bands of brass. His voice was like the male tiger's when pouring forth his deep-toned rage against his foes.

"Why are ye come out to set your battle in array? Am I not a Philistine—a freeman—and ye servants of Saul? Choose ye a man of war on your side and let him come forth to meet me! If he be able to fight with me and to kill me, then will we be your servants and the servants of Saul; but if I prevail against him and kill him, then shall ye be my servants and serve the Philistines!"

When he had thus proclaimed his challenge in a voice that was heard even by King Saul in his tent, he cast from his hand his huge iron gauntlet, so that it fell far across the brook upon the earth in sight of the Israelites. With the act he cried aloud, "I defy the armies of Israel this day! Send forth thy champion that he may fight with me!"

This bold defiance from so terrible a warrior, whom no single Israelite could hope to cope with, was heard by the whole army with dismay. I have already informed your majesty of the gloom which the condition of the king's mind had cast over the camp, and that, as one expressed it to me, "The whole heart had gone out of the men!" This challenge of the Philistine caused their spirits wholly to fail and their souls to sink within them. They knew that their enemies had heard of the king's condition, and hence took this way of defiance and showing contempt for Saul. Who in their army could have the courage to meet him save King Saul, whose lion-like courage never had quailed before man? But to their earnest and anxious questions of their captains and chief lords as to what was to be done, the answer was given, "The king sits in his tent, and the evil spirit of God rests upon his soul!"

"Has he heard the proud defiance of the champion of his foes?" I asked of his chief steward.

"Yes, my lord," he answered; "but he moves not from his seat. His brave general Abner, who has just arrived in camp from the country beyond Mount Ephraim with reinforcements from the land of Asher, of Manasseh, and of Naphtali, has repeated to him the challenge word for word, and said, 'O king, if thou wilt permit thy servant Abner, he will go forth and meet this dog of a Philistine! If I perish, my blood will in part wipe off this dishonor from our army!'"

"'Nay, Abner,' answered the king, without look up from the ground; 'nay, thou art come hither, not to be slain, but to stand in my place before my people! Thou wilt command them! If thou art slain, they will take to flight and each man seek his own home, and the Philistine will possess the land! Let him defy us! Words do no harm! We are strong within our intrenchments and they fear to assail us! Go and leave me, and put courage into the hearts of the people. Peradventure God for their sakes will yet give us victory!'"

I saw for the first time this warrior Abner, your majesty, as, when he came out of the king's pavilion, he entered my tent to visit the wounded prince. He is a man of noble bearing, with a bold, martial front and a proud, imperious air, with all the characteristics of the Hebrew race in the blackness of his eyes, the eagle shape of his nose, and full, resolute lips. He was in a rich suit of armor, and wore a helmet inlaid with gold, and a mail-shirt of golden chains with greaves of brass and a corslet of bronze. I greatly liked his appearance, and felt that the king had a strong arm to lean upon in his presence in the camp. More than once ere his arrival I had heard Saul sigh and say, "Would Abner, my general, were come! Would God Abner were come!"

The Philistine, after giving his defiance, retired and with his huge bodyguard strode back to his camp. The same evening, just as the priest who attends the king in his wars was offering up the evening incense with the prayers of the army to their Lord, the giant again made his appearance in the plain and repeated his defiance as before, his hoarse, barbarian voice almost drowning that of the priest reciting the holy service. The next morning and evening the challenge was repeated in the same terms of boasting and scorn. My own blood boiled at the repeated insult, and I felt tempted to go forth with my hundred Assyrian nobles and attack him and also his men-at-arms! But this, doubtless, would have been an act of rashness.

No mere charge of horse would avail, especially as the brook lay between. It seemed necessary to assail the monster only with stones from a catapult or other siege-artillery. In single combat no one could meet him and live! This was so evident that even the brave Abner said "that he would permit no man, if one could be found in the army to offer, to go out to him! He would be slain and we should be mocked the louder. To attack him with a strong body of horse would not only be a confession of our own weakness which compels a resort to numbers to subdue one enemy, but contrary to the rules of war, wherein the person of a champion who presents himself is sacred from surprise or treachery, and, if met at all, must be met by but one of the other side! Therefore he must defy us until he is weary! It is a bitter thing," added Abner, "to have to hear him bellowing out there morning and evening; but we must abide patiently the end, and in the meanwhile strengthen our position, in case of an attack."

The brave prince, as he lay on his couch, writhed when the voice of the giant day after day came roaring across the vale, like that of a wild Bashan bull when he paws the earth and lashes himself for combat with a rival.

After forty days had elapsed, during which the giant ceased not morning and evening, at the hours of sacrifice, to present himself before the camp of Saul, he appeared with new rage and fresh terms of defiance and hatred. Up to this time the king had remained in his tent, and the dark cloud hung upon him with but little change in the intensity of its gloom. He ate but seldom, scarcely slept, and spoke to no man. When the hour for the Philistine to shout out his challenge came, the king would be seen to lift his head and pause in his walk up and down his tent, or if lying down to raise his head as if to listen for it; and when it came he would bury his face in his mantle, and mutter:

"I am accursed—accursed of God! This son of Anak is sent to curse me by his gods, and I am impotent! When will this burden of my life end! Rather would I perish by the sword of this Goliath of Gath than live! But shall the king of Israel give himself up to die like a dog that this giant may howl over his dead corpse and mock my people! No, I must live on—live on—and bear as I may this Atlas of woe God has placed upon my head!"

On the fortieth morning the giant came out, and cried:

"O Saul of Kish! Thou craven Benjaminite! son of a left-handed race! Hast thou not a man to take up my gauntlet which rusteth there, lying on the earth these forty days! Where art thou, circumcised Hebrew? Show thyself! If thy evil spirit lovest music I will play thee a sweet melody with my sword against thy buckler! Choose you a man of war and let him come down to me! Dost thou not know me? I am Goliath, the lord of Gath! I slew Hophni and Phineas, sons of your High Priest. I am he who carried off the Ark of the Lord, and set it up in the temple of my gods! Come and slay the man that did it, and avenge thy God and his sacred taber-nacle which I defiled!"

This taunt, your majesty, filled to the brim with the last drop the cup of his insults he had from day to day made the ears of the Hebrews drink! Saul sprung to his feet, seized his sword, crying, as he marched forth from his tent:

"Is there not a man here whom God is with who will rid me of this Philistine?"

Jonathan, who was still lingering (for his excitement on account of his father and the Philistine retarded his con-valescence), rose and hastened to meet his father, who was wholly without mail, helm, or shield, armed only with his naked sword in his left hand. The king no sooner saw him than he dropped his sword, fell upon the prince's neck, and said hoarsely and pitifully:

"Lead me back to my tent! I am accursed! It is not by my hand that the Lord is to avenge himself and his honor! No! all my deeds are an abomination to Him! Jonathan, lead me back! I am not mad, but I am all dead within! My lost soul is imprisoned within my body by the Lord, instead of departing to join companionship with the dark souls of my fathers!"

At length the prince, with traces of weeping in his eyes, came into the pavilion faint and depressed, and told me what had passed.

"My poor father! He is not violent, but his present mood is heart-rending. I fear the Lord God has left us, and will destroy this army by the hand of the Philistine. If He send not help soon, not a Hebrew beard will wag on these hills by noon to-morrow. The army is spiritless, dismayed, and re-bellious! Already the generals of the tribe of Naphtali and of Dan have told Abner they will leave the camp and return to their own borders, for God is surely against Israel! Oh, my dear Prince Arbaces, what can be done?"

"I know not, my prince," I answered, greatly distressed at so strange a condition of things in so vast an army; for there were not less than one hundred and forty thousand men encamped under the banners of the different tribes on the hill and plain. "Perhaps safety lies only in a bold attack on the camp of the Philistines with the whole army."

"I have thought so! The brave Abner, who is at his wit's end between his allegiance to the king and his duty to the people, spoke of it! He called a council of all the captains, lords, chiefs, and generals of the tribes, and proposed a battle! But superstition has fallen upon them. They refuse to fight unless the king leads. But alas! he is not himself, and seems to be dead while he lives, as he strongly and truly expressed it!"

"Why not send for David to try again the power of his harp?" I asked.

"I have thought of it often. But he is in the School of the Prophets and under Samuel. If my father knew that he came from the Seer he would not suffer him to enter his presence, for he will take no favor from the Prophet," answered the prince sorrowfully.

"It is two years or more since the king sent him back to his father Jesse," I said. "He was then a beardless lad you told me. When we saw him at Ramah two months ago he had a bearded lip and chin, and you remarked, in my presence, to him how tall he had grown since you first knew him at Bethlehem, and from a youth had got the air and beard of manhood. If he is so much changed, though indeed he looks still fair and comely of countenance, the king may not recognize him. Let him be sent for as a strange harpist."

"It is possible the king might not know him, as he observes and notices but little of what passes around him," answered the prince thoughtfully.

While he was speaking, Ninus came in and exclaimed, "The king is in his right mind and has on his armor, and calls for his horse, and has given Abner command to put the whole army in array, and offer battle to the Philistines this day!"

The news proved true! Saul had suddenly awaked from his deep gloom like a man shaking off the nightmare, and in his natural tone of voice and usual manner was infusing a new spirit into all who approached him. It was a joyous sight to the army to see its chief once more in battle-harness, with the light of war illumining his face, and his cheerful voice heard as of old giving his soldierly commands. The Philistines, thus seeing the army of Israel forming in battle array, also marshaled their hosts, and soon army was set against army. In this attitude they remained all day, but Saul resolved not to attack until night came on. But as evening drew near the gigantic Philistine's appearance nearer the camp than ever produced a panic along his line, and half his army precipitately fled up the mountain. The next morning Saul set them again in battle array, and the Philistines stood opposite to them ready for battle. But before Saul was ready to give the command to advance the formidable Philistine again appeared and challenged the king. Then Saul, seeing his soldiers troubled, caused a proclamation to be made that " the man of Israel who would slay the heathen champion should be made the richest man in his kingdom; should receive the Princess Michal, his beautiful daughter, to wife; and his father's house should be made all princes in the land."

This offer of reward for victory over his foe shows strikingly, your majesty, how wholly the king's piety toward his God had left him; for, by the custom and law of war among his people, it was the duty of a king or general about to give battle, to consult the Prophet of God in the land, or else the High Priest, and also to have sacrifice offered to his Lord in heaven, in order to gain the divine favor and blessing upon his arms. Here the king ignored the aid of Heaven, and looked only to human prowess. This extraordinary impiety was doubtless a part of his retributive madness.

But while the monarch sought in vain along the wavering line of his trembling hosts for a man to slay the Philistine, there was, unknown to him, approaching the camp one who was ready to accept the defiance of the Philistine, lift his iron gauntlet, and do battle with him in the name of his God!

But, your majesty, I will defer until my next letter, which I shall shortly write, my narration of the events that subsequently transpired.

Your faithful
ARBACES.

LETTER VIII.

ARBACES TO THE KING.

YOUR MAJESTY:

In my last I prepared you to hear that a champion was found who was about to meet the Philistine lord and avenge the insulted honor of his God and country. It will not be in your power, O king, to form the remotest idea of the person, although his name is not unfamiliar to you, having been often mentioned in my letters; nay, he is one of the chief persons who have figured therein.

You will remember that we left the youthful David at the School of the Prophets in Ramah. But when he heard that his three older brothers had gone to the wars, and that a fourth was ill, having been severely torn by a wolf, he requested of the Seer permission to go and see how it fared with the old man his father, and if his services were needed by him. The prophet, pleased with this filial feeling, granted his request, and dismissed him with his blessing.

The young shepherd had been but a few days at home, where he found his aid needed about many things, especially in his familiar duty of tending his father's flocks, which by neglect had been reduced to a very few, when one morning the venerable Ephrathite called his son to him and said:

"I desire to hear from thy brethren in the camp of Saul! Lade thee a small sheaf wagon with provisions for them, and gifts for Joab the brave young captain of their thousand, and take thee my Canaanite servant to drive it, and go to the king's camp in the valley of Elah, and see how thy brothers fare; and take receipt for what thou givest them; but take no such pledge from Joab! Keep thyself from harm, my son; and shouldst thou find the battle waging, take no part in it! for thou art consecrated to God, and thy life is not in thine own hand."

Before day the following morning the young man left for the camp of Israel. The distance was but twelve miles westwardly over hills, through defiles, and across plains. At length, as the sun rose, he caught the glitter of the arms and armor of the Hebrews encamped on the hills above Elah. He hastened on pleased with this warlike sight! Ere long he emerged from a glen and came full in view of the two armies. It was a grand spectacle to his brave heart, and he stopped to gaze on the martial scene. Lo! as he looked, he saw both armies move toward each other, heard the clangor of shields, the clash of spears and swords against bucklers, the bray of trumpets, and the preliminary shouts of battle. But after a show of attack both armies retired to their former positions, but still in array of battle.

The young shepherd continued to approach the camp of the Hebrews, and as he came near the outer trench in search of the entrance, he was directed by the sentry to the part of the camp where his brethren stood in the "thousand" of Joab. He found their phalanx, and came and saluted his brethren and made known to them upon what errand he had come. They frowned at first on him, but gladly accepted what he told them he had brought in his carriage, and speedily sent out to have the provisions taken in! While they were talking with him about home and their father, he was surprised to hear a voice like a man's, yet loud as a lion's roar, while at the same time the Israelitish soldiers around him manifested a disposition to fly; but their fierce young captain, Joab, with his spear in his hand, swore by the Ark of the Lord that he would slay the man that fled; nevertheless, from other battalions great numbers retreated sore afraid. David looked round when he heard this strange and terrific voice, and beheld the Philistine champion, Goliath of Gath, come forth upon the plain out of his army and stand as heretofore and defy the armies of the living God, and calling upon Saul to send him a man to fight him! When the young shepherd had listened to these words he asked of those about him:

"Who is this son of Anak? Doth he thus defy the king and all his hosts?"

"He hath done this for forty days! For forty days he has defied Israel, the king, and the Lord of hosts. No man can stand before him!" they replied to him.

"And the king hath made proclamation," said a man of Judah, "that the man who killeth him shall be enriched with great riches, marry the king's daughter Michal, and that all his family shall be free nobles and princes in the land!"

"Sayeth the king so?" exclaimed David. "What said he?

That the man who slew him should have his fair daughter in marriage?"

"So shall it be done by the king to the man that killeth him," they answered, interested in seeing the comely shepherd manifesting such a deep interest in what they told him.

Joab now approached and thanked David for the present he had brought him, and said:

"If thou goest back to Jesse, thy father, tell him not, young man, that thou sawest the army of Israel put in fear by one man, though a giant! It is not that, but there is a cloud from God upon all our hearts, and we dare do nothing! A strange fear hath fallen upon us all from the Lord! My courage oozes from my finger-ends at the voice of this Goliath! We are bound by a spell! We know heaven is against our king! So we are but an army of women, while this giant of Gath insults us! The dark shadow of God's hand is upon us!"

"How fares the king's mind?" asked David. "Hath he lost heart?"

"He has been for forty days under a cloud. Yesterday and this morning he was like himself! But he no sooner gets the army in array for battle than he gives the order, not to 'advance,' but to 'retire'! We know not what to do! The prophet aids us no more! The High Priest is not consulted! No sacrifice burns on the altar!"

"And he who slays the Philistine shall be rewarded with the hand of the king's daughter?" interrogatively repeated the graceful shepherd to the men about him, as the champion filled the air with his voice, calling to the combat.

"What is that to thee, stripling, what the king will reward with?" cried angrily his eldest brother, Eliab, his eyes kindling with scorn. "Comest thou hither to do him battle, boy? With whom hast thou left those few sheep in the wilderness? I know the pride of thy vain heart. Thou didst come only to see the battle, for thou hast ever the conceit in thee to play the soldier! Go back and fight the wolves and chase the conies of the rocks! What is it to thee, proud boy, what the king offers?"

"Dost not thou tremble," spoke his brother Abinadab, with light laughter, "to hear the voice of this Anakim? Go, lad! Thou art fitter to look after sheep than fight a giant; yet, by the king's head, brothers, the boy's words smack of a wish to try his hand to win the king's daughter!"

Here Eliab and his two brothers laughed loudly, and openly scorned their younger brother, so that he turned from them, and said to Joab:

"If there be none to step before me to meet this blasphemer of God and defier of Israel, I will go!"

"*Thou?*" exclaimed the captain of the thousand, regarding him; while all around made themselves merry at David's bold words; seeing he was but a mere youth without armor, dressed in his blue shepherd's tunic and carrying only his cross-hafted crook in his hand. "I fear Goliath would hardly notice thee, my brave youth! If thy height were at tall as thy heart, thou hast courage enough!"

In the meantime someone went and told the king that a young shepherd in the camp spoke boldly, and expressed no fear of the Philistine, and seemed ready to fight with him.

"Haste and bring him before me," cried Saul.

The king walking up and down before his pavilion was gloomily deliberating in his mind what to do in his present great trials, when the son of Jesse was conducted by Joab before him.

"Is this youth he?" he demanded, with a glance of derision. "Why dost thou mock me to lead this stripling hither?"

"Let no man's heart fail him, O king, this day because of the champion of the Philistines," said David, who at once perceived that the king did not recollect him as the beardless youth of two years before who had soothed him with the harp. "Thy servant will go and fight this defier of the armies of Israel and of the king!"

"Thy words are brave, young man; but thou art not able to go against this Philistine to fight with him," said the king, regarding him with a kind expression and speaking with gentle condescension in his tones, as if there were a mysterious influence over him exerted by the voice and presence of the sweet harper who had aforetime laid the evil spirit in his soul. "Thou art but a youth, and this Goliath of Gath a man of war from his youth! I love thee, child, for thy courage; but thou wouldst no sooner come near him, ere he would toss thee in the air as a wild bull would toss an antelope that crossed its path."

Then David answered firmly, but yet with modesty:

"Thy servant kept his father's sheep, and there came a lion and a bear, and the bear took a lamb out of the flock, and I pursued and smote him and delivered the lamb out of his mouth; and when the lion rose against me, I caught him by the beard and smote him and slew him. Thy servant slew both the lion and the bear; and, O king, this uncircumcised Philistine shall be as one of them, seeing he hath defied the armies of the living God!"

The king and his captains and all present looked with surprise and a sort of awe upon the fearless and noble countenance of the youth, on which the loftiest courage sat enthroned.

"Young man, thou hast a lion's heart—but thou canst not slay the Philistine," said Saul.

David answered, "The Lord who delivered me out of the paw of the lion and out of the hand of the bear will deliver me out of the hand of this Philistine. Let the king command me to go!"

"*Go*, and the Lord be with thee, for he hath departed from me and all my people!" said Saul, with a sigh. The king then led the young shepherd into his pavilion and said to his armor-bearer:

"Put on him my royal armor!"

Joab, who loved him for his courage, hastened and brought the king's helmet of brass and would have placed it, all too large, upon his head; and clasped about him the king's coat of scale-mail; and girded his own sword upon his thigh: but they proved so much too large for him that they got a suit of Prince Jonathan's armor which was hanging in the armory of the pavilion and put it on him, with the helmet also; and David girded the sword upon his thigh; but unaccustomed to be mailed in full armor, which he now only suffered to be put upon him by the order of the king, who stood by, and even clasped his helmet for him, he could not move at ease, and turning to King Saul, he said respectfully:

"May it please my lord the king to let me put off these, as I have not been used to them. I will meet Goliath with my own weapons."

The king consented to his request, and he took off all his armor and laid aside the sword, and said quietly, "With my lord the king's permission I will now go forth!"

By this time it was noised about that a mere youth, a shepherd's lad, had presented himself before Saul and offered to do battle with the giant. The news did not reach my pavilion until after he had left the king's tent and begun to descend the hill, when looking from the door, and noticing a great movement of the people in camp, I followed the direction of their gaze and perceived the young shepherd, staff in hand, crossing the outworks. The prince, who had been sleeping to invigorate himself, for he was not yet well, rose up and came to the tent door to look at the youthful champion on whom all eyes were fixed. After a second glance he caught my arm and cried:

"It is David! It is my dear, dear friend! What madness has possessed him? Let me fly to detain him!" he exclaimed, overwhelmed with grief and amazement as he saw the young Hebrew boldly advance into the plain at a rapid step, as if impatient to meet his foe. "Fly!" he called to his armor-bearer and others; "go and by force turn him back!"

"*I* will obey you," I answered, seeing no one moved, while all eagerly watched the youthful hero.

"Nay, hold, Arbaces!" he cried hesitatingly; "I have not forgotten that he is consecrated and his person is sacred! The Philistine dare not harm the anointed of God! But see! What does he?"

As he spoke we saw the young champion stoop and lift the iron gauntlet from the ground and throw it down derisively and walk over it. The Philistine, who had ceased his bellowing, and now stood watching the approach of the unarmed stripling with curiosity, no sooner saw this act than he advanced with a great cry of rage.

David was by this time at the brook. We saw him bend down and carefully select from the stones in its bed several pebbles, which he placed in his shepherd's bag at his girdle. He then crossed the brook, and taking from the bag a shepherd's sling, he went forward swiftly. The Anakim was all the while slowly and heavily advancing, his armor-bearer going before him.

"Wherefore comest thou, boy?" called Goliath, in his loudest tones deepened by rage. "Doth Saul mock me by sending some message by thee to me! Go and tell Saul the lord of Gath holds speech only with mailed warriors!"

"I come to meet thee, not for Saul, but for my own pleasure, thou vain boaster and defier of Israel!" answered David.

"By the gods of Ashtaroth, am I a dog that thou comest against me with a shepherd's staff?" called the Philistine. "May the curses of Dagon and Baal light on thee! I call for a man to fight with, and Saul sendeth me one more fit to dance with women! Cursed be thou by my gods!"

David, fearless and cool, continued to approach him, when the giant, as if scorning any fear of him, sat down upon a rock in the plain and said:

"Come to me, and I will give thy flesh unto the fowls of the air and unto the beasts of the field! In my hand thou wilt be as a lamb in the grasp of the lion!"

Then answered David in a clear voice, "Thou comest to me with a sword, and with a spear, and with a shield; but I come to thee in the name of the Lord of hosts, the God of the armies of Israel whom thou hast defied! This day will the Lord deliver thee into my hand; and I will smite thee and take thine head from thee; and I will give the carcasses of the hosts of the Philistines, this day, unto the fowls of the air and to the wild beasts of the earth, that all the earth may know there is a God of the armies of Israel. And all these Philistines and Israelites shall know that the Lord saveth not with the sword and spear; for the battle is the Lord's, and He will give you into our hands!"

These words so greatly enraged the Philistine that he arose and strode forward to meet David. Then we all trembled for the safety of the young shepherd; and when a thousand voices said, some, "He will be slain," others, "He will fly," he hastened forward still faster toward Goliath, and when within half bow-shot he stopped, put his hand into his bag, and took thence one of the stones of the brook and fitting it to his sling, slung it! The stone, as if Heaven-directed, smote the giant in the forehead and sunk deep into the skull. With a terrible death-cry, heard in both armies, he fell over with his face toward David flat upon the earth. At his fall the very skies were rent with a shout from the whole Hebrew army.

As there was no sword in David's possession, he ran swiftly and stood upon the prostrate Philistine, and took hold of the huge hilt and drew his sword out of the sheath thereof, and seeing he was only stunned by the stone, he drove it through a joint of his coat of mail into his body, killing him. He then cut off his head and held it up in the sight of both armies. The armor-bearer, dropping the monstrous shield, was the first to flee away, and then the bodyguard of giants stationed further back in the plain, seeing their king and champion dead, turned and fled toward the army, which, taking fright and struck with consternation at the sudden fall of their king, broke their line of battle and took to flight.

It would be impossible to convey to your majesty the scene that now followed. The whole army of Hebrews with the wildest shouts of joy and with fierce warlike cries arose, and pouring like an inundating river from their intrenchments pursued their foes across the plain, armed with vengeance. Saul remained on the hill in his tent giving the command of the pursuing army to his generals. It was a wild and terrific spectacle. The whole army, to a man, was engaged in the pursuit, so that but for the king's bodyguard, which never left him, and my Assyrians, the camp would have been emptied.

In an hour both armies, the pursuing and the pursued, were lost to view far beyond the hills upon which the Philistine army had encamped; only the dead strewn over the plain, here singly, there in heaps, showed where the flood of battle had rolled along its sanguine tide.

When David was advancing into the plain to meet the Philistine, Saul was heard to inquire of his general, Abner, who the lad was, and whose son he was, so bold and that seemed to have the Spirit of the Lord upon him? Abner answered him:

"As thy soul liveth, O king, I cannot tell."

"Inquire thou whose son the stripling is," commanded the king.

After the death of the Philistine Abner found the hero in my pavilion, whither Jonathan (forgetting his wound) and I with Joab and others had brought him, having hastened to meet him as he was returning from the plain with the head of Goliath in one hand and his sword in the other. The prince embraced him on meeting, weeping with joy, and again and again drew him to his heart! Eliab and Abinadab, his now proud brothers, came with us and took up the head to carry after David, and Shammah bore the giant's sword! After the great wave of battle had swept over the plain, parting at the giant's headless body, I dispatched some of my men-at-arms with Jonathan's to strip the dead champion of his armor and bear it to the tent. It took four men to carry his coat-of-mail, three his spear with its staff, and two his helmet, while his target of brass and shield were a heavy load for three men! Such, your majesty, was the monster slain by this fearless youth! What a godlike hero! In Assyria he would be ranked with the warlike gods! Yet how modest after his victory! He blushed when I praised him.

The fall of the Philistine amazed the king.

"Do my eyes deceive me?" he called out. "Is the champion down?"

"Down, O king, and the youth's feet upon his neck!" cried a hundred voices. "See, he cuts off his head!"

The king looked, and then overcome by the reaction of his feelings, he would have fallen to the ground if he had not caught by the shoulder of his armor-bearer.

"God still fights for us," he murmured, "and I am not cast off forever!"

Overcome by his emotions, he desired to be led to his tent. When he came to himself he sent for Abner his general, and bade him bring the young conqueror before him. With the head of the Philistine in his hand, David entered his pavilion.

"Whose son art thou, young man?" asked Saul, as David placed the gory head of Goliath at the feet of the king.

"I am the son of thy servant, Jesse, the Bethlehemite," modestly answered the young conqueror.

Then Saul, looking closely at his face, recognized his skillful harpist, and extending his hand to him, David reverently bent his knee, and kissing it, said:

"Let the lord my king long live and prosper in his kingdom, and let the spirit of wisdom and power rest upon him forever, and let him triumph over all his enemies, as he hath over the Philistine this day."

"What!" cried the king, "givest thou *me* the glory? To thine hand alone is owed the glory of Israel this day. Rise from thy knee! All men shall do thee honor!"

Prince Jonathan, as David rose to his feet, rushed forward and folded him to his heart, and with expressions of the warmest affection called him "his brother," saying:

"I love thee, David, I love thee even as my own soul. Thou hast saved my father! From this hour we will no more be separated!"

"Nay, did he desire to return to his father's house," said the pleased king, "I would forbid it. From this day, young man, thou shalt be to me as a son and dwell with me!"

"Promise the king to remain, O David!" cried the prince, seeing he hesitated.

"For thy sake, my beloved prince," he at length answered, "I will dwell with the king."

"Then from this moment we are one!" exclaimed Jonathan. "Between us my father will make no distinction, unless to love and honor thee more! As a seal of our covenant take thou this robe which I put upon thee."

Here Jonathan, with my aid, divested himself of the flowing broidered robe which his sister Michal had sent him, and placed it upon the shoulders of the beautiful youth; called to his armor-bearer to fetch his Damascus sword, his silver inlaid bow and his golden girdle, and his undress helmet of scarlet silk wrought with needlework of divers colors (all prized gifts to him from friends at court or fair maidens, companions of his sister), all of which he put upon his friend. The transformation was singularly becoming to the young shepherd! By nature of a princely air and noble countenance, with a graceful carriage of his body, he now looked a true prince! Jonathan gazed upon him with proud delight and admiration. Saul cried, not witting how truly he spoke:

"The young Bethlehemite looks as if he were born to a throne! Young man, I here appoint thee head over the royal guard which ever stand in my presence. Thou shalt be second only to Abner my general in my armies, and Joab shall be next to thee and serve thee. Thy father shall be a prince in Israel, and thy brethren lords in the land! and thou shalt have in treasure ten talents of silver and five of gold for thy own and their maintenance, even as I said! and thou shalt dwell with me in my own palace and stand next to my throne!"

HEBRON, AMBASSADOR'S CAMP.

I had written thus far, your majesty, the evening of the day on which the wonderful Hebrew, David of Bethlehem, slew the champion of Palestina, when a portion of the conquering army began to return across the plain, sounding their victorious trumpets from afar. I left my tent to hear the intelligence. These, however, were the plunderers, laden with spoil, the main body of the fighting men having continued the pursuit, thinking only of the slaughter and extermination of their enemies. It was noon next day before the warlike battalions began to reappear. All the latter part of the day the plain was filled with their exulting companies, each man laden with some trophy of victory. At their approach the lynxes, wolves, and wild dogs of the desert, with the carrion eagles and vultures which in clouds covered the plain, devouring the carcasses of the dead, scarcely moved aside, so absorbed were they by their voracity. Upon the carcass of the Philistine giant I had seen wild beasts and fierce, flesh-eating eagles feeding all day, and their savage howling over it as they fought with each other reached the camp. How truly herein were the words of the youthful Hebrew champion fulfilled!

On the third day the whole army of Saul returned from the slaughter of their foes, having pursued them to the gates of their sacred city, Ekron, and to Gath, and their utmost borders, slaying great numbers by the way, capturing all their tents, much treasure, and horses, and chariots, and prisoners, and great spoil. Saul received them with great honor, and the following day prepared to return to Hebron in triumphal march. It was a grand spectacle, the sight of the warlike hosts winding among the dark, wild mountains. They were five hours passing the height on which I stood to witness their passage. From all the garrisons, walled towns, citadels, and cities there came forth the people to welcome the victorious king and his army. Maidens with sounding timbrels and graceful dances welcomed the conquerors, and preceded them with songs of triumph.

As we approached the gates of Hebron the prince and David rode near Saul, by whose side I also had the honor of riding. The king looked more noble and majestic than I had ever seen him. His countenance had wholly lost its sadness and wore a proud expression, while his fine eyes were lighted up with pleasure. He enjoyed the happiness of the people, and gave himself up to the excitement of this hour of glory for himself and for his kingdom. David, with that becoming indifference to public notice which characterizes him, rode by the side of his friend, pleasantly conversing, and seemed to have forgotten that he had performed any unusual feat of valor. At times he would turn as his name with that of the king caught his ear, and blush and smile as the enthusiastic multitude, all of whom had heard of his prowess, closely crowded the way to catch a look at the youthful hero who had slain the champion. As we came under the towers of Hebron two bands of virgins from the city issued from the portal, one led by Michal the fair daughter of the king, and the other by Adora the beautiful "Princess of Tadmor," if I may so term her, your majesty.

As they drew near they played on tabrets, harps, and cymbals, and other instruments of music; and sang a song of welcome to the conquerors. Saul's eyes flashed with pleasure as he heard, while David looked at the lovely sight with unusual interest. Before we came to them they had formed on each side of the way, while other maidens strewed with fresh flowers the path along which Saul rode.

"Thou seest Michal, my sister, dear David!" said the prince in my hearing. "She knoweth not yet that she is thine, by thy valor won! What, does the color mount so confusedly to thy cheek and brow! Thou hast good claim to her, and I will be the first to join your hands when we reach the palace! Hark! They chant!"

We had now come up so near to the double line of virgins that we could distinguish their words. Thus they sang, one company answering the other alternately:

MICHAL, AND HER VIRGINS.

Saul hath slain his thousands,
Honor to the king—Israel's mighty lord!

ADORA, AND HER VIRGINS.

Saul hath slain his thousands,
And David his tens of thousands:
Slain the lord of Gath,
Slain the foe of God.
Honor be to David, and honor to the king,
Saul hath slain his thousands,
David his tens of thousands.

MICHAL.

Hail to the Lord's anointed,
Israel's mighty king!
Hail to Israel's champion,
David, loved of God.
Saul hath slain his thousands,
David slain his ten thousands.

ADORA.

Saul hath slain his thousands,
David his tens of thousands.

Here I perceived the king's brow blacken with a frown dark as night. In a displeased and angry voice, and in great wrath, he turned to Abner, who rode close at hand, and cried:

"They have ascribed unto David ten thousands, and to me

they have ascribed but thousands. What can he have more but the kingdom?"

From that moment he rode in silence, paying no heed to the salutations of the elders of the city and others who came to meet him. The cloud gathered over his soul; and when he alighted at the palace, his last glance on entering rested upon the youthful David with looks of hatred and implacable jealousy. The arrow had entered into his soul, and his happiness at the overthrow of the Philistines was destroyed by the sight of the honored victor receiving the homage and praise due to his courage.

That night the king slept not. He paced his chamber gloomily, and refused to be spoken to. At sunrise I visited him at the earnest request of Jonathan, who said all the elders and the council of the city with the priests would soon be assembled to do him honor; and he urged me to prevail upon the king to receive them. The guard at his door did not hesitate to admit me, but said, "He prophesieth, my lord prince." King Saul was addressing himself (when I entered) to empty space, in a tone of mingled anguish and wrath.

"Behold, and see if there be any sorrow like my sorrow, which is done unto me! Behold how the Lord hath afflicted me in the day of his fierce anger:

> "He prevaileth against me!
> He hath spread a net for my feet!
> He hath poured his vials on my head!
> He hath bound me with the yoke of my transgressions
> He hath made my strength to fail:
> He hath brought mine honor to the ground.
> He hath shamed me in the sight of my people;
> He hath given mine honor to another!
> All mine enemies have heard of my trouble;
> They are glad that thou hast done it!
> I am the man that hath seen affliction!
> By the rod of his wrath hath he smitten me!
> He hath led me into darkness, and not into light.
> He turns his hand against me all the day.
> He hath hedged me about: I cannot move:
> He hath put a chain upon me and bound me:
> Also, when I cry he shutteth out my prayer!
> He is as a bear and a lion lying in wait for me.
> He hath set me as a mark for his arrow.
> The arrows of his quiver have pierced my soul.
> I am a derision to my people. They make their songs of me:
> My strength and my hope is perished
> I lift my hands unto the Lord, and say to my God—
> I have transgressed and rebelled and thou forgivest not;
> Thou hast slain—thou hast not pitied.
> Thou hast covered thyself with anger,

Thou hast covered thyself with a cloud,
That my prayer should not pass through.
My warriors scorn me—as for my soldiers,
I am their music. All men hunt my steps,
I cannot go into the streets ! They talk of me :
The Lord has utterly rejected him—let his name perish—
Let his inheritance be turned to strangers—
His house to aliens."

"O king, live forever!" I cried, interrupting his prophesying, which was an appeal between a prayer and a complaint to
some invisible one.

He turned upon me:

"Is it thou, Prince of Assur? What wouldst thou?"

"To ask thee to meet the elders and council of this and
other cities, who desire to honor thee."

"Where is the shepherd, Jesse's son?" he asked fiercely.

"With Jonathan!"

"Aye! aye!" he responded sneeringly, "with the prince!
No, no! I give no audience to-day! I am ill! Where is this
harp player?"

"Dost thou mean the chief player of instruments?" I asked.

"No, David; he who once played before me, when they said
I was mad!"

"I will send him to your majesty," I answered.

"Do so—thou wilt befriend me, O Assyrian, if thou wilt bid
him come and bring his harp! Hark ye, my lord of Assur,"
and the king approached and whispered in my ear, in a low,
strange whisper, "tell him not I sent for him! The lad is
vain enough now, and mind Jonathan come not with him!
Bid him bring his harp and play before me!"

I looked in King Saul's face attentively, his manner and
tone were so singular. But he suddenly veiled all expression,
so that his looks were divested of all meaning. It was the art
of madness, so completely and suddenly to empty the eyes of
all intelligence. It seemed as if he sought to hide a thought
he feared I might read. But I then suspected nothing. I may
still do him injustice; as what subsequently occurred, O Belus,
may not have been premeditated, but only the impulse of the
moment; but I fear it was premeditated. I obeyed the king,
and David soon appeared in the king's presence. Neither he
nor Jonathan had heard the king's remark about the song of
the virgins, and had no suspicion he felt any malice or
jealousy.

I went in with David, and so also did Jonathan; and while the youth stood near the wall on the west side of the room playing a noble hymn, we remained not far from the entrance. The king sat upon the lower step of his throne, his face leaning upon his left hand. He did not raise his eyes when David entered, who, striking a few noble preluding notes, thus began:

> " O sing unto the Lord a new song,
> Sing unto the Lord all the whole earth.
> Declare his glory among the heathen,
> His wonders among all people.
> Honor and majesty are before him,
> Strength and beauty are in his sanctuary.
> O sing unto the Lord a new song,
> For he hath done marvelous things;
> *His* right hand and his holy arm
> Hath gotten him the victory.
> Sing unto the Lord with the harp,
> With the harp and the voice of a song."

At this instant, while the last glorious words were yet echoing through the hall in divinest melody, the king rose to his feet and cast with all his force a javelin, hitherto unseen in his hand, straight at the heart of the youthful player! The prince and I both uttered a cry of alarm, but David, whose eyes were upon the king, saw the act and stepping aside avoided the blow. The flying javelin, whizzing through the air, struck the wall close behind him and buried itself deep therein, vibrating like a leaf.

The prince rushed forward and caught his friend in his arms, and burst into tears.

"God has preserved you," he said. "But forgive my poor father."

"It is nothing," answered the young man, with a smile.

We at once drew him forth from the king's presence.

From this time Saul took no pains to conceal his jealousy and hatred of David. He saw that the Spirit of the Lord, as said Abner to me, was upon him; and probably foresaw in him the future prince of the people. The king, singularly, was sane from the moment he discharged the javelin; and went forth and received the deputations in his natural manner. The people, however, could talk only of David; and of the thousands who came from all the cities of Judea to congratulate Saul, their first inquiry was not for the king; but for David who slew the mighty Philistine of Gath! All this came to Saul's ears, and increased his gloomy displeasure at him. David behaved himself wisely and prudently. Saul dismissed him from his high command, and made him captain only of a thousand. He would, without doubt, have sent him away from his court if he had not feared the people, especially the army, who idolized their young hero. David tried to turn all the adulation from himself to the king, and in his whole conduct in a situation so trying proved himself wise, discreet, and worthy of all honor. But the more Saul saw of his wise and modest behavior, and that he did not commit himself to any imprudence or folly, the deeper his hostility became, and his dread of him increased.

CAMP, SOUTH OF HEBRON.

Your majesty will be gratified to learn that the overthrow of the army of the Philistines has opened the way to Egypt, and that I have already made one short march, having yesterday broken up my long encampment in the plain of Mamre, and passing round Hebron, pitched my camp a league south of it. This I have done in order to wait for a company of Jewish merchants who desire to embrace this opportunity afforded by my strong force to go down into Egypt to carry merchandise, and bring from thence the productions of the land of the Nile. King Saul has encouraged this traffic hitherto, but the late wars have put an end to it for some years. There is now, thanks to the valor of David, security of travel. At the request of Prince Jonathan I have consented to permit the seventy Hebrew merchants to go and return with me. To-morrow they will all be ready; and I know your majesty will be pleased to have me to do all that lies in my power to cultivate friendly relations with this singular people.

As I have some leisure this evening in my tent, I will devote it to an account of an interesting visit I paid, three days ago, to the tombs of the four kingly Patriarchs, Abraham, Isaac, Jacob, and Joseph, the founders and fathers of the Hebrew nation. Prince Jonathan and David accompanied me, or rather I went with them by the invitation of the former. Mounted upon horses, we rode a little while along the plain of Mamre until we came to the face of a rocky eminence, broken and picturesque in appearance, parts of it towering in gloomy grandeur. In advance of this cliff was a lower rock, before which was a massive house of stone many feet thick. It was venerable with age, and seemed to have been erected more for perpetuity than beauty of proportion. It was stern, massive, and solemn. Before its stone gate grew four majestic palm trees, each sacred to one of the patriarchs. The path to the entrance was broad and well trodden by the feet of the thousands who continually go to the place; for it is a reproach to a Hebrew to have lived to his fortieth year without having visited the tomb of the patriarchs of his race. There stood several old men, youths, and maidens about the portal, who with silent reverence gazed upon the gate; for no one can enter without permission of the king or High Priest.

We alighted, and leaving our horses in charge of the prince's armor-bearer, we approached the entrance. An old man, noble in aspect, opened the gate to the prince. We took torches and a guide, who was a Levite, whose office it was to show the sepulchers, as well as to keep trimmed a lamp which burned night and day over each of them.

The passage for the distance of a few cubits was artificial, inclosed with walls of stone, but soon joined the entrance of a cave, which was irregular and gently inclined. The surface of the rock was blackened with the smoke of the torches of pilgrims for nearly a thousand years; for Abraham has been buried there but little less than nine hundred years, Isaac about one hundred years later, and Jacob but thirty later. The bones of Joseph, having been detained in Egypt and in the wilderness one hundred and ninety years, were only placed here about four hundred and ninety years ago. Thus this cave is what we in Assyria would call the "House of the gods of the land." As I moved along the echoing passage under the everlasting rock, I felt the spirit of ages impressing my soul. Awe filled my mind at the idea of approaching the last "abodes of rest" of the mighty dead.

At length we came into a chamber of the rock. It was wide and large. The torches faintly revealed its size and form. At its extremity we saw a solitary lamp suspended by bronze chains from the irregular roof.

We removed our shoes from our feet, as we trod on holy ground, and reverently drew near. The silence which filled this cavern of the dead was profound. Neither of us spoke. The guide reverently led us first to a tomb on the left or west of the entrance, about seven feet long, of dark porphyry, and by the side of it another of smaller size; the lamp above shed its calm, soft light upon them,

"Who sleeps here?" I asked of the prince, who had often visited the sacred sepulchers.

"This is the tomb of Isaac," he said solemnly. "He died at the advanced age of one hundred and eighty years. You perceive his name graven upon the top in ancient Chaldaic characters. The tomb next to it, north, is that of the virtuous Rebecca, his wife. There they have reposed nearly seven hundred and fifty years. Their bodies are within stone coffins inclosed in these outer tombs."

From thence we passed westward along the cave, and through an opening in a thick wall, which led into a spacious and lofty chamber where two lamps faintly revealed a gigantic tomb beneath each of them. We drew reverently near, and stopped before the first one, which was of dark stone, five feet high and twelve in length—like the sepulcher of a giant. By the side of it was a tomb of equal size.

"This," said the prince, who courteously volunteered all the information I required, "is the mausoleum of the mighty patriarch Abraham—the monarch of our race! Sarah his wife lies in the tomb next to him, and here for nearly nine hundred years they have slept undisturbed! And here, tradition says, he will sleep until a descendant from his loins shall be king of the whole earth, and come hither and bid him rise and walk forth; when he will hear his voice, and rise from his sleep of death, and receive from this son the scepter and crown of all the kingdoms of the earth, and reign thereon forever."

"And dost thou, O prince," I asked, "have confidence in this prediction?"

"I know not, Arbaces," he answered. "I have already told you we are a nation of mysteries, and that we are but instruments working out some divine problem for God's glory and the benefit of mankind."

Now I stood for a few moments in silent meditation by the tomb of this potentate and father of a mighty people; and then followed our guide across the cave to a part of it where two more tombs, both larger in size than that of Abraham, and more elaborate in workmanship, and constructed of marble, met our view.

"Here is buried Jacob, the patriarch of our people and father of twelve nations," said the prince.

David gazed upon this sepulcher, as he had upon the others, with reverent contemplation. His aspect seemed elevated and ennobled by this vicinity with the mighty dead of his race. He spoke but once or twice, but his words were striking, and expressed the depth of his emotions; for this was the first time he had come to this spot so honored by his countrymen.

"And here is buried Leah?" he asked of his friend, pointing to the other vast tomb by its side.

"No," he answered; "here is buried Rachel, his best beloved wife. Leah is also buried in the cave where you see this lower tomb on the right of the patriarchs, and farther removed from it than Rachel's. It is sunken and out of repair; for though more of our tribes descended from Leah, yet Rachel's memory is more cherished and honored by the nation; perhaps, because she was more honored by the patriarch."

"Where," asked David, looking round, seeking to penetrate the gloom of the vast subterranean chamber, "was the brave and noble Joseph buried?"

"This way," said the Levite; and turning to the left he conducted us through a narrow opening in the south wall, partly rock, partly artificial, which was nine feet in thickness; and we found ourselves in a narrow apartment hewn partly out of the rock, and with a cavernous roof, lighted dimly by a single lamp of Egyptian form.

Here we beheld a tomb about eight feet long and four wide, purely Egyptian in its style, even with the winged sun sculptured upon its side, and the figure of Osiris on one end. Upon the top was written in Hebrew and in Egyptian characters:

"JOSEPH THE VIRTUOUS.
THE WISE—THE GREAT.
FRIEND OF GOD, AND GUARDIAN OF EGYPT."

"This is the tomb of the patriarch who was lord of Egypt," said the guide. "Within this outer tomb is a sarcophagus in which the embalmed body was brought up from Egypt. There are times in the heat of summer, when the cave is not so cool as now, when the subtle aroma of the spices with which he was embalmed fills the whole place!"

After lingering here some time and talking of Joseph, we returned through the main chamber of the cavern, visiting again each of the tombs of the immortal dead!

"Are any of the twelve patriarchs buried here?" I asked of the prince.

"None of them! They all lie buried in the land of Goshen in Egypt," he answered, "unless the tradition be true that Joseph sent the body of his brother Benjamin thither, when he was in power, for sepulcher. There are five other tombs in another and remoter part of this cave of Machpelah. One is said to be that of Benjamin, and another that of Judah, sent here by Joseph. The third is known to be that of Zobar, the father of Ephron, of whom Abraham bought this cave for a burying-place; and the fourth that of Heth, the first king of Canaan, a thousand years ago; and the fifth where Ephron was buried, he having reserved a burial place for himself here. It is a branch of the main cave, walled off from it and never visited in this day and generation."

Having at length emerged from these subterraneous sepulchral abodes of the majestic men of the past, we regained the chief outlet, and remounting our horses rode toward Hebron, which is at this day called "The Castle of Avraam" by the Canaanites. Here the patriarch once dwelt and held his power as king after he had conquered five heathen kings. In Salem, or Solima, twenty-four miles north of this, at the time reigned Melchisedek, a king whose name is spoken with veneration by all the Hebrews as the friend and ally of Abraham.

And this reminds me, your majesty, that I have not informed you of a visit I made to this ancient capital of the land in the days of Abraham. I have already written of the remarkable castle of the Jebusites which covers a rocky height south of the town of Solima, called, usually, Jebusolem from the castle which commands it. In this town of Salem there is an armory or temple of war in which all trophies taken by the Hebrews are kept. In Nineveh it would be called a temple of the "god of war." But the Hebrews recognize but one God, who governs, controls, and performs all things, who thunders in the skies, who sends forth lightning, who rides on the storms that lash the seas, who fights their battles, who ripens their harvests, who causes the sun and moon and stars to rise and set, who created not only the mountains, but the pebbles in the brooks, who made even the lily of the valley, and equally the eagle and the fly! This one idea of a supreme God, who condescends from the highest to the lowest, pervades all their religion, and is its foundation. When I said to the prince, one day as we were talking in my tent, that we Assyrians had higher ideas of a supreme God than to attribute the creation of flowers and singing birds to so majestic a Power, he replied: "That to an infinite Being there was no such thing as great or small! noble or mean! That He himself was the measure and standard of all things existing." He asked me who created the flowers according to our Oriental faith. I replied, "We believe there is a supreme Cause of all! that He was *not* created! for if there were a time *when there was no God*, there would *never have been* a God! and if there *never* had been a God there would be *now* no God! Therefore, if there is a God, He has always existed! We believe He created the heavens and the earth, and that his dwelling place is in the sun, which we honor as the temple, and throne, and visible presence of the Supreme. Hence our emblem of God is fire. We believe that He created man, because we are intelligent and reasoning beings as He must be himself; but we deny that He stooped to create the soulless brutes and meaner things; that he formed the mountains, but left the trees and plants thereon to lesser divinities; that He created the ocean, but not fountains: hence we have a deity to every fountain and to each lesser thing."

He heard me with great patience, and asked me if I would read the books of the sacred mysteries of their Uni-Deic faith. I have promised to do so, your majesty, and if I am convinced that there is but one God alone, I will not hesitate to change my faith. If there is but one God, I cannot but perceive that He is the mighty Deity who guides the destinies of the Hebrew people, as they assert; for two such mighty Powers could not exist in the universe. I can conceive of none superior, and if there were an equal in power they would destroy each other: that is, become One.

But to my visit to Salem. After David reached Hebron he was reminded by Jonathan that the trophies he had won should be conveyed to the temple of arms in Jerusalem, as the prince terms the name of the town. We, therefore, one morning rode thither, David bearing the head and sword (assisted by his three brethren), and others conveying the coat-of-mail, helmet of brass, greaves, and trousers of iron chains, flexible as woven cloth. We wound along the deep valley under the wall of the garrison of the Jebusites, who covered their battlements to behold the trophies.

"The day will come," said David, as we glanced at these ancient foes of his race, yet unconquered, though living at peace with the Hebrews, "when some brave king of Israel will drive these vultures from their rock, and plant above the fortress the standard of God! This Salem, and not Hebron, ought to be the capital of the kingdom!"

He seemed to speak as by inspiration! His eyes were bright and flashing, and his voice rung like a trumpet! We were all surprised; it was so unlike his usual manner, which was retiring and quiet. If, your majesty, the conquest be effected, I felt it would be by his arm when he shall become king! "And," I hear your majesty say to yourself, "and does my Arbaces believe in all this vaticination? Does he have faith in all that is told him of the future of this youth?"

I have, your majesty, I answer. He is yet young. Saul may live many years. But if you or I will watch his career, we shall yet, if we live, see him or hear of him as king of the Hebrews! If so, he will no doubt make Jerusalem the capital of his dominions. If he becomes king, with his valor, wisdom, prudence, sagacity, and friendship with his God, he will elevate this nation to the first place among warlike and powerful kingdoms.

After going round the steep rock of Sion, held by the Jebusites, we passed the base of a lofty hill, called Moriah, or the "far-seen top," on which, and its adjacent region, the chief part of the city is built, and where stands the armory. We were admitted on the north side by a gate strongly guarded, and received with shouts of a thousand troops which, under their captain, garrisoned the place to hold it against the Philistines and Jebusites. The armory was a strongly built edifice of Canaanitish architecture, having once been a temple of Baal, and then the palace of the king whom Joshua slew when he took the city. David's trophies were received by the keeper of the citadel, the sword and head being delivered with his own hand to the lord of the armory. He himself was treated with the greatest distinction, and Eliab, and Abinadab, and Shammah took great pains to make known aloud to the admiring soldiers and citizens that they were brothers to the hero!

Here we were shown the throne of Melchisedek, cut in the face of a rock over which was erected a mausoleum of stone. It bore no inscription. Of this king there is a tradition that he descended from the clouds when an infant, borne earthward by seven white doves, sustained by their united wings; that they laid him upon an altar of white marble at which a priest of Baal was offering incense; that the priest preserved and nourished him, but he was fed by the doves with olives and grapes, and so grew to manhood, when he taught the pagan priest the knowledge of the true God, and converted the whole people to the pure worship of heaven. He became king, priest, and prophet of the kingdom, and after ruling in wisdom and love for a long life, he drew near his end.

Then he comforted his subjects by promising to them another king from heaven, who should, after a brief reign, be slain by the evil powers of the earth, but revive, and establish a kingdom which should extend from the rising to the going down of the sun, of which Jerusalem should be the capital forever. Thus speaking, and when they expected to see him expire, there came seven bright angels to his couch, and lifting the majestic king upon their wings, communicated to his form the glorious illumination of their own splendor, and bore him out of sight into the heavens.

Therefore the empty stone-throne and the vacant cenotaph in remembrance of his reign!

I have written, your majesty, a long letter; but I desire to give you all the information I myself possess of this land and people, and I do not shrink from the labor of writing whatsoever I think will contribute to this end. I introduce into my letters no incidents merely for the sake of their interest, but because they in some way illustrate the past and the present of the Hebrews, and give you a knowledge of their manners, customs, and peculiarities as a nation.

I shall to-morrow proceed on my march toward Egypt, after three months' detention in the land of Judea. I hope to be in Egypt in twenty days' easy travel. I am on the road taken a thousand years ago by Abraham, by Jacob and his sons during the famine, by Joseph when he came up to bury his father Jacob, with a great retinue of Egyptian lords and men-at-arms. It is therefore a highway well known and full of interest.

I shall, early in the morning, after seeing my caravan well in motion, ride into Hebron to take my leave of the king, of the noble prince to whom I am greatly attached, of the valorous and wonderful David whom I love scarcely less, of the valiant Abner, Saul's general-in-chief, of the ambitious and fierce young Joab, who seems fit only for a man of war, and lastly not least, of the princess Michal, and Adora the beautiful and captivating daughter of Isrilid of Jericho.

I may write, your majesty, on the route, if a caravan should

meet us: otherwise I shall not send you another letter until
I reach Egypt. Once there, I trust I shall so succeed with the
important and agreeable mission your confidence in me has
intrusted to me, that I shall speedily return with the lovely
prize you are so anxious to possess.

With the prayer that the gods of your royal House may have
your majesty in their sacred keeping, I am, as ever,

Your faithful

ARBACES

LETTER IX.

BEERSHEBA, BORDERS OF IDUMEA.

YOUR MAJESTY:

I am to-night encamped by the " Well of the Oath," in a palm grove opposite the gate of this southern border-city of Judea. By this well, a thousand years ago, Abimelec, a king of Gerar, and Abraham, the father of the Hebrews, made a covenant of amity. Here at this fountain the ancient Chaldee used to lead to water his thousands of camels and tens of thousands of sheep. It is regarded as a sacred place by the Hebrews, who, with fine feeling, honor every place made historical by association with their " three great patriarchs."

The dark-walled town of Beersheba frowns down upon my encampment, and trom within it I hear the voices of singing women and the sound of the nebal and the harp, as if there were rejoicing going on in some happy home.

This place is twenty miles south of Hebron, and we have been since sunrise coming from a league this side of that city, where my last letter left me encamped. Therein I informed your majesty that I should march the following morning. At dawn, therefore, our tents were struck, and at sunrise the chief captain of the caravan had the whole body in motion. The seventy Hebrew merchants, mounted on mules and horses, joined in good time, and I soon had the satisfaction of seeing my people move southward. First went four hundred horsemen of my legion, then followed the two hundred camels laden with the bridal gifts, with their drivers, and after them the three hundred led Assyrian horses, save twenty of the handsomest I had presented to the king, two to the prince, and two to David. Behind these was the long train of four hundred mules laden with provisions and tent equipage, and the eighty wagons of armor as presents to the king. These were protected by two hundred armed horsemen who rode behind them. Now followed the two hundred chariots of war, with their charioteers, swordsmen, and beautifully caparisoned steeds two and three abreast, and behind them came three hundred horsemen of my legion as a rear guard. My guard of nobles had no particular place in the long procession, but kept near my person, as I sometimes would ride in the van, sometimes in the rear, and at other times in the center, or to the right or left over the plain! The seventy Hebrews merchants, with a motley company of others who attached themselves to the caravan for protection, took places in the column as suited their convenience. The whole line of march extended half a mile, and, seen from an elevation, had, with its gay colors and its shining steel, an imposing and brilliant, if not warlike appearance.

When I had seen it fairly on the highway I galloped at the head of my nobles back to Hebron to take leave of the king. I was received at the entrance of the house where he dwelt, while his palace was being finished, by the prince, whose face as he saluted me appeared so sad that I could not withhold saying:

"I fear, my lord prince, the king is again ill?"

"Far worse, Arbaces," he answered, with trembling accents. "He has again attempted the life of David! This morning he sent for him to play before him. He fearlessly and benevolently, for he is all goodness and love, obeyed. While he played, the king a second time launched a javelin at his head, his face being turned from him. It was not steadily thrown in the passion of the act, but passed close to his cheek, fanning it with its wind. David at once came to me, and said:

"'It is necessary that I should leave the king's presence forever! The sight of me increases his malady. It is no longer within the power of music to soothe him, as it was two years ago!'

"I could not, O Arbaces, gainsay his words. We embraced, and he was about to depart when the king my father suddenly stood before us! He extended his hand with one of those fine smiles which in his best days so often won the hearts of his people, and said:

"'Nay, go not away, son of Jesse! I meant not to slay thee! I will no more test thy courage with making thee a mark for my javelin. The mood is gone! How is it thou hast not asked my daughter yet? The order for the talents of gold and silver, at thy request, when thou refusedst them, I sent to thy venerable father! Wilt thou have my elder daughter, Merab, to wife,

young man, even as I promised the victor over Goliath of Gath?
I will give her to thee to wife according to my kingly oath on
the plain of Elah!'

"'Nay, your majesty, I am but a shepherd,' replied David
modestly; 'who am I that I should be son-in-law to the king?'

"Then said I to my father, O Arbaces, 'My eldest sister is
betrothed to Adriel of Meholath. If thou givest one of my
sisters to David, let it be Michal!'

"'What! doth he refuse Merab?' demanded the king fiercely,
striking his hand upon his sword. 'Let him take her and I
will give him five thousand men, and he shall go forth and
fight my battles!'

"Here Doeg, his armor-bearer, spoke aside to the king and
said, so that I could hear:

"'The youth loveth the younger and fairer one, my lord
king.'

"'Sayest thou?' answered my father. 'So much the better!
He shall have her! This news pleaseth me vastly, O Doeg! I
will give her to him, and she will snare him, and I will play
him into the hands of the Philistines. Let not mine hand be
upon the youth, but let the Philistines slay him!'

"Thus answered the king in the ear of his wily armor-
bearer," continued Jonathan, in relating the conversations and
events; "and turned to David, who had not overheard their
private discourse, and said:

"'If thou preferrest Michal, I will give thee her. Thou shalt
this day be my son-in-law in one of the twain. I desire no
dowry! All I ask on thy part is to bring me the heads of one
hundred Philistines.'

"At these words David, who would risk his life a hundred
times for love of Michal," added Prince Jonathan, "answered
the king, with his eyes bright with mingled love and valiancy:

"'The words of the lord, my king, please his servant well.
I will, O king, receive thy fair daughter on these conditions
thou hast named!'

"I at once saw, O Arbaces (for I conceal nothing from
thee)," said Prince Jonathan, "that my father hoped to cause
David to fall by the swords of the Philistines. Therefore I
said to him, 'O king, my friend David hath already won
Michal by the death of Goliath. Wherefore demand a second
trial?'

"'What!' cried my father; 'art thou leagued against me,

young man? Thou nourishest in thy bosom a ewe that will by and by show the teeth of a young wolf, and tear out thy heart.'

"Thus saying, my father strode away, leaning on Doeg, the crafty Edomite, and looking back with bitter envy upon David. You ask me, O Prince Arbaces, why I sorrow? My father seeks relentlessly his life. The brave young man has already departed, and taken with him one hundred men to invade the Philistine country. My tears and entreaties could not prevail. I have just seen from the walls his company disappear in the gorges of the hills over against the gate to Gath. What will become of my father? What will become of the kingdom? How will all this miserable condition of things end?" he added, in a paroxysm of mingled grief and shame.

Your majesty may perhaps regard it as singular that the prince should speak with me so freely about his father's conduct. But the condition of the king is the common talk of the land; and every new outbreak is fresh news for the curiosity of the people. Besides, the intimacy between Jonathan and myself, by our frequent intercourse, is become very close and confidential; and he speaks with me as freely as if I were a brother. I, therefore, expressed my deepest sympathy for him, and assured him that the young shepherd would ere many days return with the trophies of victory which were to win him his lovely bride.

I accompanied the prince into the house where his sister Merab, a tall, dark, stern-looking princess, was seated at a distaff surrounded by her maidens. She silently received my courteous homage to her presence; while Michal, gentle and beautiful, though now pale and anxious at David's departure on so dangerous an expedition, met me with friendly cordiality. She expressed her regret that I was to leave for Egypt, and said that she hoped that I should return this way with the fair daughter of its king, saying she had heard the loveliness of the maidens of the land of the Nile greatly commended.

While she was speaking Adora, the superb daughter of Isrilid, and at present guest of the king's daughters, appeared. She took my hand with great kindness, and expressed her sorrow that I was about to go away. For a moment I made no reply, I was so struck with her appearance. She was dressed most gorgeously in attire that wonderfully became her style of form and face. She wore a scarlet cap broidered with gold, confining her raven tresses. The shape and fashion of it was graceful and elegant beyond description. Her veil was thrown partly off from her face, revealing features of the most perfect outline, and eyes before the splendor and glory of which I dropped my own. A luxuriance of beauty, if I may so express myself, enveloped her. Every motion was a grace—every look a dangerous charm. I felt too that those noble eyes looked kindly upon me, and that my departure lent the sadness to the smile with which she greeted me.

After lingering half an hour in the society of these charming Hebrews, I took leave of them, I fear not readily to forget one of the two, my dear Belus.

Having taken leave of the brave and warlike young Joab, the splendid general Abner, and others, I sought the king to pay to his majesty my parting respects. I found him at his new palace superintending the construction of the throne room. Seated upon the just completed throne-chair of ivory inlaid with silver, he received me with stately courtesy, expressed the satisfaction he had received by my visit to his dominions, wished me a pleasant journey, and desired me, if I returned through his kingdom, to pay my respects to him and give him the news from the court of Egypt; which I promised to do. With dignified hospitality he accompanied me to the door of the palace, and I there took a second leave of this extraordinary man, kissing his hand and wishing him a long and happy reign. He replied only by a cold, strangely sounding laugh and turned away, his iron heel ringing as he crossed the paved hall, while I heard him repeating with muttered, fierce, mocking tones my last words: "Long and happy reign."

Alas, a mad king! Oh, what a calamity to a people, your majesty! With what greater chastisement could the gods afflict a nation? Prince Jonathan accompanied me half a league beyond the city gate, and embracing, we parted, my heart bleeding with the profoundest pity for the noble young prince, doomed to such a life of woe—to end with disinheritance from his rights as prince royal of Israel. His fine frank countenance has of late lost its cheerfulness, and a fixed sorrow seems to have impressed itself upon his princely features. What will the end be?

I overtook, after two hours' galloping, my caravan as they were resting for a space by a brook which crossed the highway. At the close of the day we reached this well of Abraham before the ancient walls of Beersheba. As I shall to-morrow, your majesty, enter the land of Idumea which lies south of Judea, I shall have little leisure for using my pen, as it is a dangerous land for strangers to traverse, even all the way to Egypt; and I shall have to be on the alert against foes, and keep up a strict war discipline in my camp. At this time, especially, the defeat of the great Philistine army has disengaged hordes of Idumean cavalry, which are prowling along all the borders and hovering over the roads to plunder caravans. My next letter, or the continuation of the present, may be written you from the land of the pyramids. Until then, your majesty,

Farewell.

ARBACES.

. . . .

The events connected with the embassy of Prince Arbaces to the court of the Pharaohs will herewith be narrated until he again resumes his pen to write, in person, to the King of Assyria.

After a journey of eighteen days, varied by occasional attacks from the bands of desert-warriors, who sought booty rather than battle, Arbaces reached the capital of Egypt. The imposing character of his retinue, the long procession of camels and wagons laden with treasure, the splendid appearance of his Assyrian bodyguard, and the nature of the mission which had brought him so far, created no little interest in the Egyptian court.

He was received by Pharaoh with great honor, and for several days banquets and fêtes were given in his honor, attended by all the princes, lords, viceroys, governors of Nomes, and generals of armies, while the most brilliant and beautiful ladies of the court graced the festal scenes with their presence. Above all her sex, superior in loveliness as well as in rank, was the charming princess, Zaila, the only daughter of the king.

At length Prince Arbaces in due courtly form presented the royal letter of King Belus to Pharaoh, asking the hand of his fair daughter. The king required seven days to consider the matter, and lay the business before his supreme council. The princess in the meanwhile was permitted to see Arbaces and ask him a thousand and one questions about the young king who had sought her hand in marriage. She was so pleased with the answers of the handsome ambassador, and he plead so eloquently for his royal master, that, unwittingly, he inspired the beautiful Egyptian with such love for himself that when the king, her father, came to her on the evening of the seventh day to say that by and with the advice of his ministers he had consented to the matrimonial alliance with Assyria through her marriage with its king, she answered him that she was very willing to marry the ambassador whom she had seen, but never the king she had not seen!

Now the princess was an only child, and her royal father loved her as the apple of his own eyes. He had never denied her the indulgence of a wish; nay, studied daily to anticipate her least possible desires, and had even proclaimed, only a few days before the arrival of Arbaces, that he would confer a gold ring, a robe of state, and a post of honor on whomsoever would discover in the princess a want which his love and pride had not already provided for! A beggar, at length, who had sat for years by the pedestal of the statue of Osiris before his palace gate, came and said:

"Live forever, O king! brother of the sun and lord of the whole earth. Thou hast made proclamation that whosoever shall discover anything the Princess Zaila yet needeth which thou hast not thought of for her, thou wilt place a ring of gold upon his finger, invest him with a robe of state, and elevate him to a place of honor! I, O son of Osiris, have come humbly to claim these three honors. The Princess Zaila is in want of a husband, which thou hast not provided for her!"

Upon this the king, greatly pleased at the wit of the beggar, acknowledged that he was in the right, and rewarded him with the three honors according to his royal promise.

When the princess heard of the affair she blushed and said, laughingly, to her maidens: "The beggar has more wisdom than Pharaoh, the king!"

This speech was taken to the ears of her father, who presently swore by the head of Osiris that he would marry her to the first prince that came into his dominions; for, by the laws of Egypt, she could not marry a subject of the crown!

Now only a week elapsed after this when arrived our Assyrian ambassador with his proposition from the king of Nineveh for the hand of the lovely princess! Her father was so long, however, in making up his mind among his venerable counselors, that he gave the lady in the interval an opportunity, as we have seen, of losing her heart irrevocably to Arbaces. When, therefore, she answered her royal father that she would marry the prince ambassador he looked greatly perplexed,

"Nay," said she, "didst thou not swear by Osiris, dear father, that you would marry me to the first prince who came into thy dominions?"

"But he came as a messenger from his powerful king," answered Pharaoh. "When the royal master asks thy hand, wilt thou prefer the servant?"

"He is a prince in his own land! said not the King Belus in his letter so, and he calleth him his cousin!" answered the maiden. "I cannot think of marrying a person I never saw! He may be jealous, blind, ugly, and of a wicked disposition! No, dear father, I will marry the noble-looking Arbaces! He is the handsomest prince in the world! Then he is so good of heart! He plead so warmly for his king! While he thought he was gradually winning me for his master, I was only thinking of the ambassador. 'Surely,' I said, 'one who can love and defend the cause of his king so well must make a loving and faithful husband.' I will marry him instead of his king, were Belus as splendid as Horus and beautiful as Isis!"

Pharaoh represented to his willful daughter the advantages of an alliance with Assyria, that eventually, perhaps, Egypt might govern both nations, as Babylon and Nineveh by intermarriages had come under one crown, but all in vain. The maiden's heart had gone out to Arbaces, and at length the king yielded to this argument advanced by her:

"Let my hand, O my father, be given to Prince Arbaces! You have no son! At your death, if you will previously adopt him, he will succeed you, and we shall reign king and queen of Egypt! This will be a great deal pleasanter than being queen of Assyria with Belus its king! Thus, dear father, you can keep me at home (and you know it would break your heart for me to go to the ends of the earth into Assyria, and perhaps never see me any more), and I shall be happy, and you will have a son-in-law to succeed you instead of your cruel and envious nephew, Menesis, who is only waiting for your crown; and, dearest of fathers," she continued, seeing he was fast yielding, "this horrid King Belus only wishes me to be his wife, hoping when you are no more to claim the crown of Egypt in right of his wife; for he must know how the deformed and cruel Menesis is feared and hated of the Egyptians, and how gladly would they exchange his yoke for that of the husband of their princess."

Pharaoh resisted no longer. The princess had conquered.

She threw her white arms about his neck and thanked him in the most affectionate and charming manner, so that when he left her he was ready to take the head off of Arbaces if he should refuse to marry his daughter!

The young ambassador was not immediately informed of the honor which was in store for him. For two months the princess almost daily gave him audience, or invited him to escort her abroad, and sought by every art and device of maiden archery to pierce his heart. To the last she saw with mingled grief and angry pride that he plead only for his king, that all her looks, and attentions, and smiles of pleasure and of love he unselfishly interpreted in favor of his master. How little the faithful and ingenuous young ambassador suspected that the warmth and glow of feeling his words and presence ever enkindled were wholly on his own account, may be seen from the following extract of a letter to King Belus, written two months and a half after his arrival in Egypt:

COURT OF PHARAOH, CITY OF MEMPHIS.

This unlooked-for and unusual delay, your majesty, in accepting thy royal nuptial gifts, and in giving me a final answer, I am at a loss to comprehend, as I am satisfied by daily audience with this charming princess that she is deeply interested in you. All my ardent descriptions of your person and eulogiums upon your heart and character have captivated her imagination; and I never discourse of you that her eyes do not beam with the splendors of the torch of love, while her sighs and virgin emotion betray the impassioned ardor of her attachment to your majesty. What a prize shall I have the honor of presenting to you, O Belus! Such personal beauty as she possesses is seldom met with! Besides, she is endowed with the most delicate wit, mirth, intelligence, and wonderful grace of speech and manner. No woman I have seen, save, with your majesty's permission, Adora of Isrilid, can compare with her in that nameless fascination which so often captivates and bewilders the strongest masculine minds.

So far as the grace of courtly forms will permit, I have urged the king to name the day when, as your majesty's proxy, I shall have the honor to receive the fair Zaila's hand; but Pharaoh hitherto has always referred me, with a smile, to the princess! I have not been rude or bold enough yet to press her, in so delicate a matter, for her answer, but unless in a few days I receive some definite response to your majesty's suit I shall firmly require a decision on the part of the king. The four months I intended to be absent from Assyria are rapidly expiring in my delay here. In the meanwhile I have been royally entertained. Pharaoh every day distinguishes me by some new honor! He has had chariot-races, maneuvers of his Nile fleet, processions and feasts, reviews of his armies, and gorgeous entertainments for me; and no court in the world can exceed in magnificence these exhibitions. Your majesty in person could not be received and entertained with more kingly attentions than your humble ambassador. Everything, therefore, promises a favorable issue, if not a speedy one, to my important mission!

I will in the interim here give your majesty an extract from a letter which reached me yesterday by a caravan from Syria which passed through Judea on its way hither. It is written by the amiable and excellent Prince Jonathan, who, after expressing a doubt whether his epistle will find me in Egypt, and wishing the happiest success to my embassy, goes on to say as follows:

"Your absence, dear Arbaces, has been deeply felt by me, and by all your friends. You remained with us long enough to show me how necessary your society and friendship are to my happiness. My sister Michal has you in kindly remembrance, and the elegant Adora, now returned to her father's house in Jericho, 1 am sure, will not soon forget you. My dear, unhappy father has spoken of you but once. Shall I, dear friend, without being thought to be unfilial, tell you in what manner? But to show you how his mind still is, I will repeat his words. He said:

"'He has gone to Pharaoh. He will tell the proud Egyptian what a mad, God-accursed king he has left in Judea, with a war upon his hand and a shepherd stripling putting him to open shame and public disgrace by his deeds of valor. He will hint to Pharaoh that my kingdom will now fall an easy prey to the Egyptian armies! By the gods of Moab! had I thought of all this, the Assyrian should not have left my borders, hoof nor sandal!'

"Thus you see, dear Arbaces, my father's malady changes not! Since the death of Goliath he is more gloomy in his mind, more dangerous to others than ever! The evil spirit, if such it be, has settled upon his soul forever. There is now no gleam of sunshine, no kind word, no pleasant look, though it were but for a passing moment! Do I speak of him too plainly? But it is that I feel the need of, and know that I shall have, your kind sympathy!

"You will be interested to hear of the result of my beloved and brave David's foray into the fastnesses of the Philistine country. On the evening of the second day he drew near the gates of Ekron, having concealed his one hundred men-at-arms in a wood, and being challenged from the walls he answered that he came after one hundred heads of the Philistines! By the captain of the guard stood Malic, the armor-bearer of Goliath, who at once knew David, and hastened to the lord of the city, and told him 'David, the slinger and champion who slew my master, standeth over against the gate and challengeth all the garrison!'

"When the governor looked from his battlements and saw only a young man in armor standing alone, he said with contempt:

"'Is it by such a stripling the lord of Gath was overthrown? I will go down and take his pretty head and hang it above my gate.'

"The tall Philistine lord then issued from his portal and advanced sword in hand to slay David, when he discharged a spear and transfixed his heart, so that he fell dead. Thereupon David ran and smote off his head, and lifting it up as a signal, his one hundred men appeared and followed him sword in hand into the gate which the Philistine lord had left wide open, with the portcullis up and the drawbridge down. Taken by surprise at the death of their chief captain, and at the sudden rushing in of the Hebrews, the soldiers which kept the gate fled. David and his hundred men pursued them from street to street, slaying and beheading all who opposed them; until each man in his company held two Philistine heads in his hand. Not until then did David give the word to stop the battle, when he left the city without a wound either on his own body or on those of his followers. The next evening he re-appeared with his trophies before Hebron, and entering the port of the city, the gory band presented itself before Saul with David at their head; and as each man laid his double burden at the king's door the son of Jesse said:

"'Behold, O king, twice the tale of the price of thy daughter's hand! I now claim the maiden as my wife!'

"The brow of my father grew black! Alas, I fear he had hoped the Philistines would that day have had the young hero's head spiked above their highest gate! He heard, too, the murmurs of applause from the people. He felt all this was against him. But he had too much kingly honor, with all his hatred of David, to deny his given word! for, with all my father's strange conduct, he has never lost a certain native nobility of soul, which in earlier years made him worthy to be the king of a brave and free people. He said to David, 'Follow me!'

"Leading him into the house and calling for Michal, who had just heard of David's success, and was flying half timidly, half joyfully, to hide herself in her own chamber, he took her by the hand and said to David as he placed it in his:

"'She is thy wife! Thou hast valiantly won her! Let not men say Saul hath denied his oath!'

"A few days afterward the nuptials were celebrated, not with any festivities, but quietly. The new palace had been the day before taken possession of by the king and his whole household, and David was given apartments therein; and the next day receiving from my father a command of two thousand men, became a resident of Hebron, and daily we were happy in each other's society.

"The week following the marriage of David the Philistines grew brave enough to invade the land with a force of four thousand men, and even menaced Bethlehem. They were emboldened to this because they were aware our Hebrew laws enjoin that a newly-married man be not sent to the wars for one year after his marriage. The prowess of David alone had, without question, hitherto kept them back. The twentieth day after his nuptials news came that a company of the Philistines had carried off the flock of Jesse his father, and slain one of his brothers.

"'Hearest thou this war news?' cried the king, in a tone, I fear, of exultation, entering David's room, where he sat singing a sweet hymn of his own composition to his young wife and myself. 'But what is it to thee, that art tied to thy wife's distaff for a twelvemonth? Why should I talk to a bridegroom of arms and war? Play thy harp, boy, and let the men of Ekron in revenge burn thy father's house, slay thy brother, and bear off his flocks as spoil!'

"'What is it thou sayest, O king!' cried David, letting his harp fall, and starting to his feet.

"'What I have said!' answered my father, with a cold tone of voice; 'but it concerns not thee! Go on with thy harping and psaltering, and stay at home and please thy young wife!'

"That very hour David tore himself from the arms of his bride, and at the head of his two thousand men pursued the Philistines, who were leisurely retiring with their booty. He came up with them, and attacked them with terrible vengeance, slew nearly every man of the four thousand men, recovered his flocks, and retook all their captives and spoil, with which, on the third day, he returned to Bethlehem, the inhabitants of which received him with open arms and unbounded joy. All this, my dear Arbaces, went against my poor father, and since the news of the victory, and these fresh laurels won by the young bridegroom, he has shut himself in his inner chamber, and allows no one but Doeg his Edomite armor-bearer, a wily and unprincipled sycophant to all the king's humors, to come into his presence.

"Thus affairs remain, my dear Arbaces. If I have been too open and undisguised in my expressions about my royal father, attribute it not to want of veneration for him who gave me being, and who is the anointed of God, but to perfect confidence in your sympathy, and to a feeling of relief in being able to speak of my sorrows to one who can appreciate my position, administer to me wise counsel, and strengthen my heart with his consolations.

"By a caravan from Damascus, that is to-night encamped in the plain of Mamre, and leaves in a few days, I shall send this epistle. Michal, my sister, desires to be remembered to Prince Arbaces, whom she greatly esteems as the friend of David and Jonathan, as well as for his own virtues. I will not seal up this letter until the day the caravan leaves, as I may desire to add a few lines more, should anything of sufficient interest to narrate to you, transpire."

Thus far, O Belus, continued Arbaces, the letter of the Hebrew prince, when another leaf of parchment folded within it drew my attention. It was closely written over in a bold, handsome script, which I recognized instantly to be the writing of Heleph, the brave and intelligent armor-bearer of the prince. I copy here, your majesty, what was recorded therein by his ready pen; for being the son of a Levite mother, he had, before taking up the profession of arms, assisted his maternal uncle in transcribing the sacred records of his people. This

Heleph I have before spoken of, in my account of the bold attack on the Philistine garrison. He is much older than his young lord, and holds, as it were, a paternal protection over him, being in battle his defender, in peace his friend, and at all times his sagacious counselor. His parchment begins thus:

"To my lord, Arbaces, Prince of Nineveh, Heleph the armorbearer:

"My lord will pardon his servant for his boldness in presuming to take up his pen to write to my lord; but my dear master Jonathan, after having written the foregoing epistle, and before he could seal it up, was suddenly called from Hebron. As he left he gave into my hands his letter to you, saying that I might add in it that he had not time to seal it with his own signet, and affix his superscription, and commanded me to bind it up and put his seal thereto, and give it in charge to the chief captain of the Syrian caravan for you. My lord will therefore understand why the prince, my master's name is wanting over the seal, albeit thou didst behold it at the commencement of the epistle. Will my lord now pardon me, if his servant makes known to him the events which, since the Prince Jonathan terminated his letter, have taken place, and which have caused him to leave the city so suddenly? for I know how deep is the interest felt by my lord of Assur in all that concerns my dear master and his friend, the valiant David, son-in-law to the king.

"Three days ago, on the day my master ended his letter, the king sent for him to appear presently before him. For several days my lord, the king, had kept his apartment, and by the windows which looked toward the sepulchers of Machpelah he would stand for hours gloomily gazing upon the tombs, and speaking to no man but the vile Doeg, his armor-bearer; who, by maliciously bearing every idle and wicked tale to his ears, greatly increases his malady, and arms him more and more bitterly against those about him. It was Doeg who told him what Jonathan and all others would have had kept from him, that is, the honors that were paid David at Bethlehem. When my noble young master entered the king's presence, modestly and humbly, the king, his father, said to him, while I stood by, for I was afraid to trust my lord in the presence of his father alone, knowing how he felt so sorely displeased at him because he loved David:

"'Who is this with thee? For my sight of late sorely fail-eth me!'

"'It is Heleph, my faithful armor-bearer,' answered my master.

"'*Faithful!*' repeated the king angrily, striking the javelin he held in his hand against the stone floor; for when he received us he was walking to and fro in the paved corridor that opens from his private chamber into his gardens. Doeg the Edomite was set down not far off upon a bench, burnishing his helmet as indifferently as if he were not in the presence of his king. '*Who* is faithful? Even a man's own children are traitors—who shall call a servant faithful? I trust no man but' —and here he glanced toward the gigantic Edomite—'Doeg! *He* would do my bidding were I to command him to drag the High Priest Ahimelech from the horns of the high altar and slay him at its base! Wouldst not, man?'

"'Thou hast only to try me, by giving the command, O king,' answered the armor-bearer, with a dark smile; not even looking up from his pastime.

"'Where is thy bosom friend and brother-in-law?' now demanded the king of Jonathan. 'He putteth airs on himself in receiving honors in my own dominions. I dare to say these base lords of Bethlehem sang the old song to him: "Saul has slain his thousands, and David his tens of thousands." This young shepherd, who has come into alliance with my royal house, will next step into my throne. This son of Jesse is a traitor! He shall die! I have sworn it by the oath of God! 'I have sent for thee to seize him and slay him for me! Thy obedience will prove whether thou lovest him or me the more! Take thy armor-bearer and go forth and slay him, though he were in his bed asleep by the side of his bride, my daughter!'

"The prince at first made no reply. He looked into his father's fierce eyes, and plainly saw that they meant certain death to his friend. At length he said:

"'Let the king remember justice and clemency, and not meditate this great sin against David, who hath not sinned against thee; but whose works have ever been for the king's good, and the glory of his kingdom.'

"'Plead not for him!' answered Saul, in a voice of rage. 'Doeg my armor-bearer will obey me; but I have sworn *thy* hand shall kill thy friend as proof thou lovest me more than him. By one or the other he dieth ere to-morrow's sun.'

"The prir ce sorrowfully departed from the king's presence and hastened to his friend, whom he found discoursing with Abiathar the son of the acting High Priest of Nob, Ahimelech, who had come to be present at the feast of the New Moon, and offer sacrifice for the king and royal household before the feast. By the advice of Jonathan David immediately went out of the city and remained concealed in the house of a friend until he should hear from the prince, who resolved not to cease pleading for the life of David with his father. The zeal, courage, and eloquence of his appeals for his friend softened the king, and before Jonathan left him Saul revoked the order which he had given to Doeg and others to find and slay David, and made an oath to the prince in these solemn words: 'As the Lord liveth he shall not be slain!'

"The prince with great joy hastened first to his sister, David's young bride, and made known to her his unexpected success, filling her heart with joy, and then went forth to where his friend waited to hear from him, and brought him back to the city, and openly before Doeg and others conducted him into the presence of the king, who received him with words of favor and bade him, as heretofore, go in and out before him without fear.

"The morning after this happy reconciliation rumor came to the gates that three thousand Philistines had marched out of their country and were laying siege to the king's granaries at Gedor. David, desirous of manifesting his gratitude to the king, at once marched out to war with the two thousand men over which he was captain; and this morning news has reached us that he has overthrown them and is driving them back to their own land with great slaughter.

"Jonathan accompanied David in this expedition, my lord Arbaces, and it was at his departure he intrusted to me his letter to seal and send to your highness."

"SIX DAYS AFTER THE ABOVE WRITING.

"My lord Arbaces is hereby informed that the sickness of the captain of the caravan has detained it a week longer, and I have, therefore, time to add that the conquering son of Jesse returned four days ago from the war against his foes; but, in order not to awaken the king's jealousy, he came privately into the city and sought his house. The same night Saul sent for him to play a hymn of victory before him. The instant, my lord, I entered, for I followed him, I perceived by the peculiar expression in the king's eyes that the evil spirit from the Lord was upon him. David accompanied himself upon the harp, and thus sang before him:

> " ' O give thanks unto the God of gods :
> For his mercy endureth forever:
> O give thanks unto the Lord of lords :
> For his mercy endureth forever :
> To him who smote great kings :
> For his mercy endureth forever:
> To him who slayeth our enemies :
> For his mercy endureth forever.'

" ' Then let the mercy of the God of gods save thee, thou thorn in my side—shadow upon my path!' shouted the king; and with the rapidity of lightning he launched a spear from his hand. It shivered in the wall, and David fled the presence, followed by the indignant Jonathan. In a moment the voice of the king was roaring through the palace, calling on his guards to pursue and slay David.

" A dart sent after him by Doeg was caught upon my shield, and I covered the escape of the noble young man not without great difficulty. The king dispatched swift messengers to the city gates to detain him, and forbade anyone harboring him in all the city on pain of death. Jonathan was familiar with the avenues of the new palace, and by crossing the terrace and descending to the garden he succeeded in gaining a secret place for David, where we remained hidden until the king had searched his house; after which we secretly went thither and left him in temporary safety. Thence the prince went and prepared fleet horses outside of the walls, and that night Michal let David through the window upon the wall to the moat beneath. There Jonathan met, and silently embracing him, they rode together across the plain of Mamre, when the two friends parting, one proceeded on to his venerable teacher and friend, Samuel the Seer, for protection and counsel, while the other hastened back to the city before he should be missed by the king: who, finding that he could not accomplish David's death by craft, hath thrown off all dissimulation and openly and publicly commands his son and his whole court to destroy him as a traitor to his throne; substituting for the veil of private murder the cloak of a public execution. Whether he swore deceitfully, my lord Arbaces, when he made oath not to slay David, or whether in his madness he held no responsibility for his words and acts, is not clear. The more services the noble youth did his country, so much the more did King Saul's envy and hatred increase against him.

"I had remained in the city to assist my master to return into the palace by the window from which his friend had been let down. It was now midnight! Jonathan, after gently comforting his weeping sister, and assuring her that God would protect her husband, and that Samuel, the prophet, would gladly give him shelter, took his departure from her chamber. We had not been many minutes gone away when Saul, who believed David to be in the city, and concealed by his wife, suddenly sent an officer with a guard to surround the wing of the palace where she abode in order to surprise him. Michal, to gain time for her husband's flight, did not deny but that he was there. Before admitting the king's captain she placed on the couch David's cuirass and shirt-of-mail, and apparel arrayed like the image of a person, placed a pillow to elevate it at the head, and spread over the whole a coverlid, so that it had the appearance of a man asleep in bed, with his head and face covered.

"'See,' said she, 'is he not sick? Let him die quietly in his bed! Tell this to the king and see if he will do more!'

"But the king, on hearing it, cried in a rage:

"'He feigns sickness! But ill or well, were I sure, if left alone, he would die before sunrise, I would not spare my vengeance! Go bring him to me, bed and all, that I may slay him with my javelin!'

"Doeg hastened with the captain and men-at-arms to obey the king, and when they had reached the chamber Michal had hid herself; but Doeg carefully approached the couch, his sword held in hand (for he feared the valiant youth, although sick and in bed), and with a cry of savage joy threw back the coverlid! Lo, instead of beholding the brave son of Jesse, they were mocked by the sight of the image with which the king's daughter had deceived them. Without doubt the young and devoted wife would have been slain by the wrathful Edomite on the spot had she been exposed to his fury. When he made this discovery Saul was not long kept ignorant of the deception. Kindling with anger he hastened to her room, and when he beheld the cheat which her love had conceived to aid her husband's escape, he said to her:

"'O woman, subtle daughter of a rebellious wife! Thou

hast all thy mother's craft and guile in thy heart! Why hast thou deceived me thus! I had hoped the wife would have forgotten herself in the daughter when her husband proves mine enemy!'

"'He is not thine enemy, O king,' she answered firmly. 'He never offended thee! He has always studied to please thee! Thou didst once applaud him! Thou didst honor him greatly when he slew Goliath and delivered thereby thy whole realm out of the hand of thine enemies!'

"At this moment, my lord, Jonathan, who had heard what was taking place, came in and said:

"'My sister speaks truly, O my father! What unjust action canst thou charge against David, son of Jesse, that thou thus pursuest him to the death like a hunted deer—a man who hath delivered our nation from the derision and reproach which, for forty days, they endured from the champion of Gath, and who alone had courage enough to meet and destroy him? And after that, in order to receive my sister in marriage, although justly his reward for his valor, at thy command he brought twice one hundred heads of the Philistines and laid them at thy feet! a man who has ever been courteous, humble, and prudent before thee, and ever ready to go forth to meet the enemy which he never has once failed to overthrow! Wilt thou make a widow of this thy daughter, just made a bride by thine own gift of her hand to the noble hero of God whom thou wouldst now slay? Do not mischief to one who has done us the greatest kindness. Show, O king, a more considerate, generous, and merciful disposition toward him. Thinkest thou his brave but yet tender heart does not feel thy displeasure? What has he not done for thee, O my father? When the spirit of evil and malicious demons have seized upon thee, his wonderful skill in music drove them from thee, and restored peace and repose to thy torn and stormy soul!'

"Saul listened unmoved by this address, which, or similar ones, had aforetime moved him to swear David should not be slain. But now he gave no ear to his son. He answered him not by look or word, but turning to his daughter said:

"'Thou art my enemy, O woman! I believed when I gave thee to him thou wouldst have been a snare to him!'

"'I deceived thee, therefore, to give him time to fly far from danger,' she answered. 'I knew and told him if the sun when it rises should find him in Hebron, it will be the last time he would see it rise; for,' said I, 'if my father find thee here, thou art a dead man! So I aided his escape, as became a wife, and then prayed God to lengthen the night for his sake!'

"'*Thou* deservest also to die!' said the king.

" Nay, forgive me, my father!' she cried, with touching earnestness. 'I cannot believe thou wouldst rather have thy once dearly loved daughter, hardly a month married, widowed, than that thy son-in-law should escape death!'

"'Go! Thou hast thy life,' he gloomily answered, and left her to return to his own chamber.

" By sunrise the morning after his escape, the persecuted yet innocent fugitive was safe in Ramah, the ancient abode of the Judges, where Samuel dwelt. The prophet, being early walking by the walls, met him near the gate of the city, and received him with such warmth of affection and pride that David felt he had still a powerful friend in the 'Friend of God,' and he was thereby strengthened in heart and spirit. Without reserve he told Samuel all that Saul had done, the snares he had craftily laid for his destruction, and his frequent attempts in person to slay him, while he was unarmed playing before him upon the harp.

" When the venerable Seer had heard his touching narrative, he embraced his young disciple, and assured him of his protection. Samuel then rose up, entered the gate of the city, and went with him to the old palace of Naioth which is in Ramah, the place in which the prophet dwelt, and where he oversees the School of the Prophets. From thence David, by one of the youthful prophets, Nathan, sent secretly to Michal news of his safety. The king also heard the same evening that his son-in-law had escaped to Ramah, and that Samuel had sheltered him in his palace.

" This information filled the king with indignation and fierce resentment against Samuel.

"'Dare Samuel of Ramah beard me thus?' he cried. 'Hath he not wronged me already, till I am mad with my grief and troubles? Let an armed company go to Ramah and seize David, though the Seer himself hold him back by his girdle!'

" When they came into Ramah and stood before the gate of the House Naioth, they were admitted into the Hall of Praise, where they beheld Samuel with David by his side, and the seventy young prophets with their seven teachers, all with harps, and nebals, and cymbals, and dulcimers, and with voices

engaged in singing and playing before the Lord; Samuel himself sublimely prophesying, and the singers answering with
their voices. When the king's messengers saw this, they were
seized with a sudden inspiration, and throwing down their
swords and spears they caught up sackbut and viol, and joined
in the loud chants of divine praise. These men at length returned to the king and said: 'That the Spirit of God had come
upon them, and they had no power to take David, but on the
contrary they could not but join him in his hymns to God, and
leave him at peace.' The king sent other messengers, who were
similarly affected and returned to him. A third time, yesterday, he sent others, led by Doeg, all fierce and cruel men, and
when these came in the presence of the Seer and of David, instead of arresting him, they commenced dancing to a sweet
melody which he at the time was playing upon the harp, striking their swords against their bucklers and making the Hall of
Praise ring with the fall of their iron-shod feet. At his will
the young psalmist moved them by his skill; now they would
move slowly at his slow measure; now he would strike his harp
with quick strokes, and compel them, unable to resist the power
he mysteriously had over them, to fly along in dizzy circles
around him, wildly and violently agitated and foaming at the
mouth, and shouting as if demoniacally possessed. At length,
when they were utterly exhausted, he released them from this
spell by ceasing to play, when they reeled from the hall like
men drunken with wine, and made their way to Hebron to report to Saul how the harp of David had made them mad, and
compelled them to prophesy like demoniacs. When Saul heard
this he turned pale with anger, and said: 'I myself will go
to Ramah and take him! Saul shall not be found among the
prophets, let the proverb say what it may!'

"The same day he left Hebron with five hundred mounted
men of his bodyguard at his back, and hastened to Ramah.
He rode all night, and at daybreak came to the well of Sechu
by the twelve oaks, and there heard that Samuel and David
had gone from Ramah. But while he was trying to learn the
truth of the report, there came to the well a water-carrier, who
said, 'Lo! Samuel and David are still at Naioth in Ramah!'

"Then the king rode swiftly to the city, which he entered in
haste, lest David should escape him. Ere he drew near the
house of Naioth, or ever Samuel beheld him, he dismounted,
and all at once began to act like a man suddenly become de-

moniac. In a loud voice he called upon Dagon and Baal, the gods of the Philistines, after their manner, and seemed all at once to have become a pagan priest before his own people! His madness had never taken this form before, and filled them with horror. Upon reaching the house of Samuel he beheld the Seer standing on the balcony with the youthful David by his side. The venerable prophet did not speak to him, but his brow was stern with displeasure mingled with pity. Saul fiercely called out to David by the gods of the Philistines to come down and deliver himself into his hand. But David, at a sign from the prophet, struck his harp. Immediately the insane monarch began a heathenish dance before the house, to the shame of all Israel! As he danced he prophesied like the prophets of Baal, not like the prophets of God. As David played on, the wild impulses of his limbs and the extravagant ecstacies of his manner increased, so that it seemed as if the evil demon, who possesses him since he was forsaken of God, and which the divine harp of David once drove from him, had now by the same harp been summoned to enter into him; and not only to punish him for his intentions against his innocent son-in-law, but to expose him to the derision of all who saw him or heard of his shameless performances; for he had not danced long ere in his frenzy he flung down his helmet, divested himself of his cuirass and greaves, then stripped off his tunic, rent his royal robe, and cast it to the ground and trampled upon it; and so continued to deprive himself of all his clothing, until there alone remained his woolen under-garments. In this indecent undress he continued to dance and prophesy to the gods, until exhausted he sunk to the ground, and lay there wallowing and foaming like a wild beast of the desert.

"It was a fearful spectacle, O Prince Arbaces! All men saw in it the judgments of God; for His real prophets, when under inspiration, were never torn by such contortions and wild agitations of the body; but calmly and with dignity pronounced their sublime vaticinations to the people. Thus all men perceived that he was inspired by a demoniacal spirit, such as possessed the false prophets of Baal and Ashtaroth; and they turned from him with horror and fear; all save Doeg the Edomite, who remained by him and kept watch over him all that night; for the degraded and lost king lay there on the ground the whole day and night in a trance, and no man approached him, but all stood aloof awaiting the issue with awe and shame. It is said that when Saul had thrown off his kingly robe to the ground, Samuel commanded David to go down and take it out of the dust; and that he did so, throwing it across his arm as he bore it to the prophet. This is said by our wise men to foreshadow the reign of David on the throne of Israel; for there is a tradition that if a king let fall his royal robe, whosoever taketh it up will, by and by, lawfully wear it. All eyes are therefore turned toward David with new interest.

"While the king lay thus in the deep trance which followed his violence, David secretly left the palace of Naioth, and escaping from Ramah, accompanied by his friend Nathan the prophet, he came to Gibeah, where he met Jonathan, who was on his way with his whole bodyguard of one thousand men to protect him, having not heard of his father's secret and sudden departure by night from Hebron until he had waked the following morning. When Jonathan beheld him approaching alone and safe, he leaped from his foaming charger to the ground and ran forward and embraced him long and tenderly, weeping upon his neck for joy at his escape. Then dismissing his bodyguard to go back to Hebron, he escorted him privately to Bethlehem, his father's house, and left him there until he should learn whether the king would cease his persecution and permit him to return to Michal and his home.

"Such, my lord Arbaces," concludes this epistle of Heleph, the prince's armor-bearer, "is now the present state of affairs. Saul is on his return with his five hundred horsemen, looking, say those who have come faster than he, like a corpse riding, his face rigid, his eyes stony, his mouth sealed like a sepulcher. All his men are afraid of him. He left Ramah this morning, without speaking to the Seer, or beholding him more. Without a word he had resumed his disordered and torn apparel, asked not for his royal robe, and like a warrior defeated and smitten in sore warfare, he slowly rode along the streets and out of the gates of Ramah toward his capital.

"As I close this letter, my lord, I hear someone, passing, say, 'The king's escort is in sight beyond Mamre!' Pardon this long epistle, noble Prince of Assur; but the continued delay of the caravan by the lingering illness, and at last death of its captain, has tempted me to keep the letter open, to add to it the history of the progress of events as they have been day by day developed. The person who is to take it to Egypt assures me that a new captain has been chosen, and that the caravan will leave at sunrise without fail! Written, O Arbaces, by

"Your humble servant,

" HELEPH,

" The armor-bearer."

Here, your majesty (resumed Arbaces to King Belus), here ends the twofold letter of Prince Jonathan and of his military servant Heleph. It reached me in eleven days, for the Damascus caravan was composed wholly of camels, and came on swiftly; thus the events transpiring in Judea are brought up to a period six or seven weeks after my departure, there having been now almost nine weeks since I left Hebron. In that period what extraordinary scenes have been enacted! How persistent the vengeance of Saul! How wonderful David's numerous escapes from death! How remarkable all that transpired at Ramah! There was surely a divine power which interposed for David, and brought upon the king such a strange malady. Truly the God of the Hebrews yet lives, and is powerful to defend his chosen ones! David is evidently under his care, and Heaven-defended in all his paths. Only a madman would continue to combat against one so plainly sheltered under the wings of his God.

But let me not forget my mission here in Egypt, your majesty, while giving so much attention to what passes in Judea. As I stated at the commencement of this long letter (or letters within letters), I have been delayed here more than two months in a state of uncertainty, waiting for a formal answer to my proposal on behalf of your majesty for the hand of the beautiful princess Zaila. Without doubt she has already made up her own mind to the marriage; for she never wearies hearing me discourse of you and Nineveh; and for your sake she confers upon me the greatest attention; while Pharaoh is courteous and friendly, and seems never weary inventing some new entertainment. I have resolved that on the third day from the present, which will close one of their high festivals to Apis, I will ask of the king a final reply to your majesty's suit.

Your faithful and affectionate

ARBACES.

. . . . .

The third day after writing the preceding letter to his king the Assyrian ambassador sought an audience with Pharaoh, and formally asked the king for his final answer.

The monarch, with great amenity of manner and tone, assured the ambassador that the princess had already made up her mind, and that if he would wait upon her she would communicate to him her determination.

The beautiful Zaila received the prince in her pavilion on the Nile, amid her garden of flowers. She was seated in a chair of ivory, inlaid with gold, and covered with velvet, woven with the richest pictures. An exquisite odor of perfumes was diffused throughout the atmosphere around her. Her dark cloud of hair was elegantly decorated with bands of pearls and her graceful neck was resplendent with a collet of gems. Her beautiful shoulders were covered with a transparent net of silk, spotted with silver and edged with a border of gold. Her soft eyes beamed with the gentle fire of the startled antelope's, and her mouth was like a cloven pomegranate for sweetness and brilliancy of color. Pendent tresses, black as the wing of the raven, flowed down her neck, which looked "like a tower of lilies" to the Oriental imagination of the handsome young Assyrian. Bracelets of wrought gold clasped her perfectly molded wrists, and upon her small fingers sparkled rings and signets set with topazes and emeralds. She was arrayed in a graceful robe of virgin white, light as a zephyr, floating around her, over which, not concealing it, was a scarlet bodice, clasped across her dovelike breast with ouches of diamonds; and her gracefully shaped ivory feet glittered in exquisite.sandals of sweet-scented wood. Arbaces thought her the most elegant of women! A captivating smile, bewildering and fascinating, yet half veiled in maidenly coyness, greeted his entrance. She was alone, and the charming retreat in which she had chosen to receive him was perfectly secluded from the curiosity of ear or eye.

"Be seated, my lord Arbaces!" said this lovely woman, whose looks betrayed that certain consciousness of power which is the birthright of personal beauty. He drew near with downcast eyes, and kneeling before the Egyptian princess, touched her hand with a respectful salute.

"I have come, noble lady," he said, rising, "to ask of you, to whom the king your father has referred me, the fate of my beloved master. It is in your hands, lovely princess. Shall I return to him bearing the fair prize he pants to clasp to his heart, or sadly go back to him and convey to him a message of denial of his royal suit?"

Her bosom palpitated! Her color came and went! Her eyes beamed with the ardent splendors of love. She laid her hand on the wrist of the handsome young ambassador, and said with emotion:

"Thou needest not return at all to thy king, O prince! I cannot become his wife! From the first I have not cared for him—*only for thee!* Plead for thyself, O Arbaces! How dull hast thou appeared to me not to know that I have all along loved thee, thought of thee, listened to *thee* alone! While thou didst foolishly believe thou wert winning my heart for thy king, thou wert winning it for thyself! My hand is thine only! I can love only thee! Here, as my wedded lord, thou shalt one day rule over Egypt, and wield the scepter of the Pharaohs. My father is with me in this! Remain thou in Egypt! Send back his gifts to the King of Assyria. Accept my hand, which I freely offer thee, and——"

Arbaces could listen to no more! His whole countenance evinced amazement, grief, and horror! With a pale cheek and bright fires in his indignant eyes, he cried:

"Dost thou, O princess, tempt me to turn traitor to my king? Not all thy beauty, and thou art the most beautiful among women, not the throne of Egypt, nor the scepter of all the Pharaohs, can tempt me to betray my trust!"

"It is no betrayal! I positively refuse ever to wed King Belus!" she answered. "How then canst thou regard thyself a traitor, when thou weddest one who can never become his?"

"No! no! Oh, fair and wise princess, do not refuse the love of Belus!" he exclaimed.

"How can he love me, whom he has seen not?" she answered. "Thee I love! Thee I will wed, O Arbaces!"

"Never!" he cried, in a loud tone. "Never, lady! By all the gods of Egypt, and by the throne of Nineveh, I swear I will never prove so false to my master as to wed thee! I should deserve to perish basely."

"Dost thou despise the hand of Egypt's daughter?" she demanded, with flashing eyes.

"I despise thee not, O princess," he answered sorrowfully; "but I love my master's honor more!"

"Go!" she said imperatively.

He left her presence. He felt that his mission was defeated, and by himself, yet innocently! With a heavy heart he sought his apartments. Without delay he sent Ninus, his armor-bearer, to bid Nacherib, the chief captain, to come before him.

"My mission has failed," he said. "We must leave Egypt to-morrow. Hasten thy preparations!"

He then made known to his officers the condition of affairs. After a little reflection Nacherib said:

"Since the princess doth refuse my lord the king, and offers thyself the throne of Egypt, O Prince Arbaces, there can be no betrayal of thy trust in taking her thyself to wife!"

"Talk not thus to me," answered Arbaces; "I know my duty. Belus would believe to the last I had sued for myself rather than for him! To his dying hour he would regard me as a traitor! No, let us leave Egypt on the morrow!"

On the morrow Arbaces found himself a prisoner! The love of the princess developed into resentment, and the proud Pharaoh lent his power to her revenge, and placed the ambassador in the Castle of On!

Nacherib, after waiting many months, trying to obtain his release, sold his camels and horses, and all the royal gifts of the King of Assyria, and hired a ship of Phœnicia that was in the Nile, and sent forward to Tyre all the servants and men of the caravan, whence by land they gained the valley of the Tigris, under the escort of a Syrian company of merchants. Nacherib and the nine hundred men of the bodyguard of Arbaces, with the chariots, sorrowfully then left Egypt by the desert to seek again their far distant country. Ninus, the faithful armorbearer of the prince, with his personal guard of one hundred nobles, remained in Egypt, resolved never to leave it without their leader. Pharaoh did not molest them, but allowed Ninus and his band to occupy a small garrison near the Nile. He did not wish, by taking the life of a single Assyrian, to bring on a war with the powerful Belus of Nineveh. Weak in purpose, and irresolute and timid, the King of Egypt had no desire needlessly to offend him. His own wish would have been the union of the two empires in friendship by the proposed marriage. But his daughter's will controlled his own. For her own pleasure she held the prince two years and a half in prison! During this interval the fair tyrant frequently had him before her, and offered him liberty at the price of her hand! But the faithful and stern Arbaces refused her terms, and preferred imprisonment to suspicion of treachery!

When at length the King of Assyria heard by the returned

persons, who had formed a portion of the caravan, that his ambassador had failed in his mission and was in prison, he resolved to declare war against Egypt, and advance to the rescue
of his ambassador and friend. At length the indignant Nacherib also arrived at Nineveh with his legion, and made known
to the monarch all the particulars. When Belus heard all, and
understood how the noble and trusty Arbaces had sacrificed
himself to the revenge of the disappointed princess, he began
to assemble his armies, and soon marched to invade Egypt.
Belesis, viceroy of Babylon, taking advantage of his departure
from the kingdom, instantly raised the standard of revolution,
declared Babylon the sole capital of the united empires, and
proclaimed himself king. Intelligence of these events was
brought to Belus in the desert, as at the head of three hundred
thousand men he was crossing it between the Euphrates and
the Jordan. He did not hesitate to turn back in the very hour
to recover his dominions. A war of two years' continuance absorbed all his attention, employed his armies, and prevented
the conquest of Egypt. At length, when he had reduced Babylon, taken and beheaded the traitor Belesis, and restored the
peace and integrity of his vast dominions, he was about to take
up his Egyptian quarrel (for he had not ceased to think of his
beloved Arbaces a prisoner to a revengeful woman on the banks
of the Nile), when the courier of the semi-annual Damascus
caravan brought him a letter. The superscription was in the
well-known handwriting of his beloved and long-lost ambassador! With a countenance radiant with joy he cut the bands
and tore the seals of the envelope, and began eagerly to read it.

It was dated, to his great surprise as well as unfeigned pleasure, not from a prison in Egypt, but at Bethlehem in Judea!
The letter, which is given on the opposite page, will, doubtless,
be perused by the reader with an interest little less than that
experienced by the king.

LETTER X.

ARBACES TO KING BELUS.

BETHLEHEM, KINGDOM OF JUDEA.

MY BELOVED AND HONORED KING :

Once more, O Belus, your Arbaces resumes his long-silent
pen, and addresses your majesty from the country of the Hebrews. Of my long imprisonment in Egypt you have heard
by Nacherib, as I know by your kind letter which was conveyed to me in my prison by your faithful courier. I will not
here enter into the causes which led to the failure of my mission; but when I visit Assyria, which I shall do ere many
months, I will go into a full explanation of the circumstances,
and take the due share of blame which falls upon me. Your
declaration in your kind letter that I was free from all censure,
and worthy of the highest honor, filled my heart with profound
joy, and lightened the weight of my long bondage.

How can I condemn in strong words the woman whom *love*
prompted to treat me so cruelly! It was only at the death of
the princess, three months ago, that my prison doors were
opened by Pharaoh, who, in giving me my liberty, desired to
exculpate himself from all responsibility; assuring me " that he
entertained the warmest admiration for your majesty and myself, and trusted that the ' trifling love passage between me and
the deceased princess ' would not lead to warlike issues." I
promised the king I would represent all the facts to your
majesty; and so, with an escort of honor to his eastern borders
given me, and with my guard of nobles, reduced to ninety-two
men, I left his kingdom.

At the end of five weeks, often resting by the way to gather
strength, for my health had suffered by the confinement and
climate of Egypt, I reached Hebron after an absence of nearly
three years. In that city I remained a few days, and then, by
the advice of the skillful Arabian physician who accompanied
me from Egypt, and by invitation of former friends, I came

hither to the city of Bethlehem, famed for the salubrity of its air.

I am a guest in the house of Joab, the Captain, who is married to a fair maiden of Jericho, and is become one of the chief warriors among the Hebrews.

What extraordinary changes have taken place since I was last in Judea! How different the state of affairs! As I have been deeply interested in hearing relations of all the principal occurrences which have transpired since I received the letters written to me by Prince Jonathan, and by his armor-bearer, Heleph, and as I know your majesty will also take an interest in their recital, I will employ a portion of my slow convalescence in making you acquainted with these affairs.

If your majesty will refer to the letter of Heleph, the armor-bearer, a copy of which I sent you from Egypt nearly three years ago, and but a few days before my imprisonment, you will find that he closed his narrative as King Saul was approaching Hebron, after his mortifying and unsuccessful attempt to seize David in Ramah while protected by the Seer. You will there learn how David, taking advantage of the trance into which the king was thrown by the power of Samuel and by David's harp, fled from Ramah, and met Jonathan with a thousand men coming to his relief, and that by him he was secretly escorted to his father's house at Bethlehem.

After Saul returned to his palace David privately came to his own house by night, and sent Michal for her brother. From him he learned that the king had in no degree changed his mind against him; but, on the contrary, was more bitter than before in his denunciations of him.

But Michal, his wife, went and entreated her father so earnestly, and with such a flood of tears, to forego his vengeance against her husband, that he relented; and in her joy she told him David was with her.

"Let him remain, and go in and out before me as heretofore!" he said.

But David did not feel secure, though he remained several days in the palace, and sought to please the king in every way, and three times a day sitting at meat before him. At length he said to Jonathan:

"A feeling of insecurity is ever present with me! A look the king cast upon me to-day troubles me! If thou knowest the king's mind toward me, hide it not from me! I am sure in his heart he seeks my life! I dare not appear in his presence again until I know his feelings toward me! I fear he will kill me!"

"God forbid! Thou shalt not die, my beloved David," answered the prince. "Do not think my father again evil-disposed toward thee! I should know it. He hides nothing from me!"

"But the king knoweth that I have been so honored as to find such grace in thine eyes as to be chosen by thee thy bosom friend, and will he not say, 'What I do I will withhold from my son, lest he betray it to David'?"

Then said Jonathan, seeing his friend was feeling deeply, and living daily in such a state of suspense:

"What shall I do for thee, O my friend and brother? Whatsoever is in thine heart I will do!"

"Behold," said David, "to-morrow is the new moon and the three days' feast beginneth. I will absent myself from the table of the king to be present at the sacrifice which my family at Bethlehem always makes at this season, and to which my brother. Eliab hath sent me pressing word to be present. With your permission I will go. If thy father at all miss me, then say I obtained thy consent to be at Bethlehem with my family. If the king say, 'It is well!' and makes no further remark, I shall have peace for the future; but if he shows great wrath at my absence be sure he has not changed his disposition toward me, and only waiteth the hour to do me evil! Pardon me, O Jonathan! but my heart is heavy. If I have done evil to the king, I am ready to die at the hand of the king's son! Slay me here! But if I am innocent, by the sacred covenant of friendship and love between us so long, let me know if thy father determines evil against me!"

As David spoke tears filled his expressive and earnest eyes, and brushing them away he continued:

"It is not *fear!* I do not fear death! But it is hard for my king, the father of my wife and of my best friend on earth, to hate me so bitterly and seek my life! I would prefer meeting in open battle a thousand Philistines than remain in this jeopardy of momentary murder!"

"Nay, dear David," said the prince, "if I knew certainly that evil were determined by my father to come upon thee, would I not tell it thee? Canst thou doubt it, friend of my soul? I see that thou fearest I would hide my father's wickedness, loath to tell it any man for his and my sake! But painful as it would be to me to expose my father's sin, I would not fail thee!"

Here the prince raised his right hand to heaven and swore before the Lord that he would certainly ascertain his father's mind and make it known to David!

"The Lord bless thee, my friend," answered the persecuted young man. "I will no more mistrust thee! Forgive me! But I know as a son thou honorest thy father and lovest him, and would naturally seek to hide what in him mortifies and pains thee! Forgive me if I feared thou wouldst think more of thy father's honor than of my life! I have wronged thee! Thou art placed by thy friendship for me in a painful position!"

"If it please my father to do thee evil," answered the prince, "then will I show it thee, and we will separate, thou going in peace where thou canst find safety, I remaining with him, which I will do to the last! I stand or fall, O David, with my father's fortunes! The Lord be with thee, if thou goest away to escape his hand, as he was with my father in the former years when God and the Seer were his friends, and all men honored him for his virtues and admired him for his valor. And, O David, with whom will be the power of this realm, by our covenant of friendship, forget me not when thou art in my father's throne, if then I am alive! Cut not off thy kindness from my father's house when thou art in glory and they in humility! Remember all my kindred for our friendship's sake, and may the Lord cut off all thine enemies from the face of the earth!"

This touching language deeply moved David! What a sublime, moral spectacle, your majesty! A young prince, his father still on the throne, tenderly suing with words of trusting faith the youthful shepherd (a fugitive from his house, his life sought by his own royal father), for the protection of his scepter, when he should by and by be king in his father's place! What a beautiful scene! What noble attributes of character the young prince displays! How touching his ready and unquestioning submission to the destiny of disinheritance which he knows has been pronounced against him! David, with emotion, made the promise, and clasping the hand of his prince he raised his right arm to heaven and confirmed it by a solemn oath: "If I fail thee or thine in this, let the Lord requite it upon me, and let the enemies of Saul become David's adversaries!"

The young men then renewed their noble covenant of love and friendship, and their souls were knitted closer together from that moment!

David immediately left for Bethlehem, but previously arranged how Jonathan should give him information without visiting him, and thus exciting Saul's suspicions; for next to his hatred against David was aroused his indignation at the firm and unshaken friendship which existed between his son and his foe. He felt that Jonathan did him a great injury by not making the quarrel also his own, and he had, the very morning on which the conversation I have just given (as it has been reported to me), charged him with being "Saul's enemy, because he was David's friend." The prince, therefore, held this interview with his friend with the greatest secrecy.

The day of the holy feast came, and David's place was empty. The king was observed to look steadily at the vacant seat, but he made no remark. This was a favorable omen; and Jonathan's heart felt lighter. On the morrow, also, David's seat was empty at the king's table. Abner, his general, sat on his right hand, and Jonathan on his left. Ishbosheth and his two brothers sat opposite to him. At one end was Joab, at the other was the vacant seat of the absent son-in-law. At a lower table sat Armoni and Mephibosheth, two sons of Saul, by the proud and beautiful Rizpah his favorite, and also the husband of Merab his eldest daughter. The women held the feast in their own apartments. Thus, all the royal family being present, the absence of David, to whom everyone believed his father-in-law was fully reconciled, was the more marked! It certainly was likely to prove a sound test of the sincerity of the king's goodwill toward him.

"Wherefore cometh not the son of Jesse to meat, neither yesterday nor to-day?" demanded Saul, in a loud tone, which made all present start!

The guests looked at one another, and then at Jonathan, in silence! The attendants appeared alarmed. The dark-browed Prince Ishbosheth, who disliked his brother-in-law, whose manly piety rebuked his vices and excesses, said with a sneer, "Doubtless, his friend Jonathan, who seems to keep advised of all his movements, can answer!"

"David earnestly asked leave of me to go to Bethlehem,"

answered the prince; "for his family have a sacrifice there to-day, and his elder brother commanded him to be present there. I gave him the permission he sought. Therefore his place is empty at the king's table!"

Upon hearing this the monarch sprang to his feet, and seizing his javelin, which he never went without, he shook it fiercely across the board at the prince, and cried with kindling anger:

"Thou son of a perverse mother! A rebellious wife was she to me, and a rebellious son hath she borne to me! Thou hast chosen this son of Jesse to thy own confusion and the shame of thy father! For as long as this son of Jesse liveth upon the ground, thou shalt not be held in honor, nor thy kingdom established! Thou warmest a viper in thy bosom that shall sting thee! Thou protectest a base hind, who will one day step on thy neck to climb up into thy throne! Go! Send, and fetch him unto me, for by the throne I sit upon, he shall surely die the death!"

"Wherefore, O my father, should the innocent person be slain? What hath he done worthy of death?" interceded Jonathan.

"Thou art even like unto him!" answered the king, his eyes burning like coals of fire; and without hesitation he cast at the prince, his son, the javelin from his hand, intending to slay him. It flew past his shoulder, and flying through a distant casement, was heard to strike and shiver into fragments against a column of porphyry in the lawn, which had been erected to the memory of Ezel, a youth who, twenty years before, had saved Saul's life in battle.

Thus Jonathan's bold friendship for David had brought his own life into jeopardy. The prince in great and just anger rose from the table, grieved more for David than for himself, for he now plainly saw that his friend's death was determined upon. Without doubt, your majesty, King Saul had received some intimation that it was David to whom his offended God was to give his forfeited throne, and hence his persistent and relentless purpose to slay him! But in vain will man attempt to overthrow the decrees of the heavenly Powers! Death cannot touch the life of one whom the gods determine shall accomplish a foreordained destiny! Spear and sword, javelin and dagger, subtile poisons, and crafty devices, all fail against him! Neither fire can burn, water drown, earth en-

tomb, or pestilence in the air harm such a child of destiny!
King Saul might as well have cast his javelin against the
rocky sides of Mount Hor, hoping to overturn it, as aim at the
life of the God-shielded youth, to whom the fiat of Heaven had
given his throne.

Upon leaving the king's presence the offended prince sought
his sister, David's young wife, for sympathy; and together they
discussed the danger of David. While she said that he must
no more come to Hebron, she expressed herself ready to go to
him and accompany him in all his wanderings. But Jonathan
dissuaded her from this step, saying that she would at present
be rather a burden to him, as he had nowhere to lay his head,
though heir to the kingdom of Israel; for it was no secret to
Michal now, that God had promised to set her exiled husband
on the throne of Jacob! Yet how mysterious to them were
these trials and dangers through which he was to reach it!
How strange that the "chosen of Heaven" should be permitted
to suffer such humiliation before his exaltation! It is singularly analogous with the trials of the Israelites as a nation
under the hatred of Pharaoh, and their wanderings in the wilderness! The dealings of their God seem to be always the
same! If it be an honor to be chosen by Him for any great
end, that honor, lest it should lead to pride of heart, is com-
pensated by corresponding humiliations. It would appear to
be his Divine policy, that those whom he will distinguish above
others must first descend lower than others; first suffer ere
they possess the glory and honor in store for them! and that
this great, wise, and holy, and dreadful God, O Belus, is the
God of all gods, and the Supreme Deity of the world, I am
almost prepared to believe!

The next morning, while the king slept, Jonathan left the
palace, and, by a private gate in the city wall, entered the garden beyond it accompanied by his page. David was concealed
in this suburban garden behind the stone pillar of Ezel, as had
been previously arranged between them. The prince carried
in his hand a bow and a quiver of arrows as if he were to
practice archery. The place was full in sight from the windows of the palace. When he came within hearing of David,
he cried to the lad, "Run, find out now the arrows which I
shoot!"

As the page ran forward, he shot three arrows far beyond
him.

It had previously been agreed upon by Jonathan with David that, if he heard him call out to the page, "The arrows are on this side of thee!" he would understand that it was peace between his father and him, and he might return into his house without fear; but if he said, "The arrows are beyond thee!" he must in haste make his escape; and if he did so go away, he must not forget his vow to be a friend to his kindred for the sake of the love between them.

When, therefore, the page hastened after the arrows the prince cried, "Is not the arrow beyond thee?" he then added, for the ears of David, still addressing the lad, "Make speed—haste—stay not!" The page made haste to gather up the arrows, not suspecting the twofold signification of the words spoken to him. David heard and understood that they were for his own warning, and knew, thereby, that his life was certainly sought by the king. When the youth had brought again the arrows to his master, he said to him, "Go—take the bow and quiver within the gates, and await my coming."

As soon as the page had disappeared, Jonathan, now that he had turned aside suspicion by his archery pastime, went forward, and David met him at a place where they were sheltered from the palace by a group of oleander trees.

"My lord," said David, with looks of deep sadness, "I am, then, to be an exile! But my heart is full of gratitude to thee for this kind warning." As he spoke, feeling his own loneliness and humiliation as an outcast, he bowed himself thrice toward the earth, as was the custom of petitioners to the prince or the king, and said, "Say farewell to my beloved bride! Comfort her, O my lord prince, and let her not come to evil from the anger of the king."

"Thou shouldst not so bow down thyself to me, O David! Let not thy sorrow break thine heart! Forget not that thou art a true prince, a son of the King of kings, crowned of God! This humiliation prompted by thy great woes becomes not thee! Be courageous! I will defend thy wife Michal from all evil! I will send thee news of her from time to time. Alas! alas! that my father should seek thy life, and make both thee and me so unhappy! But thou art no longer safe in Hebron, nor anywhere from his power, for he will seek thee as the tireless hunting leopard pursues the antelope. Your only shelter, since Samuel could not protect thee, is to fly to the altar of God!"

"Thither I will fly," sorrowfully answered David, "till this calamity be overpast. Ahimelech, the priest, will receive me, and, in the sacred shadow of the holy tabernacle, not the sceptered sword of Saul can reach me!"

"Oh, that I could retain and defend thee here!" said Jonathan. "But God will be with thee! Blessed are they that dwell in His house, and sit under the shadow of his footstool!"

"I am weary of flying from this death," said David, with deep feeling. "My heart and flesh fail me, and my soul, like a dove pursued by the falcon, now longeth for the courts of the Lord, even the sheltering and peaceful altars of my king and my God! There I shall be at rest! There even the sparrows find shelter from the stormy winds, and there will I abide."

Jonathan's heart swelled as he listened to this touching and tender language; and he gazed tearfully on the pale and suffering visage of the persecuted yet innocent young man, whom he loved as his own soul; and, with a sudden outburst of grief, he threw himself upon his shoulder. For a few moments the two friends stood, locked in each other's embrace, weeping, for their sorrows were one. At length Jonathan kissed his friend on both cheeks with the love of a brother for a sister. This lovely expression of affection and tenderness unmanned the heroic conqueror of Goliath. He fell upon his friend's breast, overcome with the depth and tenderness of his feelings, as he thought of his double separation, both from his young wife and the brother of his soul, and recalled the deadly enmity of him who caused all his grief, to whom he had only done good. Jonathan felt the weight of David's form suddenly become heavy as he rested upon his breast, and looking with alarm in his face, he saw that he had fainted away.

With a cry of anguish, and bitter thoughts rising against his father, he gently let the lifeless form of his beloved David down upon the green grass. The suspension of life was but momentary. The young heart, too full of its woes, was not crushed, only bruised. The earnest, kind, entreating voice of his friend recalled him to consciousness. He rose to his feet stronger, and said:

"Forgive me! I am greatly afflicted. The sorrows of death have compassed me! My soul cleaveth even to the dust, and hath melted for very heaviness. But it is past now! I can put my trust in my God! It is better to trust in the Lord than to put confidence in princes. The king hath thrust at me sore that I might perish; but the Lord will help me! I will hasten to pay my vows to the Lord in his tabernacle, and humble myself before his footstool! The Spirit of the Lord is upon me to help me, and he hath seen my tears, and will give me rest and peace! Farewell! I go forth weeping, bearing precious seed, but doubtless I shall come again with rejoicing, bringing my sheaves with me!"

"Truly," answered the prince, "the Highest will perfect that which concerneth thee! I know the Lord will preserve thy going out, and thy coming in, from this time forevermore! And when thou art in power, forget not to befriend my father's house! Go in peace, my brother! May thy house and my house forever be even as Jonathan and David!"

"May my name be cast out as evil, may I become as Moab, and base as Ammon, ere I forget my vow to thee, about thee and thine," answered the houseless wanderer, receiving and granting prayers, as if he were already seated upon the throne of the kingdom and Jonathan stood a suppliant at his footstool.

A few more words of tenderest affection, and the two friends folded each other in a final embrace; and, silently disengaging themselves, they separated; David going away by the path which led to the hills, and the prince (after following him with longing looks of love, as the wanderer often glanced affectionately back to him), slowly, and with a heavy heart, re-entered the city.

Such, your majesty, was the last interview and parting of these two noble friends! In all the history of the past such a pure and unselfish friendship is unknown! On the part of each, it was surpassing the love of women! How tender, how delicate, how full of sweet and holy dignity was their attachment! If one is to be preferred before the other, perhaps the prince deserves the highest admiration; for he loved him, who, he knew, was to deprive him of his throne! loved him whom his father hated! loved him homeless, wandering, outcast! trusted in him in his humiliation as his future monarch, and with a beautiful faith, plead for his kingly care over, and lasting protection of his mother, his brothers, and sisters, and all near and dear to them and to himself! What august trust, what deathless love, what sublime hope, what godlike humility! Worthy was such a prince to rule in his father's stead! but the inexorable law of the God of the Hebrews, written on the sacred tablets of Moses, kept in their holy Ark, reads, " The sins of the fathers shall be visited upon the children unto the third and fourth generation of those who hate me." This virtuous prince is therefore sacrificed for the guilt of his father; and even his children's children may feel the evil consequences of the fierce and impious king's folly, sacrilege, and pride of heart! Already has the first blow been struck, as your majesty will by and by learn as you proceed in the perusal of my narrative.

But the trials of this prince of God, David the son of Jesse, on account of Saul, were not yet over; for when he had reached the strong place called Nob, over against Jerusalem on the north, to which place the tabernacle, or high temple of the Hebrews, had recently been removed by Saul, and which hence became the center of the national worship, Ahimelech feared to receive him for dread of the king's anger.

This temple had been constructed by Moses when in the wilderness, and after a pattern sent down from heaven, taken from a celestial house, in which dwelt from eternity God himself! This temple was erected to be the palace for the visible presence of their God, *as their King*, and also as the place for the people to worship before Him! I have already alluded to it in a previous letter to your majesty. Its magnificence was, and is (for it still exists, though every seven years its hangings are renewed with undiminished splendor), of the most novel and elaborate description. It was constructed in all its particulars with the greatest care, as every part answered, said Moses, to something in heaven. The costliness of it was incalculable, and defrayed by the voluntary gifts of the Israelites, who brought out of Egypt spoils in jewels of gold, and jewels of silver, and precious stones, of untold wealth, given them by their Lord, who surrendered to them the riches of the people of Egypt. The architects were divinely inspired. I will describe to your majesty this wonderful movable temple which I saw when I was here a few years ago. Nob is but twelve miles from this place, Bethlehem, where I now sojourn. I copy from a description which I wrote at the time for your majesty, and now have by me: It is pitched like a pavilion within the castle of Nob, upon a broad area, inclosed by the dwellings of the priests; the chief of which is the Palace of Ahimelech, now occupied by his son Abiathar, who hospitably received me, and suffered me to see as much of the sacred structure as was permitted to a stranger. A space one hundred and fifty feet in length, and seventy-five feet in breadth, is inclosed on the four sides by beautiful brazen pillars, eight feet in height, ten at the ends, and twenty at the sides, sixty in all, richly filleted with silver. From pillar to pillar extend rods, from which hang fine twined linen curtains to the ground. This parallelogram, thus curtained, stands east and west. The entrance is on the east, from the rising sun, and on this end the curtains are of blue, and purple, and scarlet, and pure white linen. Crossing the soft verdure of the plain, which is kept spotlessly clean, and is as a carpet of velvet to the tread of the sandal, I was conducted by a youthful Levite of the family of Abiathar to this eastern entrance, beyond and over which, in the interior, appeared the Divine Tabernacle, or Temple. Leaving my sandals with a Levite at the entrance, another drew up with silken cords the brilliant curtains for our admission into the court, inclosed by the sixty pillars. Here I stood, and contemplated with religious awe the spectacle before me!

Immediately in front of the entrance, and near the center of the vast area, stood the brazen altar of burnt-offering. It was between six and seven feet in length, and four and a half feet high, overlaid with massive plates of brass, with brazen-plated horns affixed one at each corner. The perpetual fire which had been kindled five hundred years before, by a torch lighted for Moses for this purpose by the angel Gabriel, at the altar of heaven when the Jewish lawgiver was in the mount of God at Horeb, burned thereupon, fed night and day with fragrant wood by attending priests. As I looked, a lamb just slain was placed upon the sacred fire, and the dark red smoke of the burnt-offering rolled high above the heads of the priests, and was borne away by the wind over the top of the outer wall of the curtained tabernacle, to mingle with the somber cloud which almost constantly hung about the towers of Nob, rendering the "city of sacrifice" distinguishable all the country round as the "pavilion of God."

I was permitted to go near and examine the altar. It was hollow, so that the ashes of the wood that burned on the iron bars upon which the lamb or bullock was laid, fell through the grate into a huge pan beneath, leaving the roasted sacrifice upon the top. Every morning and evening the attending Levites in linen tunics, who are the servants of the priests and of the altar, and taken from a tribe set apart by Moses for these holy duties, draw out this pan of ashes and empty it on the outside of the tabernacle. For the service there were placed by the altar shovels of brass, and tongs, and brazen hooks to turn the victim on the fire, and vessels to receive the blood as it poured from the wound in the victim made by the sacrificial knife of the officiating priest, who is of necessity to be a descendant of the High Priest Aaron. The eldest son of this consecrated family, in succession through the ages, takes this lofty rank by right of birth! All the other priests are descended from Aaron also, but by younger sons. The Levites are men who are sprung from Levi, and of the same tribe with Aaron, kindred of the priests, but inferior to them in rank, being forbidden to sacrifice or offer incense, but only to serve the priests and tabernacle. The priests are in number many hundreds, and serve by companies or course morning and evening, while the Levites are numbered by thousands. (The High Priest, at the time of my visit, was Abiathar, also called Ben-Ahimelech, being the son of Ahimelech, who was priest when I was last in Judea, and whose tragic death I have yet to record.)

Upon this high altar a holocaust of sacrifices bleed continually, nor ceases the flow of innocent blood for the sins of men from morning until evening. As with us, a part of the victim is sacred to God, a part given to the priest, and the rest of the flesh distributed among the families of the priests by His command. Upon the altar four kinds of sacrifices are offered, termed burnt-offerings, sin-offerings, trespass-offerings, and peace-offerings.* The first three are expiatory: that is, make atonement for the transgressions of those who bring the victims. The poured-forth blood of these sacrifices is solemnly consecrated to the Lord of heaven to be an expiation for the soul, to which end He has pledged himself to receive it. The peace-offering is a thankful sacrifice to God for benefits. There are free-will or voluntary offerings that depend on the heart and piety of the giver; and obligatory offerings, such as the presentation of the first sheaf, the first lamb, the first fruit of any increase, with the natural tithes and sin-offerings. No one can avoid these last two without guilt and punishment. Wine, oil, bread, salt, and many things are offered to the Lord by this religious people; and, as everything offered must be laid upon the altar by the priest, the concourse of worshipers

* *Vide* first seven chapters of Leviticus.

to the tabernacle is every day very great, and the immense numbers of priests on duty hardly suffice to serve them. This is emphatically a worshiping nation! Their whole life and polity revolve around the altar! Sacrifice is the center of their system.

Their most extraordinary sacrifice is that of the Great Day of Expiation. The High Priest, on this occasion, bathes with unusual attention to purity of person, invests himself in a plain robe of white linen as a "penitent," laying aside his purple robe and ephod of office; as first he is to expiate his own sins as a man, before he can offer as High Priest the Great Expiation for the nation. With solemnity he now approaches the high altar, and a bullock and a ram being brought before him, he lays his hands upon the heads of the victims, at the same time confessing his sins and those of his priestly house, by which act it is supposed that his sins and those of the priests, by virtue of a foregone covenant between their God and them, are transferred to the heads of the brutes about to be slain! He then slays with the sacrificial sword these sin-laden victims, whose blood poured out unto the Lord is to expiate the sins of the order of the priesthood.

The High Priest is now regarded holy, his sins all washed away by the blood of the victim, and he is now ready, without sin, to offer sacrifice acceptable to God for the people. Two of the most venerable elders of the nation hereupon bring him two goats, which are to be victims in behalf of the whole nation. Both of them, however, are not to bleed. Lots are cast by the priests to ascertain which of the two is to be slain.

But, before I proceed to describe to your majesty one of the most remarkable features of this sacrificial expiation, I will narrate what I further beheld within the four linen walls of the tabernacle. Passing reverently the altar of burnt-offering, I came to a gigantic Laver of elaborate workmanship standing upon a brazen feet of lions. Its sides were of brass, so brightly polished that they served the priests for mirrors wherein to see to rearrange their disordered costume when they came there to wash after sacrificing. Here several priests were engaged performing their ablutions preparatory to sacrificing, who regarded me with no surprise, as I was attired like the Levites, and hence attracted no particular attention in the vast concourse which moved in and out and through the court of the tabernacle.

After passing the magnificent Laver, I saw before me, about fifty feet distant, the front of the inner or true Tabernacle of God; for where I now stood was but the inclosure or court of sacrifice, inclosed to veil, by the range of curtains, the priests and their offices from the common eye. But the *real temple* was within this great court and before me! It was about ten cubits or eighteen feet broad in front, and as many high, extending back thirty cubits to the west curtain of the court of the tabernacle. It had the appearance of a long and narrow pavilion, with five pillars in front overlaid with plates of gold, and fixed in sockets of silver. Across these five costly pillars was partly drawn aside a magnificently embroidered curtain of the richest colors, giving, between the columns, a glimpse at the dark and mysterious interior. Nearer to it than where I then stood I was not permitted to advance, as its sacred vicinity is forbidden to every foot except that of a certain class of priests. It is called the Sanctuary, the peculiar abode of the Hebrew's God on earth, and where he makes his Presence visible by a bright flame which floats mid air above the inmost altar of its most secret chamber. Once in a year only does a human tread awake its solemn echoes, when the High Priest on the Day of Expiation enters it alone!

Unlike the outer curtained wall of the tabernacle, this lesser temple within it is inclosed by four curtains hanging over side walls of fragrant wood closely ceiled, save at the entrance, where, for these closed sides, stand the five columns with open spaces between. "Of these four curtains," said my guide, describing the forbidden temple to me, "the first and inner one is composed of fine linen, richly embroidered by the cunning art of needlework with figures of Cherubim (that is, your majesty, winged gods), in exquisitely arranged shades of blue, purple, and scarlet."

This magnificent curtain not only hangs along the two sides and western end, but it extends overhead, forming the expanded ceiling as well as the walls, and a gorgeous and glorious inner roof does this extension make with its tasteful borders and the beautiful central figures. This inner covering of the sacred tent is all covered by a curtain of closely woven goats' hair to exclude from it dust and damp, by a third of carefully dressed leather of rams' skins dyed red, and by a fourth of skins skillfully prepared to shed rain, also colored in the richest manner, and lending to this singular temple an aspect of novel magnificence. The front before which I stood had separate curtains of the most beautiful embroidery; which could be raised for admission or lowered so as to rest upon the ground.

The interior of this celestial pavilion is divided into two apartments, by means of four pillars of precious wood, overlaid with plates of gold, and standing in sockets of silver. Upon these pillars is hung a heavy and ample veil of blue, purple, and scarlet fine-twined linen. The outer apartment of the pavilion occupies two-thirds of the interior area, and is called the "Holy Place"; while the remaining lesser space is named (ever spoken by Hebrews with awe), the "Holy of Holies." This sacred interior chamber ever remains in mysterious darkness, save the soft illumination which perpetually glows within, beaming from a visible Glory resting above the altar, whereby their God manifests his awful presence. This holy Light is said, by some, to appear like a lambent flame; by others, like a serene star; by others, like a fiery blaze; but no man has ever beheld it save the High Priest, whose lips are forever sealed as to what he beholds in that dreadful and glorious sanctuary— the visible terrestrial throne of God. Thus much, however, is known, that the splendor or obscurity of this presence of fire within the Holy of Holies is affected by the holiness or wickedness of the nation; hence, at times it may blaze like angry lightning, or shine subdued and soft like the evening star. This glorious visible manifestation is said, by Abiathar, to be the continuation of the divine presence of the Pillar of Fire; which once, a column of splendor rising above the Ark of the Covenant, lighted up the whole camp of Israel in the wilderness, now, with lesser starlike glory, limited to the inner sanctuary of this Most Holy Place, is still shining above the same Ark of the Covenant.

Are not these wonderful mysteries, your majesty? How sublime, how awe-inspiring the idea that this lamp of God has continued to burn since it took the form of the fiery Pillar until now in the luminous Shechinah! and will shine on from generation to generation as a token of their God's presence with them, "unless," as the High Priest sorrowfully said to me, "the nation forgets God and commits gross iniquity, when the divine light will suddenly go out and leave the inner temple in darkness forever."

There is, your majesty, believed to be a prophecy which pronounces that such extinction will take place at the close of a period of seven hundred years from the first king that reigns over Israel. That after more than three hundred years of darkness and humiliation there shall descend an angel from the upper heaven, bearing a star, with which he will alight upon one of the hills of Bethlehem, when the last Prince of the House of Israel shall then be an infant in its cradle, who will rise and by inspiration seize it from the hand of the angel, and suddenly entering the temple, once more light up therewith the glory of the inner House, and illuminate the whole earth with the dazzling splendor of the rekindled Shechinah.

There being no window, and strictly no door but the raised curtain on the east front in the tabernacle, and as in the outer apartment there are services performed at the Altar of Incense therein by the priests, it is necessary to have lights. Moses, therefore, directed to be made a Candlestick of pure gold with seven branches, one in the center, five feet in height, and three on each side, of similar proportions, with equal spaces between. They are represented by Abiathar as very elegant in form, each one adorned with golden flowers, and lilies of raised work, and with apple-shaped knops, and almonds of wrought gold. Instead of cups for candles, upon the end of each branch is a gold lamp. These lamps are fed with pure olive oil, and lighted every evening at sunset, and all but the west one extinguished at sunrise by the priests on duty.

This golden, seven-branched lamp stands on the left of one entering the Holy Place, while on the right of the entrance is an elegantly shaped table, called the Table of Shew Bread. Between these two objects, and in front of the curtained entrance, stands the Altar of Incense! The seven-branched candlestick is so placed as to throw its light upon the Altar of Incense, and upon the golden table of Shew Bread at the right of the entrance. This beautiful table, which is about three feet and a half long and two feet and a half high, is overlaid with plates of pure gold of Ophir, and a border or crown of gold a hand breadth high surrounds the top; and at each corner are four rings of gold, to contain the bars of sacred wood by which the priests bear it from place to place; upon it are vessels, and dishes, and spoons of gold. Upon this table, every seventh day, the Priest places twelve loaves of unleavened bread, covered with leaves of gold, the number representing the twelve tribes

of the Hebrew nation, in whose behalf this extraordinary perpetual offering is made to their Lord. Wine is also placed as
an offering upon the same table, also salt and incense at certain times.

These loaves are separated by dishes of gold, so that air
may come to the bread, and mold be prevented. Every Sabbath four priests go first into the Holy Place, and take away
the twelve loaves which have remained there seven days,
presented, or shewn before the Lord, and other four follow and
replace them instantly with twelve others, hot from the oven;
thus the table is never without bread before the Lord. The cakes
of bread are placed six in a pile near each end of the table, and
between is a richly chased vase with a golden cover, and containing sweet incense. The bread removed becomes a portion
of the daily bread of the officiating priest, by whom alone it
is lawful to be eaten. The purpose of keeping this bread in
the presence of, and always " shewn to, the Lord," was in grateful remembrance of his care in ripening their harvest: in a
word, it may be called a continual thank-offering that famine
hath not fallen upon the land; and is a beautiful and appropriate recognition of the good providence of their God. Abiathar termed the loaves " the presence Bread," because it was
always present before the " Lord of the Harvest."

The Altar of Incense, which is also called the Golden Altar,
stands farther in from the entrance than the golden candlestick and golden table, between which two the Priest passes to
approach the Altar of Incense, which is very small, being but
eighteen inches square, and three feet high. It is overlaid with
gold, golden horns project from the corner, connected by an
openwork border of gold, the whole very rich and elegant.
Golden rings are also attached to its sides, to hold the rods
by which it is carried by the priests; for the tabernacle, temple,
altars, tables, and all the furniture appertaining thereto are
portable, and so constructed as to be taken to pieces and put
together again; and in this manner have changed places from
city to city several times since they were first placed at Gilgal,
after the crossing of the Jordan. It was exposed thereby to
capture, and its Ark was, a generation ago, actually seized and
carried off by the Philistines, who, terrified by the judgments it
brought upon them, were glad to send it back. It is in intention to remove the whole tabernacle once for all to Jerusalem,
when the Jebusites shall be driven out of its southern castle.

which ere long will be effected by him who now wields the scepter of this kingdom!

Upon the golden Altar of Incense the most fragrant incense is burned morning and evening perpetually. Neither burnt-offering, meat-offering, nor drink-offering is permitted on this Altar, which is never stained with blood, save but one day in the year, when the High Priest makes atonement on the great Day of Expiation; to which subject I shall now soon return, delaying only to add a few words about the inner sanctuary, the Holy of Holies, which is ever hidden from mortal eyes, save on that one Day of Expiation, when the Chief Priest, in the execution of this, the most solemn and awful duty of his high office, removes the terrible veil and disappears within, and stands alone with God! What does he behold therein?

"With reverence," says the younger brother of Abiathar, who was part of the time my guide, "these holy things may be spoken of!" From him I learned as follows: In this Most Holy Place are the Ark of the Covenant, the Mercy-Seat, and the Cherubim. That wonderful Ark! That consecrated Coffer, which, borne on the shoulders of twelve priests, stayed and held back Jordan "upon a heap," is preserved behind that mysterious curtain! It is a sacred chest three feet and three-quarters in length, and two feet and a quarter in width and height. It was made in the wilderness under the eye of Moses, covered with plates of gold, and rimmed with gold. The lid is a plate of purest gold, seven times purified, and is termed the Mercy-Seat, and is the holiest point on earth! At each end of this golden lid and upon it, are two figures of glorious heavenly creatures called Cherubim, with golden wings, which, as they face each other inwardly, looking down upon the Ark, are curved forward, and meet above the Mercy-Seat, forming a throne, where, in rays of divine splendor appears the mysterious symbol of the Presence of God, shining in glory unspeakable; illumining the Mercy-Seat and guarding Cherubim, and filling the secret chamber of the Holy of Holies with light ineffable, before which the Hight Priest veils his eyes, and prostrates himself with fear and trembling.

Your majesty will pardon me for entering so fully into this description; but in order to understand this people it is necessary to understand their religion. How wonderful is their worship! How sublime, how glorious, how dreadful is their God!

Within this Ark are placed a golden vase, in which is preserved some of the manna or heavenly bread which sustained their fathers in the wilderness; the divine rod of their first High Priest, Aaron, which miraculously budded and blossomed at once, and the two tables of the Law or Covenant, written with the finger of their God in the Mount of Horeb; and hence the appellation of the sacred chest.

Your majesty will be surprised that a powerful and opulent people should, for nearly five hundred years, be contented to worship and sacrifice in a temple of this frail description; which, while they were wanderers in the desert, was appropriate to their circumstances; but which, now that they are established in their kingdom, seems to be illy-adapted to their permanent condition. But their adherence to it, because the pattern of it was given them by their God, and it was erected by Moses, is a beautiful illustration of their piety and reverence for the old paths in which their fathers walked.

I will now, your majesty, proceed to the completion of my account of the scenes and acts of the great Day of Expiation, all of which will now be intelligible to you.

When the High Priest, by lot, has ascertained which of the two goats brought to him is to be sacrificed, he receives a censer from an attendant, puts therein burning coals of sacred fire from the Altar of burnt-offering, and taking sweet incense in his hand, he solemnly moves toward the Holy Place alone, while all the priests and people stand in attitudes of silent reverence.

He enters with awe the outer chamber of the sacred pavilion of his God, and passing between the golden Candlestick and table of shew-bread, leaves the Altar of Incense behind him with its ever-smoking censer thereon, filling the place with fragrance, and stands before the mysterious Vail which for three hundred and sixty-four days no mortal hand has lifted. He pauses, perhaps turns pale with holy dread, as he slowly raises the curtain of God's Holy Abode. He hesitates—enters —*dares* to enter—because he is *commanded* to enter.

If the nation of which he is High Priest has been the year past obedient and virtuous, he beholds the mysterious Glory of the Shechinah, enthroned above the Mercy-Seat, resplendent and serene; but if the people have greatly sinned it shines with a pale light. He hastens immediately to cast the incense from his hand upon the coals of fire in the censer, the smoke of which at once ascends and covers the Mercy-Seat, and veils the

glory of God above it, or he would die with the sight. Having
thus by the offering of incense filled the holy sanctuary with
the sacred and sweet fragrance acceptable to his God, he slowly
retires and reappears, his face and garments all resplendent,
before the great Altar of burnt-offering, on which he had sacrificed the bullock. With a sacred vessel appertaining to the
altar he takes up a portion of its blood and returns again to
the Sanctuary, and going within the Vail sprinkles it, with his
finger dipped in the blood, before the Mercy-Seat, seven times.
He now returns a second time to the Great Altar, and taking
the one of the two goats which is to be slain, he sacrifices it
thereon. When this is done all the priests leave the tabernacle,
he alone remaining. The blood of the goat he now puts in a
sacred vessel and bears it into the inner Sanctuary, and sprinkles it seven times, also before the Ark and the Mercy-Seat,
and before the Lord of Glory. Thence he returns to the court
of the Tabernacle, sprinkling the sides of it as he comes, in
order to purify it with the blood of the goat. Then advancing
to the High Altar he wets the four golden horns thereof with
the blood of the young bullock and of the goat, and sprinkles
it seven times therewith.

The Sanctuary, the Court, and the Altar of burnt-offering
being thus purified, the priests, who are not permitted to remain
during these ceremonies of purification, are readmitted; and,
at his command the other goat is now brought to him. In the
most impressive manner he puts his hand on its head and
aloud confesses his own sins and the sins of the people thereon,
thereby solemnly affixing to the victim their personal guilt.
The goat, thus accursed with bearing the transgressions of a
whole nation, is handed over to a base person, who is angrily
driven forth with it to the desert, where he is to let it escape.
The High Priest in the meanwhile puts off his penitential
garments, bathes again at the Laver of the Tabernacle, and
resuming his robe of purple, his ephod, and other insignia of
his rank, sacrifices two rams, and offers them smoking to
Heaven, one as a burnt-offering for himself and the other for
the nation. Thus terminates, your majesty, the chief ceremonies of the great Day of Expiation, which is also held as a
day of rest and of rigid fast by all the people.

"There is a profound and divine signification to all these
extraordinary rites," says Abiathar. "They teach symbolically
that, in the coming ages, a Wonderful Man with two natures

(symbolized by the two goats), divine and human, shall appear in Israel to deliver the nation from a great bondage into which it will fall. In his human nature he will consent to die for the guilt of the people, to reconcile them to God, and will be slain by the High Priest as the goat was; but in his divine nature he will live, receive upon his head the sins of the world, and carry them forever away in his own person, so that they shall no more be found to appear against men!

"His blood as man he will sprinkle before the Mercy-Seat in the Upper Heaven, to make atonement to God there in the celestial Holy of Holies for his people; and in his divine nature he will ever stand before the Ark of the Covenant in Heaven, to make prayers, offer incense, and intercede for the whole earth! For his reward he will be crowned King of all kings, inspired above all Prophets, and invested with the High Priesthood of the Great Temple of God in Heaven, of which the Tabernacle and its Sanctuary here below are but the faint type and image!"

Such, your majesty, is a brief outline of the record I made three years ago, and which I have here carefully copied for you, of the chief religious ceremonies of this remarkable people, where all is done, not so much for itself, as to typify something yet in the future far more glorious!

I will, in my next letter, your majesty, return to the fortunes of the fugitive young shepherd David, who, flying from the persecution of King Saul, bent his steps toward the sacred city of the Tabernacle, to seek shelter at its altar, and protection from its High Priest, the venerable Ahimelech; for in all lands there is a sacred right associated with the Sanctuary that human power, however lawless, has never ceased to recognize and respect.

Your faithful friend and cousin,

ARBACES.

LETTER XI.

ARBACES TO THE KING OF ASSYRIA.

BETHLEHEM, PALACE OF JOAB.

YOUR MAJESTY:

The brief visit alluded to in my last letter, which three years since I paid to the Holy City of Nob, gave me a deeper insight into the Hebrew people than I have derived from all my former experiences and observations. As I left the house of Abiathar to return to Bethlehem the perpetual holocaust of the lamb sacrificed every morning (and a lamb also every evening), was just slain and laid upon the altar, slowly to consume by a low-kept fire all day, that the smoke of the burnt-offering might continually ascend to appease the Powers of heaven. The officiating priest had poured the cup of wine on the victim, emtied his vase of pure oil upon its head, and sprinkled its body with the finest flour, when Abiathar came forth from the Tabernacle and joined me, saying he would walk with me a few furlongs on my way. Were I to record, your majesty, his interesting conversation, I should give you a history of all the rites and ceremonies of the Hebrews; but as I intend only to narrate what will afford you such information as will enable you to have an intelligent appreciation of this people, I shall not repeat any of his words. I will, therefore, return to the friend of Prince Jonathan, in whose varied fortunes I know you take a deep interest.

David had proceeded but a few miles on his way toward Nob, which is thirty miles north of Hebron, when he came to a grove of palms, under which was a well. Here, seeing only maidens with their pitchers, he approached, and sat down to rest a little ways off in the shade. Two of the virgins, who dwelt in a village close at hand, who came to the well for water, after observing him a little while, spoke together, and then blushingly drew near him, one who was about sixteen, carrying her pitcher, and the other, a lovely child of fourteen, holding in her hand a basket of dates and figs, which she had just gathered not far off to take to her home. The youngest and most beautiful of the two, smiling with a kind benevolent expression in her soft eye, said:

"Young stranger, you look tired, and I dare say have traveled far! Will you eat some of these very nice dates and figs?"

The older girl, all confusion and less self-possessed than the other, then let down her pitcher of water from her head, and said, with charming embarrassment, in which kindness struggled sweetly with maiden bashfulness:

"You have no pitcher. Will you drink from mine, sir?"

The young wanderer and exile flying for his life, and feeling sad and desolate, was touched by this unlooked-for kindness in these beautiful strangers, and answered, with a vain effort to keep back his tears:

"The Lord hath sent you as he sent of old his angels to our father Jacob. I accept the dates, for I am hungry, and will drink the water, for I am thirsty!"

When he had refreshed himself, he asked their names.

"I," said the taller and older maiden, "am called Abigail, and dwell in this village."

"But," said the other archly, "she will not long dwell there, for she is betrothed to rich young Nabal of Judah, and is soon to be married and go to Mount Carmel to dwell."

"Nay, but thou art forward to give thy information, Bathsheba," said the comely young woman with crimson cheeks; and covering her face with her veil she hid her confusion from the eyes of the handsome shepherd.

"Thy name is Bathsheba, then?" he asked of the smiling little maid.

"Yes, daughter of Ammiel, sir!" she answered. "What is thy name?"

"David!" he replied; and seeing horsemen approaching he rose to go, thanking the two young maidens, and promising he should always recollect their kindness.

He walked rapidly on, thinking of the pleasant interview, until he came to an eminence whence, looking back, he saw that the three men, who had stopped a while at the well, were galloping toward him. He hastened to the rocks for concealment, when he recognized in the leading rider one of his own body-guard, who waved his hand to him. The fugitive stopped until three young men of his acquaintance came up to him, and, all alighting, each one saluted him with friendly warmth and respect. The eldest was a graceful and intelligent young man, called Ahithophel, famous for his wit and scholarship, as well as for his attachment to David; the next, a brave soldier and captain of horse, named Uriah of Heth, a dark, handsome young man, with Canaanitish blood in his veins, but a Hebrew from choice, who had fought thrice against the Philistines under David in his late battles, and admired him with true military devotion. The third was a kind-hearted, devoted, and courageous Hebrew youth, Hushai, who greatly esteemed David for his bravery and virtues, though he was not a soldier himself, only a rich, young citizen of Hebron, son of the chief lord of the king's treasury.

All three knew of Saul's persecution of David, and were indignant, and felt for him; and when they heard from Prince Jonathan that he had fled from the king they consulted together and agreed to follow him and join their fortunes to his. When David learned that they had come after him for this kind purpose, he would have sent them back, but they would not be prevailed upon to leave him; and as one of them, Uriah, had thoughtfully brought along with him David's own horse, one of the two presented to him by me, the young exile mounted the noble animal, and, gratefully acknowledging their kindness, thankfully accepted their company and protection, which, as they were all three well armed, was not to be despised.

The four mounted men now rode rapidly forward. Said Uriah, as he galloped along by his friend David's side:

"It was by the information of the two little maidens at the well we knew that you were in advance of us, noble captain. Upon my inquiring if such a person as thyself had been seen, the younger replied that a young stranger had been there, and asked if 'the person we sought was named David'? I replied that it was his name. She then said, 'If you are his friends, I will tell you which way he went; but if his enemies, I will not open my lips, for he is so good and looked so brave, and yet so sad, too, and he is so handsome!' I assured the beautiful little girl that we were your friends, and had brought the fine horse which I led for you to ride. She then told me the way you had taken. I was so pleased with the lovely and vivacious maid that I asked her name, and when she told me she was the daughter of Ammiel, I claimed her as my remote kinswoman, as Ammiel is my mother's second cousin. The little virgin would have stolen my heart had she been three years older," added the blunt, manly young soldier, with a smile; " as it was, I gave her a piece of my silver chain, and told her, smilingly, not to forget the man-at-arms, Uriah, the Hittite, who would one day come from the wars and woo her!"

Thus the party rode on, each one trying by conversation to cheer up the spirits of their beloved captain and honored friend, until they had passed Bethlehem, and got into the deep valley under the castle of the Jebusites. Here they were about to be met by a party of the king's troops, to escape the notice of which they turned back and remained in the hills of Bethlehem all night. The next morning they found that the whole country was full of armed parties searching for David by the command of Saul. The four friends, therefore, prudently resolved to remain among the mountains and keep concealed during the day. The following night they made secretly a circuit around Jerusalem on the east side, and remained in Mount Ephraim that day. The next night, by the light of the moon, they came under the walls of the holy city of Nob. Here they were compelled to remain until the sunrise-trumpet sounded for opening the gates, when, weary, hungry, and thirsty, having been for two days and two nights without food, they entered the city. As they were riding toward the house of Ahimelech, the Chief Priest, Ahithophel suddenly cried, " Do I not behold Doeg, the Edomite, the king's armor-bearer?"

David, looking up, saw the man named crossing the square of the Tabernacle with two men by his side. Their backs were to him; but he at once feared that Saul had sent him to take him even there; and, bidding his companions follow him, he galloped on quickly to the front of the Tabernacle, leaped from his horse, and entered the curtained door of the House of God, leaving his friends, who had nothing to apprehend, without to wait for him. At the moment there were present within the Tabernacle only the two priests who kept the fire alive upon the grate underneath the lamb laid upon the Altar of burnt-offering. David drew near, and taking firm hold of one of the horns of the altar, lifted up his voice in a divinely inspired hymn:

> " He that dwelleth in the secret place
> Of the Most High,
> Shall abide under the shadow
> Of the Almighty.
> The Lord is my refuge
> And my fortress;

He will cover me with his feathers,
And under his wings will I trust."

"Who art thou, and whence comest thou?" demanded one
of the priests; "and from whom dost thou seek sanctuary?"

At this moment David, perceiving the venerable High Priest
standing by the door of the inner Tabernacle, and recognizing
him by his robes and ephod, hastened to him and said, kneeling down before him:

"Holy Father, I have sought shelter in the House of God,
and at His altar, from the anger of a foe who seeks my life."

"Thou shalt have it! Who art thou, my son?" asked Ahimelech, regarding the prostrate youth with interest, as he raised
him from the ground.

"David, the son of Jesse!"

"The Champion of Israel!" he exclaimed. "Rise to thy
feet! I have heard much of thee, young man! Why art thou
here alone? Art thou not a chief captain of thousands in the
king's army? Why, and from whom shouldst thou flee in this
way? Hast thou fallen out with the king? I have heard that
he loves thee not! I trust it is not from him thou flyest
hither!"

David perceived by this that the High Priest feared Saul,
and that it would not be prudent to let him know the truth.
He, therefore, evaded the question, and said quickly, "I am
hungry, I and three of my men at the gate; for I am not alone.
Wilt thou give me to eat? What food hast thou here? Give
me four or five loaves, or what thou hast for me and mine."

"I have no common bread that thou mayest eat, save only
the twelve loaves of shew-bread just taken away from the
golden table and replaced by the hot loaves. I was about to
bear them to distribute to the House of the Priests. It is only
lawful for the priests and their houses to eat of them; but as
thou and those that are with thee are hungered, and thou look-
est famished and weary, I will give of them to thee if thou art
not this day, nor for the past three days, legally defiled."

He then commanded his son Abiathar to give to the fugitive
of the stale shew-bread, which was not now altogether as holy
as when it stood upon the table of the Lord, being ordained
to be eaten by the priests, and even their wives and children.
David at once hastened to give the bread to his three friends
before breaking it for himself. Outside of the entrance of the
court of the Tabernacle, as he stood therein to call to his com-

panions, he beheld, to his dismay, the dark and ill-visaged Doeg standing talking with Uriah, whom he well knew. The Edomite, who was a " proselyte of justice " to the Hebrew faith, had come to the Tabernacle four days before, not only to dispose of bullocks and lambs for the temple, being chief lord of Saul's herds, but to perform a vow, and knew not of the flight of David; nor did he suspect but that the three young men were there also to fulfill some vow; nor did they undeceive him. When, therefore, he turned and saw David, laden with the sacred loaves, call to them, he looked amazed and began to suspect something wrong. He was too profound a dissembler, however, to betray his suspicions, and saluting David with his usual cold dislike, he entered the Tabernacle. There he learned that David had sought sanctuary. The same hour news of his flight, brought by messengers of the king, reached him.

David was greatly troubled at seeing Saul's potent servant there; and after satisfying his hunger he returned into the Tabernacle and said to Ahimelech:

" Is there not in thy possession spear or sword? for I have neither brought my sword nor my weapons with me, for I came from Hebron in haste. I will go forward on my way! "

" Here is the sword of Goliath the Philistine, whom thou slewest in the valley of Elah; behold it was sent hither from Jerusalem last week by command of the king, with other weapons of the foe. It is here wrapped in a cloth behind the ephod. If thou wilt take that, take it; for there is no other save that here! "

" There is none like that; give it me! " answered David gladly; for he feared Doeg's evil eye, and resolved to arm himself against his treachery. He knew, also, that Saul's men-at-arms had reached Nob in pursuit of him; but Ahimelech was yet ignorant of it.

As soon as he received the sword he went out, and feeling that he might compromise before Saul the timid High Priest by remaining in sanctuary with him, he rejoined his friends, and the four left the city at full speed, and just in time to escape being shut in by the closing gates; for Doeg had been busy with the captain of the place, and persuaded him to hasten to detain David that he might be taken; for the fierce Edomite, David well knew, would not have hesitated to have taken him from the very horns of the Altar of the Sanctuary.

When they had ridden hard two leagues westward they came

into the passes of Mount Ephraim, and winding up the hills, they at length reached a summit, from which was visible the country of the Philistines.

"My own land is unsafe for me," said David as he regarded it; "this land of the Philistines cannot be more so!"

"My chief," said Uriah the Hittite, "thou knowest I am by descent from the ancient Canaanites allied to these Philistines. I have friends in their land. Trust yourself rather to strangers than to your countrymen, whose hands are armed for your life! Let my lord David go hence into the Philistine country. The King of Gath is Achish, who is a very generous person, and brave, and knoweth how to receive and extend hospitality to a brave adversary who seeks his court, especially to a man flying from Saul, who is his dreaded enemy!" David, after a little reflection, resolved to take shelter in the land of his hereditary foes; and the party descending the mountain rode southwestwardly in the direction of Gath.

Behold, your majesty, this young hero, who had done only good to his king and country, thus compelled to fly from it, because the very good he had done had aroused the fears and jealousy of its chief recipient, Saul. What a sad spectacle to see virtuous and noble acts of good men bring them into sorrow, as if they had been foes instead of benefactors to mankind! Truly did Samuel the Seer say in my long interview with him at Ramah:

"Such, O Prince Arbaces, is the ingratitude of man, that if the God of the Universe should leave his throne and take the human form, and go about on earth blessing and healing, and even proving his Godhead by raising the dead, the envy and hatred of man would compass his death, if so divine a person could come under the laws of death!"

Alas! without question the Hebrew prophet's words would be verified were it possible to have their truth tested.

When David reached the gates of Gath, where Goliath dwelt, he was received by the magnificent barbarian king with frankness and hospitality; for the Philistine rejoiced to have so powerful a warrior taken from Saul and added to himself. These people, being a nation of warriors, respect valor as the greatest of virtues; and although David had slain their champion, the king admired so greatly his courage that he preferred rather to pay him honor than avenge the death of Goliath and others upon him. He therefore offered him the command of a thousand men, and felt proud of having so brave a soldier in his service.

A few days afterward, as David rode by the side of the King of Gath, who displayed his armies before him, some of the captains and lords of the Philistines murmured, and said, in his hearing:

"Is not this the warrior chief of the Hebrews? Is he not a mightier king in Israel than Saul? Is not this he of whom they sang one to another when he had slain our champion, and bore his head to their temple to offer it to his God, as if it were a bullock's head, saying, 'Saul hath slain his thousands and David his ten thousands!' What doth he here, riding by the king's side?'

These words troubled David and his friends. They saw, after a few days more, that they produced an evil effect upon the king, who grew less cordial to him, and regarded him with less honor than before, and even set spies upon him! At length the constant excitement and anxiety to which he was a prey, combined with his forced exile from his country and from his father's house, from his beloved and beautiful young wife, and from his friend Jonathan, with the weight of the undeserved anger of King Saul—all these causes operating upon a body fatigued by his wandering, and upon a mind singularly sensitive and of the finest organization, threw him suddenly into a wild fever. The king, yet ignorant of his sickness, and led to believe he had come to Gath as a spy from Saul, under pretense of having been driven away by him, sent the captain of his guard to bring him before him as a prisoner, as he resolved to put him to death. The officer found the young Hebrew raving with delirium, and the foam of his mouth sprinkling his beard, while to the demand of the captain he would madly write upon the gate with his finger and laugh unmeaningly. They led him before Achish, who no sooner beheld him in this pitiable condition than he cried:

"Lo, ye see the man is mad! Wherefore then have ye brought him to me? Have I need of madmen that ye have brought this Hebrew to play the madman in my presence and into my palace? Take him hence!"

The next day at evening the fever left him, and his three friends, fearing for his safety before the king when he should recover, fled out of Gath with him that night. Holding him upon his horse between them they rode swiftly until they recrossed the border of Judah, and came to a wood in which was the cave of Adullam wherein Joshua slew its defeated king. To this cave the three young men conveyed David, it being very secluded, and also, from its elevated position in the rocks, easily defended, and its approaches' readily commanded by the eye. Here they made him a bed of skins, and, while Uriah kept guard at the mouth of the cave, Ahithophel remained by his side, and Hushai sought food from the villages or by hunting. Here they remained until he became perfectly well and strong, and fresh in heart and spirits. His brothers and others of his household were secretly informed of his abode, and came well-armed to him, besides several of his friends, and the friends of Uriah and Hushai, so that in six weeks after he had fled from Gath he found himself at the head of seventy men, five of them his brothers, all well-armed, and ready to defend him against Saul. In the meanwhile the king ceased not to hunt for him throughout all the realm, and his wrath was greatly increased against him when he heard that he had fled to the court and protection of his enemy, Achish; and it is said that the real cause of the coolness of the Philistine monarch was produced by Doeg, the Edomite, who had been sent to Gath to whisper that David was artfully there as Saul's spy upon its strongholds. When, therefore, Saul heard that his victim had escaped death from Achish, and had been seen in Judea again, he offered large rewards for his capture.

This vengeance of the Hebrew king against an innocent person created a strong feeling of sympathy for David, and when it became known that he was fortified at the rock of Adullam, not far from Hebron, numbers flocked to him, not only of his friends who had fought in Saul's service with him, but men of all classes! In a few days he was captain of four hundred men, among them certain debtors and dissolute persons, who fled to him, supposing he would protect them from their creditors for their service to him in his adversity. But he sent them away, indignantly answering "he was not become an adversary to the laws of the realm, though persecuted by its king, nor had his misfortunes made him of necessity a companion of the base. I am not at war with my people," he said to them, "nor do I intend to take cities from the king that such persons should come to gather yourselves unto me!"

Word was now brought David secretly from Jonathan that Saul, despairing of capturing him, had resolved to seize upon the persons of his aged parents at Bethlehem, and hold them as hostages until he should come and deliver himself up.

"Place them in security, O my friend," were the concluding words of Jonathan's message, brought by the lad who had gathered the prince's arrows, "and with all diligence, for to-morrow night I fear it will be too late. Providentially my father does nothing without informing me of his intentions, and hence I am able to do thee and thine this service, yet without injuring him. May the Lord bless you and guard you from all peril, and in his good time give you peace and safety. My heart is with you, I weep for and with you, but I am powerless between my affection for you, and my duty to my king and father. Michal mourns in silence your absence, and trembles when a messenger approaches the palace, lest he bring tidings that evil hath befallen you! I inclose from her hand an epistle for you, wetted more bountifully with tears than with ink."

The same hour David rose up, and taking three hundred men with him, leaving Uriah with one hundred to guard their fortified cave, he went to his father's house, and taking his invalid father and aged mother thence, he fled with them from Saul across the Jordan to Mizpeh, a city of the King of Moab. Presenting himself before the king, he said:

"I pray thee, O king, let my father and my mother be with you, till I know what God will do for me!"

"Bring hither thy father and mother, O David," answered the King of Moab; "and I will let them dwell with me! Was not the warlike Jesse, thy father, known to my father the king? Was not his grandmother a Moabitess, whom we hold in great honor? Art thou not but four removes from us? Let us be at peace!"

David gladly presented his venerable parents to the king, who gave them a house near his own palace, and entreated them for David's sake, as well as their own, with great favor. At the court of the King of Moab was a friend of David, one of the seven prophet Teachers of Ramah, whom I have already spoken of to your majesty. His name was Gad, and he was in great favor with the king, being allied to him by kindred, for the King of Moab had married a Hebrew woman, and was friendly to the nation; but Saul had offended him, and hence his friendly reception of David. The prophet Gad rejoiced to see David, but being inspired to reveal the future, he warned him that his safety and prosperity depended on his returning into the land of Judah. "If thou desirest it," he added, "I will go with thee and abide by thee, and aid thee with my friendship and by mine office."

David joyfully accepted this powerful ally; for a prophet is as a prince in rank in this religious land, and usually attends only kings; and the presence of this man he felt would give great weight to his cause; for "cause" his affair had now become, he having been forced by Saul to head a faction for his own preservation. This filial duty performed, he now returned to the cave of Adullam, in the plain of Judah, and gathering his whole band, increased by three hundred of the fighting men of the tribe of Gad, from beyond Jordan, and a score of brave Moabite warriors, he removed farther south, to the dark forest of Hareth below Hebron, to escape the attack of Saul, whom he did not desire to meet in arms; for the king with his whole army was marching upon him. But when Saul reached the cave of Adullam and found it empty he inquired of a herdsman who was friendly to David the way David had taken, who purposely said, "To the north, toward Jerusalem; with a thousand men at his back."

The king believing he had marched thither to capture his armory, hastened to defend the place. Upon reaching it he could hear nothing of him, and so continued his march upon Gibeah; and thence to Ramah, believing he had marched thither to hold counsel of Samuel the Seer. At Ramah he got no intelligence of him, and learned that Samuel himself was not in the city. He was now assured that the prophet was with his adversary, and stopping by a palm tree which stands by the well of Gibeah, over against the gate of Ramah, he said, as he leaned with a disappointed look upon his spear, addressing his lords, chief captains, and men-at-arms, who stood waiting silently around him until he should decide in what direction to continue his march:

"Hear now, ye Benjamites! Will the son of Jesse give everyone of you fields and vineyards and make you all captains of thousands, and captains of hundreds, that all of you have conspired against me? Ye know where he lurketh, yet no man will tell me! Am I become so abased in your eyes that ye mock me with your silence, when I would know where my enemy lieth hid? So my son, also, hath made a league with the son of Jesse against me, and is for him! Yet there is none of you that is sorry for me! I can trust none of you who eat my bread and receive the king's wages! Why is it that ye will not speak?"

"My lord the king will not be angry with his servant," here spoke Doeg, his armor-bearer, and lord of his herds, "because thy servant hath kept silence until now; but thy servant knew that first it was expedient the king should give himself wholly to the destruction of his foe; but now that he hath eluded my lord the king, and brought the king into these parts opposite Nob, his servant would let my lord know that when thy servant was performing his vow in the holy city, two months ago, thy servant beheld the son of Jesse come to the tabernacle, and claim sanctuary at the hand of Ahimelech, the son of Ahitub. The High Priest received the son of Jesse, inquired of the Lord for him, gave him to eat, and those that were with him, of the sacred bread, and also placed in his hands at his departure the sword of Goliath!"

Before the malicious and artful Edomite had ended his words the anger of the king kindled, and brandishing his spear in the air he swore by the Ark of God! that Ahimelech and his whole company of priests should die!

Without delay he marched against Nob with his four thousand men, nearly all Benjamites of his own tribe, to whom alone he now trusted, brave and fierce men who always fought with the left hand and held their bucklers on the right arm. As he approached the city of God the smoke of the perpetual sacrifice was rolling in dark clouds skyward, and as they drew near the walls it hung above their heads and obscured the sun. Coming before the gate, Saul sent in a messenger to command the High Priest to come out to him, and bring all his father's house and all the priests who served the tabernacle.

The High Priest with a heavy heart summoned his holy family and all the priests save those who were serving at the altars. Arrayed in miter, ephod, pectoral, and breastplate, and wearing his purple robe, and all the priests clad in their sacred vestments and linen ephods, Ahimelech led them in long procession forth to the impatient and angry king's pavilion. Saul came forth clad in full battle-armor, his spear in his hand, and his face dark with wrath. Fixing his fierce eyes on the venerable countenance of the Chief Priest, he cried:

"Hear now, thou son of Ahitub! Art thou here at last?"

"Here I am, my lord," he answered with dignity, though pale with fear.

"Why have ye conspired against me," demanded Saul sternly, "thou and the son of Jesse, in that thou hast given him bread and a sword, and hast inquired of God for him, that he should now rise against me, and lie in wait for me, as at this day? Thou hast favored the king's foe, and been at friends with him, and didst let him depart with thy blessing to take up the sword against me!"

The High Priest, though naturally timid and gentle, seemed to be inspired by his God with courage, for he replied firmly and fearlessly:

"And who, O king, is so faithful among all thy servants as David, which is the king's son-in-law, who ever did thy bidding, and was as honorable in thy house for his virtues and wisdom, as on the field by his valor and skill in defending thy crown and kingdom? If such be his high character, O king, if I received him with honor, was it not my duty, even as I would the king's son had he come to me? But I did not consult the divine oracles for him, nor did he ask me to do so, O king, for only on public and national occasions do I inquire of God, and never privately for private persons! Had I done so for David, the king might impute blame to his servant. If one inquired of God for him, thy servant knew not of this, less or more! Evil hath been spoken of thy servant about this thing."

"Thy words avail not," answered Saul. "Thou shalt surely die, Ahimelech, thou and all thy father's house!"

The king, with a countenance black with the profoundest displeasure, then turned to his bodyguard of two thousand men, who were standing in armor, sword in hand, about him:

"Abner, turn and slay this hoary priest, and all his house, and all the priests here before me, with the sword! They belong to the son of Jesse, because they sheltered him when he fled, and did not show it to me. Let them die the death, and their Gibeonite slaves with them!"

The brave and noble general of the king made no movement to obey this sanguinary order. His iron-clad men-at-arms stood immovable in their ranks. The king glared at them, and, almost speechless with passion, demanded of them whether they were going to obey him.

"My lord, the king," said Abner, "will pardon thy servant, but he cannot put forth his hand, nor will his men do so, to fall upon the priests of the Lord."

"Rebel! Art *thou* against me?" shouted the king. "By the head of Dagon there is one man here I can trust to! Where is thy sword, Doeg? Thou and thy bearded men of war turn to, and fall upon these priests!"

No sooner had the word gone out of the king's mouth than the Edomite's eyes blazed with the hue of blood, and drawing his sword he called to two hundred desperate men, of all nations, who served him, ever ready to do his bidding, to commence the slaughter.

What pen, your majesty, can portray the scene that ensued! Already anticipating their fate most of the priests had begun to fly. Doeg struck the first blow at the High Priest, cleaving his head to the brow, and laying him dead at the feet of the king. For a quarter of an hour the work of death went on, the murderers pursuing in every direction those who fled; though the greater portion who were slain received their death, fallen on their knees, with their hands folded upon their linen ephods, and their faces cast down to the earth, in profound submission to their irrevocable fate. At length Doeg recalled his monsters of blood, who slew, in all, four score and five priests wearing the sacred linen ephod.

"Now," said the king, "go and enter the city of the priests which has received the fugitives, and take it, and put to the sword all within."

This sanguinary order was executed. The sacred city was taken by Doeg, and not only were three hundred more persons slain in the city, but all the wives, daughters, and sons of the Levites, and all the remnant of the Gibeonites therein, and all the infants, were put to the sword by the vengeance of Saul against David. But one person escaped, Abiathar, the eldest son of Ahimelech, who, having remained behind in the Tabernacle to burn incense in the Sanctuary, secreted himself until the massacre was over, when he secretly fled from the ruins of the city of God, and reaching the camp of David in the forests of Hareth made known to him what Saul had done.

Upon hearing these dreadful tidings David was deeply moved, and, embracing Abiathar, with tears, he said in a tone of self-reproach:

"I knew it that day when Doeg, the Edomite, was there, whose tongue deviseth mischief and who loves evil more than good. I knew that he would surely tell Saul. Alas! I have occasioned the death of all the persons of thy father's house!"

He then said, "Abide thou with me, Abiathar; for thou shalt be very dear to me henceforward. Fear not Saul! He that seeketh my life, he it is that seeketh thy life; but with me thou shalt be safe. God will be our safeguard!"

I come now, your majesty, to a series of incidents in David's wonderful career which show the excellency and dignity of his character, his patriotism, justice, and clemency.

The Philistines, taking advantage of Saul's pursuit of David, invaded lower Judea and robbed the granaries of the Hebrews. David without delay assembled six hundred followers, marched against them, and smote them with great slaughter; and, relieving the Hebrew city of Keilah which the Philistines had laid siege to, he entered it and garrisoned it with his own men. When Saul heard this, instead of giving David praise for driving his foe from the land, and, therefore, seeing in him a faithful subject, he cried with exultation:

"God hath delivered him into mine hand; for he is shut in by entering into a town which hath gates and bars!"

Thus the wickedness of this Heaven-forsaken monarch waxed greater and greater every day; confirming the saying, "that evil produceth more evil continually, until cometh the end of evil, which is dishonor and death."

David being warned by the divine oracle through Abiathar, who was with him, and now the real High Priest of the nation, that Saul would come against him, and the citizens of Keilah, for dread of Saul's vengeance, would deliver him into the king's hand, marched forth from the city by night and sought the fastnesses of the wilderness of Ziph, east of Hebron; for in it were numerous caves and lurking places where Saul's army could not easily penetrate. Here David strengthened his retreat in a military manner, and remained on the watch against Saul, who dared not attack him in the depths of this wilderness of trees and rocks.

One evening as David was walking in the forest, going from outpost to outpost, attended only by Uriah, his armor-bearer, in order to see that all were vigilant, for Saul was in the neighborhood, three men suddenly appeared in the path. The moon shone broadly down upon them, and, with a cry of joy, David ran forward and fell on the neck of the foremost of the two, exclaiming:

"The Lord hath blessed me indeed in letting me, O Jonathan, behold thy face once more!"

"And me also, O David, in permitting me to come safely to thee," answered the prince, embracing his friend again and again, and holding him off to look into his face to see what change had taken place therein. "Thou art older and darker, and more stern in look, dearest David! Hadst thou not spoken I would hardly have known it was thee. I have come to thy fastnesses to comfort thee, and tell thee that I sympathize with thee in all thy troubles. Here also is the brave Joab, who was thy chief captain, and his younger and equally brave brother Abishai, who have come with me to see thee!"

"And to stay with thee, O my lord, if thou wilt take me into thy service," answered Joab. "I cannot serve the king any longer while thou needest my sword!"

David's heart was gladdened by the presence of these friends; and he told Joab he should be the chief commander of his men. Uriah, Joab, and the youthful Abishai now followed the prince and his friend, as they two walked together toward the camp discoursing.

"Thou art so good to come to see me," said David tenderly. "I feared I had displeased thee by taking up arms and gathering an army!"

"No, David," answered the prince. "I rejoice to know that thereby thou wert making it more and more difficult for my father to do thee harm! Fear me not, my David! I am as true to thy soul as ever! Shame for my father's hatred of thee tinges my cheek. He shall not find thee to come to thee! God will strengthen thy hand! Thou shalt yet be king over Israel, and I shall be next to thee; is it not so? and that also Saul my father knoweth!"

Before day David accompanied his friend to the verge of the forest, and there renewing their oath of perpetual friendship, they parted, Jonathan taking a memorial from the young husband to his bride in Hebron. This visit of his friend strengthened the heart of David, as did the coming to him of Joab, his hand.

Not far from the forest was the city of the Ziphites, who, fearing Saul, sent to him to offer to betray David into his hand.

"If ye know where his haunt is," said Saul, "go and find him if ye can, for I am told he is very subtle, and may not easily be taken unaware. Go and take knowledge of all his lurking places where he hideth himself, and then come to me, and I will go with you; for if he be in the land, I will search him out throughout all the thousands of Judah."*

These men returned from the king to their forests, and would have betrayed David, but being warned by the prophet Gad, and by the oracle of Abiathar, of danger, the Heaven-guarded wanderer changed his camp to the wilderness of Maon, farther south. Here his young men did good service in protecting from robberies the flocks of Nabal, who had already married the comely maiden Abigail David saw at the well, and dwelt at Maon. Saul pursued David to this place, when a messenger came bringing intelligence that an army of the Philistines, taking advantage of his war against David, had invaded his kingdom. The king hesitated for a while, whether to continue his pursuit of David, or turn back and march against the enemy of his country. Revenge and patriotism struggled for the mastery in his stormy bosom, but the latter prevailed, and he went against the Philistines, while David leisurely fortified himself in a stronghold, near the Sea of Sodoma, called En-geddi, a land of vineyards and of plenty, of wild rocks where the goats browse, and of fertile vales.

The warlike Saul having defeated and punished his enemies the Philistines, returned with three thousand men, and followed David among the very cliffs and caves of En-geddi. In these caves David and all his men were concealed. Saul, not supposing he was near them, driven to seek shelter from the sun, left his attendants without and entered a cave, in the dark recesses of which David and fifty of his men lay hidden. David saw the king enter, his tall, martial form clearly relieved against the sky of the opening. He recognized him immediately, and made a sign for his followers to remain quiet. Saul walked in for a few yards, and after looking wearily about him, lay down to rest, covering himself and his feet with his camp cloak, for the cave was cool. He soon fell into a deep sleep. Uriah then came near and said to David, " Behold the Lord hath delivered thine enemy into thine hand, to do to him as it shall seem good unto thee!"

" Nay," said David; " I am not his foe! Is he not my father-in-law, and the father of Jonathan my friend? Is he not also my king, and the anointed of God? I will not harm him, for I seek not his life. It is he who seeks mine. But I will show him he has been in my power!"

*1 Samuel xxiii. 22. 23. etc.

David then advanced to where lay the stern king whose jealous hatred had so embittered his life, and with his knife he
severed the border of his robe; and taking the piece in his
hand he returned to his men, who were grieved and angry that
he had not slain him.　But their prudent and upright young
captain said:

"Nay, but I have done wrong even to sever his robe.　My
heart smites me to have put this indignity upon an anointed
king!　I am ashamed to have put forth mine hand to touch
the anointed of the Lord.　Touch ye him not!　He is our master and lord!"

At length Saul awoke and rose up and left the cave, followed by David, who from the outlet thereof called after him:

"My lord the king!"

Saul turned and beheld David, who bowed with his face to
the earth before him, and said aloud:

"O king, live forever!　Believe no more what men tell thee,
'that David seeketh thy hurt!'　I found thee asleep in this
cave.　Thou seest, therefore, how the Lord delivered thee into
mine hand.　My followers saw thee, and bade me kill thee.
But I spared thee, remembering thou art my master and the
Lord's anointed.　Moreover, my father, behold this skirt of thy
robe in my hand! for in that I cut off this from thy robe and
killed thee not, know then I seek not to harm thee, O my lord!
yet thou huntest my life to take it!　The Lord judge between
me and thee; the Lord avenge me, not mine own hand, for as
the Lord liveth, mine hand shall not be put forth against thee!
Wickedness doth wickedly.　Judge me.　It I were evil I should
have done thee evil."

What a noble and generous speech, your majesty!　What
godlike forbearance and forgiveness!　What piety and reverence are here exhibited by this ingenuous and unselfish young
man!　How worthy in every way to succeed in the throne his
relentless persecutor!　What divine qualities display themselves
in his character!　Every trial serves to elevate him higher and
higher in all that makes a man great, wise, and good.　Now
mark, your majesty, the effect of this sublime treatment upon
King Saul.

At first he did not know David by his features, his face had
so changed by exposure and hardships; but he recognized the
noble voice which had so often soothed his melancholy, and
when David had ended he cried with emotion:

"Is this *thy* voice, my son David? I have heard thy words! They break my heart. I cannot speak to thee for my tears! I perceive thou art more righteous than I; for thou hast returned me good for evil, since, when the Lord delivered me into thine hand, thou killedst me not; for if a man find his enemy, will he let him go safely away? The Lord reward thee for the good done me at thy hand this day. I now know the Lord is with thee, and that thou shalt surely be King of Israel, and that the kingdom shall be forever established in thine hand. Swear now, therefore, unto me that when thou comest to be king in my place, thou wilt not put my children to death, nor destroy my name out of my father's house!"

David lifted his hand to the Lord and took the oath Saul required of him; himself exacting of the king no oath, as he might well have done, that he would cease his persecution of him, and leave him in peace.

Saul, without drawing any nearer to David, turned and gathered his army, and left the caves and strongholds of En-geddi, and the same day turned to go back to Hebron. But David too well knew the king's inconstancy, and that his reconciliation was the result of a momentary emotion of gratitude, and admiration of noble qualities he once possessed himself, and could still appreciate even in his enemy; and remembering the saying, " Trust not with too credulous a heart an enemy reconciled, for though he humble himself, yet take good heed and beware of him," he durst not stay in such an exposed and well-known position, and immediately removed from the caves to the strongholds of the highest hills.

When Saul reached his palace at Hebron the intelligence met him that the mighty Prophet of God, the man whom he feared above all other men, was no more! that he had died at his house in Ramah two days before, falling asleep in death with a calm serenity which was in correspondence with the piety, dignity, and purity of his character.

" Samuel dead! " repeated the king thrice, looking the messenger in the face incredulously.

" Dead, my lord! "

" Come with me, young man," he said to the youthful prophet, Asaph, who brought the news which, as he delivered it on his route to Hebron, filled all the land with mourning. The king took him aside, and placing his hands upon his two shoulders, and piercing his eyes with his own, said in a whisper;

"Who was with him when he died?"

"The Teachers and the disciples of the School of the Prophets alone stood about him," answered the young man.

"Wert thou there?" continued Saul.

"Yes, my lord!" he replied.

"What said he?" demanded the monarch. "Breathed he no message for the king? Spoke his lips naught to be told me? Sent he from his dying bed no word to Saul?"

"None, your majesty," was responded by the surprised young man.

"Not *one* word?" hoarsely asked Saul.

"Not one, my lord!"

"No sign? no attempt to say aught for me, but therein stopped by death coming upon him and preventing?"

"No, your majesty!" he replied.

Saul released his grasp upon the alarmed messenger, walked to and fro a while greatly excited, murmuring:

"Samuel dead! The light of Israel extinguished! The glory of Judea gone down to the shades of the departed, where the mighty, and powerful, and great, and wise of earth have gone before him! Dead! my counselor, my friend! Yes, these he was to me when I deserved his friendship. Now he is gone, I feel the mightiness of all his greatness and worth! Never shall a prophet again rise like him! This day Judah is shorn of her splendor, and the sun gone down in Israel! I, I am left in darkness alone! How shall Saul live, Samuel dead! for though he spoke no more with me, the sense of his presence was to me a power in the land, and I was strengthened by it! Now, like a solitary column, its companion riven by the lightnings, I stand unsupported and ready to fall! The death of Samuel is the omen of my own speedy downfall! Young man," he said, suddenly turning toward the messenger, "what ailed the man of God? Was he sick long?"

"Nay, my lord! He had no ailing. He had just closed the evening prayer, and joined in the chant, a ray of golden sunshine resting upon his majestic brow, like a crown of resplendent glory. We all noticed the unusually clear tones of his voice, as he praised the Lord in the ancient hymn of the school:

> "'My soul waiteth for the Lord,
> My soul doth wait for God,
> My Saviour.
> My soul waiteth for the Lord,

More than they that watch
For the morning,
More than they that watch
For the day.'

"While the last words were upon his lips he slowly sunk back into the ' Judges' throne '; the paleness of death succeeded the bright sunlight upon his forehead. He gathered the folds of his prophetic mantle about his breast, and committing his soul to God, murmuring: 'It is day!' he closed his eyes, and peacefully departed."

Saul listened with profound agitation, and when he had concluded, burst into tears and wept like a child! His unrestrained grief was heard by his attendants in the corridor and halls without, and all marveled when they learned how that Saul wept aloud for Samuel.

Ah, your majesty, what a noble, great wreck of a heart was in that kingly man's bosom! How fearful the power of evil in the soul to mar and destroy such a godlike nature as his! Even in its darkest and most fearful condition it responded instinctively to the best and highest aspirations of humanity! In the smoldering ashes still lingered the divine spark of sacred fire, which, too faint to be kindled into an altar-flame for God's sacrifice, yet could be fanned by the breath of penitence into life enough to burn grains of sweet incense, sprinkled thereupon by the gentle hand of piety and love.

In the death of this illustrious prophet, your majesty, the whole nation lost one who, for forty years, had been their wisest and best citizen, distinguished for his miracles, for holiness of life, zeal for God and his country, inviolable attachment to truth. He was a pattern to all judges in integrity and wisdom. His private character was without reproach. As a military leader he evinced courage and warlike skill of the first class. In the language of David to me, who wrote a noble eulogium upon his death: "He was a man of irreproachable integrity, undaunted fortitude, unblemished and unaffected piety, sincere as a friend, gentle as a man, virtuous as a Judge, and holy as a Prophet." His death threw the whole nation into profound grief, and by command of King Saul extraordinary honors were paid to his memory. He was buried with great pomp, at Ramah, in the garden of the Palace of the Prophets.

There is an interesting narrative connected with his early

life. He was a gift from God, in answer to her prayers, to his mother long childless; and in return she named him Samuel, "asked of God," and consecrated him from his birth to the service of the Sanctuary. Eli at that time was High Priest, and, I believe, the seventh in succession from Aaron, the great Hebrew Pontiff, and founder of the sacerdotal line. This chief Priest was a man of irresolute character, who failed to restrain his two sons, who were priests, in certain acts of impiety and sacrilege of which they were guilty. Instead of punishing them, he only gently reproved them, being a man of a mild temper. This parental indulgence in persons of public character, and in the sacred office, appears to be more culpable than in others. His God, therefore, showed his divine displeasure against the High Priest, by sending a strange prophet to him, who stood before the aged man and said:

"Behold, the days are come that there shall not be an old man in thine house forever! All the increase of thine house shall die in the flower of their age. And this shall be a sign unto thee: thy two sons Hophni and Phineas shall die, both of them in one day; and I will raise me up a faithful priest who shall do my will!"

Eli bowed his head in humble submission to this judgment of his God.

Not long after this denunciatory visitation Eli, whose eyes were now dim with age, was in the Holy Place lying down upon a couch where he kept watch by the Altar of Incense. Samuel, who was a mere child, and served in the temple, and waited on the High Priest, was asleep not far off upon a mat laid on the floor of the Sanctuary. There burned but a single lamp in the central branch of the golden candlestick, which was nearest to the Most Holy Place, the others being filled so as to burn only until dawn, having gone out; for it was near day. The central lamp, being left perpetually burning, was casting a soft twilight throughout the Sanctuary. While the lad slept a voice, calling him by name, awaked him. He answered, "Here am I!" and rose up, and ran to the couch of the venerable Eli, and said, "I am here, for thou calledst me."

"I called not, my child; lie down again," answered the aged Priest.

A second time the youthful Samuel was awaked by a still, small voice uttering his name.

The faithful and dutiful boy immediately ran to the side of

the couch of the old man, and said, "Here am I, for thou didst call me!"

"Nay; I called not, my son, lie down again," answered the High Priest. The lad went away and laid down again, and was ere long awaked a third time by a voice which called him by name.

He did not hesitate to rise and go to Eli as before, thinking that the aged man had some service for him to perform, but, by great age and loss of memory, had forgotten, as soon as he had called, that he needed him. This prompt obedience and patient, cheerful attendance of the amiable child are beautiful, and show the rich seeds of the noble character which were ultimately developed into golden fruit.

The High Priest now partly rose from his recumbent position. The threefold repetition of the voice he began to think could not be in the imagination of the boy; knowing that *he* did not call him, and that in that Holy Place no other human beings were, he perceived that it could be no other than the voice of God calling to the child from between the Cherubim behind the Vail. He therefore said unto the child:

"Go, my son, go and lie down again; and if thou hearest the voice call thee again by thy name, answer it and say, 'Speak, Lord, for thy servant heareth.'"

The boy returned to his little bed, and lay down in his place. All was once more still. No sound pervaded the solemn silence of the Sanctuary. He slept the profound sleep of innocence.

"Samuel! Samuel!" was again heard from the voice so mysterious. The lad awaked and answered, "Speak, Lord, for thy servant heareth." Then the voice of God said to him:

"Samuel, behold I will perform against Eli all things which I have spoken concerning his house: when I begin, I will make an end: for I have told him that I will judge his house forever, because his sons made themselves vile, and he restrained them not! And, therefore, I have sworn unto the house of Eli, that the iniquity of Eli's house shall not be purged with sacrifice nor offering forever!"

The voice of the Lord ceased with this dread sentence pronounced against the High Priest and his family, and Samuel slept no more, but lay until the dawn broke, when he rose and lifted the curtains to open the entrance to the Sanctuary. Then Eli called him and said, "Samuel, what is the thing the Lord said unto thee? I pray thee, child, hide it not from me."

And the lad repeated all the words of the Lord, hiding noth-ing from him. Then the venerable Priest bowed his hoary head with humble submission to the earth, and said:

"It is the Lord! Let him do what seemeth to him good!"

From that day Eli knew that Samuel was ordained to be a mighty Prophet and holy friend of God; and all Israel soon heard that the Lord had spoken with the child in visions of the night. From that time Samuel had other revelations from the divine Oracle of the Inner Sanctuary at Shiloh, and in-creased in wisdom and favor both with God and all the people.

This, your majesty, was the beginning of the sacred life of the great Seer. He is the first prophet that God so eminently distinguished as to converse with him in an audible voice, since the day of Moses.

Before I close this letter, your majesty, I must record the remarkable fulfillment of the denunciations of God against the house of the offending High Priest, showing that this great and terrible God regards neither sanctity of office, nor dignity of rank, but prophets, priests, and kings, alike with the basest (and more severely), are visited with punishment if they sin against Him. To punish sin it seems, in His holy anger against it, He would destroy a world! nay, hurl from His highest heaven angelic gods guilty of transgression; nay, be willing, if it could be thereby, and in no other way, banished from His universe, to give up His own Son, were He a Father, as a sacrifice in atonement for sin, if the blood of the lambs that now perpetually bleed on His altar cannot suffice to wash it away! To drive sin from the dominion of His creation, be-ginning with it in man, seems to be the motive of all His works and wonders, of all the displays of His terrible power and glorious majesty, of His ceaseless mercy to the true penitent, and inexorable justice against the offender.

Until the advent of Samuel as a prophet there had been a long period of suspended revelations to the Hebrews from their God, and heaven had set, they believed forever, its seal of si-lence upon their Oracle, and upon the Urim and Thummim by which the High Priests used to ascertain the mind of God! The Urim and Thummim are, if I am rightly informed, two sardonyx stones of extraordinary size and beauty which are set in ouches of gold and worn upon each shoulder of the High Priest. These stones represent Light and Truth. When God is present at the sacrifices the stone borne on the right shoulder shines with increased splendor, so that the rays of the illimitable glory darting from it are seen afar off; yet this stone is not naturally luminous. The stone emitted, also, a celestial brilliancy when the High Priest, entering within the Vail, stood before the Ark and sought of the Lord answers to inquiries made relative to important, public, and national events in the future, such as whether the general of the armies should give battle, and if so if he will be victorious. But of late revelation from God thereby had ceased, for the people had become careless and irreligious, and walked not in the laws.

The Oracle, also, had long been silent. This was the voice of the Lord audibly answering the High Priest, when, entering within the Holy of Holies, robed in his most gorgeous apparel and wearing his brilliant Breastplate, he inquired of Him! Standing before the Mercy-Seat he looked toward the place where, between the wings of the Cherubim, dwells the Divine Presence in the form of the "Light of Glory," and proposed what he desired to be informed about. If God answered favorably, He spoke audibly from between the Cherubim, and the twelve stones upon the Breastplate shóne forth with a splendor which lighted up the inner Sanctuary with dazzling radiance; each jewel, like a star, flashing forth its resplendent light! And when he went forth to the people the glory of the Lord still lingered on the Breastplate, so that they were all sensible of their God's presence in what they were about to undertake, whether it were to make war or defend their borders!

All these celestial manifestations and divine revelations had, for many years, on account of the irreligion of the people, been suspended! The Breastplate of Eli ever came forth from the Sanctuary as dim as when he bore it before the Lord; and until the voice of God spake audibly to the holy child Samuel, it had not been heard in the Tabernacle during that generation.

When, therefore, it was known that the Oracle of God's House was vocal once more, and that God had spoken audibly in the Sanctuary in the morning watch to the child Samuel, the liveliest anticipations were awakened in the bosoms of the desponding and humbled Hebrews. The news spread quickly throughout the whole land; and new heart was given to the nation. The Philistines at that time were masters of the country, and neither Judge nor warrior raised his head in the land.

"God is with us! The Lord hath spoken! Let Israel re-

joice! Let Judah lift up her head! The anger of Jehovah
hath ended! Lift up the standard of the people! Let us destroy our enemies! In the name of the Lord, let us redeem
our country."

Such was the cry which rang from one end of Judea to the
other. The whole nation flew to arms! They attacked the
Philistines, so long their masters, expecting without opposition to drive them from the land! But they were signally defeated, and four thousand of these confident Hebrews were left
dead on the field!

Disappointed and perplexed at this discomfiture, when they
counted upon certain victory, some of the lords and high captains cried, " It is because we asked not the Lord's presence
with us! We trusted to our own arms to bring us liberty."

Thereupon a deputation waited upon Eli, and asked for the
Ark of the Covenant to be delivered to them, with the Mercy-
Seat and Cherubim, between which dwelt the visible glory of
the Divine Presence. The High Priest, prevailed upon against
his own wishes by his two sons, surrendered the sacred Coffer
to these warriors and captains. They bore it away, attended
by his sons, Hophni and Phineas, as its keepers, with great
rejoicings, and accompanied by tens of thousands of jubilant
people praising the Lord and rejoicing in his Presence. The
House of the Oracle was brought to their camp and placed in
the center of the army. Inspired with confidence in victory, the
Hebrews now recklessly gave battle to their enemies. The result proved far more disastrous than before! The Philistine
armies were conquerors in all parts of the plain, defeating the
Hebrews with immense slaughter, overthrowing all their hosts,
and putting to death on the field thirty thousand of those who
bore arms against them. The new and young king of the
Philistines, Goliath of Gath, the giant, who was slain many
years afterward by David in the vale of Elah, attacked the
guardians of the Ark itself, with his own hands slew Hophni
and Phineas, who, dissolute and unworthy priests as they were,
as men showed the greatest courage, and died valiantly defending the Ark of that God whose holy laws they had dishonored
by their impious and sacrilegious lives.

The Ark now became the rallying point of the men of Israel,
and the elevated wings of the Cherubim became the standards
to call them to die for their faith! A thousand devoted men
fought to the last, and were slain around it, piling with their

dead bodies a hecatomb to their God, around the Sanctuary of His Presence. But all in vain these pious and sublime sacrifices! The Ark was taken by their foes, and borne in barbaric triumph from the field to the Philistine camp!

Eli the High Priest had gone out of the Tabernacle in Shiloh, to watch for news from the battlefield, for his heart trembled for the Ark of God. Weary with ninety-eight years upon his shoulders, he came to a seat by the side of the road, and which stood near to the gate of the city, and sat down. Suddenly he heard a great outcry in the direction of the gate, but his eyes being dim, he could not see what produced it. But there had just entered it a man, running from the army, with his clothes rent, and earth upon his head, and with all the signs of woe in his face, like one who bore evil tidings. As soon as he could get his breath, he cried to those about him:

"The Ark of God is taken! The Ark of God is taken! The people of Israel are overthrown in all their armies, and the Ark of God has fallen into the hands of the King of Gath and his Philistines."

These tidings spread like wild-fire throughout Shiloh, and the whole city cried out with despair.

"What meaneth the noise of this tumult?" asked the old man, with tremulous accents.

The bearer of the tidings came near the blind High Priest and answered, "I am a bearer of news from the army, my lord! I left it to-day, and have run all the way hither!"

"What has been done? Have they fought, my son?" he asked.

"They have had a battle, and our people have fled before the Philistines," answered the man; "and there has been very great slaughter of our people, and thy two sons, Hophni and Phineas, are dead, and the Ark of God is taken!"

The old man heard of the death of his sons unmoved, but at the last words he fell over backward from his seat by the gate, and died! His daughter-in-law, the wife of Phineas, no sooner heard the man's tidings than she cried, "The glory is departed from Israel; for the Ark of God is taken," and immediately expired from grief and shame.

Thus in one day, your majesty, was fulfilled in the most wonderful manner the prophecy of the Oracle to the child Samuel!

The Philistines, believing that the Hebrew God was the two

Cherubim, idols like their own, felt great exultation in robbing them of their deities; and believing that all the wonders the Ark had done for Israel, it would do for them, conveyed the Oracle with great pomp in sacred procession to their chief temple, dedicated to Dagon.

No sooner was the Divine Ark placed therein than the image of their god bowed to the earth and fell prostrate before it. Attributing this remarkable obeisance to accident, they replaced it upon its pedestal. The following morning, when the priests of the god entered the temple, they were amazed to behold their idol again prostrate before the Ark, and his head and hands broken off by the fall, and lying on the threshold. The same day the whole city, beginning at the priests, was smitten with unknown fearful diseases! * The dreadful Ark was sent away therefore by them to another city, which was similarly afflicted by dire pestilences and calamities, which followed the Ark whithersoever they carried it, until at length by the counsel of their diviners they resolved to restore it to its rightful owners, the Hebrews, which was done with great ceremony, and with trespass-offerings of gold and jewels to God for their sin in taking it, and that He would heal their diseases. The Israelites received their holy Ark with national rejoicing.

At length Samuel came to manhood and became the Judge and leader of Israel, and under his holy influences the whole nation publicly repented and confessed its long-continued sins to God, returning to Him after those years of disobedience by fasting, humiliation, sacrifice, and prayer. The Philistines, hearing of the vast, unarmed religious assembly of the men of Israel under Samuel, resolved to attack them, hoping for an easy victory. The sight of the mail-clad armies of their implacable and dreaded foes filled them with consternation, and they began to accuse Samuel, as of old their like fathers did Moses, of bringing them into their great peril. But Samuel sacrificed a victim upon the altar, and as the smoke of the burnt-offering ascended toward heaven, he called upon his God! At the prophet's voice the skies grew black with clouds above the hosts of the Philistines: thunders rolled in fearful voices along the heavens, from which darted forked lightnings down upon the foes of God, and of his people. Filled with dismay, the Philistines fled, pursued by the Hebrews, and utterly overthrown, were smitten with great slaughter. From that day of

* 1 Samuel v.

power this eminent Hebrew ruled Israel as Judge and general of its armies. For forty years, during his wise, and prudent, and powerful government, the Philistines remained within their own borders, fearing his power and respecting his courage. At length, when he became advanced in years, he divided the rule with his two sons, who, though not like those of Eli, wicked and sacrilegious, yet governed the people without prudence or wisdom. Hence arose that universal spirit of disaffection which led the Israelites to wait on the aged Seer and Judge, now three score and ten years of age, and ask him to withdraw his authority from his sons, and anoint over the nation a king, that they might have hereditary rulers, and be like the nations around them!

Your majesty will recollect that in my earlier epistles I narrated the result of this petition, which was the election and anointing of Saul! Samuel, who had been forty years sole Judge of Israel, lived more than a score of years during Saul's reign, dying at the advanced age of ninety, sublimely ending a life of honor and usefulness, and leaving to the future ages a name that will never die.

Farewell, my dear Belus,
King, and kinsman, of his faithful
ARBACES.

LETTER XII.

ARBACES TO THE KING.

BETHLEHEM, LAND OF JUDEA.

YOUR MAJESTY:

Since I last wrote to you my health has been steadily improving. I sit by an open window, from which I have a pleasant view of the olive hills, near Jerusalem, and a pleasant vale between filled with gardens and vineyards, and white-walled homes of the vine-dressers and olive-keepers. In the court of Joab's house are numerous orange trees, the golden fruits of which shed delightful odor on the air, while the odorous oleander and the pomegranate tree, with its scarlet-scalloped cups, and flowers of every gorgeous hue, enrich the prospect before me. Zephyrs blow softly in at my window, and the voices of singing birds unknown in Assyria charm my ear.

All this is very grateful to an invalid, and I do not know how better to dispose of my invigorated health and cheerful spirits than to write to you, O Belus, and continue the narrative of the events which transpired during my detention in Egypt, and which have paved the way of David, the shepherd, the hero, the poet, and great captain, to the Throne of Israel.

At the closing part of my last letter I gave you more in detail the history of the Seer Samuel than hitherto, inasmuch as it afforded a key to the understanding of one of the most important periods of the history of this people. Your majesty can now, with me, intelligently trace the progress of the Hebrews through the centuries which have elapsed since the crossing of the Jordan to the death of Samuel; while the letters of Sesostris * in your archives have given you a full history of the wonderful events connected with this nation, from the calling of Abram out of Assyrian Chaldea, to become the father of this mighty confederacy of twelve Principalities, to their forty years' march through the wilderness toward this land now occupied by them.

* *Vide* " Pillar of Fire; or, Israel in Bondage."

The reign of Saul is the foundation of the prophetic Throne of David; and no future events of David's life can hardly prove more extraordinary than those of his youth, from the time of his anointing as King and successor to the Throne (which from that day was virtually his own) of Saul, and to the scepter of Israel.

Your majesty will, perhaps, believe that the Hebrew monarch, after his reconciliation with David at the cave of Engeddi, and open acknowledgment of his right to the succession on his throne, suffered the youthful, God-appointed heir to his kingdom to remain in peace. Doubtless he was sincere at the time in what he said and did, and meant to keep his vow.

But you have learned enough of the fickleness of his temper, O Belus, to lead you to suspect that the first impulse of feeling rising against David from any cause, his persecuting wrath would reawake. Such was the fact.

He had returned to Hebron after paying royal honors to the sacred ashes of the consecrated Prophet, and shutting himself in his palace he became profoundly melancholy; a condition of his mind, which, like dark clouds rolling up the sky and casting their shadow over earth's sunshine, foreboded a tempest. Fearing to hasten the outburst of the simoom across the fiery desert of his soul, his attendants came not near him. Since the massacre of the priests he had seldom slept; if so, only where fatigue chanced to arrest him; and then his dreams were fearful, and would rouse him with groans of despair to equally terrible consciousness. His dark visions were as unedurable as his waking reflections; hence he studiously kept away from his couch, and compelled his servants to keep him from sleeping by music and constant watchfulness. "Strike the gray beard, Doeg! let not one be left alive!" he would cry in his sleep, seated upright in his chair, or leaning against the side of his throne, or by the window.

How remarkably, your majesty, the massacre of these priests, all of whom were descendants or kindred of Eli, fulfilled the prophetic denunciations of the Oracle in the Sanctuary, when God spake to the child Samuel! Seventy years had elapsed, and their God, to whom a year is a moment, makes the fierce and cruel Doeg the executioner of his judgments; but with no less guilt to Doeg the sword, and Saul the hand which did the deed. Wicked men may carry out God's purposes, when they think they are only following the dictates of their own sanguinary nature. He can make even the fury of his creatures redound to the glory of his own power and will.

His daughter, the Princess Michal, at length approached her father when he was in one of these gloomy conditions of mind. She found his face hollow and haggard, his eyes blood-shotten, his massive jaws hanging with helpless woe, and his whole frame drooping and spiritless.

"Father," she said; "I have come to ask thee to send me to David, my husband, since thou art reconciled to him."

"Thou! what dost thou ask? A husband! By the brazen gods of Ekron, thou shalt have one!" he cried, with looks so terrible that she shrank from the blaze of his eyes. "Call hither Phalti, the Danite lord, son of Laish!" he commanded his servants.

When the man appeared before him the king said to him, "I have heard thou didst love my daughter Michal ere the son of Jesse beheld her! She has no husband! I divorce her by the king's oath! Take her! She shall be thy wife!"

In vain Michal plead for mercy. Phalti was a man twice her age, and of stern countenance; but virtuous and upright. He had done his king service in guiding him to Engeddi, having possessions in the forest. He would have opposed the king's command, but feared to do so. The marriage was performed the same hour, and Phalti bore his wife to his home, saying to his mother, "This is my sister, and keep her with thee, that David may one day have her."

When David heard the news he was justly indignant, and had a good cause now for quarrel with the king. But he bore the insult and wrong with forbearance. Saul now followed up this outrage. He felt that he had thereby wronged David so that he would certainly, in his anger, come out from his fortresses and give him battle; when he hoped to slay him on the field.

He therefore went forth again at the head of his army and approached the place in the wilderness of Ziph, where his spies told him David was fortified. Here, upon a plain partly covered with wood, the king pitched his camp and slightly entrenched it, hoping David would attack on the morrow. From the top of the rock David beheld the tents of Saul, his banners flying, and his whole army in battle array.

"I will seek Saul's pavilion to-night," he said, turning to Abishai, the brave younger brother of his chief captain Joab, and others about him. "Who will go down with me thither secretly after dark?"

"I will go down with thee," answered Abishai. Under cover of the night, though aided by a new moon, David, who by daylight carefully marked with his eye the direction and path, approached the outposts of the king's camp. Without being discovered he entered within the lines and came to Saul's pavilion. His guards slept, and David advanced beyond them, and stood by the side of the king, who lay fast asleep in his unharnessed chariot before the door of his tent, the light of the young moon distinctly revealing his worn, yet still majestic features. His javelin was stuck in the ground at his head. The young warrior stood and contemplated his face with profound emotions and sad recollections. "How changed!" he said, unconsciously speaking with himself; "how deeply passion has drawn its plowshare across his kingly brow! How stern the visage! He starts and mutters! It is the name Samuel he pronounces. His dreams trouble him! Alas! I pity thee, O king!"

"My captain," said Abishai, "the Lord hath delivered thine enemy into thine hand! Now therefore let me smite him with his own spear, even to the earth at once! One blow and no more, I ask."

"Destroy not the anointed of God!" said David. "Who can stretch forth his hand against the Lord's anointed and be guiltless? Leave him to the justice of God. His day will come! Let him fall in battle, but not by my hand!" He then turned and looked for a while at the sleeping king's face, who started, feverish and ill at ease, and uttered his name in his disturbed sleep, but with harsh and bitter tones. Abner his general also slept, his head on his buckler, and his sword in his hand, not far from the chariot. "Take the spear at the king's head, and the cruse of water by his side, and let us depart," said David to his companion. "He shall thereby know, and Abner also, that he has been in my hand!"

Reluctantly Abishai refrained from slaying the king, and taking the spear and the cruse of water, with which the feverish king quenched his burning thirst, he followed David. They repassed the sleeping sentries, no man being disturbed in the deep sleep that was fallen upon them. Opposite the camp of Saul was a high hill of rock, about five bow-shots distant, to the top of which David ascended, and turning round he called:

"Abner! Hear thou, O Abner, O chief captain of King Saul! Answerest thou not, Abner son of Ner?"

His loud call aroused the Hebrew general from his sleep, and springing to his feet. he cried, looking all about him:

"Who, and where art thou, that criest to the king?"

"Art thou not a valiant man?" continued David from the hill; "and who is like to thee, O general, in Israel? Wherefore hast thou not better kept ward over thy lord the king? There but now came one near to destroy thy lord. Is this the way to keep watch and ward over your master, and the Lord's anointed? As the Lord liveth, ye are worthy of death! Who am I? Find thou first where the king's spear is, and the cruse of water that was at his head as he slept!"

Saul also awakened, and recognizing his well-known voice, and missing his spear and the cruse of water, and perceiving that the man he had wronged had been by his side as he slept, and refrained from taking his life, with that impulsive emotion characteristic of him he was touched to the heart, and called out, in tones of kindness:

"Is this thy voice, my son David?"

"It is my voice, O king," answered the noble young man. "While thou and thine slept, I stood by thy head, and with thine own spear could have slain thee! I bore it away, not to insult thee, O my father, but to show thee that the Lord gave thee into my hand. If the Lord hath now sent thee against me for my sins, then will I offer him a sin-offering, and humble myself before his footstool for my transgression; but if the wickedness of men hath stirred thee against me, let the Lord destroy them for driving me into the wilderness, and holes, and caves of the earth, and even to seek shelter among the heathen, and under their gods! Wherefore does the King of Israel hunt me thus, as a wild bird, or a coney of the rocks, giving me no rest! Moreover thou hast taken from me my wife, and given her to another! Yet for all this I slew thee not this night!"

Then Saul answered and said, "I have sinned, my son, my son David! Return to Hebron or go where thou wilt. I will do thee no harm, because my life was precious in thine eyes. I have been a fool, and a madman before thee, and have grievously wronged thee and thine, O David!"

David did not make any answer to these confessions and promises, for he knew better than to put any confidence in a prince so wayward and inconstant, and who still hated him bitterly.

"Behold the king's spear!" he called to Abner. "Let one of the young men come over and fetch it."

Saul sent a lad for his spear and cruse of water, and said:

"Blessed be thou, my son David! The Lord is with thee! Thou shalt do mighty works and deeds of valor, and over all thine enemies have the victory and prevail."

David, delivering the spear to the youth who timidly came for it, turned and left the top of the mount, accompanied by Abishai, and ere midnight regained his own camp in the hill-forest.

That the king dissembled when he spoke to him so softly David well knew, for he was not ignorant of the wickedness and weakness of Saul's character. He was sure that he would never forgive him for having taken away his spear, to lose which is a warrior's greatest disgrace. A few days afterward the faithful Jonathan sent him word that the king, finding he did not return to Hebron, had called together all his armies, resolved to destroy him, and all with him, if to be found within the land of Judea. David therefore called a council of his friends and captains. There were present the valiant and fierce Joab, his general; Uriah, his second in command; Abishai, the brother of Joab, who was now his armor-bearer instead of Uriah; Hushai and Ahithopel, both of whom bore arms with David, though war was not their usual pursuit; also, Abiathar, the priest, in his sacred robes and ephod.

At length the counsel of Uriah prevailed, who said: "That Achish, King of Gath, having certainly learned that David had in good faith and not artfully by stratagem before sought his protection and service, had sent word to Uriah that if his master desired again to leave Judea to escape from King Saul, he would gladly receive him and his followers in his own dominions, and entreat them with all honor. giving him a high command in his armies, and places according to their rank and ability for his men.

"Therefore," continued Uriah, "if my lord David refuses to meet the Lord's anointed in battle, ere Saul surrounds us with his hosts to take us in a snare let my lord pass over with all his force unto Achish, king of Gath."

David, determining to follow this counsel, a few days afterward marched from his fastnesses, and crossing the country of Judea, came to the court of the King of the Philistines, who received him gladly, and gave him a palace near his own to dwell in, and places for his followers.

Before David left his camp in the forest of Ziph, to pass over to Philistia, an interesting incident occurred which led to his marriage, Michal having been taken from him by her father. I have already alluded, your majesty, to Nabal betrothed to the lovely village maiden, Abigail, who gave David water when, the year before, a fugitive he sat thirsty and weary by the well under the palm trees. The bridegroom, who was much her senior, and whom she had married by compulsion on the part of her parents for his great wealth in flocks, herds, and lands, proved an avaricious and churlish man, and treated her rather as his slave than his wife. While David and his followers were encamped between Maon and Carmel, where Nabal dwelt with his young wife, he would have lost a portion of his flocks by the incursion of a band of desert robbers but for the assistance of David's men, who drove them away and gave protection to the herdsmen.

Some weeks afterward David being greatly in want of provisions for his garrison, and recalling the service his people had done the rich Nabal, he sent to Nabal ten men to bring whatsoever he could spare, bidding his messengers say to him: "Peace be both to thee, and peace be to thine house, and peace be unto all thou hast! Whatsoever cometh to thine hand give unto the servants of thy son David."

When the men came to Nabal, and delivered their captain's gracious words, he roughly answered them:

"Who is David, and who is the son of Jesse ye speak of? There be many servants nowadays that break away from their masters! Shall I take bread, and flesh, and water, and give it unto men whom I know not whence they be?"

When the young men returned to David and reported his words to him, his indignation was justly kindled at this treatment by Nabal of one who had done him service.

"Gird ye on every man his sword!" he cried, buckling on his own sword; and at the head of four hundred of his men of war he hastened to punish Nabal for his inhospitable conduct. News of his march came to the ears of his young and beautiful wife, and when she knew all (for she had not see David's messengers, who had met Nabal in the field), in great alarm she secretly made haste, and took two hundred loaves of bread, two skins of wine, five dressed sheep, five measures of parched corn, a hundred clusters of raisins, and two hundred cakes of figs, and lading several beasts with them, she went forward with her servants to meet David. When she came near she alighted, and bowed herself to the ground, and when he raised her up, he, with surprise and pleasure, recognized the fair face of the maiden he had seen at the well. Eloquently she entreated him to forego his vengeance, and accept the peace-offering she had brought. The young captain received of her hand her gifts, and said: "Go in peace to thine house. Thou hast prevailed, and for thy sake I spare thy offending lord!"

When Nabal on her return was informed by her how David in fierce wrath was coming upon him, with four hundred armed men, to destroy him, and how she had averted the danger, his heart sunk within him, and struck as with lightning he fell back paralyzed. Ten days afterward he died.

When David heard of the death of Nabal, and the days of her mourning were passed, he sent to her and asked her to become his wife; and not long before the departure of David to pass over to the court of Achish he married the beautiful widow of Nabal, and took her with him into the land of 'the Philistines.

At the court of Achish David remained nearly a year and a half, serving him as a captain in his wars, and increasing his own fame as a warrior. The King of Gath gave him and his followers a city in the south to dwell in, called Ziklag. Saul, in the meanwhile, no longer able to pursue David, disbanded his army and remained in his palace, ill in spirit and body, and Prince Jonathan his son never left him, but with noble, filial devotion anticipated all his wants and gave him his tenderest sympathy in all the darkness and bitterness under which his soul dwelt. Since the death of Samuel and the flight of David the Hebrew king had ceased to take an interest in anything. Few of his people saw him, and he gave audience to no one save through his son, who strove with beautiful charity to conceal his father's failing and to keep the kingdom together with some show of government. There was no High Priest, no Prophet in the land for the miserable monarch to resort to; for Abiathar, the lawful pontiff, was with David in Philistia. Without God, without prophet, without priest, and it might be said, without king, the land of Israel was in a desolate estate, and no man had heart or hope, but only a prevailing apprehension of coming evil!

Achish, King of Gath, who seems to have been a sagacious and warlike prince, with deadly hatred of Saul, and an ambition to subdue Judea to his scepter, took advantage of this state of affairs to prepare a vast army for the invasion of his kingdom. Marching northwardly, he intended to strike the Jordan, east of Mount Tabor, and so descend the valley of the river, take Jericho, and thus hold the key of the land of Israel. He desired, also, to separate the Hebrews on the west of the river from those on the east, and so place Saul between the Philistines on the Jordan, and the Philistines in their own country westward.

But Prince Jonathan, whose counsel Saul sought in all things distrustful of himself, advised the king to hasten his march to check the Philistines in the pass between Mount Gilboa on the south and Mount Hermon on the north. When King Saul, Jonathan, and his two brothers, at the head of the army of Israel, reached the foot of Mount Gilboa, Achish had already pitched his camp in the valley before it, Gilboa being on one side to the south, and Tabor also in sight, but far to the north. The two armies, the largest the hostile nations had brought into the field since the days of Eli, were encamped within sight of Saul, who pitched his camp on the sides of Gilboa, opposite the valley of Shunem, where Achish lay. Saul and Jonathan ascended the mountain behind their camp and surveyed the vast hosts of the enemy covering all the plain. Jonathan's heart failed him, because he had heard that David was in the camp of Achish in high command, and he feared to fight, opposed to him! The great numbers of his adversaries, however, filled the king's soul with dismay. He trembled as he leaned upon his spear and gazed down upon the thousands of the army of Achish.

"Is there not one of the race of Ithamar, not a priest of the house of Eli or Ahimelech, in the army that I can inquire of God?" he asked of his armor-bearer, Doeg, the Edomite, who stood behind him.

"Not one, my lord, save Zadoc, whom thou hast made priest," answered Doeg. "I finished my work that day at Nob faithfully."

"Where is Abiathar, son of Ahimelech?" demanded Saul. "Doth he yet live?"

"He is with David," replied Jonathan.

"Would I had Abiathar here to inquire of God for me; him will he hear," said Saul. "Zadoc to whom I have given the High Priesthood hath no answers from God. And David, too, is in yonder camp! It is well he hideth from my arm, under the plume of Achish and his gods!"

"Nay, my lord," said Ishbosheth his son, coming up the hill, in company with his brother Melchisua, drawing near the king; "David I hear is not with Achish. The King of Gath made him and his six hundred men come a part of the way with him; but his lords and chief captains took alarm, and told the king that he ought not to trust him, saying he would be sure in this battle to go over to his countrymen, and turn his sword against them. Achish could not prevail that he might keep David, and sent the son of Jesse back to Ziklag, his town in the land of the Philistines." This Ishbosheth was the youngest son of the king, and a young man who loved rich apparel, and indulged more in pleasure than in arms; an elegant and vain youth.

This intelligence was gratifying to the prince, who felt he should go into battle now with a brave heart.

"Doeg," said Saul, leaning on the shoulder of his armor-bearer, as he descended the mountain, first commanding his sons to go on before him, and speaking softly in his ear, "knowest thou of a woman that hath a familiar spirit? It is in vain for me to inquire of God as to the issue of the coming battle by dreams, or by prophet, by priest, or by Urim! The heavens are brass! Sleep comes not! Samuel is dead! The High Priest with the Urim and Thummim is with the son of Jesse! Seek ye, therefore, a woman that hath a familiar spirit, that I may go to her and inquire of *her.*"

Then answered the Edomite, "There is a woman, my lord, that hath a familiar spirit, who dwelleth beyond Shunem, over the hill of Hermon, in the little village of Endor, which lieth south of Mount Tabor."

"Is it far hence, Doeg?" inquired Saul.

"Ten miles in a direct route, but twelve or more to go about among the hills," answered Doeg.

That night, after the camp guard of the first watch had been posted, and the stars alone gave light upon the hostile hosts, Saul, disguised in the coarse attire of a man-at-arms, and with no sign of royalty about his person, save his kingly bearing,

which could hardly be concealed, stole from his camp. He was
attended by two men, Doeg and Amasa, the armor-bearer of
Abner, a young man, son of David's sister, but who held firmly
to Saul's side in the war he made against his heroic kinsman.

The masked king, led by Doeg, kept near the foot of Gilboa,
until they had got far enough eastwardly to avoid the outposts
of the enemy, which were extended along the plain, and then
boldly struck across the open valley to the foot of Hermon.
Under its dark shadows they followed the herdsmen's paths,
until they came to the other side of the low mountain; when,
far in the north, the black form of Mount Tabor, indistinctly
relieved against the sky, and hiding many of its stars, became
their guide. In an hour more they left the village of Nain on
the left, in silent repose under the hills, and entered the obscure hamlet of Endor. Doeg led the king to a base-looking
habitation, and said:

"This is the place!"

The king, wearied with his long night tramp over hill and
plain, through glen and mountain gorge; rejoiced at its termination. The woman timidly unbarred her gate: for Saul, after
the death of Ahimelech, hearing that the people, being without oracle or priesthood, sought wizards and diviners and familiar spirits to inquire of *them*, forbade, on pain of death, such
inquiries to be made; thereby showing that he still retained
something of the grace of his former piety. He commanded by
an edict all who had familiar spirits, necromancers, and for-
tune-tellers, were they men or women, to be slain or driven out
of his kingdom!

It must have been, therefore, with the most abject sense of
debasement that he now stood in the door of this mean habitation, whither he had come degradingly disguised, to consult the
sorceress of Endor, who had hid herself in this obscure place
of his kingdom from his sanguinary edict against her profession.

"Open, woman! Dost thou not hear me? I bring in my
hand for thee a purse of gold!" called out Doeg, who carried
with him a camp lantern, whereby he had been able to light
the king's steps through the dark defiles of Hermon.

"I fear me also a sword in thine other!" she answered.

"Nay; we be three soldiers of the camp of Saul, who come
hither to learn of thee how the battle we are soon to fight
will go!"

The door being carefully opened, after she had looked from within fixedly at the three men, Doeg went in, followed by the king, while the other stood on watch without. The rude apartment, revealed by the rays of the lantern, was scarcely a fit abode for anyone. In one corner reposed a white calf, and on a shelf above it sat a raven gray with age. The woman lighted an old Tirian soldier's lamp, which she had doubtless found on some battlefield. Saul gazed with deep earnestness upon the tall, aged dame, whose silvery hair, bound by a fillet smoothly about her lofty forehead, with her grave and modest costume, gave her an air of dignity he was not prepared for. Her dark face, once superbly beautiful, was still distinguished by large, splendid eyes, a noble and regular profile, and a firm mouth with finely shaped lips. Her face had the refined, oval contour which is characteristic of the Phœnician women, for she was a native of Tyre, as her speech and aspect proved to the king. In age she was not more than fifty. With a sort of queenly air, native to her notwithstanding all her poverty, she said, looking at Saul, and distinguishing him at once as the superior of the two men:

"For what dost thou visit me?"

For a moment the king of Israel made no reply. He hesitated to strike the last blow to sever the golden chain which bound him to his God; for the act he now contemplated had no equal in impiety. It was a voluntary and deliberate renunciation of the Oracles of God for the accursed vaticinations of an evil spirit. Alas! how had the august and once glorious king fallen! How had his proud spirit become abased to the dust! How far had he sunk into infidelity, and the absence of all moral feeling! How deliberately was he approaching the verge of the precipice, over which he was to plunge into everlasting night!

What a painful, pitiable spectacle to humanity, to angels, to God, is he, as he stands there in that low hut, his sandals soiled with his long night-walk, his coarse mantle torn by thorns, his gray locks wet with the dews of the hills, his whole appearance desolate and careworn, and in his heart a keen sense of degradation; the light of shame kindling his cheek, that even his familiar Doeg should behold him thus humbled and superstitious He hesitates for another moment ere his soul cuts itself off from God, and answers her:

"I pray thee, O Tyrian, divine unto me, by thy familiar

spirit, and bring *him* up to me whom I shall name unto thee!"

"I am here a lonely widow, O sir! I am poor, and have but this one calf in the world. I subsist by my distaff, and try to live humbly in peace, as becometh a stranger in the land. Wherefore comest thou to me to get me into trouble with the king thereof? Behold, thou knowest what Saul hath done; how he hath cut off those that have familiar spirits and the wizards out of the land: wherefore then layest thou a snare for my life to cause me to die?"

The king's conscience as well as his pride felt keenly the rebuke implied by her words; but he answered her with this solemn oath:

"As the Lord liveth, woman, there shall no punishment happen to thee for this thing."

Reassured, the woman said, fixing her mysterious eyes upon him.

"Whom shall I bring up before thee from the shades?"

"Bring me up Samuel!" answered Saul, in a voice low and tremulous; at this hour of his greatest trial, having no other trust but in him who had once guided him by his counsels, and also by his reproofs. Samuel dead was to him wiser than Saul living—Saul in his hopeless despair!

The woman, with singular solemnity, then proceeded with a wand which she took in her hand, to separate herself from the king and his companion by inscribing an imaginary ring about herself. She chanted in low voice a verse of mystic words, and then cast upon a censer of fire somes trange fragrance; retiring from the circle, her whole form dilating and majestic, and her dark eyes flashing with a sort of terrible and wicked splendor, she cried aloud in Syriac, "Appear!"

The floor of the hut within the circle seemed instantly to disappear, and in its place yawned a cavernous gulf, from the dark abyss of which majestically ascended a venerable form like a god in aspect, enveloped in a halo of misty light. Saul saw not the awful shape, but, feeling its presence, had covered his face with his mantle.

"Why hast thou deceived me?" cried the divineress, with a loud voice of mingled terror and anger, as if the shape had uttered to her the name of the king; "for thou art Saul!"

"Fear not for thyself," said Saul. "What dost thou see?"

"I see a god ascending out of the earth," she answered, with a voice of alarm.

"What form is he of?" demanded Saul.

"An aged man cometh up, and he is covered with a mantle like a prophet of the Lord."

Then Saul knew that it was Samuel, and he prostrated himself to the earth before him.

"Wherefore, O Saul," said the voice of the phantasma, "hast thou called me from the abodes of the happy dead, where in hope and peace we await the end of time, and the kingdom of God, at rest from the cares of this earth?"

Saul trembled at this solemn address, uttered in tones that seemed like echoes from the depths of Hades. He made no reply, and the shade of the Seer continued more sternly:

"Why hast thou disquieted me to bring me up?"

Then the king answered, rising to his knees, but without lifting his eyes to the mighty apparition, his voice touched with the profoundest sadness and helplessness:

"I am sore distressed, O Samuel! for the Philistines make war against me, and God is departed from me, and answereth me no more neither by prophets nor by dreams; therefore, I have called *thee*, that thou mayest make known unto me what I shall do!"

Then the voice of the form within the dim cloud of light answered, and said: "Wherefore, then, dost thou ask of *me*, seeing the Lord is departed from thee, and is become thine enemy? The Lord hath done to thee, O King, even as he spake by me to thee; for he hath rent the kingdom out of thine hand and is about to give it to David! Because thou obeyedst not the voice of thy God in Gilgal, nor executedst his command against Amalek, therefore hath the Lord ordained this thing against thee, and taketh thy kingdom, and giveth it to thy neighbor! Thou hast come hither to know what shall be thy fate in the battle to-morrow! Lo, the Lord will deliver thee into the hand of the Philistines, and to-morrow shalt thou and thy three sons be with me, and all the hosts of Israel shall the Lord deliver into the hand of the Philistines!"

When Saul heard these fatal words he fell his whole length forward on his face to the floor, and became insensible! The majestic and mournful specter, gazing upon the prostrate king with eyes of sadness and divine sorrow, slowly descended into the earth, and silence and darkness succeeded!

The woman, who had stood transfixed with horror and awe while the solemn colloquy went on, and who, by her looks of amazement, had not expected a spirit to appear in answer to her harmless incantations, now pale as a corpse sank upon the floor and shuddered with terror at what she had heard and seen; while Doeg, the Edomite, at the first appearance of the awful shape out of the abyss fled from the house in speechless horror; even the poor dumb brute tied in the corner of the room trembled all over in the most extraordinary manner, the perspiration pouring from its sides like rain.

When the woman, who really could have had no power over the dead, and especially over good men, to disturb their celestial rest, and bring them into this world when she pleased, at the call of wicked men, and who only plied her deceiving art for gain on the ignorant and superstitious—when she was finally able to rise she drew near to Saul, who lay as one dead. Her efforts, aided by his two attendants whom she called in, at length restored the king, and he stood tremblingly on his feet. But the terrible scene he had passed through, with the need of rest and food (for he had eaten nothing during all the day and night), and above all, the words of his sentence of death sounding in his ears, so unmanned him that it became necessary he should be supported by them to a bed.

"Pardon thine handmaid, my lord," said the woman. "I but obeyed thy voice, and put my life in thy hand. I knew not what terrible thing would be! Let my lord take courage and eat a morsel of bread, that thou mayest have strength when thou goest away, for thou art sorely tried!" But sick at heart, depressed and wretched in mind, and all hope buried forever, conscious of his guilt, and trembling under the divine displeasure of his God, who had numbered his days and finished his kingdom, he refused to eat or to be comforted.

At length, exhausted, he fell asleep. In the meanwhile the hospitable woman directed Doeg and Amasa, the armor-bearer of Abner, to take her little calf, that she petted and kept in her house like a child, and kill it, and dress it for their feast; while she took flour and kneaded it, and baked bread, and diligently prepared a bountiful meal for the king when he should awake. When all was ready Doeg, now knowing it was time, if they would unseen reach the camp before day should break, to call the king who had slept two hours, aroused him. To their surprise he arose calm and collected, all trace of care

and trouble gone; nay, his very voice was stronger and more cheerful than his two servants had heard it for a long time! He gladly sat down to the table which the foreign woman had so unselfishly and kindly prepared, and ate heartily; and when he arose to go, he thanked her for her hospitality, and would have rewarded her with the purse of gold which Doeg brought at his girdle. But she refused all gains from the king, and so he departed from her house strong in body and mind, to return to his camp.

Without doubt, your majesty, Saul's sudden calmness and even cheerfulness arose from that extraordinary attribute in our nature, which leads us to be more at ease under a certainty, even though it be certain evil, than in a state of uncertainty and doubt, and a restless fear of evil to come; as, oftentimes, the wild terror of a criminal at the fear of being sentenced to die ceases when that sentence is irrevocable. Thus King Saul, long torn and tossed by unspeakable fears and terrors, anxieties and guilt, dying a thousand deaths in the fear of death, enduring a thousand punishments in the living apprehension of God's wrath, tortured more keenly by the dread of losing his kingdom than the actual loss of a score of scepters would have moved him, with the consciousness that all was now determined upon him, and that on the morrow he would certainly lose his kingdom and his life, and join Samuel in the abodes of the dead—thus, his tempest-lashed bosom was suddenly calmed, as when a mighty tornado bursts upon the sea, levels the billows which lesser winds have raised, and leaves the dark ocean calm in the highest of the storm!

As the morning star above Hermon was fading into the pale golden sky of the breaking day, Saul and his companions re-entered the lines of the Hebrew camp; and unrecognized, the king reached his pavilion, his guards, and even Abner, still asleep around about it.

The monarch, as he softly entered, beheld Prince Jonathan sleeping calmly on his war-couch, in the corner of the tent, and his two brothers reposing one on each side of him. He stood and gazed thoughtfully down upon them! His eyes rested upon the princely and handsome form of his eldest son; then fell upon the face of the next oldest, Melchisua, who, from childhood an invalid in the palace, seldom left his home or went to the wars; but whom filial affection now brought to the field; for all the land instinctively knew that the coming battle was to decide the fate of the kingdom, either for Saul or against him!

His gaze rested longest on the proud and elegant features of Ishbosheth, his youngest son. "Alas, my poor boys! my brave and beautiful sons! How calmly ye sleep! The prophet said *three* of my sons are to go with me to-morrow, and be with him in the solemn shades! He named not which of the four! Is it thou, O noble Jonathan, son of my pride, worthy to wear a crown and wield a scepter for thy virtues, wisdom, and courage! or thou, my poor, delicate boy, whose misfortunes should have kept thee in thy mother's boudoir, rather than that mine should have brought thee upon this battle plain, where to-morrow Death, armed with ten thousand scythes to his chariot wheels, shall mow Israel down as the mower cuts the ripened harvest! or is it thou, lordly and beautiful prince, my brave and wayward Ishbosheth, who art to join me, and two of thy three brothers, as to-morrow night I lead the long procession of my army of the dead down to the gloomy realms of Sheol? As for thy father, he knoweth certainly that his doom is to die! God spare thee, O Ishbosheth, with thy fair mother's smile and dark shining tresses!"

At this moment Abner entered! The king instantly banished from his face all emotion. With the old look of the proud warrior in his eyes, and his voice as aforetime ringing like a trumpet, Saul called to his surprised and overjoyed general and said:

"To-morrow we give battle to our foes! Let to-day be spent in careful preparation. Let nothing be lacking to bring our whole army into the battle in the best possible condition for fighting. To-morrow, my Abner, will be fought the greatest battle between kings that ever shook the plains of Israel."

The next morning Saul put his army in battle array. His martial spirit inspired his lords, captains, and all his men-at-arms. Abner, his general, could hardly believe the change he witnessed, and said to Jonathan:

"We shall win the field, for the king has victory blazing in his eyes. He will fight to-day as he used to do battle in his glorious youth."

"Thou art sure David is not in the ranks of Achish?" asked Jonathan.

"The king hath sent him back to keep his country till his

return, for all his lords refused to fight if he were retained," answered the general.

At length the two armies approached each other, led by their kings: Achish standing up in his war-chariot, drawn by four white horses abreast, his helmet of gold and his splendid armor glittering like the sun. Saul rode a large coal-black war horse, and looked the very personation of Mars in the field, challenging to battle! His tall and commanding stature, his martial air, his warlike and courageous aspect, with the light of battle flashing from his eyes, kindled the pride of his own army and filled even his foes with admiration. By his right side rode Jonathan, clad in rich armor; and on his left hand, Prince Melchisua; while, attended by Ishbosheth, glittering like a star, and by Abinadab, another royal prince who had just arrived on the field, Abner in his chariot commanded in another part of the plain.

There is something august, if not sublime, in the moral spectacle presented by King Saul at this moment. He knew that on that day he was to die—that his long reign, the last portion of it so full of woe, and of transgression against Heaven, was to end before the sun, which then was rising above the pleasant valley of the Jordan, should set beyond the dark mountains of Megiddo; yet (as doubtless a king of inferior courage and dignity would have done) he did not seek to avoid his fate; did not for a moment shrink from his destiny! The idea of flying from his doom seems never to have entered this extraordinary man's thoughts. He felt ready, rather, to offer his life a sacrifice to his offended God, who had demanded it of him. He seemed to feel that his iniquities required a victim, and that victim, himself. Some lingering traces of his ancient piety, some fragments of the noble shrine of honor which once stood in the shattered temple of his soul, remained, and he resolved to die like a penitent, courageous, and generous man, and with the composed dignity of a king who still wears the regal robe and royal crown!

In this sublime temper he went into battle. A warrior in a position like his feels immortal—heeds neither sword nor spear, arrow nor javelin, the charge of horsemen, nor the rush of scythe-armed chariots. He carries a charmed life! He has already conquered death in resolving to die, and he fights like one of the immortal gods of old, whose life no weapon from a human forge can touch. He who knows he will fall by an arrow from the bow of God is invulnerable in soul to those of human archers. Such a sublime feeling should have borne along with it the prestige of victory, and the splendor of his battle-lit eyes should have lighted his armies on, conquering and to conquer. But alas! it was the false fires burning on an unholy and accursed altar which blazed so brightly. The coal which kindled those warlike orbs never burned on the sacred altar of God. Their false glory could only lead the army, which trusted and followed, to ruin and death.

At length the two armies, who have been slowly approaching each other, as if ambitious to outvie one another in the splendor of their battle array, were separated the space of a long bow-shot. The archers in advance had already begun to darken the air with clouds of arrows, which filled the calm air of that sunbright morning with the sound of a thousand rushing wings.

Saul now turned, and, with emotions unutterable, embraced his two sons, Jonathan and Melchisua, and bidding them fight for glory and for God, and be ready to die for their country, he ordered his trumpeter to sound to the onset. The clear musical bugle, as it gave the keynote of conflict, was joined by all the trumpets and cornets in Saul's host, breathing loud, defiant battle cries, until the hills of Gilboa on the south echoed the sounds, and Hermon on the north repeated them, until three distinct armies seemed preparing to attack the Philistine hosts. Ere the warlike notes had died away among the hills the trumpeter of King Achish had answered the challenge of King Saul's, and all his brazen bugles caught up the fierce response. The two armies in a few moments were mingled in deadly fight from one end of the plain to the other. Long and sanguinary was the contest. The superior numbers of the Philistines thrice compelled the Hebrews to retreat, and thrice Saul, with his two sons by his side, recovered the field. Where the battle waxed the fiercest there his shining helmet, with its glittering royal crest, towered as the rallying point for his bravest warriors.

All day the two armies contested the ground; now rolling towards Hermon, and breaking against its base, to recede soon afterward to dash against the cliffs of Gilboa, with a human roar louder and fiercer than ten thousand billows of the lashed ocean. Saul everywhere rode amid the battle storm, and wheresoever his sword waved, victory held the field; but where he was not, Achish conquered and drove Saul's army, pursuing them with great slaughter. At length, as the sun was near his going down, the plain was won by the King of Gath, and on every side his foes had been overthrown, save one part of the dead-strewn battleground, where not more than three hundred Hebrews were valiantly and desperately making a stand against thousands of Philistines. As the victorious Achish, mounted upon one of his wounded chariot horses (for no chariot could now traverse the plain on account of the dead men and the wreck of battle which covered it), drew near this point, he recognized the tall form of King Saul towering head and shoulders above his sons and warriors, and though covered with wounds fighting like a dying god rather than a man, so sublime was he in this last conflict with his death. As Achish drew near, Saul saw him, and, sweeping with his mighty sword a space around, he urged his horse toward the Philistine king. So terrible was his aspect, as he disengaged his charger from the heaps of dead his own hand had slain, so fierce his war-cry, that Achish feared the encounter (although he could plainly see that Saul reeled in his saddle from great loss of blood), and ordered his guard of archers to destroy him! As a majestic lion covered with wounds, whom the hunters dare not approach, is killed at a safe distance with their lances and arrows, so did the relentless archers of unpitying Achish discharge flights of arrows against the King of the Hebrews, until the joints of his mail were penetrated, and his war-horse fell to the earth pierced with a javelin. The king, standing above him, still fought on, slaying all who came within the reach 'of his sword, until he saw the brave Prince Jonathan, who had fought by his father's side all day, fall bleeding from a score of wounds and die at his feet! His son Abinadab, valiant as the eagle the plumage of which formed his crest, came tottering near to protect his brother, but, pierced with arrows, fell upon the body of Prince Jonathan, his sword broken to the hilt in his hand, and expired also before his father's eyes. Melchisua, seeing his brothers dead, lay down by Jonathan, and without a wound, breathed out his spirit, dying from exhaustion and grief. Saul stood and, as if scorning his foes, gazed upon his dead sons, and said bitterly:

"These, then, O God, are the two victims besides Jonathan, heir to my throne, I have had to offer up to thee for my iniquities, which sacrifice will be completed with my own life! Ishbosheth is then to live! My bright, beautiful boy will be safe!"

The king then turned and beheld Abner his general all red with blood, and looking like the incarnation of a battlefield, coming up at the head of six hundred mounted Benjamites, the king's own countrymen, to his rescue. By his side rode Prince Ishbosheth, his golden armor as bright as when the morning sun was reflected from it, his gay azure and white plume unsoiled, his sword in his hand still polished as when drawn from its scabbard in the morning; for the mighty warrior had kept the youth by his side and defended him, many a wound himself receiving thereby, from all the dangers of that dreadful field.

"Save the king! To the rescue!" shouted the warlike commander, who could now collect only this devoted remnant of his vast armies! On he came like a whirlwind. The Philistines, unprepared for this sudden onset, left Saul and fled, Achish in vain attempting to restrain them. As Abner rode past, Saul cried:

"God is appeased! Save Ishbosheth, O Abner! It is in vain you fight any longer! All is lost. Escape with my only son from the field, I command you! Farewell—farewell, Abner! Protect the boy! Be a father to him! Farewell, my son! I am going, I and thy three brothers, to be with Samuel this night!"

Abner heard these words, and seeing that the trumpets of the King of Gath were calling for succor, he reined up for an instant. Perceiving that Saul was dying, he waved farewell to him and took the bridle of the prince's horse in his grasp to prevent him from joining his dying father, caused his trumpeter to sound the retreat, and galloping with his followers across the valley, pursued by a squadron of mingled chariots and horsemen of the foe, he reached a gorge in the mountains, and so escaped into the valley of the Jordan the same night, with four hundred men crossing the river safe from pursuit.

Saul, after the flight of Achish and his Philistine archers, was left standing alone on the side of Mount Gilboa where it touches the plain, gazing down mournfully upon his sons. Far and wide around him lay the dead and dying. He alone stood up, leaning upon his sword, and contemplating sternly his dead! As when a mighty sirocco has swept the sea, strewing it with wrecks of brave argosies, save one, the Admiral's bark, which, shattered by the storm and riven by lightnings, still floats alone a majestic ruin, so stood Saul on that death-strewn plain after the storm of war had subsided! The impress of kingly majesty still remained upon his martial visage; but he looked like the rebel god of whom write the Hebrew books, who, rebelling against the supreme Power in heaven, with his hosts of rebel angels had been overthrown and hurled down to earth with all his followers, and now stands contemplating around him the splendid wreck of his celestial armies, still a god!

"Doeg," he said to his armor-bearer, who, having fought like a wild beast all day, lay near upon the ground, "hast thou strength in thee to get to thy feet?"

"I will try, O king," he answered, and raising himself by his broken spear he stood, blood running from his wounds.

"Come near, and with thy sword thrust me through, that I may presently die, lest these uncircumcised Philistines return and take me alive, and abuse me, and put out my eyes, and make sport with me before their gods, as they did of old with Samson!"

"Nay, my lord, I cannot kill thee! Wait patiently, and thou wilt presently die of thy many wounds," answered the Edomite, "for they are grievous."

Then the king, looking about him, and seeing no one but an Amalekite camp-follower, who was creeping along to spoil the dead, he disdained to ask one so base to slay him, and raising his sword toward heaven he cried with the countenance and air of some penitent High Priest who is permitted once more to offer sacrifice for sin to his God:

"Accept, O Lord, most mighty, this last and final offering for my crimes, even my own body, which I now sacrifice to Thee, and which Thy stern justice demandeth! Let this act of sacrifice atone for my sacrilege! Let this valley filled with my slain servants, let these my three sons who lie here dead before Thee, let the loss of this battle, let the loss of my kingdom, of my own life, which I now return to Thee, atone for all my guilt!"

Thus speaking, he rested the hilt of his sword upon the earth, and finding above his heart a crevice in his coat of mail, he pressed against the sword's point, and with all his weight, aided by his heavy armor, fell forward thereupon! The sword pierced through and through his mighty heart, and he fell dead upon the bodies of his sons, his head resting in the bosom of Prince Jonathan.

Such, your majesty, was the painful and touching end of the wonderful career of this great king, valiant warrior, and wise statesman; for he had been all these, until in a moment of impiety he offended the Divine Powers and brought upon himself and his children, and upon all his house, the vengeance of his God! But let his unhappy end, let the severity of his punishment, the bitterness of his fate, atone for all! Let his devotion to the will of his God, when that will sentenced him to die, and his regard for the glory of his country and the honor of his army, which he refused to desert, confer upon his memory everlasting fame! They serve to veil his errors with a sort of sublime virtue; and future ages, forgetting them, will rank him with its heroes. As their first king the Hebrews will honor his name and reign, and their bards will do justice to the noble qualities of the man, the valor of the soldier, and the dignity of the monarch. Under his rule their land has taken a rank among the nations unknown to it before, and won the respect even of its foes.

When news was brought to Achish, who had returned to his pavilion suffering from a wound which he had received from the javelin of Abner, that the King of the Hebrews was dead, with his three sons about him, he sent the chief captain of his guard, on the morrow, to bring him Saul's head, his crown, sword, and royal breastplate, and the heads and armor of the three princes. But when the Philistines came to the side of Mount Gilboa, where Saul lay, they found that his crown was taken from his helmet by some sacrilegious spoiler, leaving only a phylactery bound upon his brow, on which were written the words:

"Oh earth, cover not thou my blood!
Mine eye poureth out tears unto God!
Oh, that Thou wouldst hide me in the grave,
That Thou wouldst keep me secret till
Thy wrath be past."

These phylacteries are bands of parchment, on which are inscribed words out of their sacred books, either sentences from the law, or verses of prayer and praise, and are worn by the pious, in obedience to a command of God. How surprising to find this sacred frontlet crowning the brow of the king beneath his helmet! Was it piety, or was it superstition? Were they either, or were they both, how painfully they express the feelings of his darkened soul! The first line of adjunction to earth was singularly fulfilled. The Philistine captain having struck off the head of the dead monarch bore it, with those of his sons and their armor, to Achish, who after severing with his sword a long, gray lock of the king's hair, and fastening the silvery trophy amid the plumage of his royal helmet, ordered the four heads to be impaled upon the gates of the town of Bethshan, which stood near the plain, and directed the body of Saul and his sons to be fastened to the city wall in sight of the whole army encamped before it!

Achish then sent swift messengers into the land of Philistia, to publish the news of the death of Saul, and of his great victory over the Hebrews, in all the temples of his kingdom, and to the people in the remotest borders of the land. He also sent away Saul's armor to be set up in the temple of Ashtaroth, along the walls of which hang a thousand suits of mail, with helmet, sword, spear, and battle-ax taken from the foes of the Philistines during the last three hundred years!

Achish followed up his victory by crossing the Jordan and occupying all the cities and towns east of that river. In fact, his victory gave him possession of two-thirds of the kingdom.

East of the Jordan is a fortified town called Jabesh-gilead, belonging to the warlike tribe of Manasseh, and distinguished for the bravery of its citizens. King Saul many years before had delivered this people from the Amalekites. When these warriors heard of the indignity put upon the bodies of the king and the three princes, two hundred of the most valiant young men, grateful to him for his deliverance when the Amalekites were about to put out all their eyes, sallied forth at night from their gates, and by a forced march reached the town of Bethshan just after midnight. Without being seen by the guards of the Philistine camp they removed the bodies of the king and of his sons from the gate, and bearing them on litters over Jordan and along the hills to Jabesh, erected an altar, and solemnly burned them thereon! The citizens then gathered up the royal ashes and the bones of the three princes and buried them in a tomb under a sacred palm which grew near the gate of their city, and the whole city mourned sincerely for the king seven days.

Thus, your majesty, closed the wonderful and interesting history of Saul, truly one of the most remarkable men of the age. His end was strikingly in keeping with his stormy life; but it is to be hoped he atoned by his death for his errors, so far as man can do so to his God, and is at rest with his sons with Samuel the Seer in the abodes of the blessed.

Your faithful   ARBACES.

LETTER XIII.

ARBACES TO KING BELUS.

YOUR MAJESTY:

It will afford you pleasure to know that your kind epistle, dated at your palace in Nineveh four weeks since, reached me three days ago. The intelligence of your continued health and the prosperity of your kingdom is very gratifying to me, as well as the reception of so large and interesting a letter written with your majesty's own hand.

That portion thereof which relates to the beautiful daughter of Isrilid I cannot permit to pass without allusion to. My silence respecting her is not because I have become less interested in her, but because she has been absent from the kingdom for several months, having been taken by her father to Tadmor in the Desert, the queen of which, in failing health and leaving no heir to the throne, having written him a letter desiring to see him in order to confer upon his daughter, as the next heir, the crown and scepter! She had been gone three months when I returned here from my imprisonment in Egypt, and although I have been here nearly three months the invalid guest of the hospitable soldier Joab (your majesty will remember my first meeting with him near Jericho), I have had no tidings of her or her father. Thus my silence respecting her, my dear Belus, is accounted for; and not owing to indifference to one who so profoundly interested me, and whom I still regard as the sincerest friend I have among her sex.

Your majesty is pleased to say that you trust, if I marry her, I shall not delay to present my beautiful Hebrew bride to your court. If, O Belus, I had harbored sentiments of this nature for her, while I believed her to be only the daughter of the lord of Jericho, I fear I shall have to dismiss them from my bosom when I am compelled to contemplate her as the proud and powerful Queen of Tadmor in the Desert. A prince who, like your Arbaces, has his chief fortune invested in his armor and camp equipage, can hardly, if he is becomingly modest in his aspirations, hope to find grace in the eyes of a coroneted dame who has beauty enough to tempt even Belus of Assyria to lay his crown and scepter at her feet!

Your majesty is very kind to thank me so graciously for my long letters which, you say, give you so clear and connected a history of the interesting Hebrew people, that you read them with the greatest pleasure. You desire me to continue to send them to you without abatement of details. I will endeavor to obey you, and now proceed to answer your inquiries in reference to the wonderful Prince David, who at this moment sits on the throne of Saul, though not yet recognized by the whole nation as their king, Prince Ishbosheth, at the death of his father, having, by the advice of Abner, boldly proclaimed himself king in his father's stead!

Your majesty will remember that David, after being dismissed from the camp of Achish in order to appease the jealous rivalry of his lords and captains, retired into Philistia. He had not reached its borders ere news came to him that Ziklag, the fortified town in the south which the King of Gath had given him as a residence for himself and his family and the families of his six hundred warriors, had been taken by the Amalekites and burned and the women and children carried away captives. By forced marches he reached his city on the third day and found its ruins smoking and desolate. The Hebrew chief, with so small a force, hesitated before pursuing an army of six thousand fierce robbers of the desert, all mounted on fleet horses or fleeter dromedaries, men whose life was war.

In this extremity his piety came to the aid of his valor. Abiathar the Priest was with him, and he besought him, in virtue of his sacred office, formally as High Priest to consult the divine Oracle! The Ark was at this time at a place called Baale of Judah, whither it had been retaken after the destruction of Nob; as formerly it had been there many years. But Abiathar wore the divining ephod, and held possession of the Urim and Thummim; that is, retained with the hereditary authority the chief insignia of the Hebrew Pontificate; for Saul, in transferring the sacerdotal dignity after the sacrilegious massacre at Nob to a priest called Zadoc of the co-lateral princely family of Eleazar, could only confer upon him an empty title; for the priesthood really was vested only in Abiathar, representing the pontifical family of Ithamar, and the royal line of the priesthood from Aaron.

That Abiathar might "inquire of God" in due form David erected in a few hours with four ranges of sixty spears a temporary tabernacle, inclosing it with curtains; and also constructed an inner sanctuary supported by javelins, and covered with Tyrian tapestry and white linen. Into this place, secret from all eyes, entered the priest, clad in his stately robes of office and wearing the ephod; and consulted the Oracle. Very different was the result from the consultation of Saul's High Priest, the want of success with whom drove the wretched king to the sorceress of Endor. No sooner had Abiathar asked of his God the words David, who stood reverently waiting in the outer tabernacle, put into his mouth to say, than a glory filled the place from the sudden splendor emitted by the Urim and Thummim and the voice of God answered the inquiry, "Shall I pursue this troop? Shall I overtake them?" with this audible response:

"Pursue, for thou shalt surely overtake them, and recover all without fail!"

In this condescension of God David was not only confirmed in his trust in God, but was assured that the Oracle and the Priesthood, which had failed the king, was with himself. Having refreshed his men, he pursued his spoilers, and on the third day came into the desert, but a great wind had obliterated the trace of the retiring army. At this crisis David beheld a man lying on the ground famished. He saw by his features and costume that he was an Egyptian. When he had commanded food and water to be given to him, and great care to be taken of him, the man was at length able to reply to David's inquiries, and to make known the direction taken by his foes, their number, and all the circumstances of the attack upon Ziklag. The man had been left behind to perish by his companions because he had been taken ill; and now their cruelty in deserting him was about to be punished by the very one who had been its victim. If they had been humane persons they would have escaped safely with their spoil to their own country, but one act of inhumanity caused their destruction.

Pursuing them by the route pointed out, David came up with them far to the south, encamped in a plain, feasting and making merry, wholly abandoned to pleasure, thinking they were safe beyond pursuit, knowing Achish to be in the far north fighting with Saul. Like a clap of thunder heard in the sky in a cloudless day fell the shouts of the six hundred Hebrews upon their ears! Ere they could seize their arms and put on their armor David and his little band were upon them! The battle lasted the whole day, for the Amalekites were a great host; but by the time the sun went down not a man escaped, save four hundred young men that fled from the field on dromedaries, and whom he could not pursue. Everything they had taken was recovered, with the wives, and daughters, and little ones of the victors. Abigail, David's beautiful wife, Nabal's widow, was restored to him, and also a second wife he had brought with him to Ziklag; for, though it is not the custom of the Hebrews to have more than one wife, yet it is not regarded as an infringement of the divine law. It is an innovation where it occurs, and imitated from the customs of the kings and people around them. Indeed, a Hebrew informed me that the greater number of wives, horses (though the Hebrews are forbidden in the laws of Moses to have a multitude of horses), slaves, and servants a great man has, the higher is his dignity; that kings and lords ought to marry many wives, in order to strengthen themselves by alliances with numerous powerful families. It was, doubtless, this policy which led David to take two wives, as the other belong to one of the most warlike and opulent families of the land!

The conquerors returned to Ziklag and camped before the ruinous walls, for there were but few dwellings for the families to occupy they had recaptured; and prepared to rebuild their stronghold.

David in the meanwhile was filled with anxiety to learn the result of the battle on the plains about Mount Gilboa between Saul and the King of the Philistines. On the third day, as he was standing on a part of the wall looking northward for any tidings, for he knew that a battle must ere then have been fought, he beheld a man advancing with haste, yet wearily, his clothes rent, and earth upon his head, like one who bears evil tidings. When he came near David he did obeisance before him, as to a king.

"From whence comest thou?" demanded David anxiously, fearing the answer of the wayfarer would convey some ill news to him.

"Out of the camp of Israel, my lord! I am escaped only with my life!"

"How went the battle?" demanded David quickly. "I pray thee, tell me."

"The Philistine king hath overthrown King Saul and his hosts. Many ten thousands have fallen in the fight, and are dead! Saul and Jonathan his son are dead also."

"How knowest thou that Saul and Jonathan his son are dead?" asked David, doubting, yet fearing the response.

And the young man answered:

"As I happened by chance upon Mount Gilboa, behold I saw Saul lean upon his spear as if sore wounded; and the chariots and horsemen of King Achish pressed hard upon him; and looking about he saw me, and called unto me, and I hastened to him, and answered, 'Here am I, O king!'

"And he said unto me, 'Who art thou?'

"'An Amalekite is thy servant,' I answered the king.

"He then said, 'Stand, I pray thee, upon me and slay me: for I would not die by the hand of these Philistines!'

"So I stood upon King Saul, my lord, and slew him, because I was sure that he could not live after that he was fallen: and I took the crown that was upon his head, and the bracelet that was on his arm, and have brought them hither unto my lord."

When David heard these words, and beheld the crown and the bracelet, and recognized them to be King Saul's, he knew that Saul was dead; and when he inquired more closely, he was assured that his noble friend, the brave and generous Prince Jonathan, was also fallen in the fight. In his anguish he rent his clothes, in token of his deep sorrow, and wept for his friend and for his king, the manner of whose death greatly affected him; and when his followers heard the tidings there was manifested the greatest sorrow in all men's faces.

"Whence art thou, young man?" at length sternly demanded David.

"Thy servant, my lord, is the son of a stranger—I am an Amalekite."

"How, thou son of a stranger! wast thou not afraid to stretch forth thine hand to destroy the Lord's anointed? By the sword of Saul! thou shalt die the death! Come hither," he called to the captain of his bodyguard; "draw thy sword and hew this Amalekite in pieces! Thy blood be upon thine own head; for thou hast testified against thyself, saying, 'I have slain the Lord's anointed!'"

Uriah, the captain of the guard, without hesitation lifted his sword and smote the sacrilegious and boasting Amalekite to the earth; who, hoping to ingratiate himself with David, whom he doubtless heard that rumor had asserted would succeed Saul, had invented the lie for which he was justly rewarded with death. This young man, your majesty, was the same who stood near Saul, and whom Saul would not ask to slay him; but who, after his death, and that of Doeg by his own hand, robbed the king's helmet of the "war crown," which was secured thereon by a band or plate of gold. This Amalekite was even the son of Doeg, by an Amalekite wife; and had been told by his wily father, if the king fell, to hasten with the crown to David in Ziklag, as he was to be king.

Little did the unhappy Amalekite understand the true character of David. Instead of beholding his face brighten with joy at the news of Saul's death; instead of seeing him seize the golden crown and vainly put it upon his head; instead of being rewarded with a purse of gold, a rich robe, and given a place of honor, lo! weeping took the place of rejoicing, in the generous and unselfish David; the crown lay untouched at his feet; and he was rewarded with an ignominious death for touching with his hand a consecrated king. How beautiful, your majesty, is this character so admirably developed by David, at a moment which would test all men and show what was in them! Here were no ambitious hopes awakened, no unfit joy manifested at the death of his persecutor and enemy! All the wrongs he had suffered from the *man* were buried in oblivion, as he thought upon the humiliating end of the consecrated *king!* The mighty Saul to be slain by a base Amalekite! The noble traits of Saul he recalled, and also his great sorrows, the loss of Samuel's friendship, of the favor of God, the evil spirit possessing him: all these recollections rushed upon his mind, as apologies for all his conduct, and he wept bitterly, that he was no more! But what pen can portray his heart's deep sorrow for the death of Jonathan! He shed tears for Saul, and the grief passed away; but he mourned long and sore for Jonathan.

"What shall I do with these, my lord?" asked the ever richly attired Ahithophel, placing the crown and bracelet of the king before him, as he sat in his tent.

"Take away the crown!" said David sorrowfully. "Give it to Abiathar to keep. Alas!" he added, as he took the silver bracelet in his hand, in which was framed a band of inscribed parchment; "here is the poor king's phylactery which, of late years, he has worn bound upon his wrist."

"Yes," said the cynical Ahithophel, with a slight tone of bitter sarcasm; "the king, the deeper he sinned, the broader made his phylacteries, and the ampler was the blue ribband upon his fringes. He grew, like all transgressors, superstitious in his late years, and what piety was lacking in his life, he bound it in sacred verses upon his brow as frontlets, and upon his hands as bracelets. Doubtless, as he went into battle with this, he regarded it as a potent charm or amulet, which would make him invulnerable. Behold! It was upon his *left* hand. That was the king's sword-hand, by virtue of his being of the tribe of Benjamin. It was a bad omen."

"This language is an offense unto me, Ahithophel," said David. "He who regards my favor will speak courteously and kindly of the fallen king."

The next day David called a solemn fast for the death of King Saul, and when the people were assembled together, and had paid due honors to the king's memory, he took his harp before them and struck it to the chords of lamentation for Prince Jonathan in the following hymn:

" The beauty of Israel is slain upon thy high places ;
    How are the mighty fallen !

    Tell it not in Gath,
Publish it not in the streets of Askelon :
Lest the daughters of the Philistines rejoice,
Lest the daughters of the uncircumcised triumph !

    Ye mountains of Gilboa, let there be no dew,
    Neither let their be rain upon you,
        Nor fields of offerings;
For there the shield of the mighty is vilely cast away—
The shield of Saul, as though he were not anointed with oil.
The bow of Jonathan turned not back;
The sword of Saul returned not empty!

    How are the mighty fallen!
    The beauty and glory of Israel departed !

    Saul and Jonathan were lovely and pleasant in their lives,
    And in death they were not divided:
    They were swifter than eagles:
    They were stronger than lions !

Ye daughters of Israel, weep over Saul,
Who clothed you with scarlet and many delights,
Who decked your apparel with ornaments of gold!

    How are the mighty fallen in the midst of the battle!

Thou Jonathan wert slain in thine high places ;
I am distressed for thee, O Jonathan, my brother:
Very pleasant hast thou been to me;
Thy love to me was wonderful, passing the love of women!

How are the mighty fallen!
And the weapons of war perished!"

This last refrain, taken up by the warriors and the women, was heard like the waves of the sea lifting up their voices to the wailing of the winds.

The days of lamentation for Saul and Jonathan being ended, David, although he knew that it was ordained that he should be king in Saul's stead, would take no steps without humbly consulting the Oracle of his God; thus evincing that modesty, prudence, and piety which are marked features in his noble nature. He, therefore, waited upon the High Priest, Abiathar, and desired him to inquire of the Lord what he should do, whether to go into the land of Judah and to Hebron, therein, where Saul had dwelt; or whither should he go?

The answer of the Oracle was, with the usual brevity of divine revelations:

"Go up to Hebron!"

David, therefore, prepared at once to go eastward into the land of Israel before the return of the conqueror Achish should place any barrier to his departure. He took with him all his followers with their families and his own, and also many servants of the Amalekites and Ethiopians which he had captured in the desert when he avenged the burning of Ziklag.

What were his emotions, when after five days' slow march, during which he crossed the field where he had slain Goliath, he came at the head of his long procession in sight of the battlements of Hebron, from which, three years before, he had fled by night from the fierce wrath of King Saul! As he looked up at the window of the palace, from whence Michal, his young wife, had let him down over the wall, he could not but recall all the scenes, so varied and adventurous, through which he had passed since that desolate night. Flying a fugitive without where to lay his head, he was now returning a king with the power and authority of Saul himself. His six hundred followers were increased by the thousands of the men of Judah who crowded along the way he came to join him and hail him as their king, and when he entered the gates of the city he had an army of twelve thousand men, while all the valley of Mamre, before Hebron, was thronged with multitudes who had gathered there to behold and receive their young king, and escort him to his throne.

When he reached the palace of King Saul, and was tendered the keys of the grand chamberlain, pride and power were not the emotions he felt at such a moment of triumph over his enemy, but sadness! The absence of Saul, of Jonathan, of his other dead sons, of Michal, left desolate vacancies in corridor and chamber, throne-room and festal hall. Having thanked the chief men, lords, and elders of Judah who had escorted him thither, he desired to be left alone, and for a while gave himself up to the painful and solemn reminiscences of the past.

The next day he gave audience to the principal persons of the tribe of Judah, of which Hebron was the chief city, who came formally to ask him to receive the solemn rite of consecration as king, some of these old men having been present when, a few years before, he had been anointed in his father's house at Bethlehem by Samuel. That that anointing was *royal* and prophetic of his reign after Saul's death of late all Israel had understood, and this knowledge at length afforded the people the true key to Saul's jealousy against one whom he feared and hated as the man who would supplant his family.

Alas! Jonathan, the prince royal, was now where earthly crowns were valueless! Only the youth Ishbosheth of all Saul's family remained, save his wife and concubines and their sons. Thirty days after the entrance of David into Hebron, the citizens of which had received him with great joy (for he had been well known to them when he dwelt there with Saul), he was consecrated and crowned king of Judah, with ceremonies more august and imposing than ever had been witnessed in the land. The High Priest, in full sacerdotals, after solemnly anointing his head with holy oil at the foot of the throne in the presence of the seventy, the seven elders of the city, the lords of the towns, the high captains and officers of his army and of the palace, led him up the steps of the throne, and seated him thereon. Then receiving the state crown of Saul from the hands of two priests, he placed it upon his head amid the acclamations of the people, and the sound of trumpets, cornets, dulcimers, and all kinds of instruments of music from a choir placed in the gallery at the west end of the throne-room. The one thousand brilliant guards without, in homage lowered their standard of the "Lion of the tribe of Judah," and paid with

depressed spears the martial salute to their new-crowned king,
and, crossing their swords, in one voice they swore safely to
guard his body " by watch and ward, by day and by night, with
their hearts and with their lives!" The intelligence that the
king was crowned was communicated to the multitudes in the
streets, whose shouts gave information to the warders upon the
walls, who made it known to the thousands who could not get
within the city, and who filled the valley. These, repeating the
shouts of joy, conveyed the glad tidings to the hills, and the
hills to the populous vales beyond these, to fortress, tower, and
city, still farther off; until the tide of sound rolled like waves
over all Judah, died away in the mountains of Carmel in the
south, of Ephraim in the west, and of Tabor in the north, and
were echoed back by the dark hills of Moab beyond Jordan.

Abner, Saul's brave general, was walking on the battlements
of the walled town of the ancient fortified camp of Mahanaim,
east of the river Jordan, whither he had fled, attended by four
hundred Benjamites, with Prince Isbosheth after the death of
Saul. All at once he heard shouts afar off: vine-dressers calling to the keepers in the towers of the olive fields, and these
to the reapers of barley under the walls, and these again to
the sentries over the city gate; each man sending on the news
which had crossed Jordan on the wings of human voices flying
through this populous land.

"What call they?" he asked of a foot-soldier, a man of the
tribe of Gad, who stood by.

Before the man could reply a warder upon a turret above
the gate, catching clearly the words which were shouted across
the valley, cried aloud to Abner:

"David is crowned! The son of Jesse is King of Judah!
Hosanna to the anointed of God!"

These words caused Saul's general to start as if he were suddenly wounded by an arrow, instead of by a voice. His great
brow grew black as night. He commanded the warden to keep
silence, and without delay hastened to the palace of the governor of the city. As he entered the reception hall he beheld
the young Prince Ishbosheth seated there, attired with that
exquisite taste which characterized him, his flowing robes
richly fringed with gold thread, his phylacteries gorgeously
worked with the needle in floss of gold; the blue silken bands
of the border, instead of being plain ribband according to the
law, were magnificently embroidered with scarlet pomegranates

and vine leaves intermingled. His tunic was of Tyrian purple, worn with a graceful air, and confined at his slender waist
by a cincture sparkling with emeralds. A collar of pearls encircled his round, handsome neck, and his wrists were decorated with bracelets, one of which inclosed a verse of Holy
Script, each letter ornamented after the style of the Phœnicians, who love to intertwine sentences among flowers, intermingled with shells and fanciful scrolls. His hands glittered
with jewel-set rings, and the royal seal ring of King Saul, his
father, was worn, as is the custom, upon the thumb of his left
hand. His dark hair, of which he was very proud, flowed about
his shoulders in shining masses; and upon his head he wore a
sort of sparkling tiara. He was seated upon a richly lined
chair, a slender Idumean hunting dog crouching at his feet, one
of his decorated, sandaled feet resting upon his glossy hide.
Upon his wrist was perched a beautiful Arabian bulbul, which
he was teaching to imitate a warlike air he was whistling to it.

Altogether it was a striking picture. Near him sat the governor's daughter, a mere child, but with those great radiant
Hebrew eyes, at once so full of innocence and intelligence.
He was amusing her with his remarks upon the dullness of
his plumaged pupil. On his handsome olive-brown and heart-
less face there was visible no trace of grief for the fate of his
father and brothers, who scarcely two months before had fallen
at Mount Gilboa. Not far distant from him on the other side
of the room sat the Governor of Mahanaim, reading out of the
book of the criminal law, in reference to a case which he was
to decide that day.

Abner entered with a quick, heavy tread, like a man in earnest, and who has something earnest to say; the ring of his
iron heel startling the prince, frightening the bulbul from his
wrist, and causing the dog to hide behind his master.

"What, my lord!" he cried, "art thou dallying there when
the times call for thee to buckle on thy sword and do battle for
thy father's crown? The son of Jesse was this day (for the
winds have quickly brought the evil tidings) crowned King of
Judah in Hebron! This must not stand! Sir governor, call
the city together! I will proclaim the Prince Ishbosheth King
of all Israel before the sun go down! and defend his right to
the crown of his royal sire with my good sword."

Abner faithfully fulfilled his purpose. The same hour he
rode through all the city at the prince's bridle, attended by

a glittering array of men-at-arms, and preceded by a royal trumpeter, who sounded the trumpet before him, while Abner cried:

"Bend the knee! Ishbosheth, son of Saul, is this day proclaimed King over Israel!"

From Mahanaim the prince and his general rode to the cities of Gilead, to the towns of the Ashurites, to Jezreel, to the strongholds of Ephraim, and the lands of the sons of Simeon, who wield their swords with the left hand, and over all Israel east of the Jordan. These all accepted and hailed the prince as their king; and when the ambassadors of David came among them a few days afterward to give in their allegiance to him, they imprisoned or drove them from their cities, refusing allegiance to any save to the son of Saul; a devotion which had its origin many years previous, when these people east of Jordan, being conquered by Ammonites, and Moabites, and others, were promptly delivered from the hands of their enemies by the prowess of King Saul. They now gratefully returned the favor by adhering to his son.

Thus not three months after Saul's death, your majesty, two kings were dividing his kingdom between them: one chosen before of God; the other, the creature of the ambition and noble devotion to his royal master's memory, of Abner the valiant warrior and accomplished general. Losing his own rank and power at Saul's defeat and death, this ambitious and proud soldier resolved to secure their continuance by placing the king's son on the throne. Perhaps he was ignorant of David's divine claim to the crown, and regarded him as a daring usurper and his natural enemy. Without doubt this stern old veteran, blunt and honest in purpose, despised the effeminate Prince Ishbosheth in his heart; but he knew that if he could secure his seat in the throne of his father, that he, himself, Abner, would be, as his adviser, the actual monarch! In establishing Ishbosheth in his father's kingdom he was, therefore, virtually to enthrone *himself!*

Abner therefore proceeded to raise an army to maintain the pretensions of the son of Saul to the throne. This personage was perfectly passive in his hands, willing to be king, so that Abner would take all the burden and trouble necessary to make him so, and leave him to the indulgence of indolence and pleasure. Though effeminate, Ishbosheth was not a craven. He had inherited all his father's courage, and he would not have fled from the face of a lion; but instead of his father's passion for war, he loved the indulgence of the chase, of the festal hall, of the scenes of pleasure and of luxury. If Abner had permitted it, he would have joined his father on the fatal field of Gilboa, and died fighting by his side, as fearless of death as his brothers! But he had no warlike ambition. Honors he would not refuse, but they must be purchased by the toil of others. Abner thoroughly understood the prince's character; and with the personal prize in view, personal to himself, he was willing to do all the work!

When David heard that Saul's son had been proclaimed King over Israel he manifested no anger. His generous temper at once pardoned an act founded upon the profoundest impulses of our nature. The sole surviving prince, was he not the lawful heir, in his own, and in the world's eye, of his royal father's throne? Were not his claims prior and superior to those of a stranger? What were David's, which should acquit him of the charge proclaimed against him from Beersheba in the south, to Dan in the north, of usurping Saul's kingdom? The secret call of God; followed by the secret anointing of Samuel; confirmed by the oracle at Ziklag, through the High Priest commanding him to go and reign at Hebron! These were evidences to *him* of his right to the throne; but was it evidence to Abner, to Ishbosheth, to Israel, to the world? How could he prove to all these his undisputed title to the scepter and crown of Saul? All that remained for him was to wait the farther revelations of Heaven, that the world might know as well as he himself the justice of his claim, founded upon the gift to him of the kingdom by Him who is King of kings, and governs the nations of the earth by whom He will! David therefore did not hasten to commence hostilities, but waited to see how God would order affairs. Three weeks elapsed when word came to him that Abner had crossed the Jordan and taken Gibeon, near Jerusalem. He now sent for Joab, his general, who, under such a soldier and warrior as David had at length become, had acquired a fierce and sanguinary character; or more truly, numerous wars had developed a temper naturally harsh and haughty into a fierce, almost relentless disposition.

"Thou hast heard the news, my great captain," said the king, as the tall warrior entered his presence, his thick tangled locks matted upon his square forehead, and the lines of pas-

sion and care deeply cut in his worn visage (for though yet
a young man, he looked already like a veteran), and the
beard upon his lips curved like two sabers across either cheek.
" I have come to but half of Saul's kingdom. Abner has not
only set up Ishbosheth against me beyond Jordan, and made
him king of all the east, as thou hast heard, but he has crossed
the Jordan and is at this moment in the heart of my kingdom, having entered Gibeon, but nine miles from Jerusalem,
two days ago! "

" Then, by the sword of Gideon, O King David," cried Joab,
in a voice that growled like a lion's when he hears the elephant
trumpeting afar off, " I will shorten him by the head ere two
days more are gone! "

" Nay, my brave son of Zeruiah," answered the king; " we
must deal gently with them. They are in the right, had not
God set Saul aside for a stranger! They must by and by all
come under my rule. Let me not do harm to my own subjects.
Go thou, Joab, and take with thee seven hundred chosen men,
the number he has with him. When thou comest near Gibeon,
send a messenger of peace to Abner. Begin not any quarrel
with him. Meet thou and the son of Ner as of old, like friends
and courteous brethren in arms. Learn from him his purposes.
Say to him that I have sworn I will not harm the seed of Saul,
nor fight against him and his people. Offer to Abner, son of
Ner, from me, terms of honor, and the command of my armies
east of Jordan, if he will submit to my scepter; and Ishbosheth
his master, for his brother Jonathan's sake, shall dwell in my
palace and be to me as a friend! "

The next morning the general of King David departed and
came and encamped before Gibeon, and sending in a messenger
of peace, Abner and twelve Benjamites, sons of Simeon beyond
Jordan, of great stature and valor, came forth with him, his
army being drawn up in battle array before the gates. The
meeting between these two mighty men of war was by a fountain near the gate. Abner heard all the words of the stern
Joab, which David sent to him, and answered graciously, saying " he would refer the matter to the King of Israel."

" Who is the King of Israel? " demanded Joab, with high
anger in his voice.

" Ishbosheth, the son of Saul! " answered Abner, with his
usual stately courtesy.

" Now, as the Lord liveth," cried Joab, striking his iron

sword-handle till it rung again, his nostrils dilating like those of a war-charger, "I know no King of Israel but my lord David of Hebron! I will do thee battle, son of Ner, on this question—thou and I here between our armies!"

"Nay, Joab," answered Saul's general, his large, brown eyes kindling with the steely gleam of battle, "I have here twelve men of war. They are more valiant than thine. If thou hast any doubt, choose ye twelve of your most valiant young men, let them meet on yonder grassy space, and at a signal let them play the game of battle instead of thee and me, and let the conquering side decide who shall be king, and who are the bravest warriors!"

The fierce and confident Joab did not hesitate to stake the kingdom on this issue of arms. When the twelve adherents of Ishbosheth faced the twelve men of Judah, the two armies looked on, and awaited the signal, which Abner gave by waving his sword, and crying:

"For Saul and his throne!"

"For God and the king!" responded Joab.

The twofold cries were taken up by the opposing combatants, and the two parties, first casting forward their javelins, rushed upon each other only with swords. The twelve Benjamites attempted by their fearful left-handed strokes to take the men of Judea unawares, but these twelve men, selected by Joab, had been trained in the army of David also to fight with the left hand, and parrying the blows caught their adversaries by the beard and hair, and run them through the body, the Benjamites at the same time transfixing each man his antagonist. Thus the twenty-four combatants fell dead together, every man's sword sheathed in his fellow's body. At this extraordinary result, as if the men by mutual understanding had agreed to die together, leaving the question of valor and right unsettled, Abner and Joab at the same instant moved by one impulse, shouted the battle-cry for their armies to close in conflict. In a few minutes the two hosts were fiercely battling together before Gibeon, and though Abner fought with superhuman prowess, the dogged valor and stern purpose of Joab overmastered him. He was defeated, and all his army put to flight, so that he himself had to flee away on foot toward the Jordan. Joab and his victorious soldiers pursued, until Asahel, a young brother of Joab, and of wonderful fleetness of foot, came up with Abner, ambitious to take him prisoner. The old warrior warned him not to come near him, but heedless of his words he was about to lay hands upon his shoulder when Abner, by a back-stroke of his broken javelin, slew him.

Abner, leaving three hundred and sixty of his men dead on the field and in the flight, reached Jordan after retreating all that night, and crossing that river regained Mahanaim, where Ishbosheth remained behind amusing himself. The loss of Joab was but nineteen men besides Asahel, whose body he conveyed to Bethlehem, his birthplace, and there buried. Then, returning to Hebron, he reported to the king the issue of the expedition, from which David perceived that he could only obtain the kingdom by an intestine war.

Thus, your majesty, I have brought the narrative of these warlike events up to the moment at which I write; for it is yet but fourteen days since the events I have last recorded transpired, and the return of Joab to Hebron. Three months ago, when I reached here from Egypt, David had but recently been crowned, and the subsequent events rapidly followed in the order in which I have given them. From Bethlehem, where I am sojourning, I saw the seven hundred men of Judah under Joab when they marched by, in the valley, on their way to meet Abner at the pool of Gibeon; and, on their return, bearing the body of the light-footed Asahel. Joab and his brother Abishai stopped here one day to bury the body in the sepulcher of his fathers. From him I learned all the particulars of the meeting with Abner as I have narrated it; and also from King David, Joab, and others, who were intimately connected with the events I have recorded, have I received the chief details of the histories which have filled my letters to your majesty.

My health is now so much improved by more than two months' sojourn in this salubrious region, that I shall, to-morrow, leave the house of the stern, but hospitable Joab, and proceed to Hebron, to pay a visit to the king, in order to take leave of him before departing from his kingdom. Ever since my return from Egypt his majesty has shown toward me the greatest kindness. Upon my arrival by the caravan from the land of the Nile, and, coming to Hebron, I found that Jonathan's friend held the scepter; being too ill to leave the camp outside of the walls, I sent to King David a message of congratulation on his accession to the throne. What was my surprise the next morning, your majesty, to behold the curtain of my tent drawn aside and to see the king enter! He tenderly embraced me, and insisted that I should be removed in a palanquin to his palace. He was greatly changed in three years. His figure was large and manly, and his air and bearing was that of a warlike chief; for he had learned to endure the hardness of a soldier's discipline in the severe school of his persecutor, Saul. Yet, with his brown cheek, his bearded chin, his martial voice, and military aspect, his eyes still sparkled with the soft light of the gentle shepherd's spirit, and his white forehead was expansive with the radiance of the highest order of intellect. About his fine mouth played the light of that divine inspiration which has revealed itself in some of the most beautiful odes, hymns, and psalters which human genius has composed. These this pious prince loves to sing at his window at the close of day, when the hills are just fading behind the holy veil of twilight, or seated upon his palace corridor in the light of the full moon, accompanying his grand, rich voice with his harp, producing the noblest harmony.

I remained several days a guest of this most devout and ingenuous king, and after he had heard of me the history of all my adventures in Egypt, he from time to time (for he often came to my chamber and remained as long with me as he could withdraw from his varied and important affairs) related to me all the events which transpired in Judea during my nearly three years' absence at the court and in the prisons of Pharaoh.

When at length he found that the close confinement and air of Hebron were uncongenial and unfavorable to me, he recommended the hills of Bethlehem, his native place; and Joab, who has a house here, the pleasures of which, however, he seldom enjoys, being so much away on duty at the court or with the army, civilly and very kindly offered me the use of it. I accepted the kindness, and by the advice of my physician came hither.

Though I have occupied my time so much in writing to your majesty, almost my only solace, yet I have grown better daily; and am now about to pay a visit to the king. Through his attention I have received in my convalescence every luxury. One day, purple grapes from the famous vineyards of Eshcol, in rich bunches of a size that would more than fill a helmet, are sent to me; on another, caskets of ripe figs, both blue and white, of wonderful excellence, such as no other land produceth; yesterday, a basket of delicious pomegranates came by a messenger from the aged Jesse, the father of the king, who had no sooner been crowned than he sent for his venerable parents to return from the court of the king of Moab to their own home; and to-day, raisins, apricots, and fruits with names unknown to me, and of ravishing flavor, with fragrant olives from the Mountain of Olives, not far distant, are bountifully poured upon my table; while the rich wines of Idumea, of Egypt, and Damascus tempt me to temperate indulgence, and invite to strength and health.

This land of Judea and of Benjamin, of which Hebron and Bethlehem are the centers, is rich and fertile beyond conception; beautiful and bold in scenery; abounding in grains, fruit, and flowers; noble forest trees, and fountains; and groves, gardens, and thousands of pleasant and foliage-shaded homes; with numerous snow-white sepulchers, gleaming amid dark groves.

HEBRON, COURT OF KING DAVID.

Your majesty will see by the change in the date of my letter, that I fulfilled my intention to leave Bethlehem, to visit the king. I was received by the young monarch in the kindest manner. He expressed his great joy at my restoration to health, and said that he trusted I would now make a long visit at his court. With what pleasure did I meet here on the day of my arrival, Isrilid, the stately, gray-haired lord of Jericho! He was accompanied by his fair daughter, and they are occupying the palace in which Abner once dwelt. They insisted that I should become their guest; and the king reluctantly gave me up; but as his palace, in this crisis of his reign, is filled with courtiers, ambassadors from the various Hebrew tribes, lords of cities, senators of the Sanhedrim, and war officers, all seeking position and place, or offering services, or presenting letters of adhesion to his rule, and congratulations upon his accession, it was far more agreeable for me to be in a private house; I therefore accepted the offer of the noble Isrilid, who at once took me to his home, which is not far from the palace.

On the way thither he informed me that when he reached Damascus with his fair daughter he was delayed some weeks for the caravan, and arrived at Tadmor in the Desert, after many delays, to learn that the queen had been dead four months and that her brother, a young soldier of Parthian blood, had seized the crown. "I found him," said Isrilid, "maintained in his usurpation by a body of wild barbaric soldiers in steel helmets, and armed with gigantic bows, that

carry steel-headed arrows five cubits long. It would have been
madness to have made known my errand. I remained at Tadmor privately lodged a few weeks, during which time I learned
that the new dynasty was hateful to the people, and that they
would aid a leader with an army, to displace the splendid savage whose yoke pressed heavily upon them. I therefore resolved to visit Nineveh, the kings of which I knew had received
for a hundred years tri-annual tribute from the kings of Tadmor; not that I hoped King Belus would overthrow the new
dynasty at my poor solicitation, or, that so long as the tribute
was regularly sent to him, he troubled imself as to who wore
the crown; but I expected, my lord Arbaces," continued Isrilid, " to find *you* at the Assyrian Court, long since successfully returned from your embassy to Egypt. I therefore waited
for the next caravan, when a company of merchants of Nineveh arrived, from the captain of whom I learned that your
mission had failed, and you had been held a prisoner in Egypt
by Pharaoh more than two years. As I was informed from
this veteran captain, that he was the maternal uncle of your
armor-bearer Ninus, I gave credence to his story, and reluctantly returned by the first opportunity to Damascus, when
three weeks ago we arrived in Judea to hear of King Saul's
death, and the wise and brave David, the friend of God, on
the throne. Here I learned, O prince, with joy, how you had
escaped from your Egyptian prison, and were in Bethlehem,
where, had you not so opportunely come to Hebron, I proposed
to visit you. As I am no longer lord of Jericho, but a private
citizen, I shall dwell here with my daughter, having taken the
palace of Abner, which Saul, to whom it belonged, though permitting Abner to occupy it, gave me three years ago in part
security for the talents of gold I loaned to him to carry on
the war against the Philistines, when Goliath of Gath and his
armies came against him!"

By this time, your majesty, we had reached the gate of Abner's palace, which stands not far distant from the " Tabernacle of Shelter," where the refugees who seek this city from
the avenger of blood are lodged for protection.

Three years had changed the Princess Adora, not in taking
away from her beauty and grace, but developing and ·finishing
that which was not fully matured in mind and person. Heretofore she was the opening rose which one hesitated whether yet
to call it a bud or a flower. But the full-blown rose of Sharon,

brilliant with the morning dews, was not more beautiful than the fair daughter of the house of Isrilid, as she now appeared when she advanced to meet me! She extended her hand, partly with the freedom of an old friend, partly with the affection of a sister for a brother, partly with a gentle look of sympathy (for she had heard of my sufferings in Egypt), partly with blushing consciousness that though she might regard me as a brother, I was not her brother! These conflicting, embarrassing emotions made her look far more lovely than my brightest recollections since our last meeting had ever pictured her.

It took the hours of three moonlight evenings spent upon the terrace-like roof of the palace, the soft breeze from the mountains of Judah laden with the mingled fragrance of fruit and flowers cooling the air the while, to interchange our stories. It is wonderful how often she desired me to describe the beauty of the Egyptian princess! At length she said: "I wonder, O prince, thou didst not marry her! Thou hadst better have sat on a throne than been chained to the floor of that dreadful dungeon!" There was a tremor in the tones of her voice that plainly betrayed she did not mean all she said.

"I had no heart, fair Adora, to give her," I answered her.

But here, your majesty, I paused, for I dared not venture on ground from which, if circumstances should render it necessary, I might be unable to retire with becoming self-possession and dignity. From what I leave unsaid, your majesty will be so kind as not to imagine there are passages of the interview I desire not of confess. What the future may reveal, I cannot say. Whatever it does develop shall not be withholden from thee, O Belus!

I am now a daily guest at the dinner table of the king. One after another the Hebrew tribes on this side Jordan are giving in their adhesion to his royal scepter; for, to the people at large the title of David, the son of Jesse, to reign over them is of the same value (in that it is from the same high Source of all authority and power, their God himself) of that by which Saul, the son of Kish, became their king! Both equally were called of God, and both were anointed by Samuel! But for the ambition of Abner, still the firm friend of the dead king, his master, who claims an hereditary right to the throne on the part of the king's son, the whole nation, both sides of the now dividing river, would ere this have submitted cheerfully to his scepter. So long as Abner lives and stands by this young and indolent prince, Ishbosheth, so long will there exist in this nation of one blood a state of internecine war, but aggressive only on the part of the adherents to Ishbosheth.

As I was about to close this letter, your majesty, King David sent for me. Upon presenting myself at the palace, he said:

"My dear prince, I trust our long and frequent intercourse has made us friends. I will, therefore, frankly commune with you. You inform me that it is your purpose in a few days to return to Nineveh, contrary to the advice of your own physicians and those of my court, who say the heat and exposure of the Oriental desert will bring back your disease, and perhaps forbid a second restoration to health. Before you incur so great a risk, I pray you reflect whether you cannot be of more service to your monarch and to his interests by remaining here and representing Assyria in the character of resident ambassador at my court. It is true my kingdom is yet in its first estate, and but a fragment of the empire God will put into my hand. But it is my purpose to enlarge its borders and raise it to a rank among the powers of the earth that the nations shall no more say with derision, 'Your God, whom you call the Lord of the earth, rules over but a little kingdom without seaports, commerce by caravan or ship, without treaties, and without the friendship of a single king of the earth!' Remain here, O Arbaces, and let me address a letter to your king, your account of whom has led me to hold him in great esteem, asking him to consent to an interchange of commerce and of royal courtesies. Such a message I shall direct to Pharaoh of Egypt, to the King of Sheba, to the Dukes of Idumea, to the Prince of Tadmor, to the noble young King Hiram of Tyre, and even to the Lord of Askelon. War is not prosperity, but peace is power! I shall cultivate amity and friendship with all nations. With an army of four hundred thousand men, which I can bring into the field when I have consolidated my power, I shall be able to command peace in my borders. The friendship and alliance of the powerful King of Nineveh will enable me to secure more readily that of all the others. If you consent, O Arbaces, to remain at my court, I will dispatch a courier with a suitable escort to your king to be the bearer of my letter, and of any message you may desire to forward to him."

When King David had ended this candid revelation of the policy which should govern him in his reign, I thanked his majesty for his confidence and royal friendship, and desired three days to make up my mind.

In coming to the determination which I have done, I was materially influenced, O Belus, by two words spoken by the Princess Adora. These words were in reply to a question which after an hour's interview I addressed to her; a question founded upon good evidence which I believed I had of her partiality for me. I said:

"And will you, O Adora, share the residue of my life with me, if I consent to remain, by my royal master's permission, resident ambassador at the court of your king?"

Without hesitation, but with trembling joy, the glory of love resplendent in her radiant gaze, and its sacred cadences trembling musically on her tongue, she answered:

"I will."

Therefore, O Belus, do you receive this letter by the caravan instead of Arbaces in person. Let not my lord prince be offended. If your majesty will turn a favorable ear to the request of King David for an alliance and representation, and will confer upon your Arbaces the position of ambassador, the king will send to you in return, one of his lords, Ahithophel, a person of great abilities, scholarship, wit, and knowledge of men, a nobleman of wonderful sagacity of intellect and penetration, and with that high personal character which will command for him your majesty's esteem.

Be assured, O my liege lord and prince, Belus, that I do not in the least withdraw my allegiance from you, my lawful king, even in taking the oath of homage (as I shall do if your majesty accredits me to this court) to the fair Queen of Tadmor, whose only empire I fear will be that which she will wield over the loyal heart of

Your loving and liegiant subject,

ARBACES.

[There is an interval of seven years between the date of the preceding letter
and the present, during which civil war raged between Abner, the general
for Ishbosheth, Saul's son, and King David; but without any notable battles
being fought. David, however, steadily gained power and strength, while
Saul's party became weaker and weaker, daily diminishing in numbers and
influence.]

LETTER XIV.

ARBACES, AMBASSADOR AT THE COURT OF JERUSALEM,
TO BELUS, KING OF ASSYRIA.

COURT OF DAVID, JERUSALEM.

YOUR MAJESTY:

I once more take up my pen to resume, after nearly seven
years' intermission, my narrative of the events of the reign of
King David. My long silence in the interval is owing to the
fact that nothing has transpired worthy of transmitting to your
majesty outside of the regular routine of my official, diplomatic
correspondence, in which I have diligently kept you advised
of what concerns you as the ally of this realm to know. I
rejoice at your majesty's approval of my whole course at this
court, during the seven years I have resided here; and especially do I feel complimented by your approval of the position
I took in promising your aid, when last year Pharaoh, King
of Egypt, insolently demanded tribute of King David, on the
ground that the Hebrews had despoiled Egypt when, five hundred years ago, they departed from it; a charge so absurd at
this time that King David said, "This Egyptian seeks this
cause of quarrel in order to go to war with me, and subdue my
kingdom to his scepter with his countless hosts."

But when I pledged to the Hebrew monarch the assistance
of an Assyrian army, your majesty, if Egypt invaded his borders, and sent to Pharaoh word that a war with King David
involved a war with the powerful King Belus, the haughty
Egyptian withdrew his insolent demand. I was sure your
majesty would approve of the responsibility I assumed at such
a crisis. Since then King David has withholden nothing from
me, but consults me in all his affairs.

Your majesty has kindly offered to march an army against Tadmor, and drive the Parthian king from its throne, of which he is now seven years an usurper, and hold it for the Princess Adora. I thank your majesty, and so does Adora, my wife; but since the death of the ambitious Isrilid, her father, two years ago, she has dismissed from her mind all aspirations after a throne which can only be won by a conflict of armies and maintained at great expense of treasure and of blood. Nor, your majesty, have I any desire to become king, by virtue of Adora's title, of the realm of Tadmor. I have been so long in this pleasant land I feel at home therein; and having been nearly seven years wedded to one of its loveliest daughters, I have all the happiness my heart or my ambition requires. We dwell in a charming palace on the side of the Mountain of Olives, facing Jerusalem, with terraces and gardens, groves and fountains, and all the luxuries which the vast wealth that Adora inherited from her father can command. I am respected by the lords and elders of the Sanhedrim, and have the confidence of the king. No, your majesty, I am perfectly happy, and my wife confesses that she is. Let the magnificent Talarac reign in barbaric splendor. I sleep sounder than he, for crowns are full of troubled thoughts, which no opiates can put to rest. The life of David is full of care! My little kingdom of seven acres, on the side of Olivet, with its little snow-white palace for me and Adora, its king and queen; our realm of groves full of bulbuls and other singing birds; our pastures enameled with a thousand flowers; our orchard abounding in fig, pomegranate, apricot, apple, tamarind, and date trees in rich profusion; our vineyard purple and gold with clusters of grapes; our olive garden, called of old Gethsemane, shining with its fragrant fruit, its olive press half hidden among the ancient olive trees; all these constitute our kingdom. We also have servant men and servant women, among them two poor Gibeonites who served Ahimelech at Nob, and escaped from the slaughter of their people by Doeg; a few lambs; a dark-eyed gazelle that feeds out of Adora's hand; a tame coney, white as snow, and a few kine, besides half a dozen beautiful Assyrian horses. Before our door, across the valley, tower the walls of Jerusalem, the battlements of the fortress of David, late that of the Jebusites, and the warlike outline of the whole of the city where, of old, Melchisedek, the descendant of the gods, reigned cotemporary with Abraham. In a clear morning, from the roof of my villa, I can also see the mountains of Ephraim in the west, the city of Kirjath-jearim at their base, where the Ark and the Tabernacle have been since the death of the priests at Nob; the turrets of Ramah, farther north, the city of the Seer and now his sepulcher; and, southwardly, the misty and azure heights of Bethlehem. What more do I need, O Belus, to render me happy? What lacketh in the dimensions of our kingdom we find in the boundless empire of one another's affection. The realm over which love reigns hath no boundary but the earth around and the heavens above.

Therefore, O Belus, suffer Talarac to reign in Tadmor, and Arbaces and Adora to reign on the side of the Mount of Olives over their gardens, birds, and gazelle, and flowers.

It is true, your majesty, I respond in reply to your inquiry, I have solemnly consecrated myself to the worship of the one God of the Hebrews; and by adoption, ere I married Adora, I became a proselyte to their grand and mysterious faith. But in departing, O Belus, from the worship of Assarac and Ninus, and the gods of Assyria, do not suppose I have withdrawn my allegiance or devotion from its lord. My heart still beats as loyal to thee as ever, my beloved master and king; and I trust you will yet bear testimony that I can be faithful to the God of David without failing in loyalty to Belus. I should have been unworthy of Adora if I could have refused to acknowledge her God, and take her faith to my heart.

During the seven years past, your majesty, Abner, with wonderful talent and influence over men, has held the fragmentary kingdom of Ishbosheth together. For the first two years this indolent and luxurious prince maintained a royal court at Mahanaim, and kept up a sort of kingly estate; but Abner could not prevail upon him to lead his army against King David. He declined to take the field, so that he could indulge, unmolested by David, in inglorious ease in his palace, surrounded by sycophants and flatterers. All the while the most warlike of his adherents were calling upon him to march against Hebron and take from him the throne of his father Saul. Disappointed by his indifference, many of the best warriors in his camp went over to Joab and tendered him their allegiance and swords for King David. At length the patience of the lionlike Abner was wearied out; and after the prince had nominally reigned two and a half years, the ambitious son of

Ner ceased longer to recognize him as king, or refer any mat-
ters to him, but took the reins of government in his own bold
and sagacious hand. He raised a large army to invade Judah,
when Ishbosheth, led on by rival warriors, jealous of the power
of Abner, forbade his march. Abner in anger refused to obey
his king; but his captains and men-at-arms becoming dissatisfied at this dividing of power, dissension arose, and the whole
host dispersed, save four thousand men. With these Abner laid
waste parts of the country which had submitted to David, but
Joab marching against him caused him again to retire beyond
the river. In this desultory and resultless manner nearly five
more years elapsed, when affairs were suddenly brought to a
crisis between the inefficient Prince Ishbosheth and his discon-
tented and long-enduring captain.

One morning Abner presented himself in the chamber of the
prince, who, broken in constitution by luxurious indulgence,
and bloated with banqueting and wine, was reclining on his
embroidered couch, listening to the voice of a beautiful Ish-
maelite singing-girl, sent him by the King of Ammon.

"What now, Abner!" he said, looking displeased at the
abrupt entrance of the veteran commander. "Thou treadest as
heavily as an elephant, and comest before us helmed and mailed
as if thou wert entering thy battle tent! More ceremony, even
if thou art my father's uncle, old man, when thou comest into
a king's presence! What now?"

"The King of Ammon's ambassador waits for thy reply,"
answered Abner, repressing his ire. "Wilt thou accept his offer
of alliance, and the eighty thousand men he offers us to go up
against David, and stablish thee on the throne of thy father
at Hebron?"

"Nay; I am content to reign this side Jordan," replied the
prince. "It is too much trouble to go to war! Let the son of
Jesse be content with his side! I will not quarrel with him for
what he has! Go, Abner, thou hast caused me to lose the
sweetest trill, when at the most critical note, I e'er heard from
human voice! Go on, girl! Sing me that song again! These
thick-headed war-men have no ear but for a trumpet or the
neighing of a charger."

The gray-haired, grand old warrior who had fought a hundred battles with Saul felt this insolence of his son, but com-
pressed his lips and left the room in silence. As he passed along
the hall he beheld a stately, beautiful woman about forty-five

years of age, who seemed awaiting his return. She fixed upon the sorrowful and angry visage of the commander her large, inquiring eyes. Abner answered the look by shaking his head sadly, and then said:

"Rizpa, wilt thou give me brief audience?"

"Come in, O Abner; I will, if it will please thee, talk over with thee this matter of the King of Ammon's alliance thou has so greatly at heart! What hast thou to ask of me?" she inquired, as he took a seat by the window of her room while she sat upon a carved gilt chair before it.

He then eloquently urged upon her the duty of exerting her influence with the prince, which, he said, he felt was very great, to induce him to accept the aid of Ammon. The woman promised to do so, and he was about to leave her apartment when Ishbosheth entered. His face was flushed with wine and jealousy! Fixing his inflamed eyes on his general, he cried:

"How, son of Ner! What doest thou here? Darest thou insult the memory of Saul, my father, by seeking to make his widowed concubine thine? Thou wilt next affect the kingdom! Hast thou of late grown so great that thou hast thought thou couldst even look to the king's wives?"

These words, embracing so grave a charge against him, roused the soldier to great wrath.

"Am I but the keeper of thy dogs, son of Saul," he cried, "that thou chargest me with this base thing?—me who have maintained thee on thy throne, and showed kindness to all thy father's house, and made myself strong for thee and thy crown, and have not delivered thee, as I have had the power to do, into the hands of David? What! am I a dog, that thou chargest me with fault concerning this woman? Now is my cup full! And may God, who once swore to David to translate the kingdom from the House of Saul, and to set up the throne of David over all Israel, and over Judah, do unto me as he hath done unto Saul and his three sons, if I do not henceforth give my help to carry out this oath of God toward David, and presently bring all Israel away from thee unto him! So help me the God of my fathers, but that I do it!"

The terrible anger and fatal oath of Abner caused the prince's face to change from the crimson hue of wine to the whiteness of parchment. He essayed to reply, but the words clove to the roof of his mouth, parched by fear. Abner without another word strode from the chamber, leaving his mantle in the grasp of Rizpa, who with tearful eyes would have detained him to pacify his fierce wrath and get him to change his mind against the House of Saul, which he had for seven years so faithfully served with his sword and his voice.

The best of kings cannot be sure of the permanent devotion of their courtiers. Ishbosheth deserved to lose this one, the defender and sole supporter of his pretensions to the crown of his father.

The first intelligence King David had of the matter was the sudden appearance of a courier from Abner before the gate of Hebron, for Abner, having made the breach irreparable between him and Ishbosheth, was too prudent a diplomatist to delay the execution of his threat, for the prince with Abner's envious enemies might combine for his immediate destruction. Instead, however, of going himself to David, he kept at home in his own palace, well armed and watchful, while he sent to him a messenger. When David heard that a courier with the banner of Saul's House on his spear asked an audience, he sent for him to appear before him.

"Whence comest thou?" he demanded of the fleet-footed Gadite runner.

"From beyond Jordan, and from Abner the head of the armies of Israel," answered the man; and with the word he delivered a sealed and tied roll into the hands of King David's cup-bearer, who bore it to his royal master upon his silver tray.

The king, quickly breaking the seal and cutting the silken thread, unrolled the parchment, and read as follows:

"To David, King of Judah at Hebron; Abner, Son of Ner,
     Counselor and General of the House of Saul: Greeting.

"That God hath sworn to thee to take the kingdom from Saul, and set up the throne of David therein, thy servant knoweth, and so doth all Israel. Wherefore should man fight against God? Whose is the land of Israel but thine, the anointed of God's? Let thy servant, therefore, make a league with thee, O king, and behold my hand shall be with thee henceforward, and thy servant will bring over all Israel to thee, so thou shalt reign over Israel and Judah, as God hath appointed thee. Make a league, O king, and secure to thy servant and his, and to the House of Saul, and to all Israel, safety and honor, and what thy servant hath covenanted to do he will do."

The King of Judah was greatly rejoiced at this unlooked-for turn of affairs, as your majesty may well perceive. He at once replied as follows:

"David, King by the grace and order of God, sendeth these to Abner, son of Ner:

"The king granteth the league. Come thou and all Israel over to me, and bring me the keys of the rebel city of Mahanaim in token of its submission. The son of Saul may depart whither he listeth, or come and dwell in Hebron with safety and honor, and Saul's wives and their sons with him; also Mephibosheth, the little lame son of Jonathan, whom for his sake I will adopt, and he shall be even as a prince in my house. But hear, O Abner, thou nor thine nor none of these shall see my face, except thou first bring Michal, Saul's daughter, whom he gave me to wife ten years ago, when thou comest. Without her come not before my face."

In addition to this reply to Abner King David sent a courier with a letter to that prince, demanding his wife, whom Saul in the first year of her marriage had divorced from David and given to Phalti of Laish, the just and virtuous man I have before named. This Phalti, upon receiving her, had committed her to the charge of his mother, as if she were his sister; for being a friend of David, he resolved at some future day to restore her to him in purity and honor.

The letter to Ishbosheth, whom David well knew, having long dwelt in the palace of Saul with him, as well as married his sister, ran thus:

"King David to Prince Ishbosheth.

"I write with my own hand this letter to thee, demanding my wife, thy sister, Michal. Deliver her to me without delay, for I hear she is in thine hand."

When Abner received David, the King of Judah's, reply, he went to Ishbosheth with fair words, for the prince, finding he had not departed from the city to David, following the sensible advice of Rizpa, made friends with him by acknowledging to him the injustice of his angry suspicions; for if Abner remained his enemy, on whom could he lean? Taking advantage of this truce, Abner waited upon him, after he knew David's messenger had delivered his letter to him, without appearing to know that such a courier or letter had come to Mahanaim. As he expected, he found Ishbosheth in a tornado of passion, cursing David by Urim and Thummim, by Altar and Cherubim, and making oath that he would slay his sister with his own hand rather than give her back to the son of Jesse!

Abner waited until this storm had subsided, and then urged him to obey the king by persuasions backed by representations of David's power, and his certain vengeance if this, his first and most beloved wife, should be refused him. The irresolute prince yielded, and sent to the house of Phalti the friend of God, as he was called, and brought Michal from his mother's care to Abner. The parting was a sorrowful one. The mother of Phalti loved her as a daughter, for the amiable and faithful princess had been as such to her; while Phalti loved her both as a sister and as a daughter, and while he felt the justice of David's claim, he could not but go with her a long ways, mourning with deep grief her departure from his roof.

Ten years had ripened the beauty of the daughter of Saul, now in her twenty-sixth year, who after so long an absence, was about to be reunited to him. That David should still retain the warmth of his youthful love, after such scenes of war, and persecution of sorrow and trials, lamenting her as dead, reflects upon him the highest honor, and is singularly creditable to the tenderness and devotion of his heart!

Did her attachment, perhaps your majesty will inquire, survive that long period of separation? I can assure your majesty that its fires were as bright as those which warmed the bosom of the king. I was by chance present at their meeting, when Abner, leaving his bodyguard of twenty men at the gate, brought her into the presence of the king. With what a bound of joy and love, after a moment's doubt as his strange aspect met her gaze, at the sound of his voice, did she fly to his heart and rest upon his shoulder! But there is a sacredness in love which can convert mere curiosity into a sort of sacrilege, and I will not describe the beautiful and touching emotion each exhibited at their reunion; for both were still young, King David being but thirty, and his recovered wife five years younger! From that moment I loved him even more than before I had esteemed him.

But how shall I describe to your majesty the interview of David with his ancient friend, Abner, who had restored to him the wife of his youth! For four hours they sat together and talked over all the past. Especially did David inquire about Saul and Jonathan's death, and hung on each particular; and tears came into his eyes, even seven years after he fell on the hard-foughten field of Gilboa. David, a brave and skillful soldier himself, respected Abner. He knew the honest purpose of his heart, and the singleness of his character. He honored him for his devotion to the House of Saul, for it became him as a faithful servant of that unhappy monarch to stand up for his house and the glory of his name, and the royal inheritance of his son. David loved him not less, but rather honored him the more for his generous devotion to Ishbosheth and his fortunes; both so unworthy of him.

When King David had done discoursing with the valiant warrior and statesman of Israel, he sent for his score men-at-arms, and had them well cared for and feasted; and placed Abner at his own table, in the presence of his lords, governors, captains, and chief officers, giving him the place of honor next to his right hand, and sending him a portion five times greater than to all others. I was present, your majesty, at this feast. I was struck with the modesty and good sense of the simple-hearted and majestic old warrior. He spoke out his sentiments bluntly and to the point. He seemed to fear no man; yet there was a native, manly courtesy about him which was very captivating. He was full sixty years of age, if not older, with a grand, heroic head, massive and stern, his eyes dark hazel and piercing, yet capable of a woman's tenderness of expression; his heavily burdened and mustached lip and chin had a lion-like aspect; while his voice had the deep energy of the rumbling bass notes of the king of beasts. If he had been Saul's son instead of being his uncle, and so been heir to the throne, King David would have sat, for the last seven years, more in his war-saddle than on his throne, slept oftener in his pavilion on the field than upon his couch in the palace.

The following day Abner took leave of King David, saying, "I will now depart and go over Jordan and gather all Israel unto my lord the king, that the lords and elders thereof may make with thee a league of submission, that thou mayest reign over them and over all the kingdom of Saul, according to thy heart's desire, and the oath of God to thee."

King David dismissed Abner at his palace gate with an embrace of friendship. It was remarked by the officers of the court that he had never shown such affectionate regard for Joab his own general. The observation of the courtiers was correct. Abner was by nature a noble character, not only brave, but generous, manly, gentle, and honest, possessing qualities of character which even his enemies could respect. Of him once said the King of Moab, where David's parents found shelter, and who fought against Abner and Ishbosheth for David's sake, "I love the son of Ner above all men, and though he be my enemy, I would give the revenue of half my kingdom to have him my friend and commander of my armies."

In Joab there was nothing to love, no trait of character to command admiration or win affection. He had no heart but his sword, no sympathies, no loving-kindnesses, no charities. He was only a man of war, iron within and iron without. A thorough soldier he was, an invaluable commander of the armies of King David; but there was no soul to be found underneath his corslet and brazen cuirass. Abner's smile would have won the most timid child to his knee; the frown of Joab would have sent it in terror to its mother's side. Therefore David embraced Abner his foe, but never embraced Joab his friend! and this was observed and commented upon. Whether the busy tongue of malice poisoned Joab's ear thereupon, I know not, leading him to the step which followed; but Abner had not been an hour departed with a safe conduct from the king, on his return to the other side Jordan, when Joab and his younger brother Abishai entered the gate from a successful onslaught against an invading band of Idumeans from the south. He had no sooner come within the city than some of the busy courtiers told him that Abner of Ner, viceroy beyond Jordan, had been three days with the king, feasting and holding audience, and had made terms of peace with him; and but an hour had left! Upon this Joab, his sword yet red with slaughter, and his armor stained with the conflict, stalked into the palace, and stood in the throne-room before the king. His raven black hair hung in tangled masses over his shoulders, his armor was indented with Idumean battle-ax strokes, and his helm cloven with a blow from the sword of a lord of the desert, whom he slew. He looked like war in all its sanguinary terrors embodied; while his red-shotten eyes, and thick voice, husky with shrieking his war cries, betrayed how great his passion raged.

"Abner the son of Ner," he shouted to the king, menacingly

and defiantly, " hath been here, and thou hast sent him away in peace."

" He came in peace," answered David firmly.

" Nay," cried Joab; " thou knowest this son of Ner came to deceive thee, and to be spy upon thee, and to know thy going out and thy coming in, and all that thou doest. Thou hast not done well to let him go from thee in peace. Thou shouldst have put him to death, and then the crown of all Israel would have been thine! "

Before King David could reply to his irate general Joab went out of the presence. Without making known to any man his purpose, he sought out his chief captain and bade him send two swift runners after Abner in the name of the king, to bring him back. The messengers overtook Abner at the well of Sirah, where ten years before David had sat down and drank water from the pitcher of the virgin Abigail, the betrothed of Nabal, and now the king's wife, and ate figs from the little basket of Bathsheba, now since become the wife of his great captain Uriah. Abner, suspecting no treachery, returned with the messengers. As he re-entered the gate of the city of Hebron, Joab met him and said:

" I knew not thou wert the king's guest, O Abner, or I would have hastened from the wars to show thee hospitality as becometh thy rank and the errand on which thou camest! Wilt thou remain and dine with me to-morrow? We are old soldiers in one sense, and we will talk our battles o'er."

With this talk Joab, who was closely followed by his brother Abishai, had got him to a corner in the wall behind the gate, when, suddenly turning upon him, he drew his dagger and struck him between the corslet and the belt to the heart at a single blow, crying:

" *That*, for my brother Asahel, whom thou didst slay between Gibeon and Jordan, with a back stroke of thy spearhead, when he followed thee to overtake thee as thou fleddest! "

The brave warrior, without a word, so suddenly was he smitten to the death, fell over upon his face and died, a victim to the basest treachery, and a sacrifice also, perhaps, to the jealous fears of the assassin; for Joab suspected that if David pardoned and took the noble Abner into favor, he would, ere long, from his superior age and experience in war and military rule, take the highest place in the army of David, and displace himself. Without doubt the last was the chief and ruling motive for his putting Abner to death; for Asahel was fairly slain in pursuit of a retreating foe, and his death could not call for such a deed of vengeance.

When King David heard the tidings he was greatly overcome, and at length said, in a voice trembling with indignation and mortification:

"As the Lord liveth, let all men hear and know that I, and my house, and my kingdom are guiltless of the blood of Abner. I sent him forth in peace. Let his blood be upon Joab, the sole author of this great crime, and on all his father's house. Let his sons be lepers, and lame, and die by their own hand, or perish with hunger, no man giving them, because he hath dealt treacherously, and slain him whom the king let go in peace and with an oath of safety."

There were not wanting malicious men, your majesty, who denounced the king as having openly sent him away in order secretly to destroy him. The king therefore in every manner sought to clear himself of all such suspicion. He publicly proclaimed his innocence. He denounced, and charged Joab with the crime. He invested himself with the habiliments of grief, and put on sackcloth, and clad his whole court in mourning. He buried Abner from his palace with the most solemn and magnificent funeral obsequies. He caused all the governors of cities, lords of towns, the Sanhedrim, or Senate of Seventy, the municipal judges, the chief men, and civilians, and half his army, in battle order, to precede and follow the body, which was placed in a richly decorated coffin upon a war-chariot, drawn by four white horses; the bier covered with an embroidered purple pall and blazing with precious stones, while his sword and helmet reposed upon it. The king, on foot, followed the bier, and the thousands of Judah prolonged the weeping procession, which, issuing from the northern gate, crossed the valley and came to the place of sepulchers before Machpelah, where the lords of Hebron lay buried. Here, with great pomp and solemnity the old warrior, thus basely murdered by the hand of envy and hatred, was entombed. Joab was compelled, by the king's stern command, to be one of the chief pall-bearers, and assist in laying his body in the tomb. Then the monarch, with feeling and eloquence, pronounced a noble eulogium upon the virtues of the deceased, boldly reviewing the manner of his death, and feelingly denouncing the act and the perpetrator thereof.

The people could no longer doubt. The innocence of the king was apparent to all. Twenty thousand warriors now marched in battle order around the tomb where the dead soldier lay, chanting a funeral war-song in a mighty voice, and accompanying the refrain by striking their swords against their bucklers, till the echoes from the hills were like sounds of armies fighting together upon the plain.

King David then, standing by the tomb, with great dignity recited the following hymn for the dead, seventy white-robed priests answering him in alternate verses, the whole sounding grandly and sublime, accompanied as it was at intervals by fourscore players on martial instruments of music, making the noblest and most solemn harmony:

> "LORD, thou hast been our dwelling place
> In all generations.
> Before the mountains were brought forth,
> Or ever thou hadst formed the earth and the world,
> Even from everlasting to everlasting, thou art God.
> Thou turnest man to destruction;
> And sayest, Return, ye children of men.
> For a thousand years in thy sight are but as yesterday when it is past,
> And as a watch in the night.
> Thou carriest them away as with a flood;
> They are as a sleep.
> In the morning they are like grass which groweth up.
> In the morning it flourisheth, and groweth up;
> In the evening it is cut down, and withereth.
> For we are consumed by thine anger,
> And by thy wrath are we troubled
> Thou hast set our iniquities before thee,
> Our secret sins in the light of thy countenance.
> For all our days are passed away in thy wrath:
> We spend our years as a tale that is told.
> The days of our years are threescore years and ten;
> And if by reason of strength they be fourscore years,
> Yet is their strength labor and sorrow;
> For it is soon cut off, and we fly away.
> Who knoweth the power of thine anger?
> Even according to thy fear, so is thy wrath.
> So teach us to number our days,
> That we may apply our hearts unto wisdom."

"A prince and a great man is fallen in Israel this day," said the king to me, as we were retiring to Hebron. "I am yet weak, and not firmly seated on the throne for which I was anointed, and this fierce Joab and his brothers and men-at-arms, these powerful sons of Zeruiah, are too strong with the army for me to punish them for the death of Abner. I am compelled to forbear! But as the Lord liveth, the doer of this wickedness shall be rewarded according to his deed!"

When the news reached the Prince Ishbosheth that Abner had been slain in Hebron, and as rumor had it, by the command of King David, his heart failed, and he shut himself up in his palace, fearing each moment he should be assassinated, and trembling at every footstep. Two men, animated by the same selfish motives which governed the Amalekite who brought Saul's crown to David, hastened to find the prince, in order to put him to death, and be the first bearers of the tidings, that he "was no more," to King David. They found his palace unguarded in the confusion, and reached his chamber where he lay on his couch, too bloated and heavy to flee far. His sword was in his hand, and his looks showed that he knew their errand, and that he would not die without defense. The conflict was brief. He fought his assassins with courage worthy of his father on the field of Gilboa; but he fell back at length, pierced to the heart by their swords, and died upon his couch. The two desperate men, Rechab and Baanah, who were brothers, then beheaded him, and hastened with the head concealed under a cloak from the palace, and that night crossed the Jordan. Keeping the valley southwardly they traveled till they came at noon the next day to Hebron. Being, at their desire, led into the presence of the king, Rechab said, displaying his ghastly prize:

"Behold, O king, the head of Ishbosheth the son of Saul, thine enemy, who sought thy life. Lo! the Lord hath avenged my lord the king this day, of Saul and his house!"

Then the king rose up, his noble and beautiful countenance lighted up with a sort of divine anger, and sternly said to them:

"As the Lord liveth, who hath redeemed my life from all adversity, when one told me, 'Saul is dead,' thinking to have brought good tidings, I hewed him in pieces in Ziklag, who thought I would have given him a reward for his tidings! How much more when wicked men have slain an unsuspecting person, more righteous than themselves, in his own house upon his bed? Shall I not, therefore, now require his blood of your hand, and cut you off from the earth you dishonor by your deed? As the Lord liveth, ye shall both die the death!"

At a sign from the king his guards drew their swords and put the two young men to death before him; and, severing their hands and feet, hanged them up in the public gibbet by the pool of the city.

The king, having thus expressed his abhorrence of their deed, ordered the head of the unfortunate prince to be placed in an urn of porphyry and conveyed by a company of Levites and priests to the sepulcher of Abner near the cave of Machpelah, where it was reverently placed by them in a niche at the head of the warrior's coffin. Thus, at last, together the ambitious soldier and his faithless prince sleep, where the viol of pleasure and the trumpet of war are alike unheard and unheeded.

King David, who had previously commended the inhabitants of Jabesh Gilead for the honor paid to the bodies of Saul and Jonathan, with like reverence for the last of Saul's sons, sent messengers to have the headless body of Ishbosheth placed in a stone coffin at Mahanaim, intending by and by to have all the bodies removed to the ancestral sepulcher at Bethel.

Thus this excellent young king, under every circumstance in which he has been placed, has exhibited the noblest evidences of being a great and good man, who not only cheerfully pardons his enemies, and remembers no more the wrongs they have done him, when death at length casts over them the sacred shield of the tomb, but honors their ashes by funereal pageants and mourns rather than rejoices at their sad end.

Nor did the generous regard for King Saul's memory and for his house terminate with the tomb. David remembered his oath to Jonathan that he would not only do good to his father's family, when he should become king, but that he himself and his seed after him should be held dear to him. Your majesty will recollect this oath which Jonathan caused David to take when they parted under the walls of Hebron, at the time David fled from Saul; for the prince, knowing that it was the custom of new dynasties to put to death all the members of the former royal family, feared that David, perhaps, in the flush of power, and influenced by evil counselors, might put to death all his father's house. In remembrance of his oath King David sent a messenger to Mahanaim to inquire if any were left of the family of Saul that "he might show them a kindness for Jonathan's sake," for he had married the beautiful daughter of the lord of Bethel, and David had heard that a son was born to him; and to know if this child were alive and where it dwelt he now sent away his servants.

It is a beautiful trait in his character that, amid the absorbing duties which now pressed upon him at this crisis, he should have given a moment's thought to this little child. But he is a man who religiously performs all duties, equally the least with the greatest.

In the meanwhile the men of Israel from beyond Jordan, and of all the remoter tribes, hastened to send in their submission to him at Hebron, bringing him gifts of gold, silver, jewels, fine linen, corn, wine, and oil, so that David was soon thereby made very rich. On a fixed day, surrounded by his guards, his lords, and captains, the national senate and civic elders being present, with the High Priest and a train of Levites, David, seated upon the throne of Saul, received the ambassadors from all the tribes, provinces, cities, towns, and citadels, and accepted their allegiance and took their oaths of submission and loyalty in the presence of the High Priest Abiathar. In his turn the king entered into a league with them, to forget and pardon the past, to rule them wisely and justly, to lead them to battle, to defend their borders against their foes, and in all things regard their peace and prosperity. This solemn league and covenant, being duly inscribed on parchments, and signed by the twelve ambassadors, one from each tribe, and also by the king, was sealed with the royal seal. The roll was then committed to the custody of the High Priest, to be preserved in the tabernacle, with other public and sacred parchments. No sooner did Abiathar take hold of them than the sardonyx stone upon the ephod on his shoulder emitted rays of resplendent glory, showing God was present and approved.

Then, in the presence of the august and venerable assembly of the elders of Israel, the High Priest, attired in his splendid pontifical robes, wearing the dazzling miter, and the ephod, and bearing in his hand a golden cup, advanced toward the throne, upon the lowest step of which the King of Judah stood. Kneeling before the vicegerent of the Lord, David was solemnly anointed by Him with holy oil poured from the golden cup upon his head, the rich ointment flowing over his locks and down his beard, and even dripping upon his robes, and filling all the throne-room with its rich perfume. Thus consecrated the third time king, he was crowned by the High Priest, robed with a purple royal vesture by two attendant priests, while a most venerable senator, the chief of the Sanhedrim, presented to him his scepter. The highest lord of the Levites placed in his hand a scroll of the laws, and another bound to his thigh the sword of state.

He then ascended the throne and seated himself amid the

clangor of trumpets and cries of "Hosanna! hosanna! Hail, David, the anointed king! Long live the Lord's anointed— the King of Israel!"

Thus, three several times had David been consecrated: the first time, as the youthful shepherd of Bethlehem by Samuel the Seer; the second time, by the High Priest as King of Judah, soon after Saul's death; and now the third time, as King of Judah and of Israel, sole monarch of all the Hebrew people.

Absolute now in his dominions, King David prepared to consolidate his throne and firmly establish his authority. There was but one place within the whole kingdom over which Saul had reigned, and which was now under his own rule, that did not send a delegate to Hebron to do homage to him. This was the citadel of the Jebusites, which, as I have already said to your majesty, was still held in the midst of the land by the original inhabitants. These people were of the race of Canaanites and sons of Heth, of whose family Abraham bought the burialplace of Machpelah; at the time of the purchase of which, he entered into a covenant, sealed by an oath, with the children of Heth, that the castle of Jebus, their chief stronghold, should remain untouched by his posterity, not only when they should come in to possess the land, but forever. Joshua respected this oath of Abraham, and left the castle unbesieged. The long line of warlike Judges respected the oath, and even Saul left this hereditary garrison in quiet possession of its formidable stronghold, though the city around it was in his hand.

King David, however, resolved to be king over all Israel as God had appointed him. He therefore sent a peaceable messenger to the lord of this fort of Zion, demanding its surrender. The haughty Canaanite answered, in the confidence of long possession and of the impregnable nature of the defenses:

"The lame have never scaled these rocks on which we dwell, nor the blind found their way into our gates. So shall thou and thine be, if thou comest to war against us; for thou canst not come in hither!"

When the king's messenger brought back this insolent answer to him, he forthwith called Joab, his general, and commanded him to take Uriah, the captain of "a thousand," and lay siege to the fortress of Jebus, and destroy all within; "especially," he said, "fling over the battlements their gods that see not and walk not, for as the Lord liveth, the blind and lame of David shall destroy the blind and lame gods, in whom these idolators and enemies of the true God trust."

When Joab reached the valley beneath the walls he saw that the Canaanite lord had, in derision, placed the lame and the blind persons of his garrison upon the battlements, and now called to him, saying:

"It is meet that the lame and blind should defend a castle which the lame and blind come against."

When Joab heard this he became greatly enraged, and exerted himself all in his power to take the castle. The third day came David the king to look on, and, seeing how high the walls were, and how difficult of access, he cried to all the army, and said, "Whosoever shall first mount the walls shall be chief in command over all my armies both of Israel and of Judah!"

Upon hearing this Joab, who was the general of his hosts as King of Judah, divested himself of his heavy armor, and helmet, and greaves, and back-piece, and tying his sword only about his neck, grasped a sharp pointed javelin and began to ascend the height, climbing by aid of the spear inserted into the crevices of the rock. Other bold hearts, following his example, climbed after him. In the meanwhile King David kept the garrison employed, and their attention fixed upon himself and his soldiers, by making feint of an attack at another part of the wall.

At length the valiant warrior gained the citadel, and raised himself above the parapet by the aid of a line which was let down to draw up water; for those who held it left and fled at the apparition of the Hebrew chief. In a moment afterward he stood on the top of the wall, and, waving his sword, called out to King David far below:

"I have reached the battlements, my lord! I claim the chief command of the armies."

The boldness of the man, and his unexpected appearance behind them, with the terror of his voice, which they all knew, for they had often seen the terrible warrior pass and repass with his armies, inspired them with fear; and as he was soon joined by others, they were filled with the greatest consternation. Confident that their citadel was impregnable they were unprepared to defend it! Joab and a score of his men rushed first to the gates and threw them open to King David, who entered sword in hand (for in the king he had not forgotten the soldier), and the Jebusites, overpowered, were slain in great numbers, each man refusing to surrender. Before the sun went down the whole citadel was in the hands of David, its gods cast over the battlements, and upon them Joab affixed the royal standard of the "Lion of the Tribe of Judah." Thus fell the last hold of the ancient inhabitants of the land; held by them for five hundred years, only out of the respect the Hebrews had to the oath of Abraham, given to the sons of Heth. But, your majesty may ask why David, a man so just, and virtuous, and prudent should break the oath of Abraham, so long held sacred, and which time had consecrated. I ventured to put this inquiry to Abiathar, who is my friend, and who has instructed me in many things concerning the faith of this people. He answered me as follows:

"This act of David does not imply a want of reverence for Abraham and his oath. But among us one period or dispensation is to succeed another; and each is the divinely-ordained foundation of its successive one. The call of Abraham led to his settlement here. This was followed by his removal to Egypt; that, by a bondage; that, by a dispensation in the wilderness; that, by the rule of the elders, by that of the Judges, and by that of the two kings. One form gives way to another. In David commences a new era of things. In David terminates all that belongs to the first great Abrahamic period of a thousand years. The traditions and power of Abraham die in the inauguration of the Throne of David, who is to be the founder of a new dynasty. David does not destroy Abraham and the promises in him: but gives them new directions through himself and his posterities. He is to be to the Future what Abraham has been to the Past. As the Hebrews of to-day call themselves the seed of Abraham, the true Israelites of the future shall call themselves the sons of David; and the title of their king shall be the Prince of the House of David, ordained such in the mystery of God before Abraham was! King David therefore has not broken the oath of Abraham; for Abraham's power and the limit of his oath were only until David should annul it. The royal Abraham saw David's day, and bequeathed him, and his house, his scepter. The destruction, therefore, of the fort of Zion was that sort of destruction which takes place in the seed before it germinates, a death out of which is developed a new life. This stronghold of the Canaanites was the last link that bound the present to the past; and its destruction has paved the way for the future glory of the House of David, before the sword of which all idols on earth shall be overturned, and all enemies of God utterly perish. By this act he foreshadowed the conquest of the pagan earth by the last Prophet and Prince of his house, according to the prophecy of Moses! In all that we Hebrews do, O Arbaces, we do but make copies for the future! Adam, Noah, Abraham, Moses, David, each of these are founders of new things, beginnings of new creations, heads of eras, each advance elevating our race, and bringing us nearer and nearer to the splendid era of Him of whom the patriarchs all have spoken, as the last wielder of the scepter of David, and occupant of his throne; the Shiloh whom Adam walked with in Eden; Abraham saw in his tent in Mamre; Jacob wrestled with for a blessing; Moses spoke with in Horeb; Joshua met at the fountain before Jericho; who was in the Pillar, and in the Cloud, and whose visible glory dwells in the Shechinah between the Cherubim; Him the express image of God, the out-going of His Presence, the Son of His right hand, who in the fullness of time shall be born to David's line; as to his nature, human, as to his person, divine and immortal; an incarnation in the flesh and blood of a virgin of the House of David, by the mysterious union therewith of the invisible power and Godhead; a wonderful, glorious, divine man from heaven, invested with godlike power, whose throne shall be set in Jerusalem, and whose dominion shall fill the whole earth!"

Such, your majesty, is the sublime character of David, according to the information of the High Priest, who is supposed to read the future by his near presence to the ear and voice of the Oracle of God. Fragmentary prophecies of some mighty Being to descend upon earth are not only scattered through all the Hebrew writings, but glitter in their obscurest traditions. The whole national mind seems to live in an expectation—not so much dwelling peacefully upon the present as looking restlessly to the future; not like a nation who realize their high hopes: a nation not so much possessing a positive good, but expecting one to come! That their kingdom is to be the first of all kingdoms, their kings the Kings of all kings, the meanest Hebrew family believes. This coming glory, they assert, will be achieved by a divine youth of celestial beauty, whose nature is a union of that of angels and of man; but who is to be born of a Hebrew woman in the coming ages. So deeply is the national faith impressed with this idea, that every wife in the land for five hundred years has hoped to become the mother of the celestial child-prince; but Abiathar asserts that this honor will be limited to the House of David, and to a virgin princess, most blessed among women, of that royal line. Upon pressing Abiathar closely, he expressed his opinion that, as a thousand years had elapsed from Abraham to David, a similar period will elapse from David to this celestial and powerful Prince of his royal House.

Who, your majesty, would not wish to live upon the earth at that day, when this glorious god, or angel, shall take upon him our flesh, and, through infancy and childhood, advance to manhood, veiling from the eyes of men the splendor of his divinity under the carnate veil of his humanity—a diamond hidden in a casket of clay! How, when in the majesty of his heavenly dignity he shall be crowned King of the earth by the hand of God out of Heaven, will the astonished and happy nations bow down before him, and all kings cast their crowns at his feet! What honor will earthly monarchs feel it to be, to be ruled by a heavenly Prince who yet, as man, can sympathize with their humanity! Of all eras of time, I would rather, your majesty, live in that day and behold the glory of this divine and wonderful Prince. It will be the realization of the fable that the supreme God once came down to earth and abode here as the King of the world; but was so indignant and grieved at the sins of men that he returned to the heavens and commanded men henceforth to be ruled by men. Will the Prince of the House of David, when he cometh, find the earth so wicked that he will reascend; or will he reform it by his power and wisdom, and make it worthy of his throne?

Pardon, your majesty, these reflections. It is difficult not to have the mind full of subjects which are the common theme of those one discourses with. I will now return to King David, who seems to understand that he is chosen by Heaven for some mighty purpose, in carrying out the mysterious history of his people.

Having subdued the citadel, he proceeded to enlarge and improve it, and when he had made the noble edifice on the Mount Zion a suitable royal residence, he publicly proclaimed it as the seat and throne of his kingdom, and gave to it the name of "The City of David on Mount Zion." In a few weeks afterward he removed thither from Hebron, and having also improved and beautified the town north and west of it, he inclosed with walls and towers a greater space, comprising three hills, and gave it the name of Jerusalem, it having hitherto borne the names Jebusalem, Solyma, Salem, and the city of Moriah.

From this time his reign began to prosper. The kingdom, united, was at peace; and the Hebrews everywhere lifted up their happy faces and walked with pride and contentment, each man sitting under his vine and fig tree without fear.

The lesser kings about him sent congratulations to a monarch they perceived that God was with; and a brilliant embassy came to him from Hiram, King of Tyre, proposing a league of friendship and commerce, and bringing presents of cedar, and metals, and precious stones, and purple cloth, and stones, and artificers cunning in the making of all kinds of carved work. David received the presents, and entered into the league of mutual assistance in war, and sent to the Tyrian king word that he desired presently to build a royal palace, and that he would gladly have him send to him skillful builders and workmen, as the artificers of Tyre were famed in all the world.

King David soon afterward commenced in Jerusalem a palace unrivaled for splendor, surrounded himself with a magnificent court, increased his army, and put in defense all the cities and fortresses of his kingdom.

Everywhere prosperity and industry now prevails. The land is blessed with abundant harvests, and peace in all its borders. Jerusalem grows in grandeur and beauty. The brave Joab is placed at the head of its strong garrison, and lives in a superb palace, with a military court about him like a prince.

Ahithophel is the sagacious minister and counselor of the king; Hushai is the lord of his palace; Uriah is the commander of the army in the field, but dwells in a stately house not far from the new palace of the king.

Of this prosperity the Philistines became jealous, and fearing the too great power of David, they secretly raised an army and marched against Jerusalem, intercepting and destroying the trains of wagons laden with Tyrian cedar from Joppa, on the way to the city. David, trusting only in Heaven, never alone in his own courage and numbers, would not attack them without God's permission, which he asked for through the ephod, and by the High Priest. The response of the oracle was a command to go out against them. These perpetual foes of Israel were defeated, even before David's hosts under Joab came up with them; for an army of angels in the air swept above a forest of mulberry trees, in the rear of the Philistines, with a noise like the swift advance through the wood of a great army upon them, of chariots and horses, footmen, and archers! and struck with terror the enemies of the Hebrews fled, and were easily destroyed. This final blow against this formidable power has secured to King David peace in all his realm.

His palace is now completed, and the court of David has become settled, and in all its appointments is finished with a magnificence equal to that of Tyre or of Syria. His throne surpasses that of Egypt of the Pharaohs; his bodyguards are clad in steel armor inlaid with gold; his palace officers are numerous and richly attired; and all the luxury and splendor of an ancient court appertains to this of Jerusalem.

The site of this city is very commanding, being composed of several eminences of unequal height, which are on nearly all sides precipitous. Deep ravines separate them, or abruptly inclined valleys. On all sides the city is inclosed by hills, save on the north, which seem to shut it in like a wall.

By the courtesy of the king I have free entrance to his palace at all times. Yesterday his majesty sent for me to come and see him. After I had been a few minutes with him, and he had dismissed his cup-bearer, there being left in his presence only a noble looking Levite, whom he called Uzziah, he said to me:

"O Arbaces, who art become one of us in Israel, and worshipest with us the one true God, I have determined to establish the worship of the nation I govern with a degree of magnificence in keeping with the dignity of my kingdom. My first step will be to transfer the Ark of God to Jerusalem. I shall take thirty-six thousand men with me to guard it in solemn procession hither, three thousand from each tribe, and call all the people of Judah and of Benjamin to be present to do it honor. It is now reposing at Kirjath-jearim, where it has been kept since the death of the priests at Nob. Aside from the honor of God in this movement, the coming together on such an august occasion of all the tribes will enable the people to see their king, and cement the great confederacy of which I am now the political head! Uzziah," he added, turning to the Levite, "go back to Kirjath-baal, and make ready all things for the removal of the Ark of the Covenant hither, on the day I have named, two months hence! I leave the arrangement of all the ceremonies to thee, to whom has been intrusted the care and safety of the Ark since the day of Ahimelech!"

The Levite shortly took his departure; and the king then invited me to accompany him and his armies of Israel on the day he should march forth from Jerusalem, to receive the Oracle of God, and escort it to his capital.

The foresight of the king in removing his court to this naturally intrenched city, which can easily be rendered impregnable, is in character with the profound sagacity which governs all his actions. Not satisfied with making it the political and military head, his camp and court, he resolves to make it the religious center of his realm, the place of sacrifices, the site of the Tabernacle, and the abode of the High Priests. Thus he will gather about him the leading courtiers, warriors, priests, and eminent men of his kingdom, and render it, if his reign be prolonged, one of the most brilliant capitals upon the earth.

But it is time, your majesty, that I bring this long letter to a close. Adora never fails to desire to be commended to a king I so much esteem as a friend, and honor as a monarch.

Your faithful
ARBACES.

LETTER XV.

ARBACES TO KING BELUS.

CITY OF DAVID.

YOUR MAJESTY:

A year has passed since the accident by which I was thrown
from my horse, and it is with very great pleasure I can resume
again my pen and interrupted correspondence; albeit, my wife,
as your majesty is pleased to say, proves not "by any means a
poor scribe." I have no doubt, indeed, that her letters, did
they go beyond the mere form of my diplomatic correspondence,
would prove far more agreeable to peruse than my own: for
our sex does not possess that talent for epistolary writing which
women so eminently display. If you find in my letters any passages more brilliant and graceful than usual, your majesty must
refer them to the tasteful suggestions of the daughter of Isrilid.

The proposed removal of the Ark to this city took place on
the day appointed. The whole ceremony was conducted with
great pomp and magnificence. It was my privilege to accompany the king and his court. When we arrived in the valley
before the citadel of Kirjath-jearim, which used to hold a magnificent temple of Baal, the king advanced at the head of the
lords, governors, chief captains, elders, and priests toward
the gate. A splendid guard of thirty thousand men, which
he had assembled, were drawn up before it in a hollow
square opening toward the town. Every soldier had a sprig of
olive leaf in his helmet or wreathed about his sword, and all
the officers wore a scarf of fine-twined white linen over their
corslets, in token of the sacerdotal character of their present
service. The standards of the captains of hundreds and of
thousands were decorated with blue fringes, the sacred color
of the priesthood. The day was cloudless. Heaven seemed to
smile on the scene. Thousands and tens of thousands of people
in their festival attire lined the walls of Kirjath-baal, and extended along the valley up the highway to Jerusalem in endless
lines. The whole spectacle was grand and imposing. It was
a nation, headed by its king, about to perform the highest

honor to its God by removing in solemn procession the House of his Holiness from an obscure village to the capital of the kingdom of his people. In this devout act how eminent is the proof of David's piety! referring all his glory and power to God, and resolving thus publicly to honor Him as the Giver of all things which were in his possession.

The king advancing to the gate with the High Priest at his side was met therein by the noble-looking Levite Uzziah, who, richly attired, stood by the Ark, which rested upon a car, whereon it had been brought thus far from the Tabernacle in the town where it had been kept. Behind it was a long train of four hundred Levites carrying the Tabernacle, in separate portions, the heaviest part being permitted to be placed on wagons and drawn by heifers.

To the surprise of King David, the Ark itself, which ought to have been borne on the shoulders of twelve Levites wearing their linen ephods, was elevated upon a chariot drawn by oxen.

"How is this, O Uzziah?" he cried with indignation; "where are the Levites whose duty it is to bear the Ark of God? Dost thou not know the Ark of the Lord shall rest only on the shoulders of *men*? The Philistines, when they sent it back to us, ignorantly placed it upon a cart; but those who received it, instead of putting it upon the shoulders of Levites, according to the Law, rested it upon the ground, touching it with sacrilegious hands; and all Israel knows how this departure from the law of the Lord caused the death of seventy of the elders of the people!"

"My lord, the king," answered Uzziah, "there are no staves to carry the Ark with; and I found no Levites. I therefore placed it reverently on this car, to take it to the city of David."

The king appeared very greatly distressed at this sacrilegious neglect on the part of the guardian of the Divine Oracle; but, as no man dared (not even a king) to lay his hands upon it, and as no consecrated rods could now be had, he commanded that the Ark should go forward as it was.

It was received, as it passed the gate, with the waving of a censer of incense by the High Priest, who went before it, while seventy priests, holding trumpets of brass in their hands, immediately escorted it, walking on each side of it and behind it. David, as it moved on, giving his sword to his armorbearer, took a golden harp from his servant and struck a noble hymn to his God, accompanied by a choir of priests, who played merrily upon harps, psalteries, cymbals, cornets, dulcimers, timbrels, and all manner of instruments of music. When the Ark had reached the center of the military square of thirty thousand men, they faced, at the command of Joab, toward Jerusalem, and the priests sounding their seventy brazen trumpets, which were responded to by all the war-bugles, the host commenced their march as guardians of the Oracle of God. The thousands of people who followed it from the citadel and town of Baal, and the countless numbers who lined the ways, caught up the chorus of praise, and filled the air with hallelujas to the Lord who dwelleth between the Cherubim.

At length the Ark rested at a place called the floor of Chidon, and when it was about to move forward again, the car whereupon it was borne, meeting with some rough places over which one of the oxen fell, was shaken so that Uzziah, who, with his assistant, Ahio, walked close by it, fearing the Ark would be shaken to the ground, put forth his hand to steady it, touching the Ark itself. This act of sacrilege was instantly punished by the divine glory which dwelt between the Cherubim, for he fell dead, as if smitten by lightning! This divine judgment upon a man whose act showed want of faith in God, as the protector of His own tabernacle, filled the whole host with consternation. David stood in silence, gazing upon the dead man. The High Priest remained immovable, and all who were with him. The instruments of music ceased, and a dread silence and awe prevailed! Every eye rested upon the king. His face looked dark and heavy. I could read from his looks that he regarded it as an evil augury for such a thing to happen at the beginning of his reign. It was a fearful interruption to the joy of such a solemnity. He felt, also, that he had been to blame for not personally attending to the proper carrying of the Ark ere it left Baal of Judah. The seventy priests looked as if they expected instantly from Heaven still further judgments, as of old, upon themselves. I saw the king remove his helm, and bow his head with humble submission, as if prepared to receive also the lightnings of the Lord, who had been so grievously offended. But *one* victim appeased the celestial anger! No second stroke of His displeasure fell!

The king was now at a loss what to do! He feared to move the Ark any farther! No man dared approach it! All stood aloof gazing upon it with terror, equal to that with which the infidel Philistines, fifty years before, had regarded it.

"What shall be done, O Abiathar?" he asked of the High Priest.

Opposite the place where they were stood the house of a poor but pious Hebrew, called Obededom. Into his humble dwelling the High Priest advised the king to have it taken. Removing the oxen, Abiathar, with solemn awe, protected by his sacred office, conducted it to the gate, drawing the car in! There it was left still in the chariot, within a courtyard, under the shelter of a pavilion which the priests erected above it, inclosing it from all eyes. David then appointed a guard of Levites to keep watch over it night and day until he should know from the Lord what he ought to do with this House of His Majesty. With sad hearts the long procession returned to Jerusalem, the people sadly seeking their homes, shaking their heads, and prophesying evil to the king and to the nation.

This unhappy event greatly depressed David, and humbled him before the Lord, so that for many days he fasted and withdrew himself from all public affairs.

At length at the end of three months it was told him that the poor man in whose habitation the Ark had been sheltered was becoming greatly favored of the Lord; his fields bore an hundred fold; his flocks and herds wonderfully increased, and all that he put his hand to prospered; so that it was said: "Who prospereth and is blessed like Obededom in all Israel!"

"Truly the blessing on this poor Gittite should be upon Jerusalem and all Israel," said the king. "I will go and bring again the Ark of the Lord, but not, as before, without holy preparation, but with sanctified hearts, as becometh those who enter the presence of God!"

The same day he made proclamation that all the Levites in the land should assemble themselves together on a certain day at Jerusalem. He also commanded the priests, and also the High Priest, to sanctify themselves seven days before the Lord. When the twelve thousand Levites and seven hundred priests came together, Abiathar offered up sacrifices in the most solemn manner, making an expiatory offer for all, from the monarch to the humblest Levite. The king then said to Abiathar, "Associate with you the pious Zadok, who was Saul's High Priest, as second to yourself, and all the sons of Aaron, and the chief priests, and all ye who are the chief of the fathers of the Levites, and sanctify yourselves, that ye may go and bring up the Ark of the Lord God of Israel unto the Tabernacle I have prepared for it. For it was because ye were not sanctified before, and I chose armed men to guard the Ark, and made a display of God's glory to please the people, and show my own pomp and greatness, the Lord hath humbled me and you! Let us now seek the holy God, after the due order of our holy priesthood of old, for in these last years we have greatly neglected the honor of God, and been remiss in our sacred duties. See that staves be provided, with Levites who are of the house of Kohath, to bear them according as Moses commanded, and let none come near or follow the Ark but the sons of Aaron, and the Levites who are sanctified! Let it be a solemn and religious day for all Israel!"

At the appointed time the sacred procession of priests and Levites went forth from the gates of Jerusalem and approached with solemn tread the place beyond the hills where the Ark of God rested. David and his court followed, with all his great officers, but no armed hosts were with him.

A choir of sacred choristers, consisting only of sons of Levi, who played on all manner of instruments, accompanied David, also his own harp-bearer. The king himself wore an ephod, and laid aside all his armor; for he wished it to appear altogether a religious and peaceful ceremony, at which he was about to preside in honor of God.

When David and the company of priests, with the High Priest Abiathar, and the Chief Priest Zadok, came before the house of Obededom, the singers and players upon psalteries, cymbals of brass, harps, and trumpets, at the command of David, played a solemn hymn to God. Then the High Priest sacrificed seven bullocks, and seven rams, before the Ark ere he himself or any man dared approach it, and sprinkled the blood seven times before the Ark, and before the Mercy-Seat and Cherubim, where the name of God dwelt! He then sprinkled the twelve Levites of the sons of Kohath, who were to bear the Ark, with the blood of the slain victims, and consecrated Obededom, and his servant the keeper of the Ark, also with blood. Now with his own garments all red, and his vesture dipped in the blood of the sacrifices, protected on all sides by the mysterious defense of blood, he drew near the dread Ark of God's presence, which, without sacrificial shedding of blood, no man could approach and live. Pale and trembling, the twelve sons of Kohath raised the Ark by the staves placed through its rings. As they advanced, Zadok the Chief Priest went before swinging the censer of incense, and the High Priest followed him sprinkling the path of the Ark with blood!

King David stood and earnestly beheld to see if the men who bore it lived! When he saw them march seven steps he commanded them to stop. The favor of heaven was then supplicated, and the High Priest sacrificed a lamb before the Ark! At every seven steps a victim bled, and the blood sprinkled the way, while the deprecatory incense continually ascended and the low solemn chant of humiliation of the singers filled the air. The Ark having advanced seven times seven steps, the high sacred number, and no signs of Divine displeasure apparent, and seven victims having bled before its progress, the king with looks of joy cried aloud:

"The Lord is gracious and merciful, long suffering, and of great kindness: he keepeth not his anger forever! Let the people lift up their voices and shout for joy! Blow ye the trumpets, ye priests, for the Lord hath received our prayer! Let all Israel praise him with cornet and harp! Let all the people shout, and praise the name of the Lord!"

The Ark now advanced, no longer regarded as a center of terror, but as the beloved and glorious presence of their reconciled God.

It would be impossible, your majesty, to convey to your mind a just conception of the profound happiness which possessed the Hebrews of all ranks, at the favorable progress of the House of their Divine Oracle, toward Jerusalem. The king, wearing the sacred linen robe, went before it on foot, attended in this humble manner by his whole court. Seven times the Ark rested during the day between the house of Obededom and the gate of Jerusalem, and seven times sacrifices were offered unto the Lord, with continual waving of incense before the Ark, while the king and the singers, with their harps of gold, chanted praises to God in solemn and joyful voices.

As the sacred procession drew near the city the walls were lined with the rejoicing citizens, and multitudes stood on the hills which stand round about Jerusalem, gazing upon the sublime spectacle. The presence of the Ark was indicated to the eyes of those who were the most remote, by the bright, mysterious halo of glory which appeared between the Cherubim. The last and seventh rest and sacrifice was made at a place outside of the city, where the Levites rested the Ark, previous to the march into the city of David. It was a hill north of

Mount Zion, and separated from it by a narrow valley. Here, tradition says, Isaac was laid upon the altar, and near here, if not on this spot, prophecy declares the future throne of the last Prince of the Hebrews shall be erected, upon a high altar consecrated by the blood of the last High Priest of the people, whose great sins (beyond the atonement of the blood of bulls and goats) will cry aloud for that of the High Priest himself!

When the Ark passed into the gate of the city of David a resplendent light illumined the Mercy-Seat, and to the songs of the priests there were heard angelic voices in the heavens, as if the sons of God on high rejoiced with the sons of men below in the presence of the Lord, coming to dwell within the city of the king of his people. They now came in sight of the palace, and also of the Tabernacle on Mount Zion, which the king had previously ordered to be put up according to the pattern shown to Moses in the Mount of Horeb; the inner Sanctuary being inclosed within the curtained walls of the outer Tabernacle or Court of Sacrifice.

Here the High Priest changed the march into a religious rite, moving with measured steps to the sound of the most solemn music played upon harps, the king himself leading, striking the chords of his golden psaltery. In this religious dance, if so majestic a movement may be termed such, and which one of the wives of David witnessed from the palace and ridiculed, the king and the priests participated until they came before the Tabernacle. Then the Ark was borne amid clouds of preceding incense into the Tabernacle. Here, upon the Altar of Burnt-offering, a fresh victim was slain, with the blood of which the High Priest sprinkled the way to the Sanctuary, in which Holy Place, after taking their sandals from their feet, the bearers of the Ark entered and set it down in the midst thereof; the golden Candlestick being on one side, and the Table of Shew-bread on the other; while the Altar of Incense stood in its place farther on. Here, first consecrating the way with incense, the two High Priests, Abiathar and Zadok, taking the Ark between them, bore it with silent awe into the Holy of Holies, and placed it reverently behind the Vail. As soon as they reappeared the king, who stood in the court of the Tabernacle, struck his harp to a sublime hymn of praise and thanksgiving at the happy and prosperous termination of his pious duty.

The next day the king proceeded to appoint the order of

worship, re-establishing the ancient rites and ceremonies, and inaugurating them with increased splendor. He appointed the High Priest over the priesthood, and Zadok his second in order; and the courses of the Levites, and the companies of singers, and directed the manner in which morning and evening worship should be performed. To his chief singer he gave the following Psalm, with which the sublime services of the Tabernacle were formally opened; one company answering another company with psalteries, cymbals, harps, and cornets; while a choir of priests, with trumpets of silver, brass, and ivory swelled the pæan of praise.

DAVID, THE KING, WITH THE HARP.

Sing unto the Lord all the earth;
Show forth from day to day his salvation.

SINGERS AND TRUMPETS.

Declare his glory among the heathen,
His marvelous works among all nations:

KING.

For great is the Lord, and greatly to be praised,
He also is to be feared above all gods:

CHOIR.

For all the gods of the people are idols,
But the Lord made the heavens.

KING.

Sing unto the Lord all the earth;
Show forth from day to day his salvation.

CHOIR.

Glory and honor are in his presence,
Strength and gladness are in his palaces.

KING.

Give unto the Lord ye kindreds of the people,
Give unto the Lord glory and strength.

KING AND CHOIR.

Give unto the Lord the glory due unto his name.

KING.

Sing unto the Lord all the earth;
Show forth from day to day his salvation.

CHOIR.

Bring an offering, and come before him;
Worship the Lord in the beauty of holiness.

KING.

Let the heavens be glad, and let the earth rejoice,
And let men say among the nations, "The Lord reigneth."

CHOIR AND TRUMPETS.

Let the sea roar and the fullness thereof;
Let the fields rejoice and all that is therein.

KING.

Sing unto the Lord all the earth;
Show forth from day to day his salvation.

CHOIR.

O give thanks unto the Lord, for he is good,
For his mercy endureth forever.

CHOIR AND TRUMPET.

Worship the Lord—praise his holy name,
Let everything that hath breath praise the Lord.

KING.

Sing unto the Lord all the earth;

CHOIR.

And show forth from day to day his salvation.

KING, CHOIR, AND TRUMPETS.

Give thanks—give thanks unto his holy name.
Give glory—give praise to his glorious name.

PRIESTS AND LEVITES.

Blessed be the LORD God of Israel forever and ever.

ALL THE PEOPLE.

Amen.

This final Amen repeated, and again repeated, by king,
priests, Levites, and people, accompanied by all the instruments
of music, with the thunder of the choir of trumpets, seemed to
shake, with its sublime chorus, Mount Zion to its foundations.

Sacrifices were again solemnly offered, and thus the inauguration of the Ark of the Covenant in the Tabernacle of David
on Mount Zion was finished. The king then dismissed all the
people with presents and with food to their homes. Now Jerusalem has become the seat of empire, of religion, and of power,
and also the center of arts and arms. The genius and intelligence of the king, his taste in all the refinements of the age,
his wonderful love for music, poetry, and architecture, his warlike education, his piety and amiability of character, all com-

bined, exert an influence over his court and empire such as few kings of the earth are able to command. He has invited to his capital the wise men, and scholars, and philosophers, as well as the poets, artificers, and soldiers of all lands, and among his own people he rewards genius and talent with the most distinguished honors, wherever it develops itself.

Yet with all the magnificence and regal power with which he loves to surround himself (for all his ideas are kingly and imperial, as if he were born to the throne, and had been educated in a sumptuous court), he forgets not the gentler and holier duties which he owed to the memory of his departed friend, Prince Jonathan! He had no sooner established, on a firm basis, the religious observances of the Tabernacle than he turned his heart toward Jonathan, to whom he remembered his solemn oath to protect his house. He again set on foot inquiries to ascertain if any remained of the house of Saul or of Jonathan, and at length a man, an ancient servant of Saul, named Ziba, said to the king's servants that if they would bring him before the king he would tell him who of Saul's house lived. When they had brought him in before the king, he said to him:

"If thou art Ziba, the servant of Saul and of Jonathan, canst thou tell me if there live yet anyone of their house that I may show kindness before God unto him?"

"Jonathan's son, Mephibosheth, yet liveth, O king," answered the man; "but will my lord the king make oath before the Lord to his servant that he will do the lad good and not evil, if thy servant maketh known to my lord the king where he dwelleth?"

"I have sworn to Jonathan, as the Lord liveth, I will be as a father to his father's house and to his seed," answered the king. "Where is the son of my friend?"

"Beyond Jordan, in Mount Gilead, where he hath kept himself safely hidden this many years, lest he should fall into the king's hand," answered Ziba boldly. "The prince, O king, is a young man of infirm health, being lame in both feet from an accident which befell him when five years of age, his nurse, terrified at hearing of the death of Jonathan and Saul, letting him fall from her hold to the ground."

"Therefore does he need more the kindness of his king and father's friend," said the generous monarch, with feeling. "Go and tell him David desires to see him, that he may show kindness to him for his noble father's sake, and also for Saul his grandfather!'"

None but a truly noble and dignified nature, your majesty, could have cherished and expressed such lasting friendship as this.

The king having thus honorably and in a royal manner prepared to redeem his oath to Jonathan when both were young men and the former a fugitive shepherd without where to lay his head, he sent a special ambassador to Hiram, King of Tyre, to make a league of commerce with him, which provided that the Hebrews, who were an agricultural people, should exchange their productions with the Phœnicians, who were a commercial people. The two kings interchanged treaties, and this has led to a friendly intercourse between them, and to a regular correspondence of personal friendship. The result of this wise treaty is already being apparent in the increased wealth of the nation, which finds a ready market for all its productions, and in the increased magnificence and comfort to be found, not only in Jerusalem, but in all the cities, through the introduction of articles of use and luxury from all parts of the world, with which opulent Tyre pays for the corn, and wine, and oil, and fruits of this land of boundless agricultural wealth.

"One thing more remains for me to do, O Arbaces," said this wise and great king to me a few days since. "I live in a royal palace of cedar, and sit upon a throne of ivory, and there is no house for the Lord God to dwell in, save the Tabernacle of curtains, the pattern of that which our fathers had in the wilderness! While we were wanderers, and afterward while we were yet at war, and were compelled to change our capital from place to place, it was appropriate to worship in a movable tabernacle. But now I have made Jerusalem the capital forever of my kingdom, and here is established my throne, and hither I have brought the Ark of Testimony to give it a place herein in all ages. I cannot rest, therefore, until I erect here, on Mount Moriah, opposite my palace of Mount Zion, a temple to God, that, as He is the God of gods, shall surpass in magnificence all the temples of the gods of the heathen in the whole earth!"

Thus did this devout man of God, your majesty, seek to honor Him who had raised him from the humble condition of a shepherd to the dignity and power of a great monarch. A truly religious prince, he prays to his God three times a day, and passes hours in divine meditations, in sacred compositions of hymns for the worship of the Sanctuary, and in pious acts. Hence it was natural to him to reflect painfully upon the meanness of the Tabernacle of his Lord in comparison with the splendor of his own house of cedar and gold, crowning like a diadem of beauty the head of Mount Zion.

This idea so occupied his thoughts that he at length sent for the Prophet Nathan, whose name your majesty will recall, who had succeeded the Seer Samuel over the School of the Prophets at Ramah. When the man of God appeared before the king David met him with that friendly regard he has ever had for him since he was with him in the School of the Prophets, where your majesty will recollect Nathan was one of the teachers of David, though not many years his senior.

"What wouldst thou, my lord, of thy servant?" asked the dignified prophet.

"I have sent for thee, O Nathan, to ask of thee counsel, for the wisdom of the Lord is upon thee. Behold I sit at peace, and in honor upon the throne of my kingdom, and God hath given me rest round about from all mine enemies. See now, I dwell in a house of cedar, but the Ark of God dwelleth within curtains. I desire to build a house to the Lord, worthy of me and of my prosperity and greatness, and that shall honor His great Name, who is the one God over all, glorious in majesty and infinite in power and holiness. Shall the gods of the heathen dwell in temples of stone, and of brass, and of costly woods, and the God of Israel dwell in tents?"

"Let my lord the king do that which is right in his own eyes, for the Lord will assuredly accept thine offering," answered the prophet, whose national pride and devout honor for the splendor of the national worship doubtless led him to assent, without that reflection and consultation with his God which became a prophet.

But the next day he reappeared before the king, and said:

"Hear, O king, and listen not to the voice of erring man, but to the voice of God. Last night, in the vision of the night, lo, the Lord appeared unto me, and said:

"Go and tell my servant David, Thus saith the Lord, Shalt thou build me a house for me to dwell in? Whereas I have not dwelt in any house since the time that I brought up the children of Israel out of Egypt even to this day, but have walked in a tent and in a tabernacle. In all the places wherein I have walked with all the children of Israel, spake I a word with any of the tribes of Israel, whom I commanded to feed my people Israel, saying, Why build ye not me a house of cedar? Now, therefore, so shalt thou say unto my servant David, Thus saith the Lord of hosts, I took thee from the sheepcote, from following the sheep, to be ruler over my people, over Israel. And I was with thee whithersoever thou wentest, and have cut off all thine enemies out of thy sight, and have made thee a great name, like unto the name of the great men that are in the earth. Moreover, I will appoint a place for my people Israel, and will plant them, that they may dwell in a place of their own, and move no more; neither shall the children of wickedness afflict them any more, as before-time, and as since the time that I commanded judges to be over my people Israel, and have caused thee to rest from all thine enemies. Also, the Lord telleth thee, that he will make thee a house.

"And when thy days be fulfilled, and thou shalt sleep with thy fathers, I will set up thy seed after thee, which shall proceed out of thy bowels, and I will establish his kingdom. He shall build a house for my name, and I will establish the throne of his kingdom forever. I will be his father, and he shall be my son. If he commit iniquity, I will chasten him with the rod of men, and with the stripes of the children of men. But my mercy shall not depart away from him, as I took it from Saul, whom I put away before thee. And thine house and thy kingdom shall be established forever before thee: thy throne shall be established forever."

"The Lord is righteous in all that He commandeth," answered David. "The Lord also hath showed me the past night that I have been from my youth a man of war and of blood, and that it is meet I should be set aside from building the house to the Lord, which I had in my heart!"

Soon after the departure of his friend, the prophet, the king left his palace and went to the Tabernacle of God, and kneeling humbly before the altar of incense in the Holy Place with his face toward the Vail which hid the glory of the Lord over the Ark of the Covenant, prayed and said after this manner:

"Who am I, O Lord God? and what is my house, that thou hast brought me to so great power hitherto? and hast favorably spoken of the glory of my house yet to come? Wherefore thou art great, O Lord God: for there is none like thee, neither is there any God besides thee, according to all that we have heard with our ears: 'Lo, what one nation in the earth is like thy people, even like Israel, whom God went to redeem for a people to himself, and to make him a name, and to do for you great things and terrible, for thy land, before thy people, which thou redeemest to thee from Egypt, from the nations and their gods? For thou hast confirmed to thyself thy people Israel, to be a people unto thee forever: and thou, Lord, art become their God.' And now, O Lord God, the word that thou hast spoken concerning thy servant, and concerning his house, establish it forever, and do as thou hast said. And let thy name be magnified forever, saying, The Lord of hosts is the God over Israel: and let the house of thy servant David be established before thee. For thou, O Lord of hosts, God of Israel, hast revealed to thy servant, saying, I will build thee a house: therefore hath thy servant found in his heart to pray this prayer unto thee. And now, O Lord God, thou art that God, and thy words be true, and thou hast promised this goodness unto thy servant. Therefore now let it please thee to bless the house of thy servant, that it may continue forever before thee: for thou, O Lord God, hast spoken it; and with thy blessing let the house of thy servant be blessed forever."

This great and wise king having now acquitted himself of the sacred duties which friendship and religion claimed at his hand, and strong in the favor of his God and the love of his people, resolved to secure the peace of his realm by putting an end forever to the power of his hereditary enemies, the Philistines, Amalekites, Moabites, and other nations which had for five hundred years warred against Israel. Recent excursions of predatory bands upon his borders, which have rendered the abode of the Hebrews along the limits of his kingdom at all times unsafe, have led him to resolve to make this aggressive war; for hitherto the Hebrews have been defenders of their land, not aggressors. While I write, the notes of warlike preparation are heard, not only in Jerusalem, but in all the kingdom. It is the intention of King David to take the field in person, and beard the Philistine lion in his own den at Gath. As I shall accompany the army, your majesty, I shall not again write to you until the war is ended.

I regret here to inform thee, O Belus, that the beautiful Michal, the daughter of Saul, has been disgraced by David, who has refused again to recognize her as his queen, and has elevated the stately Abigail to that distinction. The fatality which from the first has hung about Saul's house seems still lowering over all his descendants. The cause of the displeasure of the king her husband was as follows:

On the day when the Ark was borne into the city of David, and the monarch danced with solemn and measured step before it, playing upon his harp, according to a form of religious worship common even with us in Assyria, Michal from her palace window mocked him and laughed aloud, as if he shamed his kingly rank by exchanging the royal apparel of a king for the white linen ephod of a priest. Her excuse, haughtily given and with a good deal of Saul's fire, was that she had never beheld the King of the Hebrews before in such base apparel, and that she felt it became not his royal dignity to assume it; that she had never seen her father, the first king, think it necessary to be so religious as to humble himself in that degrading way, and that such display became more hired dancers at a festival and singing women, than a king!

The king became greatly offended and also grieved at her words, for he perceived by them that she was without piety, and despised the worship of God, which in the days of Saul had been so much neglected; he also learned that it was not until the more reverent Abigail commended the king's devout bearing before the Ark that Michal began to scorn him and deride.

Thus, your majesty, the perverseness and jealousy of Saul, coming out in the character of the daughter, has been the cause of her shame, as it was of the father's. What an illustration of the law of God, that the sins of the fathers shall be visited upon their children! From that day David has not entered the presence of the perverse and jealous woman, who publicly sought to bring upon him ridicule while in the accustomed worship of his God. She is punished, therefore, even like her father, Saul, both for irreligion and for jealousy.

The widow of Nabal is now, therefore, the first in rank in the palace as queen, and being scarcely less beautiful than when David married her among the mountains of Carmel, and possessing amiability and grace of manners, she is a great favorite with the court and people, which Michal has never been.

At length Ziba returned, and with him came Mephibosheth, the sole surviving prince of the unhappy House of Saul. I saw him when he came into the Hall of Justice, where David sat, having just closed for the day the administration of the cases brought before him. The king would not have known him as he drew near, but for the presence of Ziba, which led him to suspect who he was; for he leaned heavily, from his lameness, upon the Canaanite servant's arm. He was a slight, sickly young man, with a short neck which supported a large and intellectual head, developing the grand brows and forehead of Saul; while the mouth was singularly effeminate and beautiful, but wore a fixed, cynical smile. His face, pale and prematurely withered, was like that of one who seldom stirred abroad in the sun and air. He was attired richly and gaudily after the fashion of the princes of Moab; jewels sparkled on his wrists and breast, and he wore rings of gold in his ears, like the effeminate Ammonite lords. The expression of his white and wilted face was a singular compound of scorn and deference, hatred and fear, as if he respected the power of David, and yet felt that he sat on a throne which was justly his own birthright. The arrogance of a dethroned prince before his successor, with the humility of a dependent, struggled also in his voice, as he answered the king, who said, kindly, and drawing near to him:

"Is this Mephibosheth, son of Jonathan?"

"I am, O king," he answered, making haughty obeisance, leaning upon the hand of Ziba. "I am come in obedience to thy command!"

"Thou hast done well! Fear not, I have sent for thee to show thee kindness, for Jonathan thy father's sake; for I hear that thou hast been dependent on strangers!"

The dark, Saul-like eyes of the young man flashed at words, which, though kindly meant, enkindled his anger; and he looked as if he would have replied, "Had I my rightful inheritance, O king, thou and I would have changed places, and I should have been seated in my father's throne." But his bloodless lips ventured no word. He had from a child been trained in the discipline of exile and self-denial, and knew how to restrain his feelings, and when to keep silence. The king, without seeming to observe his looks, continued mildly:

"For thy father's sake I will restore thee all the land of thy grandfather Saul and all things that thy father possessed. These will enrich thee! Also, thou shalt dwell with me in my palace, and have a seat at my table as long as thou livest! Ziba will look after thy estates, and render to thee his yearly accounts; and thou canst dwell here in peace and pursue such a life as suits thy fragile health!"

At this unexpected kindness and generosity on the part of the king the proud heart of the exiled prince softened, his anger melted away, tears quenched the ireful fire of his eyes, and, with a voice trembling with grateful emotion, he cried:

"Thou art too gracious and good to so worthless a wanderer as thy servant, O king. I believed thou wouldst treat me as if I were a dog in thy sight, and lo! thou honorest me as a prince, giving me the royal lands of my father's house!"

"Ziba," said the king, turning to the old servant of Saul, "thou hast a score of servants and many sons. They and thou shall be servants of Mephibosheth!"

"According to all that my lord the king commandeth thy servant, so shall thy servant do," answered the gray-headed Canaanite, making lowly obeisance, after the abject manner of the men of his race, before the king.

Since then, the last Prince of the House of Saul has dwelt in Jerusalem, a guest in the palace of the king and daily sits at the king's table. He dresses with magnificence, and is imperative and troublesome in temper, showing the irascibility of Saul without his courage, and the vices of Ishbosheth without his indolence; for there is nothing escapes his inquisitive and jealous eyes that goes on in the palace; and while he seems to be full of gratitude to the king and artfully plays the sycophant, he is evidently his secret and envious enemy. Treachery plainly lurks in his covert glances at David, who, honest in purpose and knowing he ought to have his gratitude, doubts not but that he has it, and entreats him with an ingenuous confidence from which all mistrust is absent.

This letter will go to Assyria by the caravan which leaves Jericho next week. It is to be laden with rich productions of this bountiful land, and will, I doubt not, reward the king for his wise policy in opening this avenue of commerce with the valleys of the Euphrates and Tigris. Already caravans leave here for Syria, Edom, Egypt, and Tyre, and a constant influx and reflux of these commercial waves, laden with the fruits of the merchandise of those lands, have given a new impetus to the minds of this hitherto exclusively agricultural people, and are converting them into a nation of merchants; while foreign gold and silver flow into the royal coffers in abundance.

A few days hence, at the head of one hundred thousand disciplined troops, the king moves forward against the realm of Philistia. Upon the return of the army I will again write to your majesty. Farewell.

Your friend and ambassador,   ARBACES.

LETTER XVI.

ARBACES, THE AMBASSADOR, TO BELUS THE KING.

CITY OF DAVID, MOUNT ZION.

It is many months since my last epistle was written to thee, O Belus; but my long silence must be attributed not to the forgetfulness of waning friendship, nor to the neglect of my official duty, but to the warlike and absorbing condition of affairs which has existed the past eight months.

My last letter informed you that King David was about to extend his arms in the direction of the kingdom of the Philistines, who had not ceased to annoy the western borders of his dominions. The march of the Hebrew army, after it entered the land of the Philistines, was one uninterrupted series of brilliant conquests.

Always, heretofore, invaders, the Philistines knew not how to meet invasion, and so bold and formidable a one as now menaced them. Wheresoever their armies made a stand to oppose the Hebrew monarch, they were routed and pursued with great slaughter. One after another their towns fell into the hands of David, their idol temples were overthrown by his soldiers, and their fields laid waste. At length, driven to their stronghold and capital city, Gath, situated on the hitherto impregnable height of Ammah, their king assembled the whole of his army to make a final stand against the conquering progress of the Hebrew warrior-king! David encircled the city with his hosts, and took it with vast slaughter. The night of the conquest thereof David reposed (how singular the reversion of fortunes, your majesty!) in the palace of the deceased Achish, whose tomb he the next day visited, commanding it to be respected by his soldiers; for once he had received from Achish shelter and favors in his exile; and David is one of that heroic and generous class of men who never forget a personal kindness. Gaza and all the ports of Philistia soon fell into his power, and he extended thereby the borders of his kingdom even to the shores of the Great Sea. All the ships of Askelon, Jopha, and of the port by the sea over against Gaza fell into his hand, with the mariners and merchandise thereof. Having laid tribute upon the King of Philistia, Ittai; the son of Achish, whom he had taken prisoner, and received his homage as his servant, and having garrisoned the seaports, and especially Gath, the key of the subdued kingdom, David returned with his armies to Jerusalem, having in three months brought to his feet a dominion nearly as large as his own, and which had been the terror of Israel since the days of Joshua.

The sons of Anakim, consisting of a family of seventy giants of both sexes, descendants of Anak, whom Joshua fought against, King David put to death, not leaving a soul of the blood of Goliath alive, thus wisely ending a race of giants, which has long cumbered this quarter of the earth.

But he had no sooner reached his capital than he found a new war upon his hands. The powerful King of Edom, a descendant of the royal House of Esau, the elder brother of Jacob, and whose dominions lay south of the province of Judah around Mount Hor, even stretching beyond the sea of Sodoma—this king, who inherited hatred of the descendants of Jacob and his twelve sons, taking advantage of David's absence in Philistia, invaded Judah and menaced Hebron. Without delay and by forced marches King David went against him, defeated the king in battle, and also the King of Moab, who assisted him, and taking their capital city, brought both Moab and Edom into subjection to his scepter, making them tributary to his crown. Thus on the west his borders now were extended to the sea, and on the south to the desert.

This increase of dominion and power has naturally aroused the fears of other kings. Talaric, the warlike Parthian monarch of the land of Palm-Zobah, whose capital is Tadmor, fearing for his own dominions on the east, hath raised a great army, saying to his generals, "This Hebrew shepherd-king is becoming too powerful for our safety. He hath laid one hand on the sea, and placed one foot on the desert. Lo, he will stretch himself, and with the other hand grasp the east, and plant the other foot on the north, even upon the crown of Syria. Let us go against him and weaken his power, and keep him within his own borders!"

Moreover, your majesty, this usurper of the throne of Hadadezer hath heard that the true princess of his stolen scepter is in Judea, at the court of David. Unknown to me, your majesty, I learn King David sent a message to Talaric three months ago, demanding the throne of Tadmor for its lawful princess, Adora, daughter of Isrilid! for the king regards my noble wife with the most respectful friendship; and well knowing her history and her title to the throne of Tadmor, as well as the fact that we no longer entertained any undue ambition to wield its scepter, secretly sent, without consulting our pleasure, the message demanding its surrender. When, upon hearing of it, I expressed my regret, the king smilingly answered:

"It is of importance to my empire, O Arbaces, that in the country between the Jordan and the Euphrates a king should rule who shall be my friend and ally. This Parthian usurper of the throne of the royal house of Rahob of Tadmor will always be a thorn in my side. I, therefore, not only secure the integrity of my borders eastward, by placing you and your wife upon its throne, if necessary, by the force of arms; but do justice to the claims of a noble lady, whom for her own sake and her father's I greatly esteem."

The Parthian, therefore, has declared war against the King of the Hebrews, not only from fear that he will extend his conquests in the direction of Palm-Zobah, but to prevent the accession of Adora to the throne of her ancestors, and, moreover, resent the insult to his crown, which King David's demand implies.

Already, your majesty, this Parthian's hosts are rolling along toward Jordan in an army of one hundred thousand footmen, twenty thousand horsemen, and four thousand chariots. To meet this formidable army King David marches to-morrow with one hundred and twenty thousand foot, eight hundred horse, and but seventy chariots, for the laws of Moses forbid the Hebrews multiplying horses and chariots for their armies.

Your majesty cannot long remain ignorant of the march of this formidable army of Talaric, the King of Zobah, who also has taken the name of Hadadezer, the royal designation of the former kings. It is impossible for me to remain behind, when King David, partly on account of Adora's claim, advances to meet him! Adora and I, therefore, join the king at Jericho two days hence, and advance with the army.

That he will conquer I doubt not. The smile of Heaven is ever shining upon his arms. If he conquers, he is resolved to place Adora upon the throne. Hence it is not impossible, O Belus, that this letter (which I shall place in my tablets until I have an opportunity of completing it and sending it) may be finished before the walls of Tadmor, or within its royal palace itself! Although both Adora and myself have long ago made up our minds to be contented to dwell near the court of David, in our happy villa on the side of the Mount of Olives, yet I will not deny that the possibility of ascending the throne of her fathers has aroused in the bosom of my wife pleasing and new-born hopes, which have kindled into warmth my own dormant ambition.

How pleasant would it be, O Belus, if Adora and her lord Arbaces could rule a dominion protected on the east by thine, and on the west by that of King David! Three such kingdoms united by the bonds of amity, as they would be, would control the events of nations, and hold the balance of power on earth! But I am letting my pen run wild with ambitious aspirations, which a few weeks ago I would not have believed existed within my breast. Farewell, for a time. I now roll up the parchment, deferring the conclusion of my letter to a later period.

.   .   .   .   .

The army of the King of the Hebrews encountered, three weeks after the above portion of the letter of Prince Arbaces was written, the hosts of the King of Zobah in the desert, and overthrew him; pursuing him for three days with great slaughter, and taking, besides great spoils, a thousand chariots * armed with scythes, seven hundred Parthian horse-men, who carried bows of steel, and twenty thousand footmen. He then laid siege to Tadmor, within which Talaric fled, and taking it, after a month's siege, by assault, he extended the borders of his kingdom even to the banks of the Upper Euphrates.

Adora, the daughter of Isrilid, was duly placed by the conqueror in possession of the throne of her ancestors, and Prince Arbaces was crowned king-consort by her side. In the midst of the festivities with which this event was celebrated, the King of Damascus, who had entered into league with the King of Zobah to check the power of the King of the Hebrews, was advancing to his aid, when he met the defeated monarch Talaric, attended by a few wearied horsemen, flying to seek shelter in his dominions.

The sight of this great Syrian army so near his late capital, inspiring the Parthian Prince with a hope of recovering his throne, he prevailed upon Hadad, King of Damascus, to return

* 2 Samuel viii. 3. 4.

with him to aid him in regaining his capital. The Syrian monarch yielded to his importunities. From the walls of Tadmor the Hebrew warrior-king beheld the advancing hosts of Syria, and marched out to offer Hadad battle. The terrible contest continued throughout the day and all the night, and the Syrians, defeated, fled, leaving two and twenty thousand men dead on the plain, with chariots and horsemen overthrown without number.

Leaving Arbaces and Adora securely seated on the throne of Palm-Zobah, King David recrossed the desert westward into Syria, and made a thorough conquest of the kingdom of Hadad, besieging and taking his brilliant capital of Damascus on the rivers Arbana and Pharpar. Leaving garrisons therein, and receiving the submission of all the towns and citadels of Syria, he returned to Jerusalem, having achieved the greatest victories of the age, and added to his dominions four kingdoms; not including that of Tadmor of Zobah, which he declared a free crown, having sealed with Arbaces a permanent league of friendship.

The noble river Euphrates now bounded his kingdom on the east; the north was defended against the Barbarians by his fortresses of Syria; and also by Tyre, the dominion of his friend, the virtuous and wise King Hiram. On the south he held military possession of Idumea, Moab, and Philistia; while on the west he touched the shores of the Middle Sea; thus Lebanon, Egypt, the Euphrates, and the Mediterranean were the magnificent limits of his vast empire.

The following year a son of one of the kings of Ammon in the East, whose father had shown him friendship on his march to Tadmor, having ascended the throne of the Ammonites, King David kindly sent ambassadors to congratulate him. The jealous prince, suspecting them to be spies, shaved their beards as a mark of contempt, cut off the skirts of their robes, and sent them back to Jerusalem. David was not a monarch to bear with equanimity an outrage so great as this. He sent Joab with an army, and, defeating their insolent young king, reduced him to the level of a tributary prince.

The Syrians now secretly raised an army to drive out the Hebrews from their dominions, and David, hearing that a great host of foot, chariots, and horsemen was assembled to overturn his power, took the field in person, conquered them, and made many thousand prisoners, besides capturing seven thousand chariots; while thousands of horses taken by him he commanded to be put to death according to the law of Moses, which law was ordained to prevent the Hebrews from engaging in foreign wars, that they might become a domestic and defensive power. King David had, in his army of the East, a battalion of chariots and four legions of horse of six thousand men each; but this was a temporary setting aside of the law by him in order to meet upon an equality foes similarly organized and mounted.

Returned from his second war against the Syrians, the soldier-king now gave his attention to the cultivation of the arts of peace. The sword was turned into the plowshare, and the spear into the pruning-hook. Unexampled prosperity reigned throughout his wide dominions, and his court was distinguished for its splendor and dignity. Marrying Maacah, the beautiful daughter of the Syrian Prince Tolmai, he cemented peace with this dangerous tributary monarch. All eminent men sought Jerusalem; and here were founded schools and seats of learning and academies of science; and from every land, men who were the most famous in their own country in any art, flocked to the Court of David. Thus his capital became the center of all that gives glory to a monarch or illustrates the genius of the age. From farther Ind, from Tarshish in Ceylona of the East, from Ophir, the land of gold, and the isles of the sea, from Grecia, and Etruria, and Cyprus, and Iberia came philosophers, poets, historians, astrologers, magicians, and painters on wood and papyrus, and workers in gold and silver, and polishers of precious stones, and artificers of all sorts' to sit under the shadow of the throne of David, and share the bountiful rewards which he bestowed on all who conferred glory upon his empire.

More than twenty years elapsed of unparalleled prosperity and regal grandeur. His wisdom, prowess, wealth, and commanding personal influence had placed his kingdom in the foremost rank among the nations of the earth. Not Assyria, nor Egypt surpassed Judea in power, and glory, and breadth of dominion. First of monarchs of the earth, all other kings did him willing reverence and eagerly sought his alliance. Embassies from the uttermost parts of the earth, which were a year on their way, presented themselves at his court, bringing gifts and letters of respectful homage. His wealth was unbounded, so that it was said, " Gold in Jerusalem is as plenty

as iron in Syria." The powerful monarch had also strengthened his throne by alliances of marriage with the Houses of the
Princes of the nations about him, so that every king of his
tributary kingdom had a daughter married to the powerful
monarch of Judea.

At length a cloud, at first no bigger than a vulture in the
sky, darkened the horizon of his dominions, concealing thunders and lightnings which were from time to time to flash their
angry fires and mutter their condemning voices against his
throne. Seated at the head of earthly empire, the proud and
prosperous monarch lost sight of God above and his dependence upon Him. Allured by pleasure, he neglected the Sanctuary, and gratitude ceased to bend his knee, for he had all that
the heart of man could wish for; and piety no longer lifted his
hands in prayer, for he felt himself sufficient in himself without God! He had nothing to ask of Heaven, and ceased to
ask! Thankfulness lives on a sense of need; but he believed
he had no needs, and required nothing more of God, and ceased
to be thankful! In the splendid king he forgot the humble
shepherd; and the virtues, which were cherished as fine gold
by the youthful "son of Jesse" in the wilderness, were disdained by the successful king on his throne! The heart of
David was wholly changed; and though he chanted magnificent
hymns to God on festal days before the people, it was from his
passion for psaltery and singing, and not from piety.

When God is forgotten He withdraws his presence! The
void is soon filled by the Enemy of Man, and the heart is exposed to every temptation! The Spirit of God departed from
Saul for *disobedience;* but the Spirit of the Lord was driven
from the heart of David by *pleasure.* His palace became a
paradise of luxury and delights. Singing men and singing
women played and danced before him: and he introduced into
his house forbidden entertainments from the dissolute courts
of the pagan kings. Beautiful slaves ministered to the intoxication of his senses, and all the arts of refinement of pleasure
were sought for and introduced before him, to enhance the
luxuries of his hours. The stern warrior had gradually become
a voluptuary; and the righteous sword of the soldier gave way
to the gold-inlaid harp and dulcimer! New delights were invented by his sycophants, and new fountains of enjoyment were
opened for him by his base and foreign-born courtiers. He
permitted the gods of the heathen princesses he had married

to be set up in their chambers, and incense to be burned before them by their own idolatrous priests.

In the meanwhile the sacrifices burned morning and evening upon the Altar of Jehovah in the Court of the Tabernacle, and incense to the God of Israel ascended continually from the sacred censers of the Priests. Perhaps the cloud which ever climbed toward heaven from the Altar of Burnt-offering, and the ever upward rising holy incense of God (the fragrance of which entered the windows of his palace) interposed like a continual national supplication between the anger of Heaven and the head of the royal voluptuary.

Sons and daughters from time to time were born to him; of whom were Absalom, son of the daughter of King Tolmai of Syria, Tamar, his sister, and her half brother, Ammon, and others, who imitated the luxurious life of the king, and rebelled against his authority when he would reprove them; for fathers who would have their children virtuous must first set them the example of virtue; for their example is more powerful than counsel.

At length one morning there arrived at the court of David a foreign-looking young man with a noble air and in fine apparel, and with those large Oriental eyes which betray the inhabitant of the East. He was richly armed, and rode a superb Persian horse, the housings thereon heavy with gold and glittering with precious stones. He was attended by a train of servants, and lords, and captains, with a retinue of one hundred splendidly armed men.

They were from the city of Tadmor, and the young man proved to be a prince, the youngest of three sons of Arbaces and Adora; and who had been sent by them to pass a few years at the court of David, to learn the art of arms and of letters under so great a captain and wise a monarch.

The king received the youthful Hadad Isrilid with great affection for his father's sake, and at once established him as his favored guest in his own palace. The reader is referred, for the further progress of the narrative of the reign of David, to the correspondence of Prince Hadad with his mother, Adora, Queen of Tadmor.

LETTER XVII.

The Prince Hadad, to Adora his Mother, Queen of Tadmor.

Court of David, Jerusalem.

My Dear and Royal Mother:

I know how impatient you will be to receive early intelligence of my arrival in Judea, and I hasten to write to you assuring you of my safety and health. Say to my dear father that we were but nine days on our journey, which we shortened by leaving Damascus far to the right, and crossing the Jordan near the foot of Mount Tabor.

With what emotion did I traverse with my retinue the field of Gilboa, where King Saul fell; the very place being pointed out to me by a herdsman who was watching his herds on the side of the mountain of Gilboa!

The beauty of the country, and its wonderful fertility from thence to Jerusalem, was a constant theme of wonder to my escort. The faithful and good Ninus, who had already long been familiar with these scenes, enjoyed my pleasure; and said that my dear father experienced equal gratification and surprise at the rich green valleys, vine-clad hills, countless snow-white villages, numerous warlike citadels, and noble towns which he passed on his route to Hebron from Jericho—your own city, my mother.

At length we came in sight of the city of David, which, partly palace and partly fortress, towers loftily above Jerusalem, and is visible far and wide. Our entrance into the city attracted no little attention, although the numerous embassies from all lands which visit the court of David have made the dress and aspect of foreigners familiar to the eyes of the Hebrews.

My reception by the king was as cordial and warm as if I had been his own son. He was taken, at first, by surprise, as he had not expected me for some weeks. He made the kindest inquiries after you and my dear father, and expressed the sincerest regard and friendship for you both; and desired me, when I wrote, to convey his friendly greetings, and to say that I so resembled you both that he should extend to me twofold regard for my parents' sake.

I am now a guest in his palace, with my own servants, and feel almost as much at home as in your royal house at Tadmor. I take delight in contemplating the scenes which you and my father have visited, and it was with mingled joy and sadness I entered the chamber which my father occupied a quarter of a century ago in the old wing of the king's palace.

You desired me to describe the appearance of the king. He looks nearly sixty years of age, with a florid face and silvery locks, and is the most beutiful old man I ever beheld, retaining still all his martial dignity of bearing, softened by the gracious majesty of the courteous king. His eyes are singularly expressive of tenderness and gentleness, and his pleasant voice, the beauty of the tones of which my father has often spoken of, it is delightful to hear. It is richer than a harp, softer than the notes of a dulcimer; yet beneath its music reposes the warlike trumpet tone, which it requires only the field and the foe to make ring as of old. He attached me at once to himself, and the deferential affection with which I involuntarily treat him greatly pleases him.

The state of his court is in keeping with the dignity of so great a monarch. I will not attempt adequately to describe it. Yesterday I saw him holding a royal court for the reception of an ambassador from Seba.

He was seated in his magnificent Throne-room, upon a chair of ivory over-arched by a canopy of cloth of gold. On each side of him stood two beardless Idumean eunuchs, waving above him fans of gorgeous feathers. On the lower step of his throne stood his cup-bearer, the young Prince Absalom, a youth of wonderful beauty of face and person, with flowing locks of hair covering his shoulders like a glorious, shining mantle. He was not more than seventeen years of age. I was presented to him the first day of my arrival, and the amiability of his manners quite won my heart. His attire was the most magnificent I ever beheld; and was so becoming that he looked like some brilliant and beautiful god rather than a creature of earth. Near him were the other princes of the house of the king, and the artful Jonadab his nephew.

On the right of the king stood his Prime Minister, Ahithophel, a noble and elegant prince with shining silvery hair, and a face full of intellect and intelligence. My father will recollect him as one of the earliest companions of the king in his youth, and then distinguished for his acute mind and profound diplomacy, talents which in his maturer years eminently distinguished him. In his crimson robe of office, his gold embroidered vesture, his coroneted cap, and gold-headed wand of office, together with the singular dignity of his person, he looks like a king himself; and it is said that David yields much to his counsel, and commits the chief weight of government into his hand.

Next to the Prime Minister stood Hushai, the Archite, and Lord of the Treasury, a noble old man whose face showed an honesty of purpose singularly in contrast with the politic looks of the Prime Minister. Next to him was Jehosaphat, the Chancellor and Recorder of the kingdom. A little in advance of the venerable Archite stood the famous warrior and General of all the armies of Israel, Joab, whom my father has so often spoken of. Tall, almost gigantic in height, his iron-gray head covered with a helmet of steel, his rough white beard trimmed closely to his chin, while the mustache of his upper lip stood in long, stiff brushes from ear to ear, a man with a ferocious countenance, covered with battle scars, he looked dark, stern, silent, disdaining the elegancies of military costume which characterized several of his officers who were about him. Seriah, the Secretary of State and Chief Scribe of the kingdom, stood by with his secretaries to record the proceedings. Farther on in front, a little to the sides, stood the ambassadors from other monarchs, tributary princes, and high officers of the court, and governors, and lords of provinces, a brilliant assembly! On the right and left of the throne, in mitered chairs of state, sat Abiathar, the High Priest, and Zadok, the Chief Priest, the only two dignitaries who are permitted to be seated in the presence of the king on such a state occasion as this of which I speak. Farther on from the throne toward the entrance stood persons of less dignity, motionless, in two lines, facing the throne, with depressed eyelids and their hands crossed upon the breast. At the great entrance stood Uriah, the Captain of the palace guards, mailed in gold armor, and keeping ward with his drawn sword in his hand, and one hundred men of Cherith and of Peleth, gigantic archers, with Benaiah their Captain of the royal guard. Fifty tall men of Dan, armed with javelins, in brazen helmets and steel corslets, were drawn up by the gate. Seated upon his superb throne, the king holds in his hand a tall scepter, crowned with a sphere set with rubies, upon which reposes a golden lion, the symbol of the king and his royal House. Prince Mephibosheth, who is now quite gray, was not present, his infirmity and sensitiveness thereupon keeping him much secluded within. He is a man both feared and shunned for his bitterness and his jealousy of all whom the king honors.

Besides the state days, when the whole court is assembled, the king passes a portion of every morning in his magnificently decorated Audience hall, or Judgment chamber, which is open to all who wish to enter and approach his royal majesty; and here he sits to decide in person those cases which, by appeal from the courts of the governors or senate of the Sanhedrim, are brought to the foot of the throne.

I was present this morning at such a tribunal. I then observed that the beautiful Prince Absalom, who volunteers to be his royal father's cup-bearer, an honor (inasmuch as it brings the person always near the person of the king), which many royal princes have held, managed artfully to keep from the throne such persons as he did not favor, while he forwarded the prayers of those whom he desired to please. I perceived with surprise that the king was wholly governed by him in all his suggestions, and that this young man, of whom I have less regard than at the first, was the idol of his heart. Upon speaking to Ninus upon this subject, he answered that Prince Absalom was actually the power behind the throne, and that the people of Israel had recently learned the humiliating lesson that he who would find favor with the king must purchase the good-will of this spoiled, arrogant, and indulged young prince. If any petitioner approaches directly to the monarch, passing by the prince, the king, before deciding, consults his young cup-bearer. The decision in such cases is always against the prayer of the petitioner, for in this way the prince delights to punish and rebuke those persons who presume to go first to his father. Whosoever wishes to have his prayer granted comes first privately to the prince and says to him, "I know, my lord, that thou art first in the kingdom, and art to reign hereafter, and that now the king, thy father, doeth nothing without thee. I desire a favor of the king; but I come first to thee, knowing that the power to grant my petition remains with thee, and whatever my lord decideth upon that the king doeth!"

This flattery is successful, and the prince is also greatly enriched by the gratitude of the successful petitioners. At first, I was pleased with Absalom, for his beauty and grace of manners and winning ways took my heart captive; but I do not like him. His character is artful and full of duplicity. He is, however, the idol of the court, perhaps because he is feared for the terrible power he can command for life or death. To offend the prince is to embrace swift destruction.

The splendor of the palace mocks description from my unaccustomed pen. It covers nearly half of Mount Zion, and is a magnificent assemblage of reception halls, porticoes, corridors, paved courts, of fountains, hanging gardens, marble walks. Ranges of painted chambers, fifty in number in one wing, and thirty in another, are all lined with alabaster or polished stones of divers colors, and hung with embroidered curtains. In the center are the royal domestic residence, Throne-room, and Judgment hall, Chamber of Ambassadors, and Hall of Princes; all adorned by bright porticoes with brilliantly colored columns; while the walls and ceilings are decorated in the most elaborate and elegant manner, with scrolls, flowers, fruit, and wreaths.

The Throne-room itself is a wonder of glory and beauty. The interior is entirely surrounded by slender pillars plated with silver, along which trail artificial vines with leaves gemmed with emeralds, and fruit glittering with rubies and sapphires. The posts which support the canopy above the entrance are of silver, the threshold is brazen, and the lintels silver inwrought with cedar and architraved with gold. Lions plated with gold stand on each side of the entrance, while all along the walls to the throne itself stand lesser thrones for kings, princes, and ambassadors, over which are displayed the shields of gold David took from the Syrian King. Without the entrance gate lies a spacious garden luxuriant with many a lofty tree, among which are the scarlet pomegranate, the broad-leaved honeyed fig, the golden pear, the bright, blushing apple, and rich, brown-tinted olive with its polished leaves; while clustering grapes hang pendent over the noble avenues. Flowers of all hues, that bloom through all the year, are arranged along the walks with graceful taste, and guarded with constant care; while the beauty of the lovely scene is enhanced by seven welling fountains, that descend in bright showers of liquid diamonds, diffusing delicious coolness throughout the summer air. This garden is the Palace Court, open to all, and traversed by all who approach the king. Beyond the threshold of this noble garden stand the tall towers occupied by the palace guards; and near them the beautiful house of the princely soldier Uriah, the king's lord of the palace and captain of his royal bodyguard.

Farewell, dear mother, I will write you again in a few days. I am, next week, to enter into the military school of the Citadel of David to learn the art of war; since as a younger son I cannot look to the throne of my father, I can, at least, hope to serve my country, by and by, as a leader of its armies.

Say to my dear father that many gray-haired officers of the court of David have inquired after his health; and that many of them honor me with notice for his sake; especially Joab, at whose house in Bethlehem my father stayed, I believe, two months after his return from Egypt. The noble Uriah has also paid me great honor for your sake, and has desired me to become his guest to-morrow, which I have promised to do.

Prince Absalom, whose peculiar, full-lidded eyes betray his Syrian blood, has just called upon me, insisting I shall accompany him to Mount Olive that he may show me how they hunt the gazelle in Judea. I shall embrace the opportunity to visit the villa situated there and so long your home.

Your faithful and affectionate son,

HADAD BEN ISRILID.

LETTER XVIII.

PRINCE ISRILID TO KING ARBACES.

THE COURT OF DAVID, MONTH TIZRI.

MY ROYAL FATHER:

A few weeks since I wrote my dear mother, informing her of my safe arrival in this sumptuous capital of the Hebrews. I will now not so much send you a letter, as commence for your perusal, when I shall a few years hence return to your court, the "Journal of Events" you desired me to preserve. This tablet of Egyptian papyrus leaves on which I write may therefore bear, besides this present one, many dates. In the tablets I shall briefly write at leisure such events as may be interesting to you.

My residence here continues to be more and more agreeable. I am interested in studying the manners and customs of the people, reading their records, witnessing the solemnities of their religious worship, and learning the forms of this stately court; moreover, I am not indolent in pursuing those military studies of which Joab is the great master, and Uriah one of the most brilliant instructors. Even the king, whose soldierly tastes, amid all the luxury which environs him, are not yet dormant, often enters the military castle, that which is called the "Citadel of David," where three hundred of the noblest Hebrew youths, as well as the king's own sons, learn the tactics and strategy of war and the use of arms. So celebrated is this college of war that a son of the King of Tyre, two Syrian princes, three sons of the King of Arabia, and a son of the King of Cyprus are pupils herein.

The sight of the army of King David in review on the elevated plane between this and the sides of Mount Ephraim is a magnificent spectacle. The main body consists of one hundred and forty and four thousand men, twelve thousand from each tribe, and each tribic host armed and mailed differently, and carrying splendid standards, the tribes displaying thereon their peculiar insignia. Besides this central army are battalions from the cities and towns, in vast numbers, eight legions of horsemen, and four thousand chariots; troops of Moabite slingers, of Edomite spearmen, of Syrian bowmen, of Ammonite lancers, of Philistine swordsmen, and a squadron of desert cavalry, wild and barbaric riders, with spears twice the length of their horses, and whose steeds rival the eagle's flight in speed.

Besides these are the permanent garrisons of more than one hundred border towns, and the soldiers who hold the fortresses in the countries the king has conquered. The whole army which the king can bring into the field numbers six hundred thousand fighting men. But, of course, only a portion of these for state forms and garrisons remain in arms in time of peace.

In my letter to my mother I informed her that I had been invited by the princely courtesy of Uriah, who is regarded as the most gallant and brilliant officer in the army of the king, to become his guest for a day. I have stated that his palace is on one side of the king's gardens, while that of Joab, the general-in-chief of the armies, stands on the other. The palace of Uriah is as distinguished for taste and elegance in all its interior apartments, and by its exterior, as that of the latter for plainness and soldier-like severity of style. The rough old warrior disdains gardens and fountains, and gives up the ground to the exercises of his long-haired Pelethites and Cherithites, with their bows and arrows, slings and quoits. The environs of the villa of Uriah are cultivated and adorned with flowers and fountains, shaded walks, and terraces, while in the midst of the scene of beauty stand white marble bathing basins, inclosed by the curtains of silken pavilions.

Through these charming walks Uriah conducted me to his mansion. He did me the honor to present me to his wife, Bathsheba, who expressed a desire to have me brought into her apartment, as she had seen both you and my mother. Is she not the same whom David saw at the 'Well of Palms, and of whom Uriah learned the way he took? How shall I give my dear mother a description of the beauty of this noble-looking lady, who, at forty years of age, for she does not seem more, and is perhaps not so old, is still the most beautiful woman, next to my ever-charming mother, I ever beheld! She received me with infinite grace, and asked me so many questions about my own country that I was soon at ease in her presence.

After dinner, attended by her maidens, and accompanied by Uriah and by me, she walked in the garden, and we gathered fruit and flowers, and looked at the wide prospect over Jerusalem from the terrace. The palace had but just been completed, and but a few weeks occupied by them, and they took, therefore, the more pride and gratification in showing it to strangers.

TABLET—LEAF SECOND.

We are now just entering upon the great Hebrew festival of which I have heard you, my father, speak; but the arrival of which, as it recurs only every fifty years, you did not witness while you were in Judea. Their sacred number, seven, applied to years, makes a *week* of years, and this week of seven years (instead of days) long is again multiplied by seven, making forty-nine years, or one year, striking out the secular days, wholly made up of Sabbaths. This forty-ninth year is celebrated by suspension of all agricultural labor, and kept as a Sabbath of rest. During the whole year no one either sows or reaps, but all are satisfied with what the earth and trees produce spontaneously.

Nor is this the only remarkable feature of this half-century festival. Every man who has sold, or mortgaged, or in any way alienated his landed patrimony, this year resumes possession of it, the holder cheerfully resigning it, having, of course, in the transaction by which it fell into his hands calculated for the jubilee restoration thereof; hence, neither loss nor injustice is received by him. All persons held in bondage are also set free, with their wives and children.

This extraordinary law of the land coming into operation produces all at once an extraordinary condition of things. The whole kingdom is suddenly thrown into a state of excitement and motion. Years of poverty and struggle end in a night, and the houseless reoccupy the homes of their fathers, the landless become possessors of noble estates, and universal joy prevails. The varied, touching, and joyful scenes which occur every hour for the first few days are deeply interesting.

The first nine days are spent in a round of festivities. Everybody congratulates everybody, and gifts are interchanged, old feuds healed, and forgiveness and reconciliation are the rule of the day. These first nine days no manner of work is done, even within doors, and everyone you meet is crowned with leaves or flowers and arrayed in festal attire, while chants and songs fill the air.

On the tenth morning I was awakened by the loud peal of the trumpets of the seventy priests who stand in the court of the Tabernacle, and which the prince of the Senate of the Sanhedrim ordered to be sounded, it being the legal signal for all slaves to resume their freedom without further form, and all lands to revert to their hereditary owners.

"This law was mercifully designed," said the king to me, "to prevent the rich from oppressing the poor, and any one person from becoming too rich in lands to the exclusion of the natural tillers of the soil; to put a bar to the too great multiplication of debts, and to prevent perpetual bondage among brethren of one blood."

Without doubt, dear father, this is a law which could only have originated from a wise and benevolent God! It preserves the liberty of the persons of the Israelites (who can be sold for debt), conserves a due equality of fortunes, and re-establishes the hereditary order of families as they stood in the days of Joshua.

There is also a lesser festival every seven years, called the Sabbatical year, or "week of years." On this year a certain class of bondmen are released from obedience to their masters, and a certain portion of property reverts to those who have alienated it. The Sabbatical year at its close annuls debts of money between man and man, which the Jubilee year does not. Cautious rich men, this year, seldom loan to those who ask, unless fully protected against the statute of limitation obtaining during the year. Houses in walled towns built within the Jubilee period do not return to those who have mortgaged or sold them, the statute having reference primarily to the reversion of lands, in order to restore the integrity of their original division between the tribes and families.

"The appointment of the Sabbatical year," replied the intelligent Prophet Nathan to me when I inquired its object, "was to preserve the remembrance of the creation of the world in six periods, followed by an equal period of rest. Then God gave six periods of time to the earth and man, and one to Himself for repose. He now gives man six periods for himself, but demands one equally long set apart for His honor, and in remembrance of the first period of rest. These periods are 'years' in the Sabbatical week, and 'weeks of years' in the Jubilee week; and a week of Jubilees must be, therefore, about three hundred and forty-three solar years. Thus we cannot learn how long was the first period of creation and rest, called a week; for God makes 'weeks of years,' and 'years of years'! With Him a day is as a thousand years, and a thousand years is as one day. There exists a record in our ancient writings which states that the first 'day' consisted of a week of solar years, or two thousand and five hundred and fifty-five years, and that this was the length of the first Sabbath. A week of these weeks of creation will comprise, according to the Rabbinical books, seventeen thousand years, at which time the world, they say, will end, and a new order of things, with a new circle of ages, begin. If this prediction and this calculation be true, we are now only in the second day of this great week of time!"

TABLET—LEAF THIRD.

It is three months, my dear father, since I have looked at my Tablets or made any record. In the meanwhile I have received my dear mother's letter. I will proceed briefly to answer her inquiries about the ladies of the palace, whom she once knew.

The deposed Princess Michal, Saul's daughter, I ought before this to have informed you, died ere I came to Jerusalem, in the house of the sons of Kish at Bethel, whither she retired after David put her away. Her declining years were tortured with the sharp thorns of fallen pride and the pangs of impotent jealousy. She slowly wasted away; and during the last weeks of her life she became lunatic, and raved, and played the queen, and, daily crowning herself with faded flowers, she believed herself the ruler of Israel, and died calling upon Saul, her father, "to avenge her upon the Shepherd of Jesse"! It is said the king, grieved at her sad end, gave her a royal burial in the tomb with Saul and Jonathan.

The stately Abigail still lives in the palace, but takes no part in the state pageants, and is seldom seen. I have been presented to her. She looks sad and broken, a wreck only of the former splendor of her beauty. The other wives of the king are foreign princesses; each keeping her own suite of apartments, and worshiping her own gods, and all rivaling and hating each other; each vainly aspiring to the supreme place in the affections of the monarch, which Queen Abigail holds by the slender and daily fading tenure of her former beauty.

A sad event, my dear father, has occurred since I laid aside my tablets, almost a year ago. I hardly know how to record it. It reflects so severely and darkly upon the king that I am sure you will feel greatly distressed; for I know in what high estimation you hold his private as well as his kingly character. It shows, however, that "humanity," as our Assyrian proverb has it, "is a flawed vase—not a perfect one can be found on earth." The golden vase of King David has at length betrayed its human imperfection. I have already alluded to the voluptuous complexion of his brilliant and luxurious court; and that his departure from the customs of his ances- tors by marrying many wives, after the manner of the heathen kings, had insensibly broken down all the barriers which a previous life of virtue had created about his heart. The pain- ful consequences of such royal disregard to the integrity of his personal honor have been lately exhibited.

A few weeks since the tributary King of the Ammonites, who had been recently subdued and was still sore with wounded pride, came to Jerusalem to do homage to the king, his con- queror. While here, he fancied himself wounded by the imperious manner of Prince Absalom, and complained to the monarch, his father, of the insult. The king, instead of rebuk- ing his son, reproved the Ammonite Prince for taking offense where none could have been given; for David can believe no evil thing of the youth; and he who carries a report to him against him will be the only one believed to be guilty.

The angry Ammonite hid his indignant feelings at the time, and with fair outside a day or two afterwards took leave of the king. He had no sooner reached his own dominions than he secretly formed a league with the King of Syria, the King of Moab, and the King of Edom, and raised the standard of re- bellion. No sooner did David hear that the King of Syria had joined him, and that they showed front of war, than he dis- patched Joab with an army against him. The Ammonites at his approach treacherously withdrew from the field, leaving the Syrians to contend alone with the Hebrew hosts. Uriah, the king's chief captain, had also joined the army under Joab; for David had not spared even his own bodyguard in order to visit the rebels with instant chastisement.

A few days after the departure of the army King David was

walking upon the terrace of his palace, which overlooked the beautiful gardens of the villa of Uriah. While he was walking to and fro, impatient to hear news from the war, and often looking in the direction of the Jordan, to discover couriers, his eyes fell upon the person of the wife of Uriah, as, loosely arrayed and unsuspicious of observation, she was leaving her bath in the seclusion of her garden attended by two of her maidens. The king, who, rumor now saith, had long envied his great captain the possession of his beautiful wife, and often distinguished her with a place of honor when he met her among the ladies of his court, was upon the instant seized with a desire to make this lovely woman his own. With a king, to wish is to will, and to will is to obtain! Nothing can resist power and will combined! The virtuous wife of the noble soldier, who was beyond Jordan fighting, as his general's armor-bearer, the battles of his king, leaving his honor in his lord's keeping, was despised and dishonored by that lord.

The guilty secret was kept from every eye, even from the prying scrutiny, and jealous observing of all things else, of Prince Mephibosheth. But I discovered that there was some deep sorrow in the heart of the wife of Uriah, who has been ever my friend, for I have continued to be a frequent and welcome guest at her house. I attributed it to the absence of her lord, and strove to reassure her mind of his safety; but the more I talked with the noble wife the more sad and tearful she became. Little did I then suspect the wreck of honor and shame she had become through the sin of one who had forgotten his anointing of God as Shepherd of Bethlehem, the fate of Saul, the justice and vengeance of that terrible Lord, the history of whose dealings with the Hebrews from his judgments against Moses and Aaron to those against Ishbosheth, show that he winks at no sin, and leaves no transgression of men unpunished, either in their own persons or in those (a still more awful consideration) of their children. At length the guilt of this king, naturally a righteous and religious man, and who hitherto had firmly kept the laws of God, could not much longer be concealed. The war was prolonged three months, and Uriah still remained absent. The king now began to reap the fruits of his iniquity by torture of mind in devising how to hide from the world his guilt and her shame; for he was well aware that when the Chief Priest should hear thereof, he would assuredly put her to death in compliance with the letter of the law, which ordained stoning to death as the punishment for a wife who dishonors her lord. The king was not so lost to all generous emotions as to risk exposing her for whom he had begun to feel a profound attachment to so cruel a fate. She also eloquently pleaded to him to save her. There was but one way which suggested itself to his mind to protect her from the law, which was to cover his crime, which was yet their own secret, ere it would be open to all men, by the artful presence of her husband. He therefore sent a swift messenger to Joab in the field, saying:

"Send me to Jerusalem as soon as this comes into thy hand, Uriah the Hittite, my faithful servant; for I have need of him."

When Joab read this letter he showed it to Uriah, who, not pleased to be ordered home on the eve of an assault, yet made no delay; but the evening of the second day presented himself, just as he was in his travel-stained dress and arms, before the king.

When the monarch had carelessly asked of the brave soldier he had wronged with the greatest wrong one man can do to another man, news of the field and learned that the Syrians were still unconquered, he said:

"I need thee here as before in my palace. I would not have sent thee to the wars had I known I should have been without thy services so long as captain of my guard. Go down to thy house and bathe after thy journey, and I will send thee meat and wine from my own table; and in the morning come to me."

The unsuspecting Uriah left the king's presence; but instead of going down to his house met several of his military friends and refreshed himself in the guardroom with them and the officers of the king's guard; and was so occupied in giving them an account of the incidents of the war, that finding it quite late when he rose to leave, he said to his friends:

"I will not disturb my house this night, it is so far gone, but sleep here on a soldier's couch, as becomes a man of war."

The next morning King David having inquired and learned that his victim had not gone down to his house, but slept, instead, in his room in the guard-tower, he sent for him and said to him sternly, and yet coloring with apprehension lest the husband suspected the truth and his motive:

"Why didst thou not go down unto thine house and gladden thy wife with thy safety and presence, and all thy house?"

"My lord," answered the stout soldier, "the Ark of God dwelleth in a tent of curtains; and the armies of Israel and Judah beyond Jordan I left abiding in tents; and, my lord, Joab and his guard of soldiers were encamped two nights ago in the open field! Shall I then, O king, go down into my house to my wife, and eat and drink and live luxuriously and at ease? Not so, my lord the king! As thou livest, and as thy soul liveth, I will not do this thing! I came from the wars with my armor on, and I return to it when thou wilt, with it on. When the war ends I will take off my helmet and cuirass and lie down in my house in peace. If the king sent for me only to learn how Joab did and the army fared, and how the war prospered, let it please my lord the king to send me back again, for presently we are to have a great battle, and I would not be absent."

"Tarry here to-day, and to-morrow I will let thee depart," answered the king, who evidently felt the deepest annoyance and disappointment at this turn which the affair had taken.

The same day at even the king entertained his lords and officers, and also Uriah at his table, and pressed the Hittite warrior warmly with goblets of wine. When the brave soldier, who could not refuse the frequent pledges of the king, was well under the effects of the wine, the king ordered his servants to take him home and leave him there. But when Uriah found himself in the court, and breathed the fresh air, he disengaged himself angrily from the men, who fled from him. He then went to the stone hall of the guardhouse, and there lying down slept until morning.

David was foiled in this additional wrong by which he fain would have covered up the original injury; for one act of guilt begets others, and deprives men of their understanding and ordinary judgment. It alters their very nature, blinds their eyes to inevitable consequences, and debases and degrades the reason. "Especially," said the Prophet Nathan to me in discoursing of this matter, "is this true of those whose sin is sensuality."

But a greater wrong was yet to be done to conceal his guilt and protect the wife from the law of death. He who generously spared Saul, who thrice sought his life, when he could have destroyed him, now meditates the destruction of a faithful servant who had oftentimes saved his life in battle, and for years had guarded his person. So degenerate do the best of men become when once they resolve to do evil.

Commanding the unsuspecting Uriah before him, whom he now profoundly hated, not only because men naturally hate those they injure, but because the wonderful interposing providence of God prevented him from making him the instrument of hiding his crime, he said coldly:

"Deliver this letter to Joab, my general, in the field. Thou mayest remain in the camp until the war is ended."

Uriah immediately departed from the presence of the king, and hastened to return to the field he had left five days before. During this visit to the court, he had not gone to his house, nor seen his wife, whom he greatly loved. How can this be accounted for, but on the presumption that he had received intimation of the truth? Indeed, it is now said that his wife secretly sent to him confessing the whole, and imploring him not to suffer her to behold his face again, since she could no longer share his honorable love. If this be so, with what delicacy he yielded to her prayer, and with what dignity he met and answered the royal injurer!

A man less noble that Uriah would have suspected, under these circumstances, evil in a letter from David to Joab, and would have hesitated to deliver it without first knowing its contents; but he honorably executed his trust.

When Joab received the letter he opened it and read as follows:

"Set ye Uriah in the fore-front of the hottest battle, and retire ye from him, that he may be smitten and die." *

It is with the most painful hesitation, my dear father, I record this dreadful history. If Saul were possessed with an evil spirit, the same demon of murder and wrong had now entered into the heart of his successor. Well may we take up the words of his requiem over Saul, and cry:

"How are the mighty fallen!"

When Joab had read the letter he said within himself:

"This man hath done some crime against my lord the king, which he hath reasons for not punishing openly, giving him the favor of an honorable death. I must obey the king my lord in this thing."

* 2 Samuel xi. 15.

Three days afterwards, when he was about to assault a part of the wall of the city and fortress they were besieging, Joab placed Uriah at a point where he knew would be the hottest conflict, and at which place he was to put his most valiant soldiers. In order, however, that Uriah might certainly be slain, he gave orders to the soldiers, who were purposely selected few in number, to retreat if the assailants came out of their gates, which he knew well they would do, while to Uriah he said: "Let no man retreat, and if the Ammonites open their gates, enter at the head of your men and take the citadel!"

When, therefore, the Ammonites, seeing but few soldiers assaulting the gate, sallied forth to attack them, while others shot from the walls, killing several of David's men, the rest fled, leaving the brave Uriah standing alone. In a moment he was surrounded by his foes, whom he fought long and desperately, slaying many at his feet, and to the last refusing to yield. From the camp the brave and fierce Joab saw how valiantly he sold his life, and said:

"But for the command of the king I would sound the retreat, and he would yet bring his life away! It is a pity to see so valiant a soldier slaughtered like a lion at bay! There he falls! But he has piled a tomb of dead men about him, within which, like a true and great warrior, he has stretched himself in death."

So died the king's brave captain, slain by treachery and guilt. Who can forgive the king this deed of murder? The crime of blood-guiltiness, who will deliver him from? How dearly was his sin purchased! Alas for the noble and faithful soldier and husband! Who, that recalls the hour when he overtook the fugitive David, lending to him his horse, and joining his fortunes, could have believed such would have been his end? But it has ever been thus. Kindnesses in this world are almost always but the forerunners of wrong and ingratitude from the recipients. Only a godlike disposition can receive a favor and not hate and strive to injure the giver. If the highest angel should come from heaven to do good to men, he would be repaid by ingratitude and insults. If such a man as David could return evil for good, who can be called wise and virtuous?

The same evening Joab, who was deeply moved at the death of one who had for twenty-five years been his fellow-soldier and long his armor-bearer, called a messenger and said to him:

"Mount a swift horse, and ride to Jerusalem, and when thou comest before the king, give him an account of all the events

of the assault; and, I charge thee, when thou hast made an end
of telling of all things I command thee concerning the war, and
of the discomfiture of the Hebrews, and the death of many of
the king's soldiers, and, lo! thou seest the king's wrath rise
thereat, and he say unto thee:

"'Wherefore approached ye so nigh unto the city when ye
did fight? Know ye not that they would shoot from the wall?
why went ye nigh the wall?' then answer thou, and say:

"'Thy servant, Uriah the Hittite is dead also!'"

How profound the knowledge of human nature, dear father,
is evinced by the old Hebrew warrior in this last order! How
thoroughly it proved his just apprehension of the king's real
character!

When at length the courier from the Hebrew camp stood
before David, the king, hearing from him of the disaster and
loss of his soldiers, became displeased, but the words of the
messenger, "Uriah the Hittite is dead also!" acted like a talis-
man upon his anger. With a face in which high satisfaction
took the place of wrath he said in an altered and quiet tone:

"Such is the fortune of war! Tell Joab not to let this thing
trouble or dishearten him, for the sword devoureth one as well
as another. Bid him send out a stronger force against the city,
that shall not fail to overthrow it. Say thou to him that the
king hath no fault against him, and bid him go valiantly on
with the war; for his conduct of it thus far pleaseth the king
well!"

After the seven days of mourning for her husband were
passed, according to law, David hastened to bring Bathsheba
to his palace and make her his wife, which he did do in the
presence of his whole court with great pomp. But in a few
months after the marriage the whole secret became manifest,
and the purposed death of Uriah was fastened upon the king
by the indignant judgment of the whole army, by which the
valiant captain was greatly beloved.

The Prophet Nathan was asleep upon his bed in the closet
above the gate at Ramah in the Palace of the Judges when he
had a vision from the Lord, in which the fourfold guilt of David
was made known to him, and he was commanded to arise and
go to Jerusalem and stand before the king and rebuke him.
Uriah had been dead then a year, and the king had manifested
no remorse.

David at that hour sat upon his Judgment Seat in the great

Hall, and all his officers, and lords, and elders of his court and
of the city were before him. I also stood in the presence, as
I desired to study the manner in which the Hebrews administer
justice. When the king beheld the dignified and holy man of
God enter and advance up the Judgment Hall his face changed;
for he knew that the prophets are oftener the ministers of God's
displeasure than of his favor. Besides, he felt that he deserved
the anger of God for his fourfold crime of adultery, his base
intoxication of Uriah, his treacherous murder of him, and
marrying the wife of the man that he had killed in order to
have her.

The brow of the prophet was calm and his features grave,
but sad, rather than stern. With his ample sacerdotal mantle
folded about his tall person, his step firm, and his bearing noble,
as became an Ambassador from Heaven, he stopped opposite the
king and made a low obeisance before the anointed of the Lord.
All eyes were fixed upon the prophet with superstitious dread.
Not a thought in that vast hall but was recalling the guilt of
the king, and suspected for what the prophet had come into his
presence.

David partly rose, and bowed reverently before the Prophet
of the Highest, and reseating himself said:

"Wherefore comest thou, O Nathan, whom the king de-
lighteth to honor!"

"I come, O king, to crave justice," answered the prophet
mildly, "for this should be the throne of judgment and of
justice."

"Speak, O Nathan," answered the monarch, looking relieved
and as if a great weight were taken from his conscience; "who
is the offender? I trust that justice and judgment are the habitation of my throne, for all who are wronged or inflict wrong."

"There were two men in one city," said the prophet, speaking calmly and humbly; "the one rich, and the other poor. The
rich man had exceeding many flocks and herds; but the poor
man had nothing save one little ewe lamb, which he had bought
and nourished up; and it grew up together with him, and with
his children: it did eat of his own meat, and drank of his own
cup, and lay in his bosom, and was unto him as a daughter.
And there came a traveler unto the rich man, and he spared to
take of his own flock, and of his own herd, to dress for the way-
faring man that was come unto him; but took the poor man's
lamb and dressed it for the man that was come to him."

When the king heard this narrative, which the prophet gave with deep feeling, he rose to his feet, and with a countenance flushed with anger, cried in a loud voice:

"As the Lord liveth, the man that hath done this thing shall surely die: and he shall restore the lamb fourfold, because he did this thing, and because he had no pity!"

Then the prophet drawing himself up to his commanding height, and with a sublime anger kindling in his aspect, said with stern severity extending his hand towards the king:

"*Thou* art the man!"

The king stood a moment transfixed with surprise. A subdued murmur ran through the hall, which told how the prophet's narrative told home in the mind of all present.

David after a moment's agitation descended from his throne and stood humbly and penitently before the Prophet of the Most High God. The personal application of the parable was irresistible. He felt all the keenness of its piercing point. Then said Nathan:

"Thus saith the Lord God of Israel, I anointed thee king over Israel, and I delivered thee out of the hand of Saul. And I gave thee thy master's house, and thy master's wives into thy bosom, and gave thee the house of Israel and of Judah; and if that had been too little, I would, moreover, have given unto thee such and such things. Wherefore hast thou despised the commandment of the Lord, to do evil in his sight? Thou hast killed Uriah the Hittite with the sword, and hast taken his wife to be thy wife, and hast slain him with the swords of the children of Ammon. Now, therefore, the sword shall never depart from thine house; because thou hast despised me, and hast taken the wife of Uriah the Hittite to be thy wife. Thus saith the Lord, Behold, I will raise up evil against thee out of thine own house, and I will take thy wives before thine eyes, and give them unto thy neighbor. Thou didst secretly what thou hast done against Uriah, but I will do this thing before all Israel and before the sun!"

Then said the king with a manner and tone of the deepest humiliation, "I have sinned against the Lord! I acknowledge my guilt! Let the Lord do unto me as seemeth good in his sight!"

The humble attitude of the penitent monarch before the prophet, the sincere contrition manifest to all in his looks and voice, the painful spectacle of beholding a king thus humbled for sin, who should be an ensample to his people, deeply moved all present. Tears stood in the eyes of many of his courtiers at a sight so pitiful. But Prince Absalom smiled haughtily and frowned upon the prophet, and Mephibosheth sneered with his cold cynical lip and eye. Ahithophel betrayed nothing in his well-schooled features. Nathan, who had known David from his youth, and been with him in the School of the Prophets, was himself not unmoved, and his voice was uneven when he replied:

"The Lord hath put away thy sin in that thou dost humbly confess thy guilt. Thou shalt not die as thy sin meriteth. Howbeit, because by this deed thou hast given great occasion to the enemies of the Lord to blaspheme, thou shalt not altogether go unpunished. Therefore the child that has been born unto thee shall surely die!"

Then the prophet, turning from the face of the king, folded his robes about him and slowly strode from the Judgment Hall, where the king himself had been judged that day by the Judge of all the earth.

Such, my dear father, is the event which has filled the hearts of the wise and good in Jerusalem with sorrow. The king is certainly deeply humbled. A great change has come over him. He walks in his house with a lowly heart and sad but contrite looks. He ordained a public act of confession and sacrifice for his sin, and humbled himself in sackcloth. So profound was his repentance, and it showed itself in such humbleness of mind, that those who at first were most bitter against him were stirred to sympathy. His solemn act of public contrition in the Tabernacle was distinguished by the composition of a penitent psalm, which he humbly recited aloud before all the people. It was as follows:

Have mercy upon me, O God, after thy great goodness; according to the multitude of thy mercies do away mine offenses.

Wash me thoroughly from my wickedness, and cleanse me from my sin.

For I acknowledge my faults, and my sin is ever before me.

Against thee only have I sinned, and done this evil in thy sight; that thou mightest be justified in thy saying, and clear when thou art judged.

Behold, I was shapen in wickedness, and in sin hath my mother conceived me.

But lo, thou requirest truth in the inward parts, and shalt make me to understand wisdom secretly.

Thou shalt purge me with hyssop, and I shall be clean; thou shalt wash me, and I shall be whiter than snow.

Thou shalt make me hear of joy and gladness, that the bones which thou hast broken may rejoice.

Turn thy face from my sins, and put out all my misdeeds.

Make me a clean heart, O God, and renew a right spirit within me.

Cast me not away from thy presence, and take not thy Holy Spirit from me.

O give me the comfort of thy help again, and stablish me with thy free Spirit.

Then shall I teach thy ways unto the wicked, and sinners shall be converted unto thee.

Deliver me from blood-guiltiness, O God, thou that art the God of my health; and my tongue shall sing of thy righteousness.

Thou shalt open my lips, O Lord, and my mouth shall show thy praise.

For thou desirest no sacrifice, else would I give it thee; but thou delightest not in burnt-offerings.

The sacrifice of God is a troubled spirit: a broken and contrite heart, O God, shalt thou not despise.

O be favorable and gracious unto Zion; build thou the walls of Jerusalem.

Then shalt thou be pleased with the sacrifice of righteousness, with the burnt-offerings and oblations; then shall they offer young bullocks upon thine altar.

This psalm seems to exhaust the language of humble penitence. He feels his sin is too great for the blood of bulls and of goats to atone for, but casts himself outside of all these upon the mercy of his God.

He also implored day after day the favor of God to spare his infant son. He wept and fasted for its life to be given him, for it was a child of extraordinary beauty. But the fiat had gone forth and been uttered by the Prophet of God. The child died! When the unhappy king heard of its death from his servants he calmly rose up and said:

"Now that he is no more, why should I fast and afflict myself? While he was alive I said, Who can tell whether God will be gracious unto me that the child may live? But now he is dead, wherefore should I weep and fast? I shall go to him," he added, with touching tenderness, "I shall go to him, but he shall not return to me!"

Then the king, after the burial of the child, once more arraying himself in his royal apparel, went in and out before his people, and gave himself up with diligence and wisdom to the administration of the neglected affairs of his kingdom. Once more he piously observed the laws of religion and devoutly meditated in the statutes of his God day and night.

TABLET.—LEAF FIFTH.

Seven years have passed, my dear father, since I commenced these tablets. Some of the records I sent you before I left Jerusalem to visit the foreign lands from which I have a few weeks since returned. One year's absence in acquiring military knowledge in Egypt, one year in the camp in Cyprus, and two years' service with the King of Grecia, and two years at the court of Tyre, with full another year spent in journeying by sea and land have, I trust, fulfilled your expectations of your son, and resulted in that improvement in arts and arms which you have sent me from home to obtain. My letters from those foreign countries you have, no doubt, duly received from time to time, and as I am now once more here, in order, before returning to Tadmor, to look after the business connected with the estate near Jericho which my royal mother received from her father, Isrilid, and has bestowed upon me, I will while here resume my tablets, for I have interesting events to record which have transpired since my absence.

I found your letters here informing me of the death of the wise and good King Belus, and that you, my dear father, had the privilege of being in Assyria and with him at his death. As he never married, it was generous and noble in him to offer to you, his dearest friend, the throne of Assyria; and as you accepted it, upon his insisting thereupon, for my elder brother, Ionaton, and the vice-regency of Babylon for my next brother, Eldavid, I cannot refuse to hasten home at your command to be with you and my dear mother. Long may you fill the throne of Tadmor! very long may it be ere its crown is transferred by your death from the brows of my mother and thine to mine!

Great changes have taken place in this kingdom during my absence. The king, soon after I left Jerusalem, went in person and ended the war in Syria-Ammon, by taking its city, Rabbah, before which Uriah fell; and as the lords and king thereof had treated his ambassadors (whose persons all nations should hold sacred) so basely, he inflicted upon them the severest punishment, in order to show other barbaric nations how people who insult the representatives of kings are to be treated. David, having put an end to the war, was crowned king of Ammon, with its defeated king's golden crown, and then with his victorious armies returned to Jerusalem. He now devoted his time to the collection of gold, and silver, and precious stones, and cedar, and brass, and fragrant and beautiful woods, in order to build the long-desired temple to God, if God would now permit it; and if not to have the materials in readiness for his son, Solomon, who was born to him by Bathsheba, his wife, after the death of her first-born. This prince is a bright, beautiful lad, whom I daily meet in the corridors of the palace, possessing a gravity and dignity beyond his years. He is the hope and glory of his royal father's pride, who has destined him as his successor, though Prince Absalom is much older, being, I am told by the veteran Joab, tall, bearded, and the very image of his father when he was crowned king of Judah, at Hebron. But this prince had been, during three years of my absence, living an exile from his father's court, dwelling a fugitive at that of his grandfather, the Syrian King Talmai, whose daughter, Maacah, was his mother. Thither he fled from the wrath of King David, his father. This anger against him was aroused by his assassination of his brother, Amnon, who had insulted his sister Tamar in a manner no brother could lightly pardon. Thus in one day the sins of the king began to be visited upon his children and his house according to the prophecy of Nathan; for in one day one of his sons became a fratricide, another murdered for a great crime, and his daughter dishonored. Thus, though the transgression of a man may be forgiven, it seems an inevitable law that the natural consequences must still take place. The sins of David were repeated in his sons, who by sensuality and blood bore the legitimate fruit of the parent tree.

The king, however, felt no anger towards Absalom, but on the contrary mourned daily his absence, and constantly sent to hear of him. No city of refuge in his own land could have protected him, inasmuch as the murder of his brother was designed, and a long premeditated vengeance; therefore he guardedly kept himself at the court of King Talmai.

That King David did not send for his son whom he so idolized, and had in heart forgiven, was because he feared the people would be dissatisfied if he recalled him. At length, however, being prevailed upon by the eloquence of a woman who came before him at the request of Joab, and by Joab himself, who greatly desired the prince to be brought back, he gave orders as his general desired. The prince, therefore, returned with the venerable warrior, but when he entered Jerusalem so great was the indignation of the populace that he should be received, that the king, hearing the uproar, feared to see his son and openly to pardon him too freely; and therefore ordered him to go to his house in another part of the city, and dwell there, until it should be the king's pleasure to restore him by a full and public pardon to his favor.

The subjects of the king thereby seeing that David did not pass lightly over the crime of his son, prince though he was, and often beholding the comely young man walking in his gardens, grew less bitter after a year or more; and from disliking him began to admire him, and to pity him thus kept a prisoner by the king, his father.

In all Israel there is none so much praised as Absalom for his extraordinary personal beauty. "From the sole of his foot even to the crown of his head," say the Hebrews, his admirers, "there is no blemish in him." And not only the elegance of his form, the comeliness of his countenance, the brilliancy of his complexion, and splendor of his eyes render him attractive above all other young men,. but the glory of his hair, its richness and abundance, and the magnificent masses in which it falls over his shoulders and breast, fills every beholder with wonder and admiration. He is proportionably vain thereof. Daily his Nubian servants comb out his long tresses, anoint it with fragrant oils of myrrh, cinnamon, and sweet spices, and training it to flow in luxuriant waves, powder it with dust of gold, which, in the sun's rays, lend to it a starry splendor.

At length finding that the common people were more and more disposed to favor him and flatter him, the graceful and beautiful prince became impatient of his confinement, and dispatched a messenger to his mentor, Joab, asking him to come and visit him.

To this request the aged warrior paid no regard, when the incensed young prince sent his servants to destroy some of the property of Joab which was near his own abode. Then Joab, when he was told of this outrage, went to the prince where he was held a prisoner in his house and remonstrated with him: Absalom answered:

"Behold! I sent unto thee to come hither that thou mayest go to my father, the king, who hath for fear of the people, lest they should think he overlooked too lightly the death of Amnon by my hand, kept me here as if I were a robber chief of the desert he had caught in his toils, and has held me here for show these two whole years to the curiosity of all the people of Jerusalem, as if I were a caged leopard. I sent for thee to bid thee go to my father and ask him why he hath brought me from the court of Talmai in Geshur of Syria? It would have been much better for me to have remained there still. If I am pardoned by the king, wherefore this continued banishment from his face? Have not three years' exile in Syria and two years shut up in this, my palace, been expression enough of the king's anger against me? Go, therefore, to the king, and let me come before him and see him face to face. If he has pardoned me, let me go in and out before him as aforetime! If he finds guilt in me still, and my blood is required, let him put me to death; for death is preferable to this suspense."

The veteran soldier, though angry with the prince for the injury he had done in setting fire to his fields, obeyed him and presented his petition before the king.

Rejoiced to have an intercessor for his erring and beloved son in so eminent a person as his general, King David gladly consented to the permission sought, and which he had long desired to grant, and at once sent for the prince! Joab brought to his father the seemingly penitent young man, who bowed himself in humble obeisance before him, even with his face to the ground, and asked his forgiveness for what he had done. The king was deeply moved at the sight of his son, whose face he had not seen for five years; and raising him up, he fell upon his neck and kissed him in token of complete reconciliation.

When Prince Absalom went forth again into the Court of the Palace he was hailed by the soldiers with acclamations; and as he rode along upon a superb charger, the handsomest rider and most courteous and elegant-looking man in the kingdom, he could with difficulty make his way through the streets back to his house for the crowds of rejoicing citizens, chiefly of the lower class, who filled the air with cries of " Long live Absalom! Long live the Prince of Jerusalem!"

TABLET.—SIXTH LEAF.

Since I wrote the last leaf of my journal, dear father, important events have occurred, the narration of which will amaze you and cause you deep grief. King David is at this moment a fugitive from Jerusalem, an exile from his throne, fleeing from his rebellious son, Prince Absalom.

This unprincipled young man's vanity and ambition had been kindled by the flattering reception he had met with by the populace, and he harbored the idea of wearing a crown. To this arrogant presumption he was prompted by a subtle courtier, who had been his adviser and tempter in his crime, and encouraged in by the deep and artful policy of Ahithophel, the Prime Minister of David. Having firmly opposed his reconciliation with the prince, when therefore the king took Absalom back to his heart and confidence, the pride of Ahithophel, at this rejection of his wise counsel, was deeply wounded. The long-existing regard he had entertained for his monarch was in a moment destroyed. He resolved to avenge this conduct of David; for a king's counselor can be offended in no manner so grievously as by the rejection of his counsels. Courtiers are bound to monarchs only by ties of selfish aggrandizement and personal ambition. Their power consists in having power over the king. They rule by him! Ahithophel, from the hour of the reconciliation, saw that his power was gone; and that Absalom would henceforth become his father's adviser and confidant.

Mephibosheth, whose penetration and subtlety fathomed all the policy and secrets of the court, was not long in discovering this alienation. He sought an interview with Ahithophel, and insidiously fanned the spark of disloyalty; and watching his moment, he said:

"Hast thou heard that the prince has secret aspirations to reign over Israel and sever the crown, leaving Judah, as of old, only to his father? He has been for the last year stealing the hearts of the people. He has prepared horses and chariots, and fifty men to run before him. He is the most popular person in the kingdom at this moment. All eyes are fixed upon the rising star!"

The seed was dropped in a congenial soil. That night Ahithophel secretly sought the house of Prince Absalom, and from that hour was born the unnatural conspiracy which has driven the king from his throne. The ambitious prince kept secret his purpose in his own breast, and in the hearts of his counselors. He took great state upon him, rode forth from the gates and from town to town royally attended, drawing the eyes and admiration of all people unto him. He stood in the gate of the palace, and in the door of the Hall of Judgment, granting all petitions without referring them to the king, and suffering the guilty to go without judgment. The splendor of his manly beauty, the grace of his speech, the condescending courtesy with which he received and addressed the meanest citizens, won all hearts; while the unthinking populace were carried away by a show of royal equipage, such as King David had never indulged in, and which resembled the magnificence of the courts of Egypt and Phœnicia.

One day, he king being ill, Absalom sat upon his Judgment seat. He decided all cases so agreeably that, when the people applauded, he could not refrain from saying as he left the hall, and they were crowded near him to behold him:

"Oh, that I were made judge in the land, that every man which hath any suit or cause might come unto me, and I would do him justice!"

If any approached him to make obeisance, he graciously prevented him, and with his captivating smile put forth his hand, or embraced or kissed him, as if he greatly loved and honored him, although the person might be the meanest man in Jerusalem; so artfully did the counsels of the politic and wicked Ahithophel guide him in his pathway to popularity and power.

The indulgent king took no notice of this, and believing he sought only the honor and glory of his reign he let him, cunningly and by flattering words, alienate the hearts of Israel from their lawful allegiance. Some he won by his beauty and gallant bearing; some by his courtesy and civility; others he carried with him by magnificent promises; and others by his boasts of what noble acts for the glory of the empire he would do if he were king.

The king who for nearly forty years had reigned over Israel and Judah, and believed himself immovably fixed upon his throne, was not disturbed by these demonstrations of rebellion against his power, if, as is doubtful, the proceedings of the prince were all made known to him. The indisposition of the king continuing probably prevented his full knowledge of what was passing so deeply affecting his power and happiness, and at the same time gave the rebel prince full opportunity to perfect his plans.

At length his conspiracy being matured, and confident that he had enough of the people with him, the treacherous prince presented himself in the sick chamber of his father, where Queen Bathsheba sat by him, and his son Solomon, a prince in his eighth or ninth year, was waving above his head a fan of gorgeous Indian feathers.

During the whole time in which he was secretly plotting to dismember his father's united kingdoms he had not ceased daily to appear before him and outwardly manifest the conduct of a dutiful son. The Prince Counselor Ahithophel, concealing his revengeful feelings, also, as before, held his place by the throne, and when David would express any misgivings as to the state in which his son was living he would artfully put them to rest.

"My royal and beloved father and honored king," said Absalom, after kneeling and kissing his hand, "I pray thee let me go and pay my vow, which I have vowed unto the Lord, in Hebron, where I was born, and where Abraham and our fathers sacrificed: for while I was in Syria an exile I vowed a vow, saying, 'If the Lord shall bring me again to Jerusalem, then will I serve the Lord in Hebron!'"

The king, gratified at this show of piety, blessed him and let him depart. Leaving the room with a courtly bow of homage to the queen, and a word of kindness to the little Prince Solomon, who affectionately came up to bid him good-by, he departed.

The same day Absalom left Jerusalem at the head of two hundred chief men of the city, and of the king's officers, who suspected no wrong, supposing he was to return upon sacrificing to the Lord. Abiathar also went with him. After sacrificing, he took possession of the gates and of the fortress, and of the ancient palace of Saul, and where once dwelt his father, King David. Here he raised the standard of rebellion, for hundreds flocked to him, sent for Ahithophel to join him, and dispatched messengers throughout all the tribes of Israel, calling upon the people, saying, "As soon as ye hear the sound of trumpets blowing from citadel to citadel, know that Absalom reigneth in Hebron, and let every man say, 'Long live the King of Israel: Long live Absalom!'"

When the news came to the ears of King David, in Jerusalem, that Absalom had taken up the fallen crown of Ishbosheth, and had been crowned, even by Abiathar, King of Israel, with Hebron for his capital, and that Ahithophel was his Prime Counselor, and that the people increased continually with Absalom, and that many of the elders, and chief men, and warriors had declared for him, he rent his clothes and humbled himself before the Lord in the door of the Tabernacle, saying:

"Thou hast laid me in the lowest pit, in darkness and in the deeps. My sins have taken such hold upon me that I cannot look up. Thy wrath lieth hard upon me! Thou hast afflicted me with all thy waves. O turn not away thy face from thine anointed; for thou, O Lord, hast said thou wilt establish the throne of thy servant David forever!"

While he was yet humbling himself before the Lord Joab came near, in full armor, crying:

"Wherefore, O king, dost thou delay! Up and escape! for

some of the chief men who went with Absalom have fled from him hither, and say that he gathereth a mighty army, and will march against thee! Fall not into his hands, and into the hands of Ahithophel, for they will put thee to death, and reign over Judah also!"

The voice of the veteran warrior fell like the peal of a trumpet upon the ears of King David. He rose and called for his armor, and put it on; and consulted with Joab, who advised speedy flight, as there was not time to provision the city to stand a siege; and, moreover, so extensive was the conspiracy among the soldiers he said he knew not whom to trust.

That night King David left his palace, and with all his household departed on foot from the city which he could not defend. The queen and Prince Solomon walked by his side. His other wives remained behind, preferring rather to trust to the favor of Absalom than endure the perils of the desert. Abigail, the widow of Nabal, no longer lived. The city of Jerusalem that night became a scene of woe and terror. The streets were thronged with alarmed people, not knowing in what direction safety lay; some crying that it was best to remain and trust to the prince; and others, that security was with the king, as he was God's anointed. Thousands flocked after the fugitive monarch all night, while the most part remained and shut themselves up in their houses awaiting events. The garrison almost to a man shouted for Prince Absalom! The royal bodyguard of Cherithite archers, and the cross-bowmen of Peleth, and the six hundred tower-guards of Philistines of Gath, who served him for pay, and whom Ittai, a son of King Achish, commanded (for Philistia now belonged to David), were all the soldiers which accompanied him. This noble Ittai followed the king from affection, for when David was an exile in his father's court at Gath he was a lad of twelve, and became greatly attached to him; and after Philistia became tributary to him, Ittai, from his ancient regard and affection, came with six hundred men and offered himself and them for the king's service. Ittai now voluntarily accompanied his royal master in his misfortunes; and David was deeply moved that foreigners should thus show their attachment to him when his own countrymen deserted him. Abiathar, who had returned from Hebron, Absalom fearing to detain a priest of God, ordered the Ark of the Covenant to follow the king over the brook Kedron, beyond the city, that the Oracle of God might be with him in his flight.

When the king beheld the Ark, he kindly commanded them to carry it back again and place it within the Tabernacle, God's own habitation, saying humbly, "If the Lord will favor me, he can do so from thence, and bring me back again to worship there before His Mercy-seat. If he delight not in me, lo, I am before Him, let Him do what seemeth good unto Him."

The unhappy monarch, whose wonderful life of vicissitudes presents one of the most extraordinary chapters of human history, sending his people eastward over the brook in the valley, followed himself. As he ascended Mount Olivet he turned back and, gazing upon the city, the towers of which the morning sun was just illuming with golden light, tears coursed down his aged and chastened cheeks. Hiding his head in his mantle, he proceeded barefoot, followed by a mourning and weeping concourse.

At the top of the hill his ancient friend and officer Hushai, who had gone unwittingly with Absalom to Hebron, not knowing anything of the rebellious son's designs, met him, having just escaped from the prince. The two friends embraced, and Hushai said, "Knowest thou, O king, I left Ahithophel with Absalom in Hebron, giving him counsel?"

"I know it, O my friend. Let the Lord, whose servant I am, turn the counsel of Ahithophel into foolishness!" He then said to his friend, "If thou goest with me, thou wilt be a burden to me; for what can I do with all these? Return to Jerusalem. Stay there and learn all things that pass there, and in the palace, and send me word privately by the faithful sons of Abiathar and Zadok, the chief priests. It is necessary I have such a friend in the city."

While the king was hastening onward with his melancholy army of fugitives, consisting mainly of women and children, and the halt and invalid, and old men, besides his soldiers before mentioned, he was met by Ziba, the old servant of Saul, who, you recollect, brought Prince Jonathan's son, Mephibosheth, many years ago to Jerusalem, and whom David made the steward of Saul's estate, which he had generously bestowed upon the son of his friend. This wily old man, who had grown rich in farming the possessions of Mephibosheth, now brought to the wearied and famished king a present of bread, raisins, dried fruits, and wine laden upon asses, saying:

"Live forever, O king; thy servant hath brought these asses for thy wife, Bathsheba, and the young Prince Solomon to ride on, and fruit and provision for thy soldiers, and wine for such as be faint in the wilderness."

"Where is thy master's son, Mephibosheth? I have not seen him these three days! Sent he thee hither with these gifts?"

"The grandson of Saul abideth in Jerusalem," answered Ziba; "for I heard that he said yesterday, when my lord the king fled, 'To-day shall the House of Israel restore me the kingdom of my father Jonathan!'"

Behold, my dear father, the subtlety of this prince, who for so many years had eaten the king's bread, and whom he enriched. When David heard this he said bitterly:

"Yea, mine own familiar friend, in whom I trusted, which did eat of my bread, hath lifted up his heel against me. But the Lord will be merciful to me, and raise me up that I may requite them who rise up against me. When I return to my throne, O Ziba, for this day's kindness to a fallen king thou shalt have all that appertaineth to Mephibosheth. There shall not be left a place for his burial in the lands of his father I gave him! All shall be thine!"

A little farther on the king passed the habitation of a man named Shimei, who was a kinsman to King Saul; and seeing David's low estate he cast stones at him from the top of his house, and then came forth and cursed him, and all with him, shouting aloud and rejoicing in his fall, saying:

"Come out, come out of Jerusalem, thou bloody man, thou man of Belial! Lo, the Lord hath returned upon thee all the blood of the House of Saul, in whose stead thou hast reigned, and the Lord hath delivered the kingdom into the hand of Absalom, thy son!"

Then Abishai, the friend of the king and brother of Joab, who, you remember, my father, joined David forty years ago in his exile near Mount Carmel, cried in great wrath: "Let me, O king, take off this dog's head who curseth my lord the king!" Joab also drew his sword to slay him.

"Nay, Abishai—nay, Joab—ye sons of Zeruiah! Let him curse on! The Lord hath sent him, and commanded him, 'Curse David!' God knoweth what my hand hath done! What marvel that this Benjamite curses me, when my own son seeks to take my life! Let him alone, and let him curse! It may be that the Lord, seeing my humility and patience under this man's cursing, will requite me good for it!"

Such, my dear father, is the present aspect of affairs at this

moment, David being now three days gone out of the city and
encamped at Bahurim. I am still remaining in the city,
though my heart is with the king; but by his counsel I have
remained behind. Hushai is at the same house with me. What
the issue of all will be I know not. The whole capital is in a
state of confusion and excitement. The soldiers hold all the
strong places and gates for the rebel prince. Their commander
is no less a person than Mephibosheth, who secretly governs
the whole city, as if for Absalom, though he does not render
himself visible. But he is unquestionably the master spirit!
He plays a deep game. If Absalom enter Jerusalem, it will be
to fall by the dagger, or by poison; for this grandson of Saul
means, says Hushai (who is pretending to be his friend and
the adherent of Absalom, in order to counterwork the intrigues
of the crafty Ahithophel), to make the vain prince the stepping-
stone to the throne of his father.

TABLET.—LEAF SEVEN.

Many weeks have passed, my dear father, since I last took
up my pen. I will briefly record the events. Scarcely had the
king's party crossed the brook Kedron ere Absalom at the
head of a large army encamped at Bethlehem, and the next
morning, followed by thousands of the baser sort, entered
Jerusalem in triumph. He was proclaimed king as he entered
the court of his father's palace, and received the homage of the
chief men and of the soldiers. He even compelled Abiathar's
son to anoint him. Among the eminent men who approached
him was Hushai, the sage and learned Archite, who, bowing
down before him, said, " God save the king, God save the king! "
meaning in his heart King David.

"What! lord Hushai, art thou remaining? Is this thy kindness to thy friend whom thou fleddest from Hebron doubtless to
join? Why wentest thou not with thy friend David, my
father?"

"Nay," answered the Archite respectfully but subtilely, " but
whom the Lord and this people and all the men of Israel choose,
his will I be, and with him will I abide. If I have served in the
father's presence, shall I not serve in the presence of the son?"

These words gave Absalom confidence in him, and he gladly
received him into his counsels with Ahithophel, and said:

"Counsel ye together, and advise me what I shall now do."

Ahithophel, fearing a reconciliation might ultimately take place, advised Absalom to take to wife the fairest of his father's foreign wives, whom he had left behind, knowing such a step would forever remain unpardoned by the king. Absalom yielded to the dangerous counsel, which Hushai however firmly opposed. Ahithophel also counseled the usurper to choose twelve thousand men and give him the command of them, saying, " I will go forth and pursue David, and will presently come upon him while he is weary and weak-handed, and his men will flee, and I will smite the king only to put him to death, and then all Israel will submit to *thee* as king; for there is none else! "

Absalom was well-pleased with this advice, but sent for Hushai to learn his opinion.

" What sayest thou, O Hushai ? " asked Absalom; " for art thou not also one of my counselors ? Ahithophel adviseth me to pursue the king with all possible haste, ere he strengthen himself with an army. Shall I do as he counsels ? If not, what sayest thou ? "

" The counsel Ahithophel has given thee is not good," boldly replied the Archite. " Thou knowest thy father and his men with him are all mighty men of valor ! Who so brave as these Pelethites and these men of Cherith ? and who can contend with the lion-like Ittai and his formidable Gittites, when they are chafed and sore with being driven away ! Like a bear robbed of her whelps, they will, if pressed, turn at bay. Thy father, though gray-headed, is a man of war of old, as thou knowest, and his experience, too, is such that he will not be found by thee lodged in his camp, for he will fear treachery; but will retire by night into some secret place. Be sure he will conceal himself from all assassins ! Wait and gather the thousands of Israel together for the field, lest if thy men are defeated by Joab, there will be a cry, ' Absalom's people are slain,' and it go against thee and thy cause. Venture not a battle until thou art sure of victory. I counsel thee to take the field in thine own person at the head of thine army, and then shall ye overpower him and his, and if he be driven to a city ye can surround it and take it and all within it. Ahithophel's counsel is not good ! He and his twelve thousand men, if they go out, will be utterly destroyed by Joab and the king, who are like lions."

" The counsel of Hushai is good—wiser than the counsel of Ahithophel," answered Absalom, and also the elders of Israel;

and his courtiers, and officers agreed with him, even as they had before agreed with him when the counsel of Ahithophel pleased him.

Hushai then sent the sons of the priests secretly to warn David not to delay crossing the Jordan, lest the counsels of Ahithophel might yet prevail with the prince, and he be destroyed. The next night David crossed the river Jordan with all his followers, and sought refuge in the city of Mahanaim, where Prince Ishbosheth formerly dwelt, and lodged in the palace in which he was slain by the two brothers.

When Ahithophel heard of the interview which the prince held with the Archite, and that messengers had been sent to David, warning him of his own counsel, he saw at once that his power at the rebel court was gone; and that he was in peril, not only from the fickle temper of his new master, but from the diplomacy of the sagacious Archite who held his ear. The experienced diplomat knew enough of the custom of courts to be aware that a disgraced counselor is regarded by the crown as a foe. Anticipating, therefore, each moment his arrest, he fled from the palace and hastened to his own house. Here he shut himself up and surveyed his position! He saw that if Absalom ultimately ruled Israel he would put him to death; and that if David got the better of Absalom he would not suffer him to live after so treacherously betraying him. These reflections, united to the bitter idea that his rival's counsels should be preferred to his own, maddened with vexation and anger at his defeat, his passions and anguish of mind increased by wounded pride (for he was a man as haughty as he was sagacious), in a moment of fierce despair at his certain disgrace he resolved to destroy himself. This determination fixed, he set his house in order, wrote letters to the king and prince, and to others, and, just as the day dawned, he hanged himself with the cords of the curtain of his sumptuous couch.

When news was brought Absalom of this tragic termination of the career of one of the most distinguished statesmen, wisest counselors, and profoundest diplomatists that ever stood before a monarch, he expressed his surprise by a mere interjection of regret, and ordered him to be buried in the sepulcher of his fathers!

King David now organized his forces, and numbering all who were with him, found he had many thousands, both of men of Israel and Judah; for great companies soon flocked to him at

Mahanaim from all the tribes of the kingdom, while the elders and chief people beyond Jordan supplied him with all manner of camp-equipage, clothing, and provisions. Absalom in the meanwhile levied a vast army, and at the head of it marched from Jerusalem to give battle to the king, his father. Crossing the Jordan at the ford of Jericho he pitched his camp over against the strong city of Mahanaim, where the king was fortified. David's army was divided into three divisions, under the command of Joab, Abishai his brother (the same who went with David to Saul's tent and took away the cruse of oil and spear), and Ittai, the brave Philistine chief. When they were arrayed for battle, the king would have placed himself at the head of his hosts, but the army effectively refused to suffer him to expose himself, saying:

"Thou shalt not go forth, for if we are defeated they will not pursue us, for it is the king they seek! Thou art worth ten thousand of us. Therefore, remain in the city. If we are beaten, thou canst raise another army. If thou art taken, then all is lost, though none of us die!"

"That which seemeth to you best, O my children, I will do," said the aged king.

He then stood by the city gate and saw them all march out by hundreds and thousands. When the whole army had gone forth into the plain, the king called the three generals, Joab, now nearly threescore years and ten, Abishai, a few years his junior, and Ittai, who was about fifty-five.

"Go forth, my brave captains, and fight the battle of the Lord. And may the Lord of hosts and God of battles be with your arms! But I charge you, and all of your captains, and all the people, that ye deal gently, for my sake, with the young man, even with Absalom!"

How beautiful, my dear father, this charge to his warriors! How tenderly the kingly old man felt for the rebel prince, his son, who had driven him from his throne! What an exalted spirit of forgiveness! What a lovely illustration of that parental affection which no ingratitude or evil can wholly destroy. "Deal gently for my sake with Absalom." These few words alone are almost sufficient to redeem the past errors of the exiled king. The armies met at the end of the plain, by the forest of Ephraim, and before noon the battle began! For several hours the hosts of Israel, under Absalom, got the advantage against Abishai and Ittai and their thousands, but when Joab came up with his reserved division, the troops of the prince, under the immediate command of the renowned Amasa, his general, gave way and fled in all directions, but most of them seeking shelter in the wood in their rear. Thousands fell on the plain, and more still amid the trees of the forest by the swords of the pursuing soldiers of David. Absalom, seeing that the day was wholly lost, to save his life, fled; and in escaping rode swiftly beneath the branches of an oak of the forest, one of which caught him by the long hair and lifted him from his saddle, leaving him suspended thereby a few feet above the ground.

Joab, in full pursuit through the dark avenues of the oaks after Absalom, passed him unseen on one side of the wood, when a soldier cried:

"Behold, my lord, I saw the king's son, Absalom, caught in a tree by the head!"

"Why didst thou not smite him there to the ground?" cried the old warrior fiercely. "I would have given thee ten shekels of silver and a golden girdle for thy sword!"

"Though I should receive a thousand shekels in mine hand, yet would I not slay the king's son," answered the man of Judah; "for in my hearing the king charged thee, and Abishai, and Ittai, to deal gently with the young man Absalom, and harm him not! If I had slain him against the king's word, even thou, O my lord, wouldst have put me to death!"

"I may not linger here! Where sawest thou the prince?" demanded the hoary-headed old man.

When the soldier had pointed out to him the oak on the other side of the forest, Joab left him, and in a few minutes coming to the spot, beheld the prince hanging in the tree, entangled partly by his long hair, and partly by the arched crest of his helmet that caught in the fork of the branch and held him. With his sword the wretched young man had already cut off a great quantity of his idolized locks, in a vain effort to disengage himself; but the throat chain of the helmet nearly suffocated him, and he would have strangled and died there ere many hours. When Joab came up, he cried:

"So thou art at last in my power, O disturber of Israel and of Judah! This day thou shalt die for thy father's peace, and mine own revenge! for I have not forgotten the injury thou didst me in burning my field! But for this private revenge I might spare thee, boy, as the king, thy father, bade me deal gently with thee; but he who crosses the path of Joab of Zeruiah, to injure him, surely dies! Thou rememberest Abner! Likewise shalt thou perish."

The dying prince essayed to speak, but could not; but his eyes revealed his terror and anguish, as he saw the tall, stern-visaged, white-haired warrior step back a few paces and level one of three javelins which he held in his hand at his heart. As it flew on its errand of death through the whizzing air, Absalom uttered a wild, apprehensive cry of horror, which was stopped by the cleaving barb entering his heart. Another and another dart followed, and the hapless rebel hung writhing beneath the oak. Ten young men of Joab's bodyguard coming up at the instant, cried out, "Let us bear the blame also of his death," and thrust their javelins through his body and slew him.

Joab gazed for a few moments on the lifeless body, and then commanded his trumpeter to sound the recall, which from bugle to bugle echoed far and wide through the vast wood; for he wished to spare the lives of the people, who, now that Absalom was dead, had no cause of battle with each other. Thus in the very act of killing the prince he had humanely and generously a thought for the lives of the multitude, who, all of one blood, had been brought into this civil war by his rebellion. When the army of David, hearing the retreat sounded, stopped the pursuit and returned, Joab commanded that no one should that day go to the king to carry news of the war, because on the day of so great a victory he did not wish bad news to go to him. "For," said he, "the king's son is dead!" The next day, however, two messengers were sent to Mahanaim by Joab—Cushi and Ahimaaz.

The king sat between the inner and outer gate of the city, which looked towards Ephraim, waiting, like Eli of old, for news from the battle. At length the watchman, who ever stands over the city gate, reported that he saw a man running alone across the plain towards the city.

"If he be alone, there is tidings in his mouth," said the king; and he arose and saw him coming on apace and drawing near.

"Lo, my lord the king!" cried the watchman; "behold, another man runneth alone."

"He also bringeth tidings," said King David.

And the watchman said, "Methinketh the running of the foremost is like the running of Ahimaaz, the son of Zadok." And the king said, "He is a good man and cometh with good tidings." And Ahimaaz called, and said unto the king, "All is well." And he fell down to the earth upon his face before the king, and said, " Blessed be the Lord thy God, which hath delivered up the men that lifted up their hand against my lord the king." And the king said, "Is the young man Absalom safe?" And Ahimaaz answered, "When Joab sent the king's servant, and me thy servant, I saw a great tumult, but I knew not what it was." And the king said unto him, "Turn aside, and stand here." And he turned aside, and stood still. And behold, Cushi came; and Cushi said, " Tidings, my lord the king: for the Lord hath avenged thee this day of all them that rose up against thee." And the king said unto Cushi, " Is the young man Absalom safe?" And Cushi answered, " The enemies of my lord the king, and all that rise against thee to do thee hurt, be as that young man is."

And the king was much moved, and went up to the chamber over the gate, and wept; and as he went, thus he said, " O my son Absalom! my son, my son Absalom! would God I had died for thee, O Absalom, my son, my son! "

No words can be more touching, no language of passionate grief so affecting as this. When he was going up to his chamber he refused to let anyone follow him, and was heard bemoaning his son as he went, until his voice was hushed in the distant recesses of his apartments.

This depth of paternal affection has no parallel. How it exalts the character of the father and king in our esteem! There is a sublimity in such grief which commands our admiration and awakens our sympathies. The victory could not be celebrated on such a day of mourning, and all the people stood in amazed groups and talked of the king's great grief for his son. When the conquerors returned and heard at the gate how the king wept for Absalom, they hushed their shouts of victory and gat them by stealth into the city, more like soldiers who have lost a battle and are fleeing away ashamed, than conquerors.

When they passed the palace and heard through the distant windows the king's cry: " O my son Absalom, O Absalom, my son, my son! " they feared to be seen, and in silence and mortification sought their garrisons.

When Joab came and heard all this he was very highly displeased, and went abruptly to the king and said:

" Thou hast shamed this day the faces of all thy servants,

which this day have saved thy life, and the lives of thy sons, and of thy daughters, and the lives of thy wives, and the lives of thy concubines: in that thou lovest thine enemies, and hatest thy friends: for thou hast declared this day that thou regardest neither princes nor servants: for this day I perceive that if Absalom had lived and all we had died this day, then it had pleased thee well. Now, therefore, arise, go forth, and speak comfortably unto thy servants: for I swear by the Lord, if thou go not forth, there will not tarry one with thee this night: and that will be worse unto thee than all the evil that befell thee from thy youth until now." Then the king arose, and sat in the gate. And they told unto all the people, saying, "Behold, the king doth sit in the gate."

When the army heard that the king had made his appearance, their chief men and captains came before him, and were received by him with kind and commending words upon their devotion to his crown, and praised for their valor in battle.

The next day David, seeing that he was now absolute king again, prepared to return to his capital. The Israelites who had followed Absalom now vied with the people of Judah for the honor of escorting the king and bringing him back to Jerusalem; and were so zealous to repair their fault and honor him, that they would have had all the glory of his restoration if word had not been sent to Jerusalem that, unless the friends of David came forth to meet him, Israel, with its armies, would alone bring the king back to his throne. But the rebellious people of Jerusalem were doubtful as to their treatment by King David, and hesitated what to do, fearing his vengeance if he came to them, and equally his justice if they marched to meet him. Abiathar, the priest, however, assured them of David's pardon to all in Jerusalem, and that he would ask no questions of any man whether he had gone with Absalom or not. Then the whole army of Judah, headed by the elders and Abiathar, sent word to David, saying: "Return, O king, to thy throne, thou and all with thee!"

Without waiting for the monarch's arrival, they marched out, and hastened to Gilgal, near Jericho, to meet and receive him when he should come over the Jordan. David in the meanwhile was waiting in Mahanaim for the late army of Absalom to assemble to escort him back, but hoping Judah would move for this purpose before they could come together. When, therefore, a messenger came to him that all Jerusalem, with the royal banner in advance, was coming towards Jericho to receive him, he at once left the city with all his people and with a thousand Israelites under the command of Amasa, Absalom's late general, whom he had pardoned and received into his favor. It was this Amasa, David's nephew, who accompanied King Saul and Doeg on the visit of that monarch to the sorceress in Endor. He had subsequently been a soldier under Ishbosheth, and had recently been made general of the army of his rebel cousin, Prince Absalom.

The returning king was received at the fords of Jordan by the people of Judah, and escorted in great triumph back to Jersualem. On his way thither the Shimei who had stoned him now fell in abject humility (for what will not a base man give for his life?) at the feet of the king, and asked his forgiveness. The king answered: "No man shall be put to death this day of rejoicing. Thou shalt not die." Thus he began by mercy and clemency to re-establish his throne.

Ziba also was in the returning king's army, even having crossed the Jordan to meet and join him. As the triumphant thousands of Judah came to the top of Mount Olivet, and David thence beheld the city, he stopped and gave praise to God with all his people, for being permitted once more to behold the walls of Zion in peace. This eminence, which a few weeks before had been ascended by him in tears and barefooted, and with his head covered in shame, he now descended with the glory and state of a conquering monarch, the people shouting " Hosannas " before him, strewing flowers in his path, and laying tapestry and their most gorgeous robes along the way, for his steed to tread upon!

Thus the King of the Hebrews returned to his capital, and was once more seated upon his throne. His wives and concubines, which the rebel prince, in taking his father's crown, had taken as his own (thus fulfilling the prophecy of Nathan, that David's wives should be given to another), the king refused to see, but placed them in a separate house to be secluded for life from all eyes. The seventh day after his return, as the king sat on the Throne of Judgment, hearing long delayed cases, the Prince Mephibosheth came and stood before him. His beard and hair were long and undressed, his apparel mean and rent, and his whole aspect one of outward humiliation. Abishai, whom David had placed over his guard instead of Joab (whom the king had forbidden his presence since the slaying of

Absalom), not knowing him in his present wretched aspect, would have led him out of the hall.

"Nay," said the king, "take no man forth. I give judgment and justice to all men in Israel and Judah. Is not this Mephibosheth? Whence comest thou to me, and so long in coming?" he asked sternly.

"From Bethel, the house of my fathers, O king," he answered, "whither I went after Absalom took the city; for my heart was not with the young man, but with the king!"

"Wherefore then wentest thou not with me at the first?" asked David. "I heard words of thine repeated in mine ears, which were offensive to me and were worthy of death!"

"The tale told thee by my wicked servant Ziba, O king, deceived thee," answered he humbly and deprecatingly; "I would have followed thee; but thou knowest I could not on foot. I ordered my servant Ziba to saddle me an ass that I might ride thereon after my lord the king; and lo, he took two asses and laded them and deceived me, and in his own name went after thee to find favor in thine eye, and hath slandered thy servant unto my lord, the king, that he might get my estates. Let my lord the king discern, with the divine wisdom God hath given thee as a judge, between truth and falsehood in the thing. Here before thy throne of judgment, O king, I submit to thy judgment, and trust to thy mercy; for all my father's house were but dead men before thee, and yet thou didst set me at thy table. What right have I to claim anything more at the hands of the king? Mercy and justice are all I ask." Thus spake Mephibosheth, Jonathan's son, before the friend of Jonathan.

When David had regarded his abject appearance and saw the tears of humility drop down upon his neglected beard, there was evidently a struggle in his mind how to decide. Already he had given judgment against him by giving all he had to Ziba. Ziba was not present to make any defense. That Mephibosheth was wholly innocent of having favored Absalom, and looked to the restoration of the crown of Saul in himself, he was not fully assured. But he had resolved that mercy should illustrate his restoration, and as he had by public proclamation pardoned all who had followed the misguided prince in his rebellion, he could not withhold pardon from the son of his friend, even though he were guilty of treason. He therefore answered him and said:

"What thou hast done or spoken I ask not to hear, Mephibosheth. Ziba is not in Jerusalem to answer. My former grant and decree shall stand for thy father's sake; which was, that the lands shall be thine, and thou shalt be lord over them, as hitherto; and Ziba shall divide with thee the income for the farming and stewardship thereof!"

The Israelites beyond Jordan, when at length they found the king had put himself under the escort of Judah, were very angry, and sent elders and chiefs to him, saying:

"Why have the men of Judah, our brethren, stolen thee away and brought thee over Jordan without us?"

"Because," David's counselors and chief captains answered them, "the king is nearer to us in blood than to you, being born in Bethlehem of Judah. Wherefore be ye angry, O men of Israel?"

"We have ten parts, we ten tribes of Israel, in the king, and have more right to David than you who have but two parts in him," the men from beyond Jordan replied. "Why then did ye despise us in not letting our advice and aid be had in bringing the king back?"

Thus speaking, the Israelite ambassadors departed from Jeruselem in great displeasure.

This feeling, so bitterly expressed, my dear father, increased and took form in open rebellion. Sheba, a relative of Saul, and a man of unscrupulous character, of great bravery, and an adventurer in arms, living by his sword in whatsoever king's service he could find employment, and who had been second in command in Absalom's army, next to Amasa, seeing this disaffection, resolved to avail himself of it to create a revolt against David. Gathering a few desperate followers, and joined by Adonijah, a brother of Absalom, he marched from town to town, sounding a trumpet before him and proclaiming:

"We have no part in David, neither have we inheritance in the son of Jesse! Every man to his tents, O Israel!"

This rallying cry was readily listened to by the disaffected men of Israel. This chief soon gathered a small army about him, and fortified himself in a city called Abel. Against him the king sent Amasa, with a large force to besiege it, associating with him in command Joab's brother, Abishai; for Joab was in disgrace. On the march, near Gibeon, Joab appeared and volunteered to serve under Amasa; but, observing his time, he ran his sword through his body while he was talking with him, and left him dead in the road. The bold warrior and assassin then, raising aloft his bloody sword, cried unto the army, "He that is on David's side and for Joab, let him follow Joab!"

The army, accustomed to the command of Joab, at once accepted him as their general. He soon besieged the citadel of Abel, when the citizens, at the suggestion of a woman, in order to prevent the destruction of their town, betrayed the revolutionary chief, Sheba, and cast his head over the wall to the leader of the hosts of Judah. Adonijah, the dissolute prince, was pardoned by Joab, with whom he was a favorite.

Thus this rebellion was crushed in its beginning, and Joab, returning a conqueror to Jerusalem, presented himself before the king with the audacity of a man who knows that his power as head of the army is too great and dangerous to the throne for the king to dare to displace him. This fierce and turbulent chief, this man of blood, is now general over all the hosts of Israel.

Thus, my dear father, is the king once more seated upon his throne; but the prestige of his ancient glory and power is gone! Sin, and crime, and degradation have lessened the love and honor of the people for one whom God anointed to be their example in all piety, chastity, justice, and truth. Deeply does he feel the loss of the confidence of his subjects, while he has no faith in the affection of those who stand about his throne. Fearing Joab he dare not offend him, but is compelled daily to endure the insolent presence of the old chief, whose hand is dyed with the blood of Absalom, his son. The days of the monarch are passed in efforts to administer the laws of God in his realm with fidelity, in educating his noble-looking son, Solomon, to be his successor, in works of religion, and in public acts of worship.

The excited state of the country during the past few months, dear father, has delayed my business in reference to the lands inherited by my royal mother; as the Court of Elders, which presides over the settlement of estates, has not held any session since the rebellion of Absalom. The king assures me that my affairs shall receive early attention, and that those persons, who have unlawfully during your long absence, taken possession of a portion of the wheat lands near Gilgal, will be ordered to restore them.

I shall therefore be ready soon to depart from Jerusalem for

Syria, and thence proceed homeward by the great caravan. You will be complimented to know that the king, hearing of the magnificence of your majesty's Assyrian palaces and Temples, is to send with me his chief architect to visit them, and draw plans * of the most beautiful and noble, in order to decide upon the style of the Temple,† for which he is preparing the materials, and which his son Solomon will erect. If the Hebrew prince should behold the palace of Ninus, my dear father, he would hardly fail to reproduce it, with that alteration and increased majesty which becomes the Palace of God, upon Mount Moriah. So vast is the accumulation of wealth, so abundant the gold and silver of Ophir and of Tarshish,‡ and precious stones from India, and fragrant and costly woods from Arabia and Lebanon, which are collected in the king's treasure house, that, without doubt, aided by the wondrous skill of the Tyrian artists, the Hebrews may present to the eyes of the world an edifice of the most extraordinary grandeur and beauty, the wonder of the whole earth.

Farewell, my dearest father and dearest mother, until I once more embrace you in your own Palace at Tadmor.

ISRILID.

* That Solomon subsequently built the Temple after Assyrian models, says an Oriental writer, is evident from the close resemblance of its style with the Assyrian Temples. Unquestionably, Assyria furnished the most ancient specimens of true art in architecture. Greece gathered as much from Assyria as from Egypt. Among the Assyrian remains is to be found the type of architecture which the Temple of Solomon developed. The recent production of a bas-relief, found in Nineveh, represents an Assyrian palace. It gives us Solomon's Temple as we may suppose it really was. The Jewish Temple was erected very nearly at the same time with the great palace at Nimroud, when the arts of the Assyrians had already attained their highest perfection. According to Josephus, Solomon "wainscotted the [walls of the House of the Forest of Lebanon] with stones that were sawed, and were of great value, such as are dug out of the earth for the ornament of Temples." The stones were sculptured, "representing all sorts of fruits and trees." The wall was "plastered over, and, as it were, wrought over with various colors and pictures." Nothing can be more Assyrian in its style and picturesqueness than this. The Persian kings of the Achæmenian dynasty built palaces at Persepolis, Ecbatana, and Susa, upon the Assyrian model: we may safely take it for granted that Solomon did the same thing when he erected the Temple at Jerusalem.

† *Vide* Appendix III.   ‡ *Vide* Appendix IV.

CONCLUSION.

The Throne of King David being now once more firmly established, and the king reinstated in all his former power and dignity, he decided to ascertain the number of his subjects, and know the extent and weight of his power and dominion. His chief motive was a desire to learn how large an army he could bring into the field; for he had conceived, it is believed, the ambitious idea of crowning his reign by the conquest of Egypt, and thereby wiping out the stain of the bondage of Israel therein, the memory of which still rankled in the hearts of the haughty Hebrews. The result gave 800,000 warriors in Israel and 500,000 in Judah, including all the conquered nations, a host altogether of 1,300,000 men able to bear arms.

To rebuke this pride and ambition the Prophet Gad was sent by the Lord from the wildernesses of Jordan, and came before the king to denounce what he had done as displeasing to Heaven. To punish him a pestilence was sent upon the kingdom, in which seventy thousand persons perished. An angel was also seen by night with his hand stretched forth over Jerusalem to destroy it, but the vengeance of God was stayed by a sacrifice of burnt-offerings * and peace-offerings upon an altar which David erected upon Mount Moriah, the site he had chosen for the proposed temple, and which was thereby solemnly consecrated by blood.

"The remaining years of David were spent in making the most costly preparations for the building of the temple, and in securing the succession to his son Solomon, to whom this great trust was to be bequeathed. As his time drew near, those evils began to display themselves which are inseparable from Oriental monarchies, where polygamy prevails; and where among children, from many wives, of different ranks, no certain rule of succession is established. Factions began to divide the

---

* This sacrifice of a lamb averted the anger of Jehovah, and saved Jerusalem. This was a figure of the sacrifice of the Lamb of God which averts the anger of Jehovah, and is the protection of the true Jerusalem, the Church. The manner of roasting the lamb upon the altar represented the affixing of a man to a cross.

army, the royal household, and even the priesthood. Adonijah, the brother of Absalom, supported by the turbulent Joab, and by Abiathar, the priest, assembled a large body of adherents, to crown him. When this intelligence was communicated to David, without the slightest delay he commanded Nathan, the prophet, and Zadok, the priest, with Benaiah, one of his most valiant captains, to take Solomon down to Gihon, to anoint and proclaim him king.

"The young king re-entered the city amid the loudest acclamations; the party of Adonijah, who were still at their feast, dispersed and fled. Adonijah took refuge at the altar; his life was spared. David after this success assembled first the great body of leading men in the state, and afterward called a more extensive and popular convention of the people, before whom he designated Solomon as his successor, commended to the zeal and piety of the people the building of the Temple, and received their contributions towards the great national work.

"As his death approached he strictly enjoined his son to adhere to the Mosaic laws and to the divine constitution. He recommended him to watch with a jealous eye the bold and restless Joab; a man who, however brave and faithful, was dangerous from his restless ambition, and from the savage unscrupulousness with which he shed the blood of his enemies. Abner and Amasa had both fallen by his hand, without warrant or authority from the king. Solomon, *according to his wisdom*, on the first appearance of treasonable intention was to put him to death without mercy.*

"Thus having provided for the security of the succession, the maintenance of the law, and the lasting dignity of the national religion, David breathed his last, having reigned forty years over the flourishing and powerful monarchy of which he may be considered the founder. He had succeeded to a kingdom distracted with civil dissension, environed on every side by powerful and victorious enemies, without a capital, almost without an army, without any bond of union between the tribes. He left a compact and united state, stretching from the frontier of Egypt to the foot of Lebanon, from the Euphrates to the sea. He had crushed the power of the Philistines, subdued or curbed all the adjacent kingdoms: he had formed a lasting and important alliance with the great city of Tyre. He had organized an immense disposable force: every month 24,000

* 1 Kings ii. 28-35.

men, furnished in rotation by the tribes, appeared in arms, and were trained as the standing militia of the country. At the head of his army were officers of consummate experience, and, what was more highly esteemed in the warfare of the time, extraordinary personal activity, strength, and valor. His heroes remind us of those of Arthur or Charlemagne, excepting that the armor of the feudal chieftains constituted the superiority; here main strength of body and dauntless fortitude of mind. The Hebrew nation owed the long peace of the son's reign to the bravery and wisdom of the father. If the rapidity with which a kingdom rises to unexampled prosperity, and the permanence, as far as human wisdom can provide, of that prosperity, be a fair criterion of the abilities and character of a sovereign, few kings in history can compete with David. His personal character has been often discussed; but both by his enemies, and even by some of his learned defenders, with an ignorance of, or inattention to, his age and country as melancholy as surprising. Both parties have been content to take the expression of the 'man after God's own heart,' in a strict and literal sense. Both have judged by modern European and Christian notions the chieftain of an Eastern and comparatively barbarous people. He had his harem, like other Eastern kings. He waged war, and revenged himself on his foreign enemies with merciless cruelty, like other warriors of his age and country. His one great crime violated the immutable and universal laws of morality, and therefore admits of no excuse. On the other hand his consummate personal bravery and military talent —his generosity to his enemies—his fidelity to his friends—his knowledge of, and steadfast attention to, the true interests of his country—his exalted piety and gratitude toward his God, justify the zealous and fervent attachment of the Jewish people to the memory of their great monarch.

"The three most eminent men in the Hebrew annals, Moses, David, and Solomon, were three of their most distinguished poets. The hymns of David excel no less in sublimity and tenderness of expression than in loftiness and purity of religious sentiment. In comparison with them the sacred poetry of all other nations sinks into mediocrity. They have embodied so exquisitely the universal language of religious emotion that (a few fierce and vindictive passages excepted, natural in the warrior poet of a sterner age) they have entered with unquestioned propriety into the ritual of the holier and more perfect religion of Christ. The songs which cheered the solitude of the desert caves of Engedi, or resounded from the voice of the Hebrew people, as they wound along the glens or the hillsides of Judea, have been repeated for ages in almost every part of the habitable world, in the remotest islands of the ocean, among the forests of America, on the sands of Africa. How many human hearts have they softened, purified, exalted!—of how many wretched beings have they been the secret consolation!— on how many communities have they drawn down the blessings of Divine Providence, by bringing the affections into unison with their deep devotional fervor.

"Solomon succeeded to the Hebrew kingdom at the age of twenty. He was environed by designing, bold, and dangerous enemies. He saw at once the wisdom of his father's dying admonition: he seized the opportunity of crushing all future opposition, and all danger of a civil war. He caused Adonijah to be put to death; suspended Abiathar from his office and banished him from Jerusalem: and though Joab fled to the altar, he commanded him to be slain, for the two murders of which he had been guilty, those of Abner and Amasa. Shimei, another dangerous character, was commanded to reside in Jerusalem, on pain of death if he should quit the city. Three years afterward he was detected in a suspicious journey to Gath, on the Philistine border; and having violated the compact he suffered the penalty. Thus secured by the policy of his father from internal enemies, by the terror of his victories from foreign invasion, Solomon commenced his peaceful reign, during which Judah and Israel dwelt safely, 'every man under his vine and under his fig tree, from Dan to Beersheba.' His justice was proverbial. Among his first acts after his succession, it is related that after a costly sacrifice at Gibeon, the place where the tabernacle remained, God had appeared to him in a dream, and offered him whatever gift he chose: the wise king had requested an understanding heart to judge the people. God not merely assented to his prayer, but added the gift of honor and riches. His judicial wisdom was displayed in the memorable history of the two women who contested the right to a child. Solomon, in the wild spirit of Oriental justice, commanded the infant to be divided before their faces: the heart of the real mother was struck with terror and abhorrence; while the false one consented to the horrible partition; and by this appeal to nature the cause was justly decided.

" The internal government of his extensive dominions next demanded the attention of Solomon. Besides the local and municipal governors, he divided the kingdom into twelve districts: over each of these he appointed a purveyor for the collection of the royal tribute, which was received in kind; and thus the growing capital and the immense establishments of Solomon were abundantly furnished with provisions. Each purveyor supplied the court for a month. The daily consumption of his household was 300 bushels of finer flour, 600 of a coarser sort; 10 fatted, 20 other oxen; 100 sheep; besides poultry and various kinds of venison. Provender was furnished for 40,000 horses and a great number of dromedaries. Yet the population of the country did not, at first at least, feel these burthens; ' Judah and Israel were many, as the sand which is by the sea in multitude, eating and drinking, and making merry.'

" The foreign treaties of Solomon were as wisely directed to secure the profound peace of his dominions. He entered into a matrimonial alliance with the royal family of Egypt, whose daughter he received with great magnificence; and he renewed the important alliance with the King of Tyre. The friendship of this monarch was of the highest value in contributing to the great royal and national work, the building of the Temple. The cedar timber could only be obtained from the forests of Lebanon: the Sidonian artisans were the most skillful workmen in every kind of manufacture, particularly in the precious metals. Solomon entered into a regular treaty, by which he bound himself to supply the Tyrians with large quantities of corn; receiving in return their timber, which was floated down to Joppa, and a large body of artificers. The timber was cut by his own subjects, of whom he raised a body of 30,000; 10,000 employed at a time, and relieving each other every month; so that to one month of labor they had two of rest. He raised two other corps, one of 70,000 porters of burthens; the other of 80,000 hewers of stone, who were employed in the quarries among the mountains. All these labors were thrown, not on the Israelites, but on the strangers who, chiefly of Canaanitish descent, had been permitted to inhabit the country. These preparations, in addition to those of King David, being completed, the work began. The eminence of Moriah, the Mount of Vision, i. e., the height seen afar from the adjacent country, which tradition pointed out as the spot where Abraham had offered his son, where recently the plague had been stayed by the altar built in the thrashing-floor of Ornan or Auraunah, the Jebusite, rose on the east side of the city. Its rugged top was leveled with immense labor; its sides, which to the east and south were precipitous, were faced with a wall of stone, built up perpendicular from the bottom of the valley, so as to appear to those who looked down of most terrific height; a work of prodigious skill and labor, as the immense stones were strongly mortised together and wedged into the rock. Around the whole area or esplanade, an irregular quadrangle, was a solid wall of considerable height and strength: within this was an open court, into which the Gentiles were either from the first or subsequently admitted. A second wall encompassed another quadrangle, called the court of the Israelites. Along this wall on the inside ran a portico or cloister, over which were chambers for different sacred purposes. Within this again another, probably a lower, wall separated the court of the priests from that of the Israelites. To each court the ascent was by steps, so that the platform of the inner court was on a higher level than that of the outer. The temple itself was rather a monument of the wealth than the architectural skill and science of the people. It was a wonder of the world, from the splendor of its materials." *

We now bring our illustrations of the extraordinary scenes in the life of a monarch whose whole career, from the hour of his consecration as an ingenuous young shepherd to his death as a venerable and penitent monarch, is without parallel in the history of kings. If there is romance discoverable in this book, it is not of the author's creation. Many of the narratives of the Scriptures are stories of the most strikingly romantic character, with surprises and positions which the genius of Scott could never have invented or conceived, from the story of Joseph down to that of Esther, the Queen. If the perusal of these illustrations of the days of Saul and of David sufficiently interest the reader, who has hitherto had but little knowledge of the Scriptures, and sends him to those sacred pages for instruction and comparison, the author's object will have been achieved.

The reader who is interested in the events presented to his attention in this volume is referred to the book of Joshua, the First and Second Books of Samuel, and the First Book of Kings for the chief sources from which the facts are drawn; and to the " History of the Jews," by Milman, and to Josephus,

* Milman's " History of the Jews."

Books v., vi., and vii. For an account of the building of the
Temple for which David collected in the closing years of his
reign the varied and costly materials, the reader is referred to
the Appendix at the close of the volume.

The royal line of the House of David continued under various vicissitudes and interruptions until the birth of the last
Prince of the Throne of Judah in his own native city, Bethlehem, according to the prophecy of Jacob: "The scepter shall
not depart from Judah, nor a Lawgiver from between his feet,
until Shiloh come."

Of whom it is prophetically written, "He shall be great, and
shall be called the Son of the Highest; and the Lord God shall
give him the Throne of his Father, David. And he shall reign
over the House of Jacob forever; and of his kingdom shall there
be no end."

Of whom David sung, striking his prophetic harp:

> "Thy throne, O God, is forever and ever:
> The scepter of thy kingdom is a right scepter.
> Thou lovest righteousness and hatest wickedness,
> Therefore God, thy God hath anointed thee
> With the oil of gladness above thy fellows.
> Instead of thy fathers, shall be thy children,
> Whom thou mayest make Princes in all the earth.
> Thou art fairer than the children of men,
>   Grace is poured into thy lips.
> Therefore God hath blessed THEE forever.
> In his days shall the righteous flourish,
> And abundance of peace so long as the moon endureth:
> He shall have dominion from sea to sea,
> And from the river unto the ends of the earth.
> For I have made a covenant with my chosen,
> I have sworn unto David, my servant,
> 'Thy SEED will I establish forever,
> And build up thy Throne unto all generations.'
> And the House of David shall be as God,
>   As the angel of the Lord before them;
> And I will pour upon the House of David,
>   And upon the inhabitants of Jerusalem,
> The Spirit of Grace and of supplications,
>   And they shall look upon ME whom they have pierced!"

And the inspired Apostle of the Apocalypse, seeing far beyond the earthly Jerusalem to the ends of the ages, writes of
the last Prince of the House of David:

> "The kingdoms of the world are become
> The kingdoms of our LORD and of his CHRIST;
> And he shall reign forever and ever."

APPENDIX.

APPENDIX I.

URIM AND THUMMIM.

The Pyramids and other stupendous structures on the Nile bear Masons' marks, as fresh as though chiseled yesterday. Similar traces have lately been discovered on the monuments of Nineveh and Babylon, that undoubtedly have reference to the Masonic mysteries, and, among them, to the Great and Occult Name. In regard to the " Book of the Dead," which in whole or part is contained in a papyrus roll laid up with the Egyptian mummy in the Sarcophagus, there are many symbols and names, probably Masonic, and more especially the name of Deity among the Egyptian writings, which may have an important bearing upon Masonic history. The explanation of the Urim and Thummim, the lights and perfections, and of the breastplate of Aaron, is remarkable. The initial letters of the Hebrew names of the twelve stones in that breastplate, and also of the twelve tribes (by the application of a key discovered by Lanci), conveyed a meaning which the exegesis of a learned linguist would never have reached. The explanation of the Urim is, " I will cause the oracular spirit to rise at my will "; of the Thummim, " And of the Seers it will manifest the secret "; and by putting the first two letters in Hebrew together, the ineffable name is made out.

APPENDIX II.

SOLOMON'S THRONE.

The following magnificent description of the " Throne of King David," which Solomon erected, is copied from an ancient Oriental manuscript:

" The sides of the throne were of pure gold, and the feet of it were of emeralds and pearls. The throne had seven steps. On each side were delineated orchards full of trees, the branches of which were of precious stones, representing ripe and unripe fruit. On the tops of the trees fowls of the most beautiful plumage were represented, and these were hollow within, and made to utter sounds of a thousand melodious tones. On the first step were vine branches with bunches of grapes, composed of precious stones, arranged in such a manner as to give the different colors of purple, violet, green, and red, so as to represent the fruit in its various stages from green to ripe. On the second step were two lions of pure gold, and terrible aspect, as large as life. The properties of the throne were such that when Solomon placed his foot on the first step all the birds spread their wings and made a fluttering noise in the air; on his touching the second step the lions extended their paws; on his reaching the third step the whole assembly repeated the name of the Deity. When he arrived at the fourth step voices were heard addressing him thus, ' Son of David, be grateful for the blessings the Almighty hath bestowed upon thee!' and the same was repeated on reaching the fifth step! On his touching the sixth step all the children sang praises! On his arrival at the seventh step the whole throne became in motion, and ceased not until he had taken his seat, when all the birds, lions, and animals, by secret springs, discharged a shower of the most precious perfume on the king, and two of the birds descended and placed a golden crown upon his head! Before the throne was a column of burnished gold, on the top of which was placed a golden dove, which had in its beak a roll bound in silver; in this roll were written the Psalms of David, and the dove having presented the roll to the king, he read a portion of it to the people of Israel. On the approach of a wicked person to the throne for judgment the lions would set up a terrible roaring and lash their tails; the birds began to erect their feathers, and the whole assembly set up such loud cries, that for fear of them, no person would dare be guilty of falsehood, but would instantly confess their crimes! Such was the Throne of Solomon."

APPENDIX III.

The following account of the building, by Solomon, of the Temple which King David so long desired to erect, and for

which he collected countless sums in gold and silver, is taken
from Josephus:

"When Hiram, King of Tyre, had heard that Solomon succeeded to his father's kingdom, he was very glad of it, for he
was a friend of David's. So he sent ambassadors to him, and
saluted him, and congratulated him on the present happy state
of his affairs. Upon which Solomon sent him an epistle, the
contents of which here follow:

" 'SOLOMON TO KING HIRAM.

" 'Know thou that my father would have built a temple to
God, but was hindered by wars, and continual expeditions: for
he did not leave off to overthrow his enemies till he made them
all subject to tribute. But I give thanks to God for the peace I
at present enjoy, and on that account I am at leisure, and design
to build a house to God, for God foretold to my father that
such a house should be built by me; wherefore I desire thee to
send some of thy subjects with mine to Mount Lebanon, to cut
down timber; for the Sidonians are more skillful than our
people in cutting of wood. As for wages to the hewers of wood,
I will pay whatsoever price thou shalt determine.'

"When Hiram had read this epistle, he was pleased with it,
and wrote back this answer to Solomon:

" 'HIRAM TO KING SOLOMON.

" 'It is fit to bless God, that he hath committed thy father's
government to thee, who art a wise man, and endowed with all
virtues. As for myself, I rejoice at the condition thou art in,
and will be subservient to thee in all that thou sendest to me
about; for when by my subjects I have cut down many and
large trees of cedar and cypress wood, I will send them to sea,
and will order my subjects to make floats of them, and to sail to
what place soever of thy country thou shalt desire, and leave
them there, after which thy subjects may carry them to Jerusalem: but do thou take care to procure us corn for this timber,
which we stand in need of, because we inhabit in an island.'

"The copies of these epistles remain at this day, and are preserved not only in our books, but among the Tyrians also; inso-

much that if anyone would know the certainty about them, he may desire the keepers of the public records of Tyre to show him them, and he will find what is there set down to agree with what we have said. I have said so much out of a desire that my readers may know that we speak nothing but the truth, and do not compose a history out of some plausible relations, which deceive men and please them at the same time, nor attempt to avoid examination, nor desire men to believe us immediately; nor are we at liberty to depart from speaking truth, which is the proper commendation of a historian, and yet to be blameless. But we insist upon no admission of what we say, unless we be able to manifest its truth by demonstration and the strongest vouchers.

"Now King Solomon, as soon as this epistle of the King of Tyre was brought him, commended the readiness and good-will he declared therein, and repaid him in what he desired, and sent him yearly twenty thousand cori of wheat, and as many baths of oil: now the bath is able to contain seventy-two sextaries. He also sent him the same measure of wine. So the friendship between Hiram and Solomon hereby increased more and more; and they swore to continue it forever. And the king appointed a tribute to be laid on all the people, of thirty thousand laborers whose work he rendered easy to them by prudently dividing it among them; for he made ten thousand cut timber in Mount Lebanon for one month, and then to come home; and to rest two months, until the time when the other twenty thousand had finished their task at the appointed time; and so afterwards it came to pass, that the first ten thousand returned to their work every fourth month; and it was Adoram who was over this tribute. There were also of the strangers who were left by David, who were to carry the stones and other materials, seventy thousand; and of those that cut the stones, eighty thousand. Of these three thousand and three hundred were rulers over the rest. He also enjoined them to cut out large stones for the foundations of the temple, and that they should fit them and unite them together in the mountain, and so bring them to the city. This was done, not only by our own country workmen, but by those workmen whom Hiram sent also."

APPENDIX IV.

TARSHISH.

It will not improbably add considerable interest to that already felt by outward-bound passengers in the Peninsular and Oriental steamers in their first glimpse of Indian land, to know that, according to the best authorities, Point de Galle is the Tarshish which was visited by the navies of Hiram and Solomon.

" Tarshish obviously lay in the road to Ophir, the land from which Solomon procured gold. Malacca was known to the later Greek geographers, as the Golden Chersonese; and in the Malay language, *ophir* is the generic term for a gold mine. King Solomon made a navy of ships in Eziongeber, ' which is beside Elath, on the shore of the Red Sea.' From Eziongeber, Solomon's navy traded with Tarshish and Ophir. ' Once in three years came the navy of Tarshish, bringing gold and silver, ivory, and apes, and peacocks.' In a Persian poem of the tenth century, which describes an expedition from Jerusalem to Ceylon, the outward voyage is stated as occupying a year and a half—a coincidence which would be valueless, if it were not for the regular limits imposed upon unscientific navigation in the Indian Seas by the recurrence of the monsoons. Gold could have been transshipped at the main port of Ceylon from the vessels which brought it from Ophir. ' Silver spread into plates,' which Jeremiah mentions as coming from Tarshish, is even yet in use as the materials of the sacred books of the Singhalese. Ivory was, of course, from the earliest times an export from Ceylon, and even more common formerly than now. Apes are indigenous to the island, and peafowl abound there. It is curious that the very terms by which these three latter articles of commerce are designated in the Hebrew invoice, so to speak, are identical with their Tamil nomenclature in Ceylon at the present day. And those terms were so entirely foreign and alien from the common Hebrew language as to have driven the Ptolemaist authors of the Septuagint version into a blunder, by which the ivory, apes, and peacocks, come out as ' hewn and carven stones.' " *

If Tarshish be once placed in Ceylon, everything seems to

* Sir Emerson Tennent.

point to its being expressly localized at Point de Galle. This has been from time immemorial the great emporium of the island. Under the name of Kalah, it was the rendezvous for the Persian and Arabian vessels in the time of Haroun Alraschid trading with China. The impossibility of navigating the Strait of Manaar except with the smallest craft, as well as the difficulties in regard of wind and currents, which would painfully add to the length of the voyage for ships from Arabia or the Persian Gulf, in rounding the southeast coast of Ceylon, exclude the noble harbor of Trincomalee from all claim to this historical distinction. And Pliny learned from the ambassadors sent from Ceylon to the Emperor Claudius, that the great port of the island fronted the south—a description applicable to no point on the coast but that of Galle. In default of any ground of the slightest probability for a bare suggestion that the depot of general Asiatic maritime trade was silently changed in the interim (a thing utterly repugnant to the habits of timid tenacity and slowly-bought experience characterisic of Eastern sailors), it may be reasonably concluded that the great port of Ceylon, from the times of Claudius to those of Haroun Alraschid, and from his times to those of the Dutch and the Portuguese, was also the great port of Ceylon in the times of Solomon.